NEW YORK TIMES BESTSELLING AUTHOR

SHANNON McKENNA

MEN OF MADDOX HILL

Books by Shannon McKenna

Men of Maddox Hill

His Perfect Fake Engagement
Corner Office Secrets
Tall, Dark and Off Limits

Visit her Author Profile page at
millsandboon.com.au,
or shannonmckenna.com, for more titles.

You can also find Shannon McKenna on Facebook,
along with other Harlequin Desire authors,
at Facebook.com/harlequindesireauthors!

NEW YORK TIMES BESTSELLING AUTHOR

SHANNON McKENNA

MEN OF MADDOX HILL

MILLS & BOON

CONTENTS

Shannon McKenna is the *New York Times* and *USA TODAY* bestselling author of over twenty-five romance novels. She ranges from romantic suspense to contemporary romance to paranormal, but in all of them, she specializes in tough, sexy alpha male heroes, heroines with the brains and guts to match them, blazing sensuality, and of course, the redemptive power of true love. There's nothing she loves more than abandoning herself to the magic of a pulse-pounding story. Being able to write her own romantic stories is a dream come true.

She loves to hear from her readers. Contact her at her website, shannonmckenna.com, for a full list of her novels. Find her on Facebook at Facebook.com/authorshannonmckenna to keep up with her news. Or join her newsletter at shannonmckenna.com/connect.php and look for the juicy free book you'll get as a welcome gift! She hopes to see you there!

His Perfect Fake Engagement

Dear Reader,

Years ago, I was working an absurd variety of administrative jobs in New York City to pay the bills while trying to be a writer and a singer. One of those jobs happened to be for a big architecture firm in midtown Manhattan. As I typed, filed and hauled coffee, one of the architects came to my notice. I'll call him Javier, to protect the innocent. Tall and dark, with shoulder-length luscious black locks and deep, mysterious eyes, a velvet voice, and truckloads of talent. I was too shy to actually speak to the guy, other than to pass on phone messages, but boy, did he make an impression. So it's no wonder that my current hero is the CEO of a big arcitecture firm. It's an homage to sexy architects, wherever they may be.

In *His Perfect Fake Engagement*, my architect CEO hero, Drew Maddox, finds himself mired in a scandal that's risking his career, until his quick-witted sister, Ava, comes up with the perfect scheme...a fake engagement to her friend Jenna Somers.

I hope you like the first installment of Men of Maddox Hill. There's more to come, so be sure to follow me to stay up-to-date on future books in the series! Look for contact links to my socials and my newsletter on my website, shannonmckenna.com.

Happy reading! Let me know what you think!

Warmest wishes,

Shannon McKenna

One

"I was set up."

Experience had taught Drew Maddox to keep his voice even and calm when dealing with his volatile uncle, but nothing was going to help his cause today.

"The damage is the same!" Malcolm Maddox flung the crumpled handful of cheap tabloid magazines he'd been clutching in his fist onto the conference room table. "For anyone who looks at this, you're just a coke-sniffing scoundrel with a taste for eighteen-year-olds! Why in God's name were you at a party at that lowlife degenerate's house in the first place? What in holy hell were you thinking?"

Drew let out a breath, counting down slowly. The photos in the tabloids were of him, sprawled on a couch, shirt ripped open, looking clouded and disoriented, while a young woman in a leather miniskirt, large breasts popping out of her skin-tight silver top, sat astride him.

"I was trying to help a friend," Drew repeated. "She found out that her younger sister was at that party. She couldn't get in herself, but she knew that I used to run with that guy years ago, so she asked me to check up on her sister."

"We were supposed have dinner with Hendrick and Bev tonight," Uncle Malcolm said furiously. "Did that even cross your mind before you got into this mess?"

"I do remember the dinner, yes," Drew said. Hendrick Hill was Malcolm's longtime partner and cofounder of their architecture firm, Maddox Hill. Drew had always liked the guy, uptight and humorless though he usually was.

"Then Bev reads about your drunken orgy at Arnold Sobel's house at her hairdresser's!" Malcolm stabbed the tabloids with his finger. "She sees the CEO of her husband's company in these pornographic pictures. She was horrified, Drew."

"It wasn't a drunken orgy, Uncle, and I never—"

"Sanctimonious bastard," Malcolm growled. "He had nerve, sputtering at me about morals and appearances. As far as Hendrick is concerned, it doesn't matter how many architectural prizes and honors you've won if you can't keep your pants zipped. He thinks you're a liability now, and if he persuades the rest of the board, he has the votes to oust you, no matter what I say."

"I know," Drew said. "But I was set up at that party. Someone played their cards carefully."

Malcolm let out a savage grunt. "You're the one who's playing, from what I can see. And if the board fires you, all of our clients will smell blood in the water. It's humiliating!"

I was set up. He had to stop repeating it. Uncle Malcolm didn't want to hear it, so at this point he'd be better off just keeping his mouth shut.

PR disaster or not, he couldn't have done anything differently. When his friend Raisa found out someone brought her sister Leticia to one of Arnold Sobel's famously depraved parties, she'd been terrified that the younger woman would fall prey to a house full of drunken, drugged-up playboys.

Then Leticia had stopped answering her phone, and Raisa

had completely freaked out. If Drew hadn't intervened, she would have forced her way through Arnold's security and into Sobel's party by herself—with a gun.

It would have ended badly. Certainly for Raisa. Maybe for everyone.

Drew couldn't let that happen.

Of course, as he discovered afterward, Leticia had never been at the party at all. He and Raisa had been played. The target had been Drew all along.

But Uncle Malcolm didn't want to hear it.

"I was set up." He knew the words wouldn't help, but he couldn't stop repeating them. "They staged those pictures. The photographer was lying in wait."

"If there's one thing I hate more than a spoiled ass who thinks the world only exists for his pleasure, it's a whiner," his uncle snarled. "Set up, my ass. You're a Marine, for God's sake! Taken down by a pack of half-dressed showgirls?"

Ava, his younger sister, jumped in. "Uncle Malcolm, think about it," she coaxed. "Drew's not a whiner. A rebel and a screwup, maybe, but he always owned it. And this is so deliberate. The way those girls ambushed him—"

"Doesn't look like an ambush to me. It looks like a damn orgy!"

"Someone's telling you a story, Uncle," Ava insisted. "Don't be a sucker."

"Ha. All I see is that your brother couldn't care less about the reputation and the future of the company I spent my life building! If Hendrick uses his muscle to get the board to remove you as CEO, I can't stop him. So start brushing up your resumé. As of today, you're job hunting. Face Hendrick tonight like a man. He can tell you his decision then. But as for myself, I'm done, boy. Done with your crap."

Uncle Malcolm stomped out of the room, cane thudding. He tried to slam the door for effect, but the expensive hydraulic hinge made it sigh gently closed after him with a delicate click.

Drew leaned forward, rubbing his aching temples. "I'll skip the dinner with Hendrick," he said wearily. "No one needs me there to make that announcement. I've reached my humiliation quota for the day."

"No, don't. That looks like an admission of guilt," Ava said thoughtfully. "You need to come to dinner, Drew. I have an idea."

Drew gave his sister a wary look. "If anything could make me feel worse right now, it's those four words coming out of your mouth."

"Don't be a wuss," Ava scolded. "This place needs you here as CEO. You're the new face of Maddox Hill. Hell, you're the new face of architecture. Nobody else has what it takes to head up all those big carbon sink building projects you got going. You're the one who won the Global Award for Sustainable Architecture, and the AIA COTE Award—"

"You don't need to flog my résumé to me, Av. I know what's on it."

"And the Green Academy competition, and that's just the eco stuff," Ava persisted. "You're, like, Mr. Cross-Laminated-Sustainable-Timber-Is-Our-Future. Maddox Hill can't stay relevant without you. Everyone will line up to thank me eventually. You'll see."

It didn't surprise him that she would think so. His sister had curly blond hair, huge cobalt blue eyes, a drop-dead figure, charisma to burn and a very, very high opinion of herself. She could bend people effortlessly to her will, especially men. He was the only one who could resist her. She was his little sister, after all.

The whole thing was still sinking in. How much he stood to lose today, in one fell swoop. Control of all his design projects, many of which had been years in the making. Most of all, he hated the thought of losing the Beyond Earth Project. He'd put that together with the collaboration of the robotics research arm of the Maddox Hill Foundation, opening up the field to young architects and engineers to problem-solve the obstacles to human habitation on the moon and Mars.

That project would have just rung all of their late father's bells. Dad had been a dreamer.

"I'm not proposing that you charm Hendrick, or even Uncle Malcolm," Ava said. "That's a woman's job. Your fiancée will do the heavy lifting. You just smile and nod."

"What fiancée?" Drew asked, baffled. "I have to find a fi-ancée before dinner tonight? That's setting the bar high, Av, even for a wild, carousing playboy like me."

"No, big brother, the finding's done for you already. It came to me like a beautiful brain-flash while Uncle Malcolm was ranting. We need to fight this false story, and I have the per-fect counter-story. And she happens to be right nearby today, coincidentally!"

"What the hell are you talking about? Who's here?"

"Your future bride," Ava announced.

Drew was struck silent, appalled. "Av, you're joking, right?"

"Nope! A temporary engagement, of course. Just a few months, to get you over the hump. You met her once, when you were on leave from Iraq, remember? You stopped to visit me at my dorm in Seattle. Remember Jenna, my roommate?"

"The little red-blonde with the glasses? The one who dumped a pitcher of sangria all over me?"

"That's the girl. I was supposed to meet up with her for cof-fee before her Wexler presentation over at the Curtis Pavilion this afternoon, but Uncle Malcolm was in such a tizzy, I had to reschedule so I could calm him down. Not that it helped much."

"What presentation?"

"Jenna's a biomechanical engineer, and she started her own bionics company a few years ago. She designs prosthetic me-chanical limbs. Brain activated, artificial nerves, sensory feed-back. Real space-age stuff. I have been doing their PR, and she's up for the Wexler Prize for Excellence in Biomedical Engineer-ing. She gave her introductory presentation to the committee today. Her mission is to make affordable, high-functioning mechanical arms available to everyone who needs one. She's brilliant, she's focused, she cares…in short, she's perfect."

"But why?" He shook his head, baffled. "Why would she do this for me? And why would anyone buy it? And what the hell is the point?"

"They will buy it, and they will love it," Ava said. "Underestimate me at your peril, bro. I am a genius."

"I don't want to tell a pack of lies," Drew said. "It makes me tense."

"You have to fight fire with fire," Ava told him sternly. "You'd rather just give in and torpedo Uncle Malcolm's company rather than try something bold and risky? Someone is pushing a fake story about you. That you're a spoiled, entitled asshat who uses and discards vulnerable young women. Ouch. My story is much better. Handsome bad boy, redeemed by love, his social conscience shocked to life—"

"I have a social conscience already," he growled. "I'm not a complete tool."

"Shh, I'm just brainstorming. The cynical rogue with the secret hunger in his heart who falls for the smart girl in glasses. Humbled by the power of love. Oh, yeah."

"Secret hunger in my heart?" Drew tilted an eyebrow. "Really, Av?"

"Just roll with it, bro. This woman is making artificial arms for people so they can hug their kids again. See where I'm going? Pathos. Warmth. Connection. We all crave it."

"I get it just fine, and you're still nuts," Drew said.

Ava picked her tablet up from the table and tapped the screen a few times, passing it to Drew. "This is Jenna. I had my assistant go over to the Curtis to record her presentation to the Wexler Prize committee, and he already sent me the video. Take a look."

In the video, a young woman was spotlighted on the circular stage at the Curtis Pavilion, one of the newest high-profile

Seattle skyscrapers that Drew had designed. She wore a micro-phone headset. A sleek fitted short gray dress. She had nice legs. Her strawberry blond ringlets were twisted up into an explo-sive messy bun, ringlets sproinging out in every direction. She still wore glasses, but now they were cat-eye style, the frames a bright neon green.

Drew held up the tablet. The camera zoomed in on her face. The pointed chin, the tilted hazel eyes. A sprinkle of freckles. Her mouth was full, with a sexy dip in the pillowy softness of her lower lip. Painted hot, glossy red. He tapped the tablet for the sound.

"...new nerve connections, opening the doorways to actual sensations," she was saying, in a low, musical voice. "Holding a paintbrush. Braiding a child's hair. Dribbling a basketball. We take these things for granted, and don't see them for the daily miracles that they are. I want these daily miracles in arm's reach for everyone. Thank you."

There was enthusiastic applause. He muted it. Ava took her tablet back.

"Her company is called Arm's Reach," Ava said. "She's won a bunch of awards already. Most recently the AI and Robotics International Award. That one was a million bucks. But she needs more, to develop ways for people to access the special-ized nerve surgery that goes with some of her tech." Ava paused. "She's cute, too. Though I'm sure you noticed."

"Av, I'm sure this woman is too busy helping people with real problems to participate in your little theater project to solve mine," Drew said absently, still gazing down at the tablet. "Send me that video."

"Sure thing." A smile curved Ava's mouth as she swiped and tapped the screen. "Done." She picked up the phone on the table. "Mrs. Crane?" she said. "Is Ms. Somers there? Excellent. Yes, bring her in. Thanks so much."

"Jenna Somers is here, now?" Drew was alarmed. "Ava, I never agreed to—"

"Don't be silly. She's here right now, Drew. What's the point of wasting any time? Hers or ours?" A knock sounded on the door. "Come in!" Ava sang out.

It was too late to answer Ava's question the way it deserved to be answered.

The door was already opening.

Two

Jenna followed the white-haired receptionist along a suspended walkway over a huge open-plan workspace. A wall of glass three stories high highlighted the Seattle cityscape. From there, they turned into a starkly minimalist corridor, paneled with gleaming wood, lit by slanted skylight windows. She'd been wanting to check out the famous new Maddox Hill building in downtown Seattle, made completely out of eco-friendly sustainable wooden building materials, for some time now. Unsurprisingly, it was gorgeous, inside and out. The wood gave it an earthy and welcoming warmth that steel and concrete could never match. A glimpse inside an open office door showed floor-to-ceiling windows and a stunning view of the rapidly transforming city skyline. Just what she'd expect of a world-famous architecture firm.

It was all very elegant, but she wished Ava had kept their original date hours ago at the coffee shop near the Curtis Pavilion, and not strong-armed Jenna into coming up here. She'd hoped for a chance to rehearse the main points of her intro presentation with her friend before she had to give the speech. Ava had a keen ear for anything flat, boring or repetitive.

But whatever. She'd gotten through it okay, even without the dry run, and it was out of her hands now. Fingers and toes crossed. The Wexler Prize was a juicy one. Half a million dollars would kick her research forward and turbocharge all her hopes and plans.

Maybe Ava had just wanted to show off the new Maddox Hill headquarters building, and if so, she was suitably impressed. Her uncle Malcolm Maddox was the firm's cofounder, and the building itself had been recently designed by Ava's sexy brother, Drew, the infamous bad boy of modern architecture.

The receptionist stopped in front of a mahogany door, and knocked.

"Come in!" Ava's voice called.

This room, like the corner office Jenna had glimpsed, was large and featured big slanted windows, and a breath-taking view. The sun glowed low on the horizon, painting the clouds pink. Ava gave her a welcoming smile, and then the man at the table stood up and turned around. Jenna stopped short—and stopped breathing.

Drew Maddox himself, in the flesh. Ava's big brother and architect of the superrich: the tech tycoons, oil sheikhs and Hollywood royalty. Currently the focus of a fresh sex scandal.

And also, incidentally, of her most feverish and long-standing girlish crush. Because of course, she had such impeccable taste in men. Ha ha.

She hadn't seen Drew Maddox since the sangria episode in college. She'd fled the scene in a state of utter mortification, and hadn't come back with a bucket and mop to clean up the mess until he was safely gone. He'd roared off on his motorcycle into the sunset and straight into her wildest sexual fantasies.

Where he proceeded to take up permanent residence. He was her go-to. Always.

He was just as gorgeous now as he ever had been. No, even more so. Eleven years had rendered him denser. More solid and seasoned. Even bigger than she remembered. He was so tall. Broad shouldered, with that tapered waist. Hard muscular thighs. On Drew Maddox, a pair of dress pants, a crisp white shirt and a silk tie looked almost dangerous.

His face was so beautiful. Golden olive skin. Dark hair. Deep-set, tilted green eyes. Lashes longer and darker than any man needed them to be. Sharp cheekbones, a strong, chiseled jaw and full, sensual lips. The dramatic slash of his dark eyebrows was mesmerizing. He was so fine, no wonder women flung themselves at him, at least according to this morning's tabloids. She didn't blame them.

Ava looked discreetly amused when Jenna finally dragged her gaze away.

Damn. Caught gawking. And of course, now her face was red. It was the cross she had to bear, with her pale, redheaded complexion. Freckles and blushing.

"You remember my brother, Drew?" Ava said.

"Of course." Jenna tried to smile. "Our dorm room, back in college. I believe I dumped a pitcher of sangria all over you."

"I remember that." His voice was so deep and resonant. "It was sticky."

"I was telling Drew about your presentation," Ava said. "I sent him the video Ernest made for me."

Yikes. Fresh insecurity rocked her. Drew, watching her speak? She could have had lipstick on her teeth for all she knew.

"Come in, come in," Ava urged. "Shall I ask Mrs. Crane to bring you coffee, tea, a soft drink? A fresh-pressed juice? We have a juice bar."

"No, thanks. I don't need anything."

"Sit down, Jenna. There's something we needed to ask you."

"Go ahead." Jenna settled herself in a chair, tingling with nerves. Drew stood with his back to them, gazing out the window at the fading sunset colors glowing on the horizon.

Jenna wrenched her gaze away from his perfect, fabulously muscular butt with great force of will. "What is it you want to know?"

"Um… This is kind of awkward." Ava's eyes flicked over to Drew, then back to her. "But we appear to be in some PR trouble. I don't suppose you saw the tabloids today."

"I noticed a couple of silly headlines online this morning," she admitted. "But I didn't read the articles. Nobody pays attention to those rags anyhow."

Total lie. She'd read through all four articles. Every word. In fact, she'd stared avidly at the pictures until her coffee was cold wondering what a guy like Drew Maddox saw in those pumped-full-of-silicone party girls. Men. She would never understand.

"Triple Towers Starchitect Caught with His Hand in the Cookie Jar!" read one headline. A photo of Drew's Hollywood starlet girlfriend's scowling face was captioned: "Bonita Furious! Bad Boy Drew Maddox strays…again!"

Drew turned around, his mouth grim. "Uncle Malcolm is pissed. But his partner, Hendrick Hill, is the real problem. Hendrick wants me out as CEO on moral grounds. My uncle owns forty percent of the controlling shares, Hendrick has forty, and the other twenty percent are controlled by the rest of the board. With those pictures, Hendrick will be able to persuade over half of them that I'm a liability. And I'll be fired."

"Oh," Jenna murmured, dismayed. "That's terrible. I mean, I'm sure you'll be fine eventually. You're a brilliant architect. Nobody questions your talent. But still. It's awful."

"It is, particularly since those pictures were staged," Ava told her. "He was set up."

Drew made a pained sound. "Ava, do we have to go into the gory details?"

"She needs to know the situation. Be clear. You were lured into that place on false pretenses and ambushed. Those girls jumped on you and posed you for those photographs. We don't know who organized it, but they've gone to a lot of trouble to mess with you, and their plan seems to be working. That's where you come in, Jenna."

"Me?" Jenna looked from Ava to Drew, confused. "How me?"

"Well...we were just thinking—"

"*You* were thinking, Av," Drew said. "Own it."

"Okay, fine. I, Ava Maddox, was thinking, because I am a freaking genius, that a whirlwind engagement would help the optics of the situation. You know, to draw attention away from those pictures. To counter Drew's soulless playboy image."

"Whirlwind engagement with...who?" Jenna's voice trailed off. Heat rushed into her face afresh. "Wait. You can't possibly mean..."

"Yes, exactly! You! Of course you." Her friend's face was bright with enthusiasm. "You're perfect. Smart. Pretty. Respected in your field. You're out there walking the walk, helping people in ways that are concrete and personal. Your social cred would help Drew right now. Plus, Hendrick's a sucker for a romantic story. Uncle Malcolm once told me that Hendrick was quite the naughty bad boy himself, back before he met Bev. He shaped right up when he snagged her. Hendrick and Bev are the real challenge, but I think you could charm them into submission if we moved fast, with assurance. You know, if you guys act as if this were an absolutely done deal, and had been for a while."

Jenna could think of absolutely nothing to say. She forced her mouth to close.

"Of course, we're talking a temporary arrangement," Ava went on. "Just until the fuss blows over and Hendrick calms down. I wouldn't ask if I didn't know for a fact that you're single at the moment."

"Right," she muttered. "No conflicts there at all." Now the heat in her face was in full flower. The humiliation caused by her ex-fiancé Rupert's betrayal was still unpleasantly fresh. Being jilted for Rupert's curvaceous blonde intern had been a nasty blow to her heart and her pride.

"And also, as a bonus... It would not suck to be engaged

yourself while that pig-dog Rupert is getting married, right?" Ava pointed out. "Just for a few months."

"Maybe not," Jenna said cautiously. "I guess."

"Be Drew's arm candy," Ava urged. "Attend swanky parties, dressed to kill. Make contacts, rub elbows. This place is crawling with people who have more money than they know how to spend. Teach them to spend it on your research. It's a win-win for everyone. This romance is going to be the magic touch that will shoot the profile of Arm's Reach up into the stratosphere. More than any of my other efforts so far. Brilliant though they are."

Jenna shook her head. "I'm honored to be asked, but I don't think it will work."

"I'd understand if you didn't want your organization associated with this mess," Drew said, gesturing at the pile of tabloids.

"Oh, no," she said hastily. "That's not what I'm saying. Um… The thing is, I just don't think that it would be, you know. Believable. Him and me."

"Why not?" Ava asked. "You two would look adorable together. You'll be the ultimate power couple. Each with his or her own personal superpower."

"Av, get real!" she blurted. "I'm not his type!"

"Type?" Drew frowned at her. "What the hell? What type is that? I don't have a type."

"You are your own individual type, Jenn," Ava soothed. "You're utterly unique. Come on. What do you think? Will you give it a shot? For me?"

"Ah…" Jenna's voice trailed off. "I don't think this makes sense."

"Back off," Drew said sternly to Ava. "You're bulldozing."

"Of course I am!" Ava protested. "Because I'm right! It would be beneficial to both of you. My spin-doctor instincts are right on the money, every time."

Drew pulled a chair up and sat down near her. So close, she could smell his cologne. A deep, piney, spicy, musky whiff of masculine yum, overwhelming her senses as he gazed search-ingly into her face.

He glanced back at Ava. "You really think it will be worth her while? Taking on my bad reputation?"

"Once I get to work on this story? You better believe it'll be worth it." Ava's voice rang with utter conviction. "It'll send her profile through the roof."

Drew turned his gaze back onto Jenna. "I don't like to mis-represent myself," he said. "But if it genuinely makes sense for you, too, I'd be willing to give it a shot."

Make sense for her? She couldn't make sense of a damn thing while she was staring into Drew Maddox's face. *Damn, Jenna. Sharpen up.*

"How about this," Drew went on. "We can give it a trial run tonight. Ava and I were supposed to have dinner with Uncle Malcolm, our cousin Harold, Hendrick and his wife, Beverly. Come with us, just as my date, not my fiancée. We'll see how it feels. See if Hendrick and Bev buy into it. See if it makes you too uncomfortable. If it does, just say no after dinner. No harm, no foul. I will absolutely understand."

"Really? Wouldn't that be, you know…really awkward?"

His smile was so gorgeous. Subtle dimples carved deep into his lean cheeks, bracketing his sexy mouth. His hypnotically beautiful, long-lashed eyes studied her intently.

"Of course it would be awkward," he said softly. "Welcome to my world."

Ooh. Those words sent inappropriate shivers rushing down her spine.

Drew Maddox waited, eyes fixed on her. After a moment, one of those black winged eyebrows tilted upwards.

She didn't want to imagine the dazzled, starry-eyed look that must be on her face right now.

Just like old times. Ava had dragged her into lots of trouble back in their college days. But this time, it was just playacting, right? In the interests of securing more funding for Arm's Reach. Her cause was a good one. It was worth it.

And what was the harm, really? She wasn't lying to anyone but the predatory gossip rags and this tight-assed partner, Hendrick Hill. And it wasn't a lie that would damage anyone, or take anything from anyone.

Plus, she wasn't locked into it. She could bail tonight if they crashed and burned.

"Okay," Jenna said slowly. "I suppose we could give dinner a try."

Ava's delighted hand-clapping startled Jenna, causing her to sit bolt upright in her chair. "Excellent!" her friend said briskly. "You have just enough time to get home and dress for dinner. You came here in a cab, right?"

"Ah, yes, but—"

"I'll call a car to take you home, and I—hold on a sec." A guitar riff from a classic rock tune came from a smartphone on the table. Ava glanced at the display and tapped the screen, holding it to her ear. "Hey, Ernest. Talk to me…really? Three of them? They're hungry today. Okay, I'll tell them to hurry up. Thanks."

She laid down her phone, her eyes sparkling. "You guys! We have an opportunity to launch this right now with a splash. My assistant, Ernest, has identified three celebrity photographers lurking down in the front lobby, waiting for Drew. Jump on it! Use them for once, instead of letting them use you!"

Jenna drew in a sharp breath. "You mean, paparazzi? They follow you?"

Drew's mouth tightened. "They bother me occasionally, yes."

Ava waved her hand. "Ever since that thing he had with that actress who did the last dinosaur flick, what's her name? Bonita Ramon. It's hard to keep your love affairs straight. Anyhow, the tabloid sharks discovered that stories about Drew sell newspapers even without a movie star attached to him. His money, his looks, his sex life—"

"Ava, don't," he said.

Ava rolled her eyes. "Your own fault for being so damn photogenic. You're, like, walking clickbait. So? They're waiting, people! Go get 'em!"

Ouch. Jenna winced inwardly at the thought of being compared to the radiant movie star, Bonita Ramon. This adventure could prove to be more dangerous to her self-esteem than she'd thought. "You mean, just go downstairs right now? Together?"

"Wait, Av," Drew said. "We told her she could bail after dinner. If she goes out with me now in front of the photographers, she'll be in it up to her neck. No going back."

"So decide now! Call it fate, okay?" Ava pleaded. "Walk through the lobby holding hands. Laugh, smile, flirt, improvise. Seize the day! If this is going to work, you can't be tentative or coy. You have to hit it hard and keep on hitting!"

Drew glanced at her, and shrugged. "Your call, Jenna," he said. "Do not let her pressure you."

Ava clasped pleading hands. "C'mon, Jenn," she coaxed. "Don't you trust me? Tell me you do."

"Hush up and let me think," Jenna said distractedly.

Thinking was hard, with her wits compromised by Drew Maddox's proximity, which created a huge racket in both mind and body.

Drew was right. Going out now nixed any chance of changing her mind discreetly.

Ava was also right. Now was the moment to announce their fake romance to the world. If it was the plan, she should just do it. Waffling and pussyfooting was stupid.

Ava had gotten her into plenty of trouble back in the day, true. On the plus side, most of it had been a blast. The most fun she'd ever had. Before or since.

She looked at Drew, who looked back without smiling, arms crossed over his chest, and her ex-fiancé flashed through her mind. Rupert, who was currently planning his honeymoon with Kayleigh, the twenty-three-year-old intern. She of the big blue eyes that went blinkety-blink like an anime waif. Pouty lips always dangling a little bit open.

The hell with it. Her love life was in a shambles anyway. Empty and sterile and stupid. So why not put it at the service of a friend? Besides, she could use a little goddamn distraction right now. And Arm's Reach needed a good push.

"I'm in," she announced. "Let's go downstairs."

"Yessss!" Ava bounded up to her feet, jubilant. "Go, go, go now! I'll call a car to pick you up out front so they'll have time to get some nice shots of you two together. Don't walk too fast across the lobby. And remember to smile. Oh, and be sure to look up into his—"

"You're micromanaging," Drew said. "Back off. We'll take it from here."

Despite her brother's tone, the irrepressible Ava didn't stop beaming as she herded them down the hall and into one of the elevator banks. She waved excitedly as the doors slid shut.

Suddenly Jenna was alone with Drew Maddox, every angle of his big, stunning self reflected in the gleaming, reflective silver elevator walls, all the way out into infinity.

Whew. That was a whole lot of Drew Maddox to process.

He smelled so good. She was hyperconscious of how well his pants fit. The width of his shoulders. The bulge of his biceps, filling his jacket sleeves, and they weren't even a type of sleeve designed to showcase great biceps.

Say something, Jenna. Speak. "Ah, wow. That was…intense."

"Sure was," he agreed. "Too intense. Ava's classic bulldozer routine. Sorry."

"I'm familiar with it," she told him.

"Yeah? Has she dragged you into her crazy schemes before?"

"All through college," she admitted. "I was a big nerd, trying to squeeze mechanical and electronic engineering into my head, and Ava wanted to save me from myself. It was her sacred mission to get me into a respectable amount of trouble."

He laughed under his breath. "Respectable?"

"Oh, yeah," she assured him. "Only lame-ass losers never get into any trouble."

His teeth flashed, gorgeously white. "Sounds like something Av would say."

"She likes to challenge me," Jenna said. "Get me out of my comfort zone."

"I imagine that's usually a good thing. But seriously. If this makes you uncomfortable, you don't have to do it. No pressure. Are we clear?"

Aw. How sweet. She nodded.

His smile made her legs wobble. "Good. Door's opening. Last chance to bail."

The decision made itself on some deep, wordless level of her mind, just as the doors started to slide open.

She went up onto her tiptoes, cupped the nape of his neck and pulled him down into a forceful kiss.

Drew stiffened for a fraction of an instant—and then leaned into it.

His lips were so warm. She registered the silken texture of his short hair. Touched his cheek with her other hand, exploring the faint, sandpapery rasp of beard shadow, his warm, smooth, supple skin. She was vaguely aware of flashes of light from the cameras, hoots and whistles. They seemed far away. Irrelevant.

Drew swayed back. "Whoa," he murmured. "You took me by surprise."

"Sorry," she whispered back. "Snap decision."

"Don't apologize. I'm there for it. Anytime."

She waited. "So?" she prompted. "Shall we go out there? Get in their faces?"

Drew stuck his hand in the elevator door as it started to close again and they stepped out, shoulder to shoulder, to the constant flashing of the cameras on every side.

Act confident, silly girl. Smile. Act like Drew Maddox is your boyfriend.

Wow, that was some potent make-believe magic. It made her

suddenly three inches taller. Her chest swelled out, her chin went up, her face turned pink.

They wound their arms together and clasped hands. Jenna wasn't sure which of them had initiated the contact. It seemed to happen of its own accord. The building security people finally caught up with the photographers and blocked them from following them out the main entrance, and an older man in a suit hurried out after them, his face clearly anxious. "The car's waiting, Mr. Maddox," he said. "I am so sorry about this. We had no idea they were going to descend on you like that."

"It's okay, Mr. Sykes. Let them take all the pictures they want from behind the glass but I'd appreciate if you'd keep them in the lobby until Ms. Somers's car is gone."

Drew pulled her toward the big Mercedes SUV idling at the curb. "Here's your ride," he said. "We still on for tonight? I wouldn't blame you if you changed your mind. The paparazzi are a huge pain in the ass. Like a weather condition. Or a zombie horde."

"I'm still game," she said. "Let 'em do their worst."

That got her a smile that touched off fireworks at every level of her consciousness.

For God's sake. Get a grip, girl.

"I'll pick you up at eight fifteen," he said. "Our reservation at Peccati di Gola is at eight forty-five."

"I'll be ready," she promised.

"Can I put my number into your phone, so you can text me your address?"

"Of course." She handed him her phone and waited as he tapped the number into it. He hit Call and waited for the ring.

"There," she said, taking her phone back. "You've got me now."

"Lucky me," he murmured. He glanced back at the photographers, still blocked by three security men at the door, still snapping photos. "You're no delicate flower, are you?"

"By no means," she assured him.

"I like that," he said. He'd already opened the car door for her, but as she was about to get inside, he pulled her swiftly back up again and covered her mouth with his.

His kiss was hotter than the last one. Deliberate, demanding. He pressed her closer, tasting her lips.

Oh. Wow. He tasted amazing. Like fire, like wind. Like sunlight on the ocean. She dug her fingers into the massive bulk of his shoulders, or tried to. He was so thick and solid. Her fingers slid helplessly over the fabric of his jacket. They could get no grip.

His lips parted hers. The tip of his tongue flicked against hers, coaxed her to open, to give herself up. To yield to him. His kiss promised infinite pleasure in return. It demanded surrender on a level so deep and primal, she responded instinctively.

She melted against him with a shudder of emotion that was absolutely unfaked.

Holy *crap*. Panic pierced her as she realized what was happening. He'd kissed her like he meant it, and she'd responded in the same way. Naturally as breathing.

She was so screwed.

Jenna pulled away, shaking. She felt like a mask had been pulled off. That he could see straight into the depths of her most private self.

Drew helped her into the car and gave her a reassuring smile and a friendly wave as the car pulled away, like it was no big deal. As if he hadn't just tongue-kissed her passionately in front of a crowd of photographers and caused an inner earthquake.

Her lips were still glowing. They tingled from the contact.

She couldn't let her mind stray down this path. She was a means to an end.

It was Drew Maddox's nature to be seductive. He was probably that way with every woman he talked to. He probably couldn't help himself. Not even if he tried.

She had to keep that fact firmly in mind.

All. The. Time.

Three

Drew watched Jenna's recorded online speeches for well over an hour. First the Wexler Prize presentation, then the Women in STEM speech that he found online, then a TED talk she'd done a couple of years ago, then a recent podcast on a popular science show.

He listened to the podcast as he drove home. He liked her clear alto voice. The direct, lucid way that she described her techniques. Her intense enthusiasm and drive. He had friends in the service who'd lost limbs in Iraq and Afghanistan. The implications of her work for them were exciting.

He couldn't wait to get home and watch the video, along with the audio. To see the conviction shining out of her eyes. Her complete, passionate investment in what she was doing.

It was sexy to watch.

He set up the tablet in his bedroom while he was changing for dinner and listened to the TED talk again. He liked the way her voice made him feel. Strange, that he hadn't taken much note of her when they first met. But he'd been a different person back then.

Oddly enough, he'd stopped constantly reliving that fiasco at Arnold Sobel's party since meeting with Jenna. Up until that moment, he'd been seeing it over and over, smelling that foul, drugged perfume that had been sprayed into his face. Remembering the moment he woke up naked in that unfamiliar bed, head throbbing, stomach churning. The bodies of strangers pressed up to him.

He'd been violently sick to his stomach. His head had felt like a mallet slammed into it with each heartbeat. He'd felt humiliated, helpless. And so damn stupid for letting that happen to him.

He hadn't told anyone about the drugged perfume or the blackout. The words stopped in his mouth before they could come out. Humiliation, maybe. Or macho embarrassment. Who knew, but he just couldn't talk about it. Not to anyone.

Meeting Jenna had made that shame evaporate like steam. The surprise kiss in the elevator forced him to drape his coat over his erection. He'd kissed her again at the car just to see if his first reaction was a fluke.

It was not. He'd kept that coat right where it was.

Her kisses were burned into his memory. The feeling of her slim body, molding against him, pliant and trusting. The fine, flower petal texture of her skin. The softness of her lips. Her perfume was a warm, teasing hint of honey, oranges. He'd strained for more of it.

One final detail. He pulled the case that held his mother's jewelry out of his wall safe. He'd tried to give it to Ava years ago, but she'd burst into tears and run out of the room. So he'd just put the jewelry box away and never mentioned it to her again.

He pulled out the small black velvet box that held Mom's engagement ring. The kiss in front of the gossip rag photographers had committed them to this charade, so the hell with it. He was all in.

With more time to think, he might have gone out and bought

a new ring, but Malcolm would recognize Mom's ring, maybe Hendrick, too. Certainly Hendrick's wife would. Bev had been friends with his mother since before he was born. Nothing got past that woman.

Besides, it felt right. Jenna was the kind of woman to whom a guy would give his mother's engagement ring. Mom would have liked Jenna.

He put his coat on and stuck the ring in his pocket and headed for the car. Thinking about Mom and her ring had triggered an uncomfortable line of thought.

Namely, that Mom would not have approved of him using Jenna like this. Taking advantage of her hard-won assets for his own agenda.

Using her to clean up his mess, essentially.

That uneasy thought tugged on his mind. He tried to rationalize it in every way he could. He had not gotten into this trouble because of his own depraved behavior. He'd been trying to help a friend. The only thing he was guilty of was being stupid, and not jumping clear before the trap closed. His conscience was clear.

Besides, Jenna had her own fish to fry. This situation was in both of their best interests. No one had been fooled. No one was being coerced. It was completely mutual.

The accident that killed his parents was eighteen long years ago, and yet he could still see so clearly that look Mom gave him when he was less than truthful, or when she'd caught him taking a lazy shortcut. Her tight mouth. The frown between her eyes.

In spite of Mom's disapproving look in his mind's eye, the closer he got to Jenna's place in Greenwood, the more buzzed he felt. He was actually looking forward to this. He couldn't even remember the last time he'd felt that way.

Drew parked on the steep slope in front of an attractive three-story house. Jenna's apartment was on the top floor. An external staircase led him up to a comfortable wraparound deck furnished with a swing and wicker furniture. He buzzed her doorbell.

It opened after a moment, and Jenna smiled up at him. "Right on time, I see," she said. "I like that in a man. Come on in."

He couldn't think of anything to say for a moment. Sensory overload shorted him out. Her figure-hugging, textured, forest green dress looked amazing. It accentuated her high, full breasts, nipped-in waist and luscious round bottom, and the color was great for her flame-bright hair, which was twisted into an updo like a fiery halo.

Cat-eye glasses again. Amber-tinted tortoiseshell, with glittery stones in their pointy tips, which matched her drop earrings, but her huge smile outshone it all. Ruby-red lipstick. Beautiful white teeth. A gray cat leaped over his feet and darted out the door.

"You look great," he offered. "I like the glitter on your glasses. Hey, your cat just ran outside. Is that a problem?"

She beckoned him in. "Not at all. He has his own cat door. Plus, he wants dinner, so he'll be back soon. My rhinestone-studded specs only come out for the special occasions, by the way. If the paparazzi show up, I'll blind them with my bling."

"Perfect." He pulled the ring box out. "Speaking of bling, I brought this, if you feel comfortable wearing it. Since you really went for it this afternoon in the lobby."

He opened the box. Jenna blinked, taken aback. "Oh, my gosh. Is that real?"

"Teardrop sapphire with diamond baguettes. It belonged to my mother."

Jenna's eyes went wide and somber behind her glasses. "Um… Are you sure? I mean, since this isn't a real thing, maybe we shouldn't…"

"Malcolm, Hendrick and Bev will all recognize this ring," he told her.

"Oh. Well. In that case, I suppose it makes sense." There was a tiny frown line between her dark eyebrows as he took it out and slid it onto her ring finger.

It fit perfectly. Her cheeks flushed, and her gaze dropped. "It's beautiful," she murmured. "I'll be careful. I know how precious it is."

On impulse, he lifted her hand to his lips and kissed it.

Jenna froze, the color in her cheeks deepening, and tugged her hand free. "Excuse me. Gotta, um, feed my cat. Before we, um, go." She hurried into the kitchen.

Drew wandered around the open-plan apartment. A sliding picture window opened out onto the deck overlooking the backyard. City lights twinkled below it. The living room was separated by a bar from the kitchen, and a couch and a cushy armchair were angled around a TV. The rest of the room was dominated by a long worktable, lit up by industrial hanging lamps and piled with cables, electronic components and schematics. The walls were paneled with corkboard, and a mosaic of information was attached, as well as dozens of photographs. Jenna with various other people. One was a child with a gap-toothed grin, holding up two prosthetic arms triumphantly high in a double thumbs-up.

Jenna came back into the room buttoning up a long, nipped-in black wool coat.

"Is this where you do your research?" he asked her.

"Most of it I do at the Arm's Reach lab. But I like having a workspace at home. When I get ideas, I like to have everything I need to pin them down fast."

He strolled around, gazing at the schematics tacked to the wall. "Impressive."

"So is the Triple Towers sustainable housing complex in Tokyo," she said. "That's some truly amazing, forward-thinking design. Congratulations for your prize, by the way."

"You heard about that?"

"Read about it online. *Time* magazine, I think. Great profile they wrote about you, too. Fawning, even."

"Was it? I didn't notice."

She smiled at him. There was a moment of odd silence, and Jenna gestured toward the door. "Smudge can let himself in the cat door whenever he's ready for his dinner, so shall we go? I wouldn't want to be late."

"Right."

Drew got her settled into his car before getting inside himself. As he turned the key in the ignition, the podcast he'd been listening to on the drive over blared out of the speakers, startlingly loud without the car noise to cover them.

"...with artificial sensory nerves, the issues are different," recorded Jenna said to the podcaster. *"We've brought together many different lines of research in the—"*

He switched it off. Damn. That podcast was online, out in the public domain, and yet still he felt as if he'd been caught snooping in her phone.

"Holy cow," Jenna said, startled. "Was that me? The *Outside the Box* podcast?"

"Yeah. Just, you know. Informing myself about who you are. What you do."

"Oh, of course," she said quickly. "That makes sense. I should have done the same. But I probably know more about your business just because Ava keeps me up to date on the big stuff. Prizes, and all that. She's so proud of you. She boasts and gloats nonstop."

They drove in silence for a while, and finally Drew found the nerve to say it. "I saw your Women in STEM talk, too. The TED talk. And your Wexler Prize presentation speech."

She gave him a startled glance. "Good Lord. All that tonight?"

"You're an excellent speaker," he said. "I got sucked in. Didn't want to stop."

Her eyes slid away, but she looked pleased. "It was hard-won," she admitted. "Public speaking terrified me for the longest time. But I just kept at it until I could power through. I can't believe you watched all that stuff in one go."

"It was fascinating," he said. "Clear, convincing, well structured. Funny."

"Oh. Well. Thanks, that's, ah…encouraging." Jenna twisted her hands together, wrapping the strap of her purse around them. Twirling the engagement ring.

"You don't need to be nervous tonight," he said.

She let out an ironic snort. "Are you kidding? How can I not be?"

"After watching those speeches, I think you'll be great."

"At what? Presenting myself as something I'm not?"

"That's not what you're doing. You just need to be yourself. That's why we asked you to do this."

"Oh, yeah. Just act like a woman who's gotten herself engaged to a guy like you. No biggie." She laughed under her breath. "The more I think about it, the less credible it seems."

"Why?" Drew was genuinely baffled. "What do you mean by a guy like me?"

"Please," she scoffed. "Give me a break. You're a world-renowned architect. You run in exalted social circles. You're American royalty. You went out with Bonita Ramon, for God's sake, and then for your next relationship, you hook up with me? Jenna Somers, Super-Nerd? Anything sound weird about that?"

"I don't see anything," he said. "What does Bonita have to do with it? That's over." Not that it ever really began.

Jenna snorted. "If you have to ask, I don't know how to begin to explain it to you."

Drew blew out a frustrated breath. "I met Bonita at a yacht party in Greece. She was on the rebound from some asshat producer. We hung out for a couple of days, and found out fast that we didn't have much to talk about."

Bonita was also a self-absorbed whiner with a huge personality disorder, and she'd bored him practically into a coma by the end of the second day, but he would never say that to anyone. Kissing-and-telling was for losers with no self-discipline or class.

"Wow," she said. "So. Do you often party with movie stars on yachts in Greece?"

He felt defensive. "I was in Crete for work. I got a call from some friends who were vacationing there. I'm not a coked-out party animal stumbling from orgy to orgy."

"Not at all," she soothed. "I didn't mean to offend you."

"No offense taken. But after the past few days...aw, hell. Sorry to bark at you."

"Don't mention it," she said. "Relax. We'll just play our parts and hope for the best. Can't ask for more than that."

He pulled to a stop in front of the hotel that housed the restaurant and got out, giving his keys to the parking attendant. Jenna got out herself before he had a chance to open the door for her. He took her arm, and the light weight of it felt good. Mom's ring glittered on her slender, capable-looking hand. It looked like she'd been born to wear it.

Out of nowhere, he felt irrationally angry. It was humiliating that he had to hustle and con and play games to protect his professional position. To beg and plead for the help of a woman like Jenna to lend him some goddamn credibility, instead of being taken seriously by her. Courting her with class. Blowing her mind properly.

Jenna must have felt his frustration, sensitive as she was, because she shot him a troubled glance. He manufactured a reassuring smile, but she didn't look convinced.

Jenna was playing along with this scheme out of loyalty to Ava. She was sorry for her friend's screwup brother. That poor sorry bastard who couldn't keep his act together.

Play our parts and hope for the best. Can't ask for more than that, she'd said.

Like hell. He did want more than that. He didn't want to make do with crumbs.

He wanted it all, whether he deserved it or not.

Four

Jenna shook hands and smiled until her cheeks ached as Ava and Drew introduced her to the people at the table in the restaurant. Ava looked gorgeous in her skin-tight black lace dress. Ava and Drew's cousin Harold Maddox was there, straitlaced and unsmiling in his dark suit and tie. Harold had the Maddox height and good looks, but he wasn't as striking as Drew and Ava. Drew's Uncle Malcolm she'd already seen in Ava's pictures. He was an older, grimmer version of Drew, shriveled by age and twisted by arthritis. Malcolm's partner, Hendrick Hill, was bone-thin and bald, with sharp cheekbones and sunken cheeks. He studied her doubtfully with deep-set, suspicious eyes beneath thick black-beetled brows. His wife, Beverly, was his polar opposite. Short, round and friendly, she had a blindingly white pixie cut and lots of white gold jewelry dangling over her midnight-blue silk caftan. Her smile froze for only a moment when Drew introduced her as his fiancée, and all eyes fastened instantly on Jenna's hand, which she'd been quick to position so that the stunning engagement ring was visible to all.

"Fiancée?" Malcolm Maddox's bushy gray brows knit together. "What's this? How is it that I've never laid eyes on you before? Where did you come from, girl?"

"Uncle," Ava reproved him. "Manners, please. She's an old friend of mine, and you're meeting her now. Be nice."

"I was just waiting for the right moment to tell you, Uncle," Drew said. "Things got crazy."

"Hmmph," Harold muttered. "I'll just bet they did."

Ava elbowed Harold, but no one else seemed to notice. They were all staring at her. Then Bev's brilliant smile flashed as she made her way around the table to hug and kiss Jenna. "Oh, my goodness! Congratulations! How exciting. I wish you all the best."

The warmth of the older woman's good wishes made Jenna feel guilty. The benevolent older lady reminded her of her own mother, gone six years now.

The meal proceeded pleasantly enough. Jenna had Drew on one side and Bev on the other, and Ava and Bev were both masters of the art of cheerful, entertaining chitchat, to which Jenna did her best to contribute, though it was hard to concentrate with a scowling Uncle Malcolm dissecting her furiously with his eyes from across the table.

Sometime after the appetizers, Bev took her hand and lifted it to examine the sapphire ring. "The sight of that ring really brings me back," she murmured, a catch in her voice. "Diana and I were sorority sisters, back in the day. She was so special. Brilliant, funny. A real beauty. Ava is her living image. I miss her so much, even now."

Jenna smiled into the wet eyes of the other woman, and squeezed her hand. "I wish I could have known her."

"Oh, me, too." Bev dabbed at her eyes with a tissue, sniffing delicately. "So, how did you and Drew meet, anyway?"

Jenna froze, panicked, and Ava piped up. "Oh, that was my doing. I take full credit for that. I am Cupid personified, people. Arrows and all."

"Why am I not surprised," Uncle Malcolm muttered.

"I met him for the first time eleven years ago," Jenna explained. "Back when Ava and I were in college."

"I was on leave," Drew said. "In between tours in Iraq."

"He came to visit me on his way to Canada," Ava said. "He was going to do the Banff-Jasper Highway in the Canadian Rockies on his motorcycle."

"So long ago?" Bev looked bewildered.

"That was long before we got together," Jenna explained. "He was unimpressed with me at the time, particularly after I dumped a pitcher of sangria all over him. Not my finest moment."

"Oh, dear." Bev tittered into her white wine. "How awful."

"It was," Jenna said ruefully. "I wanted to die."

"I'm glad you didn't." Drew lifted her other hand to his lips and pressed a hot, seductive kiss against her fingers that sent shivers rippling through her body. "My shoes stuck to the floor when I walked for days afterward. But it was worth it in the end. Baptized by Gallo port and peach nectar."

His smile made her go molten inside. Oh, he was good. She knew it was for show, and even so it made her feel like she was the only woman in the world. And now she was staring back at him, starry-eyed, mouth slightly open, having completely lost her train of thought. The Drew effect. Whoa. Debilitating.

The waiter arrived and began serving the entrees. Bev patted her hand and waited, clearly amused, while Jenna struggled to orient herself in the conversation.

"So, when did you and Drew reconnect?" Bev asked, gently nudging her back on track.

Another split-second-panicked pause, and once again Ava jumped to the rescue.

"Actually, that was my fault, too," Ava said. "Last spring Jenna asked me to do PR for her Arm's Reach Foundation, so I went down to see the Women in STEM speech in San Francisco to talk strategy. Drew was down there, too, working on the Magnolia Plaza job. The three of us had dinner, and it all came together. Like magic."

Jenna stabbed a couple of penne with vodka sauce on the end of her fork, trying to breathe down the panic. Okay. Thanks to Ava, she and Drew now had an origin story. Yay.

Drew's eyebrow tilted up for an instant, like Ava's did when she was doubtful about something. Then he kissed her hand, going with it. "Changed my life," he murmured.

"Huh. I was down in San Francisco working on Magnolia Plaza, too," Harold said slowly. "Funny that I never ran into Jenna once that entire time. We were there for three months."

Ava shrugged. "Doesn't seem funny to me," she said. "You weren't with us on those nights."

"Evidently," Harold said. "But I did not get the impression that Drew was engaged to anyone during that time." He gave Drew a thin, knowing smile. "On the contrary."

"Women in STEM, did you say?" Bev swooped in to salvage the conversation, sensing tension in the air. "What was it Ava said you did, dear? Some sort of engineer, right?"

"Yes. I design neuro-prosthetic devices," Jenna explained.

Bev blinked. "Ah. I see."

"She designs brain-directed bionic limbs for amputees that give actual sensory feedback," Drew broke in. "It's overly modest to just say, 'I design neuro-prosthetic devices.'"

Jenna laid down her fork. "I didn't think this was the time or place," she told him sternly. "But I do know how to toot my own horn."

"Yes, but this actually is the time and place," Drew said. "Bev works with the Bricker Foundation, so she needs to know about Arm's Reach." He looked at Bev. "I'll send you the link to the Women in STEM speech. You'll be intrigued, considering your work with veterans."

Bev sipped her wine, her eyes sparkling behind her rimless glasses. "Thank you, Drew. By all means, do send me that link."

"The TED talk is fine for a quick overview," Drew went on. "But the Women in STEM speech goes into much more detail."

"And there's the Wexler Prize presentation she gave today at the Curtis." Ava picked up her phone and tapped it. "Forwarding video links right now, Bev."

"I can't wait to see them." Bev smiled, her eyes soft. "I love how he's so proud of you. That's just as it should be."

Another awkward pause. Everyone's eyes on her. She was starting to sweat.

"You certainly have been doing your homework, Drew," Uncle Malcolm said.

"Just admiring my fiancée's accomplishments," Drew said. "It's worth a look. She does groundbreaking work that transforms people's lives."

Malcolm grumbled under his breath. "I'm sure it does. Yours included, eh? So she just pops out of the woodwork, fully formed and already engaged to you?" He scowled in Ava's direction. "You plotting and scheming again, girl? I know your tricks."

Ava batted her big gray eyes at him. "Uncle," she murmured. "You wound me."

"Ha," Malcolm grunted. "Suffer."

Hoo-boy. Jenna did not want to hear them thrash this one out right in front of her. Time out. She jumped to her feet. "Excuse me, everyone. Back in a moment."

She fled toward the ladies' room, grateful for some air and a break from all that intense scrutiny. To say nothing of the mind-jamming effect of Drew's over-the-top hotness. She lingered in one of the stalls, trying to settle herself with deep, slow breaths.

This was trickier than she'd anticipated. She disliked lying on principle, and hated lying to people she liked. And she liked Bev Hill. Hendrick still had that mistrustful pucker to his mouth, and Malcolm Maddox couldn't stop frowning. Both men were hyper-wary of a trap, but not Bev. She was sweet and warm and genuine.

Jenna came out, straightened herself up, washed her hands

at the gray marble sink and tried, more or less in vain, to get her hair in order. She was touching up her mascara when Bev came out of one of the bathroom stalls. Bev waited for another couple of women who were there to finish their washing and primping and walk out.

As soon as they did, Bev moved closer and placed her hand on Jenna's shoulder.

"Honey. I have to say something to you," she said earnestly. "I don't have the right to say this yet, since we just met. But you seem like a lovely girl, so I'm going to risk it."

Jenna braced herself. "What is it?"

Bev's eyes were anxious. "How well do you really know Drew Maddox? I mean, beyond the sangria and the meeting in San Francisco. Do you really know him?"

"Ah… I, um…" Jenna stammered, groping for words. "Bev…"

"I know I just met you, and have no right to ask," Bev said swiftly. "And it was clear to everyone that you're madly in love with him, so I'm sorry to cause you any pain."

Jenna tried not to wince. So her crush was really that visible. "Bev, um… I just—"

"He's ridiculously handsome, yes. Far more so than is healthy for him. Brilliant, talented, charming. Naturally seductive. Ava, too. Their parents both were, and Malcolm was, too, back in the day. But Jenna… I don't know how to say this, but—"

"You don't have to," Jenna said. "I know Drew didn't live like a monk before we got together. His love life would be hard not to notice even if you wanted to ignore it."

"Well, thank goodness you're aware of that. But I… I just wanted you to be forewarned of, ah…" Her voice trailed off. She looked pained.

"I assume you're referring to the pictures in the tabloids lately?"

Bev's lips tightened. "I'm glad you know about them. I would hate to be the one to tell you."

"It's not what it seems," Jenna explained. "Drew got ambushed by the photographer and the girls when he got to that party. The whole thing was staged."

"Oh." Bev's lips were still compressed. "Is that a fact?"

"It is," Jenna insisted. "Really. Someone is trying to take him down."

"You truly believe that?"

"One hundred percent," Jenna said firmly. "Not a doubt in my mind."

Bev let out a sharp little sigh. "Well, then. If you're sure, then I suppose there's nothing left to say, honey. Except sorry, for overstepping my bounds."

"I know it came from a good place," Jenna said. "You're very kind. Trying to protect me when you barely even know me."

"That's a generous way for you to look at it, my dear," Bev said. "My husband and I were worried the second he introduced you as his fiancée. We just hate to see a lovely young woman with all that energy and promise running right off a cliff."

"No cliffs, I promise," she assured the other woman. "My heart is safe."

"Good luck with that, honey." Bev patted her shoulder with a smile. "But it's not supposed to be safe, you know. That's not what hearts are for."

Five

Drew gazed after Jenna as she vanished around the corner on her way to the bathroom. Bev got up and excused herself shortly afterward to follow her. Then Hendrick mumbled some inaudible excuse and fled, which surprised no one. Hendrick could tolerate mixed social situations only if Bev was by his side.

That left Ava, his cousin and Uncle Malcolm. All family. No one left at the table to constrain his uncle to basic politeness. He'd been tossed to the wolves.

Uncle Malcolm got to it without losing time, wiping his mouth aggressively with a napkin. "So, then," he growled. "Jenna Somers, eh? Quick and well-timed, wasn't it? Engaged to a scientist philanthropist, out of the blue? She's not your usual type, boy."

"I don't have a type," Drew said.

"I told you," Ava butted in. "Jenna was my college roommate. She's my best friend in the world, and she—"

"I'm not talking to you, girl. I'm talking to your brother. Why don't you run along and powder your nose with the other females?"

Ava's eyes flashed. "I don't need to pee, Uncle," she said through her teeth. "And I don't run from a fight, either. Guess who taught me not to?"

Uncle Malcolm made an impatient sound. "I don't want to fight with you, girl. I want to talk to him." He jerked his chin toward Drew. "Privately."

"Tough," Ava said. "You want privacy, make a private appointment in your office. Don't banish me from the table at a public restaurant during a dinner party. That's just rude. Jenna is perfect. There is no way that you could object to—"

"Too perfect," Malcolm said grimly. "You don't pull a woman like that out of a hat. You two are cooking up some scheme, and I want to know what's up."

"Nothing is up," Ava said. "No schemes. Just true love. What's the harm?"

"Probably none, for Drew." Harold sounded smug.

"Exactly," Uncle Malcolm said. "The harm will all be to her when she realizes that she's been sold a bill of goods. No nice young lady deserves that."

Drew stared his uncle down. "Thanks for the vote of confidence," he said.

"I'll have confidence in you when you earn it," was Malcolm's curt reply.

At that moment, Jenna and Bev reappeared, engaged in a lively conversation about Jenna's company. Hendrick trailed close behind.

"...to widen my reach," Jenna was saying as the two of them drew nearer. "I would love to meet with them. It sounds like we would be a perfect fit."

"Wonderful," Bev said briskly. "I'll get back to you first thing tomorrow about possible times, as soon as I speak to Jayne and Helen and take a look at their schedules."

"Don't forget that we'll be busy all day tomorrow," Ava reminded her. "My whole crew, along with Drew, are going to be at Arm's Reach, filming a new installment of our video series."

"Me?" Drew said, startled.

"Of course you," Ava said. "Eight thirty on the dot. Ruby's Café is the rendezvous point, on Hatton Street, just a couple of blocks from Jenna's house. My camera crew will meet us there, we'll all grab some breakfast, and off we go to shoot our video."

"What exactly are we shooting? And how long will it take?"

"You'll see," Ava said airily. "Jenna will show us all how the prosthetics function. It'll be fascinating. Don't worry, you can go back to your crazy fourteen-hour workday soon enough. I already talked to both of your assistants. They're on board."

"I can manage my own damn staff, Ava."

She smiled at him, all sweetness. "Just trying to help."

Coffee and dessert arrived, as if Ava had timed it herself, and for a while they were all taken up with sampling tiramisu, panna cotta and the pine-nut cream pastry. Hendrick and Bev said their goodbyes, and Bev gave Jenna a hug, murmuring something into her ear that made Jenna laugh.

Uncle Malcolm shrugged on his coat and made a point of limping around the table and taking Jenna's hand, frowning into her eyes. "I hope you know what you're doing, young lady. You look like a fine girl, but I believe you're in over your head with this one."

"We'll see about that." She leaned close to kiss his leathery cheek. "Don't underestimate me, Mr. Maddox," she murmured. "Or him."

"Hmmph," he muttered. For a fleeting moment, it almost looked as if he were threatening to smile. "Good night. Harold, my cane. See me down to the car, please."

Harold took Uncle Malcolm by the arm, and Drew, Ava and Jenna all watched their cousin help Malcolm down the staircase.

When they were out the door, Ava threw herself at Jenna and hugged her. "Jenna, you were brilliant. They were eating out of your hand. I would never have guessed that you two weren't wildly in love. Bev was charmed to pieces, and Hendrick will follow anywhere Bev leads. Like a lap dog."

Jenna pulled away, looking flustered. "She is a lovely person."

"And so are you! Like recognizes like!" Ava swatted her brother on the chest. "And that bit about her work, how she was underselling it? Genius, bro. Simply inspired."

His sister's words irritated him, obscurely. "I wasn't acting at all. It's just stating the truth as I saw it."

"Right!" Ava crowed. "Perfect! My plan is working. Don't deny it!"

"We're not denying anything," Jenna said. "It's just compli- cated. It's doesn't feel good, to tell a lie to a person like Bev."

Ava gazed at Jenna with a puzzled frown. "I suppose it's not ideal," she admitted. "But desperate times, desperate mea- sures, right?"

"Let it go, Av," Drew said. "It's been a long day. We're tired, and you're bulldozing again."

Ava took a step back, laughing. "Well, now. Look at the two of you, defending each other. In cahoots against me. That is freaking adorable."

"Av, don't condescend," Jenna said wearily.

Ava backed away. "Okay, okay. See you two lovebirds bright and early at Ruby's. Night!"

Drew and Jenna stood there after Ava disappeared, locked in an embarrassed silence.

"So did Bev corner you in the ladies' room?" he finally asked. "When she excused herself she had the look of a woman on a divine mission."

"She was worried about me," Jenna admitted. "Poor inno- cent maiden that I am, falling prey to a heartless seducer's hon- eyed promises."

Drew winced. "I'm sorry she feels that way about me."

"I told her you were set up. I'm not sure if she bought it, but she feels sorry for me, and she believes that I believe. I guess our performance was, um...convincing." Her eyes slid away. Her face was pink.

"I guess it was." Drew waited for a cue, but she wouldn't

meet his eyes, so he had to just throw his invite out there into the cold with no clue how she'd receive it.

"Want to go somewhere else?" he asked her. "We could get a drink. Hash it out."

She looked up and finally gave him what he'd been craving. That nerve-jolting rush from eye contact. Her big hazel eyes. Streaks of green and gold and a border of dark slate, setting all the bright inner colors off.

She caught her full red lower lip between her teeth, her delicate blush deepening. "Actually, it's been a long, weird day, and tomorrow will be another one. We'd better catch some sleep, if we're going to meet up with Ava's crew at eight thirty."

He let out a silent sigh, crestfallen. "Okay. I'll just take you home."

"Oh, no. I can call a car. There's no need for you to—"

"I insist," he said.

There was a brief struggle, but he managed to persuade her. Once she was inside his car, the self-conscious silence between them deepened. He kept sneaking quick glances, catching the curve of her high cheekbone, the glitter on her glasses. The flash of the ring on her finger. He felt as nervous as an adolescent, asking a girl on a date for the first time. Tongue-tied and struggling.

"Usually Ava drives me crazy when she lets her mouth run," he said. "But she saved the day with that dinner–in–San Francisco story. It should have occurred to me to get our stories straight on the ride over here, but I didn't even think of it."

"I forgot, too," Jenna said. "Thank God Ava thinks on her feet. I'm not much of an improviser. There was no time to think it all through."

"Sorry about that," he said. "We rushed you into this."

"It's okay," she assured him. "I agreed to this freely. No one coerced me."

He pulled up in front of her apartment and killed the engine. "Good. I'm glad you met Bev. She's a good person for you to

know. She's connected and extremely committed to her charitable enterprises at the Bricker Foundation. I want this arrangement to be useful for you."

"I'm sure it will be." She smiled at him. "Good night, Drew.
Thanks for the ride."

"Let me walk you to your door."

"Oh, no. That's not necessary—"

"Please. I'd prefer to see you safely inside."

Jenna sighed. "Fine. If you insist."

Drew followed her up the stairway and stood at the end of
the porch, waiting while she dug in her purse.

"I don't usually fumble for the key, I'll have you know," she
told him. "Normally, I'd have it in my hand, ready to jab into
an assailant's eyes. I'm a little off my game tonight."

She opened the door, and looked up, opening her mouth to
say goodbye, and wild energy suddenly arced between them.
The breathless silence felt charged with meaning. Possibility.

Jenna held the door open and shifted back, making room for
him to come inside.

She closed the door after he followed her, hung her key ring
on the hook on the wall, placed her purse on the shelf and stood
there waiting. Seconds passed. They turned into minutes.

"Is there something you wanted to say to me?" Jenna's voice
was a soft, throaty whisper.

Yes. But not in words. Words had abandoned him. Something
else had taken him over. Something hungry, restless, prowling.

Jenna made a startled sound as he reached out and took her
glasses off. He placed them on the shelf by the door, his movements slow and deliberate.

Her hands floated up, but not to push his hands away. He
touched her jaw, her cheekbones, with his fingertips. The tender skin at the nape of her neck, behind her ear. The warmth
of her hands came to rest on top of his, brushing along his fingers, then pressing his hands against her face.

Every part of her was just as soft and fragrant as he remembered from that astonishing kiss outside the Maddox Hill building.

Her arms wound around his neck. He cupped the back of her head, the thick mass of twisted curls wound up in the back, the ringlets coming loose and twining around his fingers. Breathing in her perfume.

Scolding voices in his head yapped at him. He shouldn't be doing this. It was irresponsible. He was being a self-serving tool. This was going to blow up in his face, and there would be no one to blame but himself.

The voices faded to a background buzz. Distant, irrelevant. And then he was kissing her.

Wildly, like he was starving for her.

Six

It was happening again. He'd bypassed her brain. Just reached past it into something deeper, rawer, truer. A part that didn't care about consequences. It just wanted more of that delicious, virile, wonderful-smelling man who was ravishing her mouth with slow, enthralling skill. *More*.

He lifted her up, and she just clung, like he was her center of gravity, winding her legs around him. He pressed her against the door, letting the hard, unyielding bulge of his erection rock against that tender ache of need between her legs as he kissed her, making her shift and move and moan. She held him tighter, moving over him until he was positioned right where she needed him to be, and then moving again…squeezing. Even through all those layers of cloth, his natural, innate skill was electric, amazing. The way he touched her, as if his hands just sank magically inside her senses, stroking her, changing her. Transforming her.

Jenna pulled him closer, having forgotten completely to be embarrassed about it. He was pulling the stretchy fabric of her bodice down over the low-cut cups of her bra, and she helped him do it, arching her back and holding his head against her chest. His lips felt amazing. Now he was caressing her breasts, circling her nipples through the lace of her bra. Every slow, deliberate caress a delicious lick of flame that sent shivers of anticipation through her body, jacking up the sensations to exquisite madness. She writhed against him, rocking, holding tighter—

And exploded, into pure bliss. Endless pulsing waves of it rushing through her. Sweet, pure, blinding pleasure beyond anything she'd ever felt. Or even imagined.

She came back to herself slowly, feeling so limp and soft, she could barely breathe. She was still pressed to the door, pinned by his body. Her face rested against his big, broad shoulder. Her legs were still wound around his.

She lifted her head. Her face was burning. Good thing his coat was dark, because her eyes were wet, and her mascara was in a highly unstable state.

Drew nuzzled her ear, kissing her throat. Slow, soothing, seductive kisses that promised more, more, more. As much as she could take. For as long as she wanted. His erection still pressed against her, since she was practically astride it. But he wasn't moving or pushing. He was still, waiting for a cue from her.

It took a few panting, shivering minutes to work up the courage to look into his eyes, as reality began to grip her mind again. The hard truth behind this craziness.

This could not happen. Being dumped by Rupert had already left her heart bruised. This was just a game Drew was playing. There was no way it could end up someplace real. She couldn't do this to herself.

She just…didn't…dare.

"Wow," she whispered, licking her trembling lips. "Where did that come from?"

"Let's find out." His voice was a velvety rasp, stroking all her secret senses. "Let's explore it. See how far it goes. How deep. Just say the word."

Before she could stop herself, her mind began to whirl with images of Drew Maddox, naked in her bed. She'd imagined him there often enough. He'd starred in her sexual fantasies ever since she first laid eyes on him.

But Drew always kept it superlight when it came to sex. He was famous for it, while she herself had never been very good at not caring too much when things got intimate. She certainly wouldn't be able to pull it off with a guy she'd had a massive, blazing crush on for over a decade.

Jenna knew how this would go. He'd amuse himself with her, and he'd be great in bed. It would be mind-blowing. Delicious. He would rock her world. Best sex ever.

Then boom, she'd fall for him like a ton of broken rock. He'd be embarrassed by her intensity and pull back fast. She'd be humiliated and hurt, hating herself for being so stupid when she knew the outcome from the start. Why even begin that sad story?

No. She was not going to hurt herself like that. No matter how tempting he was.

She steeled herself. "I think, um...that we've had a miscommunication," she said carefully. "I'm really sorry, but when I agreed to this, I never meant to put sex on the table as part of the bargain. That's just not who I am."

Tension gripped him. He shifted back, and she slid down his legs as he set her gently on her feet. "I never dreamed that you were," he said.

Jenna fumbled with the neckline of her dress, trying to get it up over the cups of her bra. "I'm sorry if I sent mixed messages. Made things more complicated."

"Complicated why? Because I made you come? Don't worry about it. You're so beautiful. It was incredible to watch. I'll dream about it all night long."

"Oh, stop that," she said sharply.

He looked startled. "Stop what?"

"The smooth lover-boy routine that makes all the ladies melt." She backed away from him. "I don't want to join the Drew Maddox fan club. I'd get lost in the crowd."

His face didn't change expression, but she saw startled hurt in his eyes.

"I apologize," he said. "I misread your cues. I'll get out of your way now."

The look on his face made her feel terrible. His only crime was in kissing and caressing her into a fabulous orgasm, and here she was, punishing him for it.

"Damn it, Drew," she said miserably. "I'm sorry. I didn't mean—"

"Excuse me." Drew nudged her to the side. "Scoot over, please. I need to get through the door."

He pulled it open. Jenna followed him out onto the porch. "Look, what I said was unfair," she called after him. "I wish I hadn't said it."

Drew lifted his hand without turning. "Don't sweat it. I appreciate that you're honest. Good night, Jenna."

She watched from the top of the stairs as he got into his car. The lights flicked on, the engine purred to life, and she dug her fingernails into the wooden porch railing, resisting the urge to run down the stairs after him, waving her arms.

Come back. Give me some more of that. I didn't mean it. I'm sorry. Forgive me.

She clamped down on the impulse. Her track record with men so far was spotty, Rupert being her latest disaster. She'd let him use her to further his own career and found herself ignominiously dumped, three months before their planned wedding date.

Odd how it had felt like such a huge disaster at the time, but at the moment, she could hardly remember now how she'd felt about it. All the hurt, mortification and embarrassment had been completely eclipsed by what she was feeling right now. After just a few kisses.

It hurt so badly, to shut Drew out. Like she'd just killed something beautiful and magical, full of unknown, shining possibilities.

But she had to do it. Because it was a trap, damn it. A pretty illusion. She had to be realistic. Drew Maddox would fulfill all her wildest dreams while he was giving her his undivided attention…until suddenly, when she least expected it, and for whatever reason, he no longer did.

At which point, she'd fall right off the edge of the world.

The night was so damn long when he couldn't sleep, which was often. He'd suffered from stress flashbacks for years after his deployment. Even now his sleep was often troubled and fractured by nightmares.

Drew came to a decision in the interminable darkness, as he stared at his bedroom ceiling. It sucked, to be awake in the darkest, deepest part of the night. Stiff as a board, mind racing with every shortcoming, every screwup, every wrong move he'd ever made.

This mess being the latest, and greatest, of many. He'd been insane to let Ava drag him into this. But if he was honest with himself, he had to admit that he'd done it because he was intrigued by Jenna herself. He'd wanted to get closer.

Now her words kept echoing in his head. *Stop the smooth lover-boy routine. I don't want to join the Drew Maddox fan club. I'd get lost in the crowd.*

Lost in the goddamn *crowd*? Seriously?

Man slut. Playboy. User. That was his rep now? Would that be his legacy?

Not all of it was deserved. Only a tiny percentage. He'd had a few talkative, angry drama-queen ex-lovers. After Bonita, he'd attracted the attention of the tabloid press, and this was the result. His current nightmare, Sobel's party being the crowning disaster.

The thought of that night made his gut clench. He was a decorated Marine, and a hundred-and-ten-pound showgirl with glitter on her eyelashes had taken him down with a drugged perfume bottle. It made him sick.

The best trick to beat that nausea was to think about Jenna.

Her softness, her scent, her incendiary kisses, her gorgeous eyes. But that was a pitfall now.

He shouldn't have come on to her but something huge and ruthless had reached inside and grabbed hold of him. Made him do and say things that were head-up-ass stupid.

Screw this. He couldn't go through with it, knowing what Jenna really thought of him. Let the Maddox Hill Board of Directors fire him, if that was what they needed to do. He'd survive. He wouldn't get to helm the Beyond Earth projects, or any of the other large-scale eco-building projects he'd been working toward, but too damn bad. Life wasn't fair.

With his reputation, he'd always find work. He could go someplace far away. New York, Toronto, London, Singapore, South Africa. Sydney, maybe. He'd start fresh. Try the whole damn thing again. From the top.

When the sky had lightened to a sullen charcoal gray, he gave up even trying to sleep. He took a long shower and made coffee, pondering how to inform his sister that her crazy reality show had run its course. The board could vote as they pleased. Uncle Malcolm could rant and rave. Harold could gloat and rub his hands together. Drew would be on a plane, jetting away from it all.

He could open his own company. Maybe get Vann and Zack to come with him. He'd served with them in Iraq, and then convinced them to come to Maddox Hill with him. Vann was chief financial officer, the youngest the firm had ever had, and Zack was chief security officer. Both were excellent at their jobs.

Come to think of it, maybe he should leave his friends' perfectly successful professional careers alone and not appeal to their loyalty and drag them along with him just because he wanted company in exile. *Grow the hell up, Maddox.*

The world had been trying to tell him that for a while. It was time to listen.

Ava would be furious, but Jenna would probably be relieved, after last night's cringe-worthy leave-taking. This whole thing could so easily become a huge embarrassment for her. She had to regret agreeing to it in the first place.

He showered and shaved, and had just enough time to draft a letter of resignation and put it into his briefcase before he got on the road. Traffic was no worse than usual, and he'd left plenty of time to get there. He got lucky with a parking spot, too, so he was right on schedule when he walked into the Ruby Café.

Ava and her crew were there already, occupying two tables in the back. Ava spotted him and jumped up. She was in work mode, in black jeans and a long, tight-fitting red sweater, black combat boots and red lipstick. Her hair was twisted up into a messy bun. She lifted her tablet and waved it at him triumphantly, and his heart sank.

"Good morning, big brother," she sang out. "You hit the jackpot!"

God, no. His jaw clenched until it cramped. "What's the damage?"

"Who said anything about damage? I'm talking priceless free viral publicity! Get that mopey-ass look off your handsome face and sit down. I'll grab you some coffee while you admire my handiwork."

Drew sank down into the chair and glanced at the headlines on the screen. The pictures jolted him. All different angles of the passionate lip-lock with Jenna after escaping from the lobby of the Maddox Hill building. He was looming over her, clutching her like a conquering hero while she arched back in sweet surrender.

Whoa. Hot.

The headlines made him flinch. "Lust-Crazed Architect Romances Sexy Scientist" was one. Then, "Bad Boy of Architecture Locks Lips with Brainiac Beauty of Biomed." And another gem: "Already? Billionaire Starchitect Frolics with Brand-New Plaything."

Ouch. They'd surpassed themselves this time.

Drew shoved the papers away, dismayed. So Jenna wasn't

getting out of this unscathed. At best, she'd look foolish and gullible, and at worst...

Never mind. He'd worry about the worst when it crawled down his throat.

Ava set down a fragrant, steaming mug of coffee in front of him and perched on the table next to him. "So?" she said, eyes expectant.

"So what?" he said sourly. "So Jenna's reputation is rolling downhill right after mine, and picking up speed. You want me to celebrate that?"

Ava rolled her eyes. "You're missing the point. Bev is completely taken with Jenna. Hendrick won't do anything to displease her. The board doesn't meet for another week. If we scramble, that's more than enough time to distract, deflect and dazzle, because Jenna is dazzling, right? Is she not the best?"

"Ava," he began grimly, "I've been thinking about this all night, and I've decided that—"

"Wait! Hold that thought. There she is, the Brainiac Beauty of Biomed herself!" Ava bounced up and was gone.

Drew turned, bracing himself.

Ava had her arms wrapped tightly around Jenna's neck, and was jumping excitedly up and down, which made Jenna's corona of bouncing red-gold ringlets toss and flop. When Jenna finally detached herself, smiling, her hazel eyes flicked over to his.

The buzz of that eye contact brought every detail of yesterday's encounter back to his mind. He could smell her scent, feel her softness. Taste the sweet flavors of her lips, her mouth. The way her hair felt wound around his fingers. The way pleasure made her shudder and gasp and move.

His face got hot. His lower body stirred.

He hung back, not wanting to get in her face if she felt self-conscious about last night, but there was no need. Jenna hung up her coat, ignoring him. She was dressed in a black wool sweater that hugged her curves, and a pencil skirt. A narrow gold belt accented her trim waist. Black tights. Lace-up boots with pointy toes, perfect for kicking a lightweight playboy's ass right into an alternate dimension. Her hair was free, a mane of bouncing curls. No twisting or braiding or bunning today.

"Good morning," he ventured cautiously.

Her eyes flicked to his briefly. "Morning." Her voice was offhand. Remote.

"Sit, sit," Ava urged. "Look at these!" She snatched the tablet away from Drew and presented it to Jenna. "Behold, the magic is happening. Check it out! Superhot, huh? You guys really rocked the method acting. So real! Rawr!"

"Oh, my God." Jenna scrolled through the articles, pausing on each of the pictures. "Wow," she whispered. "That's... really something."

"I know, right?" Ava crowed. "You brainiac beauty, you! Rupert's going to choke on his bran flakes. And only Kayleigh will be there to perform the Heimlich maneuver on him. The poor guy's done for."

Jenna snorted. "I doubt that Rupert follows these particular news channels."

"Oh, you better believe he has his system set to ping if your name is mentioned, that jealous little user. He's always been jealous that you're a better engineer than he is. He couldn't marry you, Jenn, because he wants to *be* you."

Jenna scanned one of the articles, a frown of concentration between her eyes. "Wow. I've never been described as a plaything before. It's like getting written up on a toilet stall in the guys' bathroom. For a good time, call so-and-so. It's a twisted compliment of sorts, but what do you do with it?"

"Enjoy it," Ava suggested. "Accept it. You might as well. What's the alternative?"

"But how do playthings even dress? Higher heels? Shorter skirts? Longer nails, brighter lipstick? Should I giggle and squeal?"

Ava snorted. "Like Kayleigh, you mean?"

"Who's Kayleigh?" Drew asked.

Jenna's mouth tightened. "My ex's twenty-three-year-old in-tern," she said. "Now his wife. Currently on a romantic honeymoon on a beach in Bali. I wish them well."

"They deserve each other," Ava said. "Rupert is a big butt-itch, and Kayleigh is a classic plaything. Big empty eyes with nothing behind them. Big oversized boobs."

"Hmm," Jenna said. "So I should stuff my bra? And the glasses have got to go."

"No," Drew blurted out.

Ava and Jenna looked around, startled. "Excuse me?" Jenna said.

"Don't stuff your bra," he said. "You're perfect. And I love the glasses."

Damn. Babbling like an idiot. He had no business weigh-ing in on this. He had a goddamn letter of resignation in his briefcase. "Which brings me to what I wanted to tell the two of you," he said swiftly. "I spent some time last night thinking it over. And I've decided that this whole thing was a big mistake."

Jenna's eyes narrowed behind her glasses. "Oh, really? Why is that?"

Her cool, dispassionate tone confused him. "We don't have time for this crap," he told her. "You, especially. You're doing real work, Jenna. Important work. You've got no business play-acting for the paparazzi."

Ava crossed her arms over her chest. "Bite your tongue," she said. "It's working, Drew. It's effortless. I'm pulling all the strings and they're doing all the work. Please remember that it's not all about you. This raises the profile of Arm's Reach, too."

"But is this really the way you want Arm's Reach's profile to be raised?" he asked.

Ava shrugged. "Who cares? You know the old saying 'there is no such thing as bad publicity,' right?"

"Big oversimplification, Av. And you know it, or we wouldn't have this scandal problem to begin with," Drew said.

He looked at Jenna. "You're no plaything. Don't bother pretending to be one."

Jenna's eyebrows climbed. "So you're chickening out on me?"

Drew was startled. "Chickening out? What the hell? You mean you actually *want* to continue this farce?"

Jenna shrugged. "Right now, I'm just a sexy plaything to the tabloids. But if you bail on me, I'll be a failed plaything. A loser plaything. One who sucked so badly at playing, she couldn't even keep the bad boy of architecture entertained for one single night. I can see the headlines already. 'Dumped by the Starchitect.' 'Sorry, Geek-Girl, One and Done.' I'll be an object of pity and scorn."

"Jenna—"

"Bev Hill will be too embarrassed by my pathetically bad judgment that she won't even want to look me in the eye, so to hell with any partnership possibilities from the Bricker Foundation," Jenna said. "Of course that won't stop my crusade, but it's still embarrassing." She crossed her arms over her chest. Chin up, staring him down.

Turning him on.

"I just thought, after what you said last night, that you'd be glad to be done with this," he said carefully.

"What?" Ava's gaze sharpened, flicking back and forth between them. "What happened last night?"

"None of your business, Av," he said. "Private conversation."

Ava's eyes widened. "Excuse me? Private conversation? About what? Clue me in, guys. Oh, wait. Am I being a bossy, condescending hag again?"

"Yes, you are, since you asked," Jenna said. "Leave him alone, Ava."

His sister started to laugh. "Oh, man. Again. It's just so cute. I'm dying."

"What's so cute?" Jenna sounded annoyed.

"You two," Ava said. "When you close ranks against me. It's just precious."

His sister kept on talking, but her voice faded into background babble. All he saw was the spark in Jenna's eyes. The jut of her chin, her upright posture. Her tilted eyebrow, silently asking him if he could rise to the challenge.

Oh, hell yeah. He'd already risen, in her honor. In every sense. He let his gaze rove appreciatively over her body. The color deepened in her cheeks, and her gaze slid away.

Good. She was aware of him as a man, no matter how low her opinion of him as a person might be. That was something.

"I give in. I can't bear to see you billed as a failed plaything," he said, leaning over and grabbing one of the breakfast sandwiches. "Let's do this thing."

Jenna pawed through the sandwiches and selected one herself, shooting him a quick, sidelong smile as he took his first bite. Mmm, smoked ham, poached eggs, melted Gruyere cheese on an English muffin. Lots of pepper. The cheese was still hot and gooey.

He suddenly felt like he could eat five of them.

Seven

"I don't understand why I have to wear makeup at all." Michael Wu flinched away from Suzan the makeup artist's bronzer brush. "It tickles, and it smells funny."

"The lights will wash you out, Michael," Jenna explained patiently, for the umpteenth time. "You'll look like a ghost."

"So lemme be a ghost, then. I'm fine with that," Michael shot back, rebellious.

Ava swept in to the rescue, perching on the chair next to him and giving him a coaxing smile. "Come on, Michael," she wheedled. "This video's going to be seen by a lot of people. You've got to look good."

Yay, Ava. Jenna left her to it. Thirteen-year-old Michael had a huge crush on her glamorous friend. It came in handy at times like these.

She glanced back when she heard Michael laughing. He was already getting his cheeks bronzed by Suzan, talking animatedly to Ava. Damn, she loved that kid.

Today, she had her three most experimental cases on display, all of whom had benefited from the expensive preparatory surgeries that had been funded by the AI and Robotics International Award. Michael had lost both arms to meningitis septicemia, one above the elbow and one below, but with the sensory reinnervation surgery, which had rerouted the nerves that had originally run down to his fingers onto the skin above his stumps, Michael now had nervous impulses running both ways. He could command the prostheses at will, and get actual sensory feedback from the sensors. Pressure, texture, grip force, heat and cold. With ferocious practice, he'd achieved remarkable motor control.

Roddy Hepner and Cherise Kurtz were the other two featured in Ava's video. Roddy was a Marine who had lost an arm in an IED blast in Afghanistan. Right now, he was seated on one of the couches by the wall talking with Drew, having already submitted, if reluctantly, to Suzan's bronzing and shading.

Drew was speaking as she approached. "...in Fallujah. First Infantry Battalion. I was the squad leader of an M252 mortar platoon."

Roddy nodded sagely. "You got wounded during Operation Phantom Fury, then?"

"No, that happened later, in Ramadi. I took a couple bullets to the back. One of them fractured my L-5 vertebra and lodged in the spinal canal, so I spent the next few months at Walter Reed. I'm lucky I can walk." Drew paused. "And that I'm alive."

"Me, too. I started out in Landstuhl and then got shipped to San Antonio." Roddy noticed her, and a huge smile split his bushy dark beard. "Hey, Prof! They tell me you're engaged to this dude. Who knew? You're breaking my heart!"

"Sorry about your heart," Jenna told him. "Word travels fast."

"Well, if it can't be me, at least you picked a Marine," Roddy said philosophically. "Way better than that last guy you had. That dude had no discernible balls at all."

She laughed at him. "Did you tell Drew about your music?"

"Yeah, I was telling him how the team here worked out some extra attachments for my arm for the drumsticks, and we're working on more bounce and flex for drumming. I've been practicing like a maniac. My roommates wanna kill me, but I can do crazy polyrhythms now that two-handed drummers can't even dream of doing." His grin flashed again. "First, the Seattle music scene. Then, world domination."

"Roddy writes his own music," Jenna told Drew. "He gave me a demo with some of his original songs, and they're gorgeous."

Roddy's smile faded a notch. "Yeah, well. That demo was recorded back when I could still play bass, guitar and keyboards. I laid down all those tracks myself. But I can still write songs, and sing 'em, even if I can't play the chords. Say, Prof, if you invite me to your wedding, I'll play your favorite song for your first dance. What's the one you liked so much? It was 'Thirsting for You,' right?"

There was a brief, embarrassed silence, during which Jenna couldn't look at Drew.

Roddy chuckled and waved his prosthetic arm at her. "Aw, don't sweat it. Cherise said your guy is, like, a rich famous architect, so it'll probably be a string-quartet-playing-Mozart kind of wedding, right? That's cool. I don't judge you. And I dig Mozart."

By now, Jenna had reordered her wits. "No, Roddy, not at all. There is nothing I would rather have for my first dance than you performing 'Thirsting for You,'" she said, with absolute sincerity. "We're on, buddy. Whenever and wherever it happens."

"Aw, shucks." Roddy grinned, but his gaze flicked speculatively from her to Drew and back again. "Maybe you should play my demo for your guy first," he advised. "He might not groove to my gritty country-rock vibe. It's all good, either way, got it?"

"I like gritty country rock," Drew told them. "I'd love to hear your stuff."

"Awesome, then. Jenna has the audio files," Roddy told him. "She can set you up."

"Great," Drew said. "I'd like to hear you. Do you play anywhere around town?"

Roddy's face fell. "Not yet," he admitted. "Haven't had much luck getting gigs since I came back without my arm. I did better when I could play four different instruments. Now I just got drums and vocals. And with only one arm, well… It's hard. Club owners, well. They don't look past that. I can't catch a break. Not yet."

"Tell me about it, man."

They all turned to see Cherise Kurtz, the third star in Ava's video series. Her makeup was gloriously done, as she was the only one to give Suzan full rein. In the last video, her hair had been teal green. This time, it was shaved tight on the sides with a long forelock dangling over her eye that shaded from pink to a deep purple.

"Love the hair," Roddy said admiringly. "You're the baddest babe, Cher."

"You know it, big guy." They fist-bumped carefully, their prostheses making a clickety sound. Twenty-five-year-old Cherise, an aspiring commercial artist and graphic designer, had lost her right arm to bone cancer. Her goal was to be able to draw again.

Cherise seized Jenna in a tight hug, patting her back with the prosthetic arm. "Hey, Professor! Ava was telling me you're engaged again! Last I heard, you'd just unloaded that useless tool Rupert. Screw that guy. Onward and upward."

"Absolutely. This is, uh, pretty new," Jenna said, flustered. "Cherise, meet Drew."

Cherise gave Drew a long, lingering once-over, and looked back at Jenna, owl-eyed. "You go, girl," she said in hushed tones. "This one is *fine*."

"Don't overdo it, Cherise," Jenna murmured. "It'll go to his head."

"I'll try to contain myself. Ava said to tell you we can get started. I go first today, boys. Before I start sweating under the lights and my mascara starts to run."

They got underway in front of the cameras. Jenna started

by filming the process of fitting the sensor map sleeve over Cherise's stump. Then they attached the muscle-reading ring, and fitted the prosthesis directly onto the titanium plug emerging from her stump that she had gotten in the osseointegration surgery. It allowed the prosthesis to attach directly to the bone without stressing her skin. Twist, *click*, and it was in place.

"Flex, and clench," Jenna directed.

Cherise did so smoothly.

"Thumb to every fingertip," Jenna directed.

Cherise did so: *tap, tap, tap, tap.* Then back again, swiftly and smoothly.

"Excellent," Jenna said, delighted. "Your control improves every time."

"You better believe it," Cherise said fervently. "I practice sixteen hours every damn day with this thing. I want my life back."

"What is it that you want to do?" Drew asked.

"I'd just applied to a bunch of graphic design schools last year when I got diagnosed," Cherise told him. "I got distracted. But I'm not giving up. Let me show you this latest thing I've been working on."

They moved closer, along with the cameramen, as Cherise hoisted up a big folder. She laid it on the table, struggling for a few seconds to open it with her prosthetic fingers.

When she finally got it open, she showed them a series of bold-colored drawings of prosthetic arms like her own, with various decorations superimposed on them.

"I have a bunch of ideas," she said, leafing through them. "These are just a few. This is Fairy Kingdom. This is Thunder Dragon. Then there's Skull Snake, Sith Lord, Starsong, Elven Realm, and this is my favorite, Goblin King. You put these on with a light adhesive so they can be switched out easily whenever you need a different look."

"Those are amazing, Cherise," Jenna said. "What a great idea."

"You drew these with your prosthetic hand?" Drew asked.

"Yes. I'm slow, but it's getting better, bit by bit. I'm training my left hand, too." Cherise looked at Jenna. "I want to propose a series of decorations for the prosthesis for your brochure and your online catalog. Amputees need to make fashion statements, too."

"Great idea," Jenna said. "We'll discuss it."

"I also really need for you guys to put some sort of base to apply decorative fingernails to the prosthesis," Cherise said. "A girl needs her fingernails."

"We're on it," Jenna promised.

"Was this project in your design school application portfolio?" Drew asked.

"No, I applied before I started these," she replied. "I've already got a bunch of rejection letters in my collection. You gotta hang on to those, you know? Every good success story has a big fat wad of rejection letters in it."

"A project like this would attract their attention," Drew said. "I bet they don't see this level of dedication and commitment every day."

"Aw." Cherise beamed at him. "Thanks, handsome. You made my day." She looked over at Jenna and mimed fanning herself vigorously. *Lucky girl,* she mouthed.

Jenna felt a clutch in her throat. It felt just as wrong to fake an engagement with Drew in front of Cherise and Roddy as it had in front of Bev. It felt disrespectful to misrepresent something that important to people whom she loved and respected.

But she'd recommitted to this strange charade herself, in the café this morning. And she'd deliberately goaded Drew into recommitting to it, too. All because being the failed plaything had stung her pride. Wow. Talk about shallow.

Nothing to do now but grit her teeth and tough it out.

Eight

Drew watched Roddy's segment with intense interest, amazed at the dexterity the other man had developed with the drumsticks.

He was impressed. Not just by the accomplishments of Jenna and her team, but also by his sister. He'd known in a general way what she did for a living, but he'd never seen her actively doing it. Ava had the air of a seasoned professional who knew what she wanted and how to get it, and she was effortlessly authoritative. Her crew snapped to it because they wanted to please her.

He could never let her know this, however. His bratty and annoying little sister was already insufferable and nearly impossible to manage. No need to fan the flames.

He got out of their way while they were setting up for the next segment. At the far end of the crowded, busy room, a skinny adolescent boy with two prosthetic arms sat on one of the couches. His black hair was buzzed off, and he was wearing an oversize *Angel Ascending* T-shirt. Two women flanked him on either side who had to be his mother and grandmother. The women looked like older and younger versions of each other, both short and slight and with long hair pulled back, the mom's into a braid, the grandma's into a bun. The mom's hair was black, the grandma's snow white.

Drew nodded politely at them as he addressed the kid. "You're Michael, right?" He gestured at the T-shirt. "You like *Angel Ascending*?"

The boy's eyes lit up. "Yeah. Cool game."

"Did you see the movie?"

"It was awesome," he said. "Lars Feehan is the bomb."

They were discussing the game they both played, though Michael had made it several levels beyond Drew, despite his prosthetic arms. Jenna appeared beside them and waited, smiling at Michael's enthusiasm.

"You gotta watch the YouTube gamer videos for clues if you want to make progress," Michael instructed him. "That was how I learned about the ancient scroll and the dimensional portal. Oh, hey, Jenna."

"Hey, Michael." She gave Michael's mother and grandmother a smile. "Hi, Joyce. Hello, Mrs. Wu. Michael, how are the flexibility adjustments working out for you? Is the writing and typing going better?"

"Not enough of the writing and typing is going at all, in my opinion." Joyce cast a stern eye at her son. "All he practices is gaming."

Michael rolled his eyes. "Not true, Mom. It's going fine. So far so good."

"Let's go take a look," Jenna said, beckoning.

Drew followed them all back to the spotlighted zone where the cameramen were waiting, hanging back to stay out of the way, but watching in fascination as Jenna and her team did the sequence of preparations on Michael's stumps; adjusting the sensor map sleeve and then snapping on the arms, which were black and chrome-colored.

"Those arms are badass," Drew commented.

Michael shot him a grin. "Yeah. I'm, like, the Terminator."

"Okay, Michael," Jenna said. "Flex…clench…thumb to each fingertip…very good. I can see you've been working hard. Let's test the sensory pads. Close your eyes."

Michael squeezed his eyes shut. "Ready."

Jenna touched his prosthetic hands lightly in a random pattern with her fingertip, and Michael announced each touch. "Right forefinger. Left pinky. Left wrist. Right heel of the hand. Right middle finger. Left ring finger. Right ring finger. Right wrist. Left heel."

"Excellent," Jenna said. "So much better than the last time, which was already impressive."

"Come try the gaming console," Jenna said. "We got it all set up for you."

Michael settled himself in the chair in front of the monitor, the cameramen shifting unobtrusively into place around him, and woke the screen with a stroke on a touchpad with his prosthetic finger and logged into his account. He grinned over his shoulder at his mother. "I can feel the pad now, Mom! I can tell that it's kinda sticky and soft."

"That's great, baby," Joyce told him.

"I'm going to try to make it through a new portal this time," Michael said to Drew as he picked up the console. "I saved this moment for your video. 'Cause it's, like, dramatic."

"Very generous of you," Ava said.

Michael shot her a mischievous grin over his shoulder as he positioned his mechanical fingers carefully over the buttons. "I know," he said. "Here goes. Wish me luck."

They waited through the logo and opening scenes of *Angel Ascending*. Then Michael's avatar appeared and began to run, bounding like a gazelle across the landscape pictured on the screen, right toward a cliff.

"Okay, here we go," Michael said under his breath. "Full power…and *jump*."

The avatar leaped. Enormous wings unfolded, glinting silver and billowing like a sail, filling with wind currents. The game had begun.

After several minutes of intense play, Michael deftly steered his avatar through the magical membrane of the portals into a blaze of golden light, whooping with joy. "*Yes!* I made it! I'm in level thirteen, and I got dragon wings now! I am killing it! Did you see me, Mom?"

Joyce Wu burst into tears and covered her face with her hands.

Michael turned around, alarmed. "Mom? What's wrong?"

"Sorry, honey," Joyce said, her voice strangled. "I'm just… I haven't seen you look that happy in a long time."

"Aw, Mom. Don't." Michael launched himself at his mother. He wrapped his prosthetic arms around her, patting her carefully. One of the hands landed on her long braid. He closed his mechanical fingers around it and tugged on it gently.

"I can feel your hair, Mom," he said, in a wondering voice.

That just made her cry harder. Drew had a lump in his own throat. Then he felt something soft bump into him from the side. Thin, wiry arms wound around him.

It was the elderly Mrs. Wu, also weeping. She, too, needed to hug someone, and he was the closest person. Whatever. He wrapped his arms around the old lady, because what else could he do? Over her white hair, he caught Ava's smile as she gestured silently for one of her cameramen to capture the moment.

Then he saw Jenna's face, and promptly forgot everything and everyone else.

She was beaming at him. Her eyes were wet. She took off her glasses, dabbed below her eyes and then sniffed into a tissue.

What a beautiful, radiant smile. It gave him an amazing rush. He could get used to this.

He wanted to chase down smiles like that every day. Endlessly. He could dedicate himself to that project and never get tired of it.

Mrs. Wu didn't let go, but nothing could embarrass him when

he was flying so high from Jenna's smile. He embraced the elder Mrs. Wu as carefully as if he were holding a baby bird, and just breathed it all in. Letting himself feel it.

He hadn't felt this good in...well, damn. Maybe never.

Mrs. Wu finally let go of him with a motherly pat on his back. He caught Michael's eyes, which were also suspiciously wet. "You play *Angel Ascending* in online mode, right?" Drew asked, on impulse.

"Yeah, sure," Michael said. "As much as Mom will let me."

"I know I'd have to up my game to play with you, but let's hook up online. I usually play after midnight when I can't sleep, but I could move it up a couple hours."

"More like four hours," Joyce announced. "He has to be in bed by ten thirty."

"Mom!" Michael shot her a mortified look. "As if!"

"Done by ten thirty, always," Drew agreed. "Hey, I play with Lars Feehan sometimes. He's a night owl, too, like me."

Michael's eyes went huge. "No way! Lars Feehan the actor? Who starred in the *Angel Ascending* movie? He games? For real?"

"For real," Drew said. "Whenever he can. He's good, too. Last I checked, he'd just cracked level eight, but that was a while ago. He might have moved up since then."

Jenna's eyes were wide with startled wonder. "You know Lars Feehan?"

"Yeah. I designed his producer's beach house a few years ago. Maybe we could all three hook up online and play sometime."

"Lars...freaking... Feehan!" Michael repeated, his eyes still dazzled. "The gold angel! That guy is so cool!"

"Yeah, and if you hook him up with Lars, we get to film it, okay?" Ava said pointedly. "The guy has thirty million Twitter followers."

"I'm sure he'll be up for that," Drew said. "He's a great guy."

"You play video games with Lars Feehan?" Jenna said. "The Hollywood A-list hottie and the bad boy of architecture, two of the busiest guys in their respective professions, have time to play video games together in the middle of the night?"

He sure did. It helped during those long and sleepless nights when nightmares and stress flashbacks kicked his ass. But that was nobody's business.

"Video games relax me," he said, defensively. "They're a great de-stressor."

"Dude. Don't even try to make her understand." Michael's voice sounded world-weary. "If she doesn't game herself, she just won't get it. They all just say, 'Oh, you're rotting your brain,' or 'Oh, you're wasting precious time that you'll never, ever get back,' blah-blah-blah."

"True," one of the cameramen agreed wryly. "That's what my wife says."

"Well, people. Be that as it may." Ava clapped her hands. "I think we have what we need for the day. Thanks, everyone. You were beyond fabulous. Until next time."

Then came a big round of emotional hugs, from which Drew was by no means exempt. "I'll look for you online," he told Michael.

"Look for CyborgStrong8878." The teenager gave him a tight, shaking hug and then hurried out with his mom and grandma on either side, chattering excitedly.

Drew figured that he was technically free to go himself, after the Wu family, Cherise and Roddy had all left, but still he lingered watching Ava's crew pack up. He wasn't ready for the whole experience to be over, and Jenna had disappeared from the room a few minutes ago. He didn't want to leave until he said goodbye to her, and maybe got another one of those gorgeous smiles as a farewell gift.

Then Jenna and Ava reappeared. Ava was on her cell phone, and she spotted him and waved him over, still talking as he approached.

"You diabolical schemer, you. A man after my own heart. I'll let them know." She pocketed her phone. "Okay, my lovelies.

Time to get back to my workshop and start postproduction. That was Ernest, and he wants you to know that A, he called in some favors to get you two a reservation at Piepoli's for eight, and B, news of this dinner reservation has been discreetly leaked to our favorite paparazzi. A few of them should bite."

"Paparazzi? I don't feel camera ready right now." Jenna looked doubtful.

"Nonsense," Ava said briskly. "You've been thoroughly worked over by Suzan, the makeup goddess, and you look beautiful. Let's keep up the pressure, people."

"Too much pressure," Drew said. "It's been a long day, Av. Let her rest."

"You still have to eat, right?" his sister pointed out. "So multitask."

Drew looked at Jenna. "No pressure," he told her. "At least not from me. I could take you straight home, or to some other restaurant where you could relax in peace and privacy. Your call. No one else's."

Ava sighed sharply. "Don't be difficult, Drew. I'm going to a lot of trouble here."

He kept his eyes on Jenna. "Don't push her around."

His sister snorted. "You know you're just egging me on when you defend her, right?"

"I'm ignoring you," he said calmly. "And Jenna decides on her own dinner plans."

Jenna gave him one of those smiles that blew his mind. "I've heard great things about the lobster ravioli at Piepoli's," she said. "I'm up for some of that."

"Yes!" Ava clapped her friend on the back. "That's the spirit! All you need to do is pretend to enjoy each other's company while eating a fabulous meal. No sweat."

Jenna shrugged, her gaze darting away from his. "I'm, ah, sure we'll manage."

Drew looked at the color blooming on Jenna's cheeks, longing to touch it. Feel the soft heat. She'd made her boundaries plain, but he still wanted more of her attention.

As much of it as he could get.

Nine

Jenna felt like she was floating as she followed the waiter through the bustling restaurant. She'd lived in this town five years and she'd never yet managed to get a table at Piepoli's. But around Drew, all kinds of impossible things became possible.

Effortless, even. He knew Lars Feehan? Seriously?

The day's emotional intensity had left Jenna feeling dangerously unshielded, but for some reason, she'd still jumped on the chance to have dinner with Drew. She didn't care if his sister had maneuvered him into it, or if he was doing it for his own selfish ends. Who cared? Tonight, she just wanted to sit across a candlelit table from Drew Maddox and drink him in. This was her chance to look her fill. Listen to his beautiful, resonant voice.

He'd been so sweet with Michael. She was beyond charmed. She'd melted into sniffling, laughing-through-her-tears goo.

And it was a bad time to lower her guard. She was putting herself in temptation's way. Throwing fuel on the fire. She was a smart woman, and she knew better, but tonight, she just… didn't…care.

The waiter seated them at a table by the window that overlooked the boardwalk outside.

"Don't look now," Drew said. "Our friends are already outside, snapping pictures."

"I guess you must be used to this by now, right?"

"More like indifferent. I barely notice them, unless they're bothering you. Here." He seized her hand. "I'll give them a dose of what they like best."

She gasped and laughed at him as he kissed her knuckles, then turned it over and kissed her palm. Intense awareness of him raced through every part of her body.

"I'm impressed that you can be so relaxed about it." She struggled to keep her voice even.

"There are worse things," he said.

Drew's tone was light, but she knew enough from Ava about what he'd been through in the military to guess what he was thinking. "You mean Iraq?"

He nodded. "I saw things there I won't ever forget. A few times, I thought it was the end of me. Once you've taken enemy fire or had your convoy blown up, people snapping pictures of you no longer registers on your radar as an actual problem."

"Ava told me you'd been wounded," she said. "I overheard you talking to Roddy about it today."

"Yeah. A bullet fractured one of my lumbar vertebrae and lodged next to my spine. That was the end of my time in the Marine Corps. I'm lucky that I can walk, and that I'm alive. I think about that every day."

"I can imagine," Jenna said. "A bullet to the spine? It must have been so painful."

"It was. Three surgeries. Months of recovery. It puts everything else into perspective."

"I bet it does," she murmured.

"I got into video games during my recovery, after I got home," he told her. "My convalescence was long and boring, and it hurt. Video games take your mind off things."

"Did you play that game that Michael showed us during your recovery?"

"Oh, no. *Angel Ascending* is much more recent. Lars sent me that last year after the movie opened, just for laughs. He's a really good guy. I'll introduce you sometime."

She laughed. "Wow, lucky me. Lifestyles of the rich and famous."

"I suppose. We're all the same when it comes to the important stuff. Getting shot in the back teaches you that. No matter how privileged you might be, you're never exempt from pain, or death. Keeps you honest." He paused. "Sorry," he said, self-consciously. "Didn't mean to get all heavy and self-involved on you."

"I don't see it that way at all," she said. "I've worked with veterans."

"I bet you have," he said.

She squeezed his hand, which she was still holding. "You were wonderful with Michael today. Roddy and Cherise, too. Michael was so excited."

"He's a great kid," Drew said. "Entirely apart from how he's overcoming the challenges he faces."

"That he is," she agreed. "I just love him. So funny. He has a great attitude."

"They all impressed me," Drew said reflectively. "The whole damn thing impressed me. Your techniques, your team, your tech, your lab. Even my sister impressed me today. Just don't ever tell her I said so."

Jenna laughed. "I won't. And thanks, that's good to hear. Now I just need to make the techniques affordable for everyone who needs them."

The waiter arrived, and they gave him their order. After the wine had been served, Jenna asked Drew a question she'd wondered about ever since she first met him. "I'm curious about something," she said. "How did you end up joining the Marines? It's not an obvious choice. Being a Maddox and all."

Drew's eyes narrowed thoughtfully as he considered his reply. "Long story."

"We're not in a hurry," she remarked.

He sipped his wine. "I don't know how much Ava told you," he said. "But after my parents were killed in that plane accident, I went sort of wild."

Sort of? Ha. That was a massive understatement.

"Ava did mention that," she murmured.

"That was my way of coping. I was pissed at my folks for dying. I didn't care about consequences. So I got into a lot of trouble. It was lucky I was a juvenile offender, and that I never actually hurt anyone. But Uncle Malcolm was beside himself. You saw how he is. He got in my face, made threats and ultimatums. He got my back up, to the point that I wasn't in the mood to trot off to college like a good boy, study hard and make him proud. I wanted to raise hell. So I joined the Marines. First Division, First Battalion. Ended up in Iraq. I learned some very important things there."

"Such as?"

He was silent for a long moment. "No need to raise hell," he said simply. "I was already there."

Jenna nodded and stayed quiet, waiting for him to go on.

"I saw a lot of bad things," he said slowly. "Things I can't forget. But it's not like it was all a nightmare. I worked hard, grew up, learned a lot. Made good friends in my platoon. Two of them work with me right here at Maddox Hill. Vann's my CFO. He's freakishly good with numbers, and Zack is our CSO. Those guys are solid as a rock. I've trusted them both with my life and they have never let me down. In the end, I'd say it was worth it just to have found them."

"You're fortunate to have friends like that," she said. "So after you got wounded, you decided to follow the family architecture tradition?"

"I always knew I'd get there eventually," he admitted. "It was destiny. I grew up around architects. My dad was one, and when I was a kid, he always talked like it was a given that I would be, too. Then after I got shot, I had all these long empty hours to think about my future. By the time I recovered and got to architecture school, I was maniacally focused. I made up for all the lost time."

"I bet Uncle Malcolm was relieved," she said.

"He couldn't believe his luck," Drew said. "Back then, anyway. Now he's changed his tune. Decided that I'm more trouble than I'm worth."

Jenna shook her head. "No. This is all just a blip on your screen. It won't hurt you in the long run."

"I hope you're right," he said. "I had some projects in the works that I was really attached to."

"Anything I might have heard of?"

"We haven't landed them yet, but Maddox Hill is in the running for the Beyond Earth project. I thought a lot about Mars when I was in the Al Anbar Province. Lots of time to stare at the rocks and sand and think about the unique problems inherent in building in environments inhospitable to man. It would involve robotics and three-D printing with local building materials. It's a long shot, with lots of competition, but I have my fingers crossed."

"Wow." She was silent for a moment, digesting it. "That's huge."

"Yeah, it is for me. My dad used to read science fiction stories to me to put me to sleep when I was small. We always said we'd build houses on Mars together someday."

That made her throat tighten up. She couldn't reply.

"I'd hate to miss out on that chance," he said. "He would have gotten such a kick out of that. If I ever do manage to pull it off, it'll be in his honor."

Fortunately for her, the lobster ravioli arrived, and food took center stage for a while. The ravioli were tender and plump and fabulous, the wine was excellent, and Drew was great company. By the time dessert and coffee arrived, the elements of the evening had combined into a magical alchemy that made her relaxed and giggly and mellow.

Then Drew glanced outside at the walkway. "Persistent bastards," he murmured. "I was kind of hoping they'd get bored and go home, but there they still are. Hanging in there."

Jenna looked out the window, realizing that she'd completely forgotten about the photographers. Which was to say, she'd forgotten the whole reason they'd come to this restaurant in the first place.

She laughed to cover her embarrassment. "Want me to do something crazy and dramatic to entertain them? I could throw a glass of wine in your face."

He grinned. "It's a little early in our relationship for that."

"I could feed you a bite of my *sporcamuss*," she said, spooning up a bite of the delicious, goopy puff pastry with cream. "That fits the narrative, as Ava would say."

He accepted the bite, and savored it. "Mmm. Wow. Good."

Whew. That smile of sensual promise unraveled something inside her. She felt like she was teetering on the brink of something dangerous and wonderful in equal measures.

Oh, boy. This was bad. She'd been prepared to be dazzled by his looks, impressed by his smarts, wowed by his talent, allured by his seductive charm. Those reactions were all foreseen and adjusted for. She was being smart. Taking care of herself, like a grown-up.

But she hadn't expected to like him this much.

That was a dirty trick.

Ten

No one ever, in the history of dining, had made a cup of espresso last as long as Drew did after they finished their dessert. He didn't want that perfect day to end.

He'd been with a lot of women, in his time, and he'd made it his business to be good at pleasing them, appreciating them, seeing them, knowing them. But apart from the sex, he'd never felt like anyone had ever successfully known him back.

Some women had tried, to their credit. He'd always assumed it was his fault when they failed. A mysterious personality defect on his part. His defenses were too high, he couldn't let anyone inside, yada-yada-yada. Big shame, but what could you do.

But he'd been open to Jenna from the start. Wide open. No choice about it. The intimacy of it stirred him up, made him feel shaky and off balance.

It was strange, how much he liked it.

Drew dealt with the bill, and they went outside and strolled together down to the street. The wind coming off the sound was raw and cold, whipping a hot pink color into her cheeks and tossing her curls wildly.

Then they were holding hands. He didn't remember deciding to do it. It felt as if the natural state of their hands was to be clasped.

She glanced up at him. "Are the photographers still following us?"

"No idea," he said. "Didn't think to look."

"Ah. So you're staying in character just in case?"

That stung, a little. "I suppose," he said. "Didn't really think of it that way."

"Hey, wait," Jenna said. "Drew, wasn't that your car? Back there behind us?"

Drew turned to look. She was right. He'd walked right past it. Lost in space.

He unlocked his black Jag with the key fob and opened the door for her.

Jenna backed away, flustered and smiling and holding her hands up. "Oh, no. That's not necessary. I'll call a car. It'll save you an hour of pointless driving."

"I can't just leave you here," he told her. "Please. Get in. Let me take you home."

She sighed, but got in without further argument, to his immense relief.

Once they were on their way, having his eyes on the road ahead instead of on her made the question he'd been wanting to ask her come out more easily.

"This mission to help amputees get the use of their hands back, it seems like more than a career for you," he commented. "It seems very personal. What's that all about?"

Jenna was quiet for a long moment, so he started looking at her profile, trying to gauge if he'd overstepped some boundary.

"It is personal," she said. "My brother Chris lost an arm to bone cancer, just like Cherise. They amputated his right arm right above the elbow."

"That must have been hard," he said.

"He was only eighteen. I was twelve. He'd just won a big

basketball scholarship, right before he was diagnosed. He was a very gifted athlete."

He winced. "Oh, God. That hurts."

"Yeah, it broke everyone's hearts that he had to give up that dream."

"What does he think of your line of work? Does he have one of your magic arms?"

Jenna was silent again. This time for so long that he suddenly guessed, in a flash of total dismay, what she was going to say and cursed himself for being so damn clumsy.

"We lost Chris about a year after that operation," Jenna said. "They didn't catch it in time. They found it in his spine, his liver. He did chemo and all that, but it got him."

He just let that sit for a moment before he said, "I'm so sorry." He wished there was something less trite and shopworn to say, but there never freaking was.

"Thanks," she murmured.

They were silent for a long time, but he finally gathered his courage and gave it another shot. "How about your parents? What's their story?"

She shook her head. "My dad was never in the picture. He left not long after I was born. My mom raised us on her own. But she never quite came back to herself, after losing Chris. She struggled for years. Then she had a heart attack six years ago. So it's just me now." She gave him a brief smile. "Something we have in common. Both orphaned."

He nodded. "That's why you do this work, right? You want to give to all these people what you couldn't give to Chris?"

Jenna gazed down at her hands clasped on her lap. "I suppose," she said. "Hadn't ever thought of it like that. Chris was my North Star, I guess. The whole world needs to be saved, and no one can save it all, since we're not comic book superheroes. But if we all do a little, maybe we have a chance. And this is my bit. Someone else can work on saving the whales and the bees and the ozone and the ocean. I'm doing the arms."

"You make me want to save the world, too," he said. "I feel like such a slacker."

She laughed at him. "Ha! You just keep doing what you're doing. Your buildings are gorgeous. You're helping make sustainable eco-friendly urban planning a reality in cities all over the world. Beautiful things make the whole world better."

He felt both embarrassed and ridiculously pleased. "Thanks."

He parked in front of her apartment and turned off the engine.

Tension gripped them. They were in the danger zone again. Every detail of last night's passionate episode, and its painful aftermath, hung heavy in the air between them.

"I really want to walk upstairs with you and see you safely inside," he said. "But I will not come on to you. I swear it. On my honor."

"That's really not necessary," she murmured.

"What? Walking you upstairs, or swearing sacred vows on my honor?"

"Both. You're being overdramatic. But if it makes you feel better, fine."

He walked her up and stopped when he saw her front door, mindful of his vow.

Jenna drifted reluctantly onward toward her door. "Good night," she said. "Thanks for everything. The ride, dinner. And for making Michael's day. It was so sweet of you."

"Don't thank me," he said. "This was a great day for me. Best day I've had in longer than I can even remember."

I could make it the best night, too.

The unsaid words vibrated between them, because apparently he hadn't learned last night's lesson well enough. The longing to touch her just kept getting stronger.

"It was wonderful for me, too," she admitted.

They gazed at each other. This was his cue, to say something lighthearted. Repeat the good-nights. Turn the hell around. Walk down the damn stairs. Left foot, right foot.

But his voice was locked in his throat. And he made no move to go.

Jenna looked tormented. "Please," she whispered. "Please, Drew. Stop that."

He knew exactly what she meant, but all he could do was play dumb. "I'm not doing or saying anything."

To his dismay, her face crumpled, and she covered it with both her hands, cursing.

He reached out. "Oh, damn. Jenna—"

"No!" She jerked back, out of range, and wiped at her eyes. "No, I'd really better not. Sorry. It's been an emotional day. I'm wrecked."

"I wish I could help," he said.

Jenna looked miserable. "I'm so sorry about what I said last night. The problem is, my reasons for saying it haven't changed." Her voice shook. "I'm extremely attracted to you, as I'm sure you've noticed, and this is hard, and awful. I'm so sorry. But I just…can't."

Ouch. He turned away before she could see the look on his face. "Okay," he said. "I'm gone. I won't put you on the spot like this."

He ran down the stairs. He felt like he'd been punched in the chest as he started up the car.

For God's sake, look at him. So last night's slap-down hadn't been enough punishment for him. He just had to come back for more. He'd practically begged her for it.

Women came on to him all the time. There was an art to steering around them, evading them, letting them down gently. He'd considered himself good at it.

The irony was painful. He'd finally found a woman he wanted to get closer to, and she'd slammed the door on him. She thought he was a train wreck waiting to happen.

It would be almost funny, if it didn't suck so hard.

Eleven

"Stop bugging me, Av," Jenna said testily. "My black-and-white gown will be fine for the presentation dinner. It looks good on me. It was expensive. We do not need to shop for another damn dress. End of story."

Ava picked a hunk of artichoke out of her salad and popped it into her mouth. "Sorry to contradict you, but you are so very wrong."

"Why? Why shell out all this money? My closet is full of nice clothes."

"You're being difficult just to be difficult. That dress is old, and done." Ava rolled her eyes at Drew. "Drew, tell your lovely fiancée that she needs a gorgeous new evening gown for the exhibit dinner at the Whitebriar Club, okay?"

"Of course she needs a new evening gown." Drew's voice was offhand. "And this is a Maddox Hill event, so it's only fair you let me pick up the tab for it. I'll give you my credit card. Knock yourselves out. Send me hot photos from the fitting room."

Jenna tried not to flinch. She stared down at her seafood salad, which she'd barely touched. Drew had been like that with her all morning. Pleasant. Polite. And completely emotionally absent.

They'd done yet another interview this morning with a podcast whose online audience was growing fast. The latest of many PR events. Too many. Ava's punishing schedule was exhausting her. The idea today had been to grab an early lunch before everyone went back to work, but Drew's friendly, indifferent blandness had killed her appetite.

She just…freaking…hated it. With all of her heart and soul. And she had no one to blame for it but herself.

"I'm putting my foot down," she said through her teeth. "No new dress."

Ava made a frustrated sound.

"Save it, Av." Drew signaled the waiter for the check. "It's not a good time to discuss it. Obviously."

"Oh, whatever." Ava shrugged, her face rebellious. "But hey. Big news." Ava's voice was elaborately casual. "We heard from the producers of *Angel Ascending*."

Jenna put down her fork, her nerves buzzing with alarm. "You did?"

"Yes. They want to feature Michael in the ad campaign for next year's game."

Jenna sucked in a sharp breath and gazed at Ava's triumphant face, heart thudding hard. "Careful, Av," she said. "I don't want him exploited. He's just a kid."

Ava sighed. "And here I thought you'd be excited at how my hard work is doing marvels for raising your organization's profile to stratospheric heights. Silly me."

"I think you're amazing at what you do, don't ever doubt it," Jenna said. "But you're doing your work too well. And I'm scared for Michael."

"Don't worry," Ava soothed. "Joyce and I will both defend him like a couple of pit bulls. It would be a nice chunk of change for his college fund, right? Stanford, MIT, am I right? This is all good, Jenn. Be excited for him. And for Arm's Reach. This is great for his future, and it's great for you, too. Michael will be fine. He's strong, and smart."

"But I wanted him to get back his normal life," she said. "Everyday stuff. Not some high-stress, high-visibility situation where people are constantly trying to use him."

"Oh. You mean, like you?" Ava's voice was crisp. "Are you tired of the limelight, Jenn? Do you think we're using you?"

Jenna locked eyes with her friend…and swallowed the sharp reply that Ava did not deserve. She shook her head. "I'm just tired," she said.

"I know, and I'm sorry about that, but buck up. Be strong. Oh, by the way. Speaking of good things. Roddy told me that he has a gig tonight. He's filling in for the Vicious Rumors' drummer down at the Wild Side. All weekend, starting tonight."

"Yes, he texted me about that," Jenna said. "I'm going to try to catch the first set tonight."

"Alone?" Drew's eyes snapped to her. "At the Wild Side? In that part of town?"

"It's fine," she said. "I'm going to the early set. It's a hip, busy neighborhood."

"You can't go down there all alone." He sounded horrified.

"Certainly I can," she told him. "I don't mind going alone, and I'm sure—"

"No way. I'll take you. Want me to get you at the lab, or pick you up at home?"

Jenna just looked at him, bewildered. "Drew. Don't feel like you have to do this. I'm sure you have better things to do with your evening."

"Not really," he said. "I want to see Roddy play."

It was the first time that Drew had looked her straight in the eyes since that disastrous evening last week, and the blazing directness of his gaze was almost jarring.

She let out a careful breath. "Fine," she said. "I'll meet you at the club. I'll be there around nine thirty."

The waiter brought his card back. Drew got up, gave each of

them a businesslike peck on the cheek and left, already focused on whatever came next in his busy day.

Jenna watched him walk away, feeling flat and dull. It had been over a week since that disaster after their dinner date. A stressful, chaotic week jam-packed with activities calculated to jack up Arm's Reach's media profile. She was exhausted, and her work was suffering... But that wasn't the real problem, and she couldn't convince herself that it was.

She'd come to dread seeing Drew. But the problem wasn't because of anything he said. It was what he didn't say. He was unfailingly polite and pleasant. Attentive, thoughtful, gallant. No one could fault him.

He was wearing a perfect-fiancé mask. But now that she'd seen the man beneath, the mask almost offended her. Being kept at arm's length felt like a punishment.

Not that she blamed him. Not in the least. She'd demanded herself that he pull back. And that didn't help worth a damn.

On the contrary, it made things worse.

It had been a long time since Drew had seen the inside of a club, but he paid no attention to the strobing lights, the pounding music or the crush of people. People tried to catch his eye, male and female, and he ignored them, having become a ruthless and single-minded scanning-for-Jenna machine. He roved through the place, sensors tuned to her and only her. Scanning for that mane of bright hair, either floating high in an explosive updo or bouncing in a cloud around her head. Cat-eye glasses. The glint of clear bright hazel eyes. Those high cheekbones. That elegant posture. That perfume.

No way could he hear her sweet-toned, sexy voice in this noise, but his ears still strained for the sound of it.

A different band was playing at the moment, not the Vicious Rumors. Roddy wasn't onstage yet. The warm-up band was winding up their last big head-banging number. Still no sign of Jenna. He glanced at his phone again. Still no messages from her.

He started another circuit, cruising the place again from the top, room by room.

Yes. A blaze of yellow light had caught her hair, lighting it up like a flame. He fought his way closer. She was wearing a tight, tailored blue coat, a black wool mini-skirt and those ass-kicking boots.

Next to her was a blazing crest of pink and purple. Cherise, talking excitedly. As he approached, Cherise threw her arms around Jenna's neck and hugged her, pounding her with the prosthetic arm. Which was now decorated by long threads of little lights inside flexible plastic tubes wound artistically around it.

Cherise saw him over Jenna's shoulder and waved excitedly, yelling into Jenna's ear. Jenna turned around and caught sight of him.

Bracing himself never worked. He couldn't get used to the rush it gave him to lock eyes with her. The contact seemed to touch him everywhere. Suddenly, he was turned on.

Exactly what she did not want or welcome from him.

"Hey." He greeted them both with a polite nod. From a safe, secure distance.

Cherise was having none of that. She lunged for him and wrapped him in a big hug.

"Drew!" she crowed into his ear. "You are the bomb!"

"I am?" he said, bemused.

"You totally are! You inspired me! I was telling Jenna about my application to the DeLeon Design Institute! They're, like, the hottest program for commercial art, and when I applied last year, they turned me down flat. But I got to thinking about what you said last week, so I applied again, and this time I included my arm decorations in my portfolio. And they called me in for an interview! The director told me that you forwarded the video link from last week's shoot to her!"

Jenna's searching eyes met his. "I had no idea you had these connections," she yelled over the noise.

"Trix DeLeon and I went to high school together," Drew said. "I just sent Trix a link. That's all."

"Aw, don't deny it, buddy. You helped, whether I get in or not. So thanks."

Cherise hugged him again and planted a loud and smacking kiss on his cheek.

"Hey! Drew!" This time it was Roddy who accosted him. He was looking bright-eyed and excited. "I didn't know you and Jenna were coming! Good to see you, man!"

"Yeah, it was a last-minute thing," he said.

"Hey, now's a great time to play that song for you, whaddaya say?"

"What song do you mean?" Drew asked.

"The one for your first dance, at your wedding!" Roddy yelled. "'Thirsting for You,' remember? I got the Rumors to try it out in our rehearsal this afternoon, just in case, and they liked it. I'll make sure it's in the first set!"

"Hey, look at you, Roddy," Cherise called out. "You're using one of my sleeve decorations. Looks supertough. Good choice."

"Yep, I went with Sith Lord tonight. Decided not to use the light strands, though. Didn't want to draw too much attention to the arm. Could look gimmicky."

"Me, I went with Fairy Kingdom today," Cherise said, holding up her own arm.

"Hey, I gotta go. We're about to go on," Roddy said. "Cherise, come on backstage with me and I'll introduce you to Bose, the bass player." He gave them a conspiratorial grin. "She has a crush on him," he added, in a stage whisper that was more like a shout.

"Nah, I'm just a big fan," Cherise protested. "Later, guys!"

Roddy and Cherise plunged into the crowd and were swiftly lost to sight.

Drew and Jenna looked at each other. She leaned forward

and yelled into his ear. "Let's go to the room near the front entrance and get a drink. It's quieter out there."

"Sure." Drew slid his arm into hers, and his body got a tingling jolt of Jenna hyperawareness, even through all the layers of fabric.

They found seats at the bar and placed their orders. One of the problems about having to keep his distance emotionally was that he no longer knew how the hell to start a conversation with her.

"I'm sorry that Ava's schedule is stressing you out," he told her. "She just doesn't know when to stop. It's the source of her superpower. It's also a huge pain in the ass."

"I can't deny that it's working," Jenna said. "My team are over the moon at how much attention Arm's Reach is getting. And this thing with Michael and the *Angel Ascending* producers, well. It's incredible, but I'm just not sure how I feel about it."

"I'm glad something useful is coming of it for you," he said. "I was afraid that all my bad press could be damaging to you."

"Not at all. I think it's more like the spice that makes it interesting. You know. The rum in the eggnog. The hot pepper in the salsa."

He snorted. "I'm glad it's good for something."

The bartender delivered their drinks. Jenna sipped her margarita, and turned to him, frowning thoughtfully. "Can I ask you something?"

"Sure."

"The guy who threw that infamous party, the one where you got photographed," she said. "He's made quite a name for himself."

"Arnold Sobel," he said. "Yes, he has. What about him?"

"I was just wondering why you would hang out with a guy like that. He doesn't seem your type. Why go to that party in the first place?"

Just mentioning Sobel's party made tension grip him, as if it had just happened. His stomach heaved nastily. "I knew him way back," he said. "In my crazy partying days, before I joined the service. I only went there as a favor for a friend."

"Ah," she murmured. "Why am I not surprised?"

"Excuse me? What the hell is that supposed to mean?"

"Nothing bad," she assured him. "By no means. It's just that helping people seems to be how you roll. It comes naturally to you."

"My friend Raisa heard that her sister Leticia had gone to that party," he told her. "She's been in some trouble already, and Raisa got nervous. Leticia wasn't answering her phone, and Raisa panicked. She knew I knew Sobel. So she begged me to go to his party and check up on her."

"Did you find Leticia?"

He shook his head.

"Ah." Jenna cocked her head to the side, frowning. "That's strange."

"Yes, it was," he agreed. "The whole thing stank."

"Did you find out if she was ever there?"

"Leticia said afterward that she was somewhere else entirely. She never even knew about that party. Someone was just winding Raisa up. For no reason she can figure out."

"What happened after they took those pictures?" Jenna asked. "You just left?"

He put his beer down, fighting the nausea. That sickening perfume stench filled his nose, even though he knew it was just a memory. Cold sweat broke out on his back. He couldn't seem to breathe. His heart was pounding triple time.

"Could we not talk about this anymore?" he said abruptly. "It wasn't my finest moment."

Jenna looked taken aback. "Sorry. Didn't mean to pry. Won't mention it again."

Damn. He'd screwed up again. "Sorry," he said. "I just—"

From the back room, someone with a mic announced the next set. Drew was grateful for the distraction. "We better get in there."

"Sure, but one second. Let me do something first." Jenna took her cocktail napkin, pressed one of her ice cubes against it and swabbed his cheek gently. "Cherise left a big red lipstick stamp on your cheek when she kissed you. Can't let another woman put her mark on my man."

The Jenna effect zapped through him at her touch, even through the cold, soggy cocktail napkin. "You're just telling me about this lipstick stamp now?" he complained. "You just let me walk around in here like that?"

"Sorry." She looked like she was trying not to smile. "Let's go listen to Roddy, now that you're decent."

Decent, ha. Drew followed her closely through the crowd as they made their way through the various rooms and toward the stage. Little did she know.

In his current state, he felt anything but decent.

Twelve

The room was packed, the band was hot and Roddy was excellent. He had loads of furious, hardcore energy, but he could be low-key and subtle when the music called for it, and he meshed with the seasoned local band as if they'd been playing together for years.

The great music and the margarita had slowly unknotted Jenna's twisted nerves. Her heart was full to overflowing as she watched Roddy play. It was a huge personal victory for her that Roddy had regained enough dexterity and flexibility with his arm to let his musical talent flow through it. That was a kiss of grace from on high. Same with Cherise's promising news about design school. The world was filled with sorrow and disaster and infamy, but tonight, she got to chalk up a few points for the good guys.

Roddy faded out expertly at the end of a song with a shimmery tinkle of the hi-hat, and the lead singer of the band grabbed the mic.

"Boys and girls, I have been informed by our amazing guest drummer, Roddy Hepner, that we have a pair of lovebirds in the audience, and he wants to dedicate one of his own original songs to them. You lucky folks are the first to hear the Vicious Rumors perform this song, but you won't be the last. So here it is, folks! 'Thirsting for You,' written and performed by Roddy Hepner! Make space in the middle of the dance floor, everybody, and give it up for our lucky lovers… Jenna…and… Drew!"

People surged and shifted, leaving a big open space around them. They stood together, ringed by a crowd of onlookers, and the light guy trained a rose-tinted spotlight right on them. Their eyes met, as the opening chords of Roddy's beautiful ballad began.

Drew had that look on his face. Like she was the only woman in the world, and he was desperate with longing for her and her alone. His arms encircled her, pulling her close. It felt so right. So natural and inevitable.

Roddy leaned into the mic angled over the drum set and began to sing. His singing voice was wonderful. Deep and slightly rough but beautifully resonant.

The desert dust is in my shoes.
A thread of hope to see me through.
I seek what's good, I seek what's true.
But now I see I thirst for you.

It was too much. She couldn't resist the pulsing music, the intense emotions. Drew's magnetism. The look in his beautiful eyes, deep and endless as the ocean.

She tried to remind herself that she was just a normal woman, not a glammed-up movie star beauty. No way could she hold this guy's interest in the long run, or fit into his jet-setting lifestyle. She was miles out of her league. Cruising for disaster and heartbreak.

And yet, she clung to him. Their bodies had their own merged magnetism. They were one single swaying entity, and they were on the brink of something momentous, and unbearably sweet. Patterns of colored lights swirled and blended over the dance floor like a dreamy kaleidoscope as Roddy sang on, his voice a tender, scratchy croon.

My eyes are burning and my throat is dry.

My thirsty heart's been seeking far and wide.

But shining from your deep and honest eyes.

I find my reason why.

Drew cupped the back of her head in his warm hand, sliding his fingers tenderly into her hair, his gaze still locked with hers. His deep and honest eyes. They made a space just for her. They saw her so clearly. Made her feel so vibrant and alive. So real.

And they were kissing again. Nothing could have stopped it. They were floating in a shining bubble, the rest of the world shut out.

Their kiss was a language in itself, passionate and direct. It spoke of hunger and longing and tenderness, it promised exquisite pleasure, it coaxed and lured and teased.

She couldn't get enough of it. She kissed him back, saying loud and clear with the kiss everything that she'd been trying so hard not to say since the moment she met him.

Yes. God, yes. Please, yes.

She could feel his erection, hot against her belly. She dragged him closer to feel it better, aching for his heat, his strength and energy as the song slowly ended.

The applause was thunderous. Hoots and howls from the crowd finally penetrated their magic bubble as the space around them dissolved.

People flooded back onto the dance floor, crowding in around them.

Jenna stared at Drew, willing her arms to loosen from their desperate, clinging hold, but they were not obeying her commands.

She finally managed it. By force, she pushed herself back, almost stumbling into someone behind her. Drew caught her and steadied her.

Careful. I got you. She saw his lips form the words, but

couldn't hear his voice in the noise. Those beautiful lips that had just kissed her into a wanton frenzy of desire right in front of a cheering crowd.

"I have to go," she said inanely, pulling away.

His grip tightened, and his lips moved again in the raucous noise. "Where?"

"Uh...uh...the bathroom. Going to the ladies'. See you in a minute. Bye."

She pulled away again. Drew hung on for a split second, sensing her panic, but then let her go.

Jenna slipped away, weaving swiftly through the crowd and toward the door.

Someone stepped in front of her as she made for it. She ran right into him.

"Sorry, Jenna! Didn't mean to bump you!"

It was Ernest, Ava's eager-beaver young assistant, with his spiky white blond hair and his big round glasses that made him look like a crazed steam-punk aviator.

"Ernest," she said. "What on earth are you doing here?"

"The usual," Ernest said, holding up a tablet. "Recording your love!"

Jenna's insides thudded two stories down. "Oh, God. Ava told you to come here?"

"She wanted me to record Roddy's gig. The romantic dance and that be-still-my-heart steaming-hot kiss was just an awesome bonus. It's gonna totally blow up online!"

"Oh, no, no, no! Ernest, do me a favor. Don't post the dance and the kiss, okay? I understand about filming Roddy, but just leave me and Drew out of it."

Ernest looked bewildered. "Why not? I thought this was the whole point!"

"It's just, um, kind of private."

"Well, duh. Of course. That's why people go for it."

"Just don't, this time," she pleaded. "Just this once. I need a breather."

"Sorry." Ernest looked anything but sorry as he lifted his tablet. "I already uploaded it to your and Drew's YouTube channel—"

"I don't have a YouTube channel!"

"Oh, but you do, and since last week, you two have already racked up twenty-one thousand followers. Let's see, I just uploaded this video of the dance and the kiss five minutes ago, and it's got…lemme see here how many views…ooh! Seven hundred and eighty-five…six…seven… It keeps going up! You guys are a hot property!"

"That's just it," Jenna wailed. "I'm not a property! Or a reality TV star! Sometimes I need to get a drink or go hear some music and have it just be for me, for God's sake!"

Ernest gazed at her, looking blank and very clouded. "Just for you? Like, what does that even mean? What do you care if people like to watch? What does it matter?"

Jenna turned her back and left before she lost her temper and smacked the guy.

The cold wind whipped her hair as she walked down the street. Her eyes stung, and her face felt hot. Her throat was tight, like a cruel little hand was squeezing it.

But she'd signed up for this insanity.

There was a taxi cruising by. She hailed it and got in, then pulled out her phone as soon as she'd given directions to the driver. Her hand was shaking as she pulled up Drew's number and texted him.

had to go. grabbed a cab. on my way home now. sorry.

A few moments later, his response appeared. wtf! seriously?

I needed to be alone. sorry. really.

Another minute passed, and his answer appeared. WHAT DID I DO

She hastened to reply. nothing. you were great. it's me. I need some space.

A long pause. Then his terse reply. understood.

Damn it. Damn this whole thing. sorry, she repeated, digging for a tissue.

me too he responded, and then after a moment. good night. stay safe.

Great. Now he was making her feel like crap by being courteous and classy and restrained about it. Damn that guy. He made it so…flipping…*hard*.

She had to run away from him, because she knew exactly how the evening would play out if she didn't. Drew would insist on taking her home. He would insist on walking her to the top of her steps to see her to her door. He would smolder at her with those deep, beautiful eyes that promised the moon and the stars and everything between, and she would lose her mind, drag him inside and jump all over him.

If they even made it inside. She might just ravish him right there on the porch.

She was nine-tenths in love with him already. If they went to bed, that would be it.

There would be no walking this back.

Thirteen

Jenna looked spectacularly beautiful when she joined him at the top of the stairs at the Whitebriar Club for their big entrance. It hit him like a blow.

She wore no glasses tonight. He'd barely recognized her for a moment, since her cat-eye specs were such a distinctive part of her look. She was gorgeous without them, too, in sea-foam green silk, with a string of iridescent beads as shoulder straps and shimmering beadwork on the neckline. The silk skimmed her gorgeous figure and showed a tantalizing shadow between her breasts. A hairdresser had tried to tame the curls into a decorous updo, but the efforts were in vain. The curls would not be contained. Some longer ones had sprung free already. Others swung and bounced around her delicate jaw.

She smiled at him, but her gaze dropped, embarrassed, as he took her slender arm.

"You look stunning," he said.

"Thank you."

"This isn't the black-and-white dress you talked about. Did

you shop for that gown with Ava? I remember you two arguing about it a few days ago."

"Are you asking if you paid for it?" Her eyes met him with a glint of challenge. "You did not. This is one battle with your sister that I actually won, I'm proud to say. I bought this dress months ago, all by myself at a vintage clothing shop downtown. I had to get the beading restored by a costume expert, but I loved the color."

Her in-your-face tone irked him. "I was not asking if I paid for it," he said tersely. "Not that I would give a damn if I had."

She shot him a repentant look. "Sorry. I guess that sounded snarky."

"Sure as hell did," he agreed.

"I just wanted to emphasize that I am not a billionaire's plaything. Even if I do play one on TV."

"It's crystal clear to me that you're not a plaything. Don't strain yourself."

She laughed under her breath, and gave him an assessing glance. "You look sharp yourself," she said. "Nice tux."

"I do my best," he said. "You look different without your glasses."

She gave him a rueful smile. "I've always had these contacts. I'm just too lazy to use them, and they make my eyes tired and red."

"You look great both ways," he said.

"It's a classic fantasy, you know," she said. "Woman takes off glasses. Man notices for the first time that she's female."

Drew looked her up and down. "I noticed it before."

Her gaze whipped away and her color rose as they started descending the stairs toward the sea of people below. Drew was frustrated and angry with himself. When he spoke to her, every damn thing that came out of his mouth sounded like a come-on.

Solution A: Shut up and ignore her. Solution B: Avoid her altogether. As in, definitively and forever, by getting the hell out of Maddox Hill. Those were his options.

She glowed like a pearl. His arm was buzzing from that light contact with her hand, even through his tux jacket and shirt.

Enough. This farce ended tonight. It was making him miserable. That night at the Wild Side had been the last straw. Passionately kissing her while slow dancing and then having her run out on him—it was the ultimate slap.

He wasn't coming back for more. He regretted the embarrassment that breaking their false engagement would cause, but at least Jenna wouldn't have to fend off his unwelcome moves. Since he couldn't seem to stop himself from making them.

He'd get through tonight, hopefully without incident, and make the announcement to everyone concerned before he went home, and that would be that. On to the next thing.

He'd met Vann and Zack last night for a beer, to give them a heads-up before he tendered that letter of resignation he was still carrying around. His friends were angry at him. They thought he was bailing on them. He couldn't make them understand that this was a desperate survival move. A last-ditch effort to salvage what was left of his dignity.

Vann looked up from the bottom of the stairs, a frown between his dark eyes, and glanced at Jenna. His brows went up in silent question. Because of *her*?

Drew kept his face stony. As he and Jenna reached the bottom of the stairs, he saw Harold bearing down on them, a woman on his arm. She was a tall brunette with a black sequined gown and glitter spray on her prominent, bulging breasts, and she was staring straight at him.

Wait. Whoa. He knew that woman. That was Lydia, an architect he'd met in San Francisco, while working on the Magnolia Plaza project. They'd had a casual affair, but he hadn't called her since leaving San Francisco six months ago.

Or thought of her at all, to be perfectly honest.

Harold steered his date so that Lydia and he were right in front of Drew and Jenna at the foot of the stairs, blocking any further progress into the room.

Then it hit him, like a freight train. Lydia's perfume. A heavy, reeking cloud of it.

The same heinous stuff that had been squirted into his face at Sobel's party. Drew's stomach turned and he broke out in a cold sweat. Heart racing. Blood pressure dropping.

"Hi, Drew," Lydia cooed. "Looking good, as always. You've been busy, hmm?"

For a moment, Drew couldn't speak, he was fighting so hard for control. "Hello, Lydia," he forced out. "This is Jenna Somers. My fiancée."

"She knows about your fiancée," Harold said. "At least, she sure knows now."

"Yes, it's so funny how I had absolutely no clue that you'd gotten engaged to this woman last spring when you were down in San Francisco," Lydia said, in a voice that carried far and wide. "You didn't act like a man who'd just found the love of his life, as I very clearly recall." She looked Jenna over, and clucked her tongue. "Sneaky Drew."

"Excuse us. We have to go work the crowd." Drew ground the words out, pulling Jenna away from them.

"We'll talk more later! We're seated right next to each other at the banquet," Harold called after them with barely concealed glee. "You and Lydia can catch up on old times! Lydia can get to know Jenna. Won't that be nice?"

Drew pressed on, putting space between them so he could breathe, but now that the memory was activated, that horrific perfume was all he could smell, and the room was wavering in his vision. Sounds seemed distorted, as if he'd been freshly dosed with whatever drug they'd sprayed on him at the party. A stress flashback, right now? God. He was furious at his own brain for betraying him like this. *Breathe deep. Chill. Control.*

"...matter with you? Drew? What is it? Are you sick?"

Jenna was squeezing his arm and frowning. Her eyes looked worried.

"I'm fine." He forced the words out.

"You don't look fine. Your lips are white. What the hell?"

He groped for an explanation. He finally got a whiff of Jenna's scent. Honey, wildflowers. It settled him. He got a deep breath into himself. Then another.

"I think I had some kind of an allergic reaction to Lydia's perfume." He threw out the first excuse that came to his mind, but it was actually kind of true.

"I think I've got you beat there. I had an allergic reaction to Lydia herself," Jenna said with feeling. "She and your cousin are quite the poisonous pair. Better now?"

"Better," he said.

Damn good thing, too, because now they were in the room where the architectural exhibits were displayed, and the crowd closed around them. The work of the evening began; the shaking of hands, hugs and air kisses, pleasantries and chitchat, posing for photos and selfies, speaking authoritatively about the projects he'd designed. Architects and engineers, board members, local politicians and businesspeople, journalists, a stream of people to interact with. He tried to fake normal, and when he faltered, Jenna covered for him as best she could.

It felt like forever, but eventually the crowd started drifting into the stately banquet room where dinner would be served and the endless speechifying would begin. By the time they got to their table, everyone else was seated, and there was no graceful way to switch out their places elsewhere without drawing a great deal of attention to themselves.

Harold and Lydia were lying in wait for them. They both stared at Drew and Jenna from the table with cold, watchful eyes. Lydia's perfume hit his nose like a foul cloud of toxic gas. The place card with his name was right next to Lydia's chair. His guts lurched.

Jenna elbowed him to the other side and sat down next to Lydia herself, giving the other woman a big smile. "Hope you two are having a lovely evening."

"Getting better all the time." Harold's eyes dropped to Jenna's chest, where it stayed like it had been nailed there, all the way through the appetizers and the first course. Drew wanted to smack Harold under the chin until his jaws clacked together to get him to look up into Jenna's eyes when he spoke to her. Disrespectful sleaze.

Drew braved Lydia's perfume and leaned closer, careful not to inhale, to focus on what his cousin was saying.

"...on YouTube. You know, the incendiary kiss. The slow dance at the Wild Side."

"Oh, God." Jenna sounded embarrassed. "That was so silly. Ava's assistant, Ernest, was filming the drummer. We had no idea he was there. So embarrassing."

Harold took a swig of his wine and licked his lips. "So spontaneous," he commented.

"Are you usually such a shameless exhibitionist?" Lydia's eyes glittered. She had a lipstick stain on her teeth. "Does Drew inspire you? I don't blame you. That man is inspiring. No one knows that better than me. He can get a girl to do any wild, crazy thing he wants. Like, anything."

"Excuse me," Jenna said, recoiling slightly. "I'm not sure I understand."

"We just wondered." Harold gave her a lascivious smile. "You know, if the two of you get off on having the whole world watch while you, ah...get busy. Is that your thing?"

Drew shot to his feet, hitting the table. His chair fell backward, silverware rattled, a wineglass toppled. Wine splattered across the table and Lydia jumped up, scooting backward in an attempt to save her dress.

"Clumsy jerk!" she hissed. "Watch it!"

Drew ignored her, addressing his cousin. "What the hell kind of question is that?"

Harold's smile widened. The room fell silent. Everyone was watching and listening.

"I'm surprised you even heard me, you're so zoned out tonight." Harold's voice was clear and carrying. "Go easy on that wine, Drew. Are you on antihistamines? Or maybe something stronger?"

"I heard what you said," Drew said. "Do not speak to her again."

"Just admiring your fiancée," Harold said innocently. "You've smeared your red-hot scorching love affair far and wide all over the internet, so I could hardly avoid admiring her if I wanted to. Don't go all caveman on me now. It's unbecoming."

"Admire someone else. Keep your goddamn opinions to yourself."

"Drew!" Jenna said in a fierce whisper. "Holy crap! Calm down!"

Harold lifted his hands, grinning widely. "Take it easy, big guy."

"What the hell is going on?" Uncle Malcolm's furious voice came from behind him.

"Oh, no biggie." Harold's tone was light. "Just the usual. Drew's had a few too many, and now he's making a public spectacle of himself. Same old same old."

"What's this?" Uncle Malcolm glared at Drew. "What's this? Is this true?"

Drew opened his mouth, but Lydia spoke up first.

"I can't take any more of this," she quavered, clutching the wine-stained napkin she'd used to clean up her dress in her shaking hand. "You lying, cheating son of a bitch. They say you were engaged to this woman last year, when you were in San Francisco!" She pointed at Jenna. "Engaged! And you never said a word about it, all those times when you were nailing me right on the desk in your office! You filthy, selfish *bastard*!"

Gasps and low murmurs of scandalized conversation followed that outburst. The waiters all around the tables froze in place, terrified, holding their trays of prime rib.

Lydia burst into tears. She hurried out of the room, weaving and bumping between tables. Sobbing, tear-blinded, but taking her toxic cloud of perfume with her, thank God.

When she was out the door, Uncle Malcolm turned back to Drew and cleared his throat. "So. Nephew. Just to be fore-warned, for the sake of my heart health, are there any more of your disgruntled chippies roaming around here on the rampage tonight?"

"Not to my knowledge," Drew said.

Uncle Malcolm harrumphed and looked around, scowling. The entire room looked back, waiting for their cue. Malcolm made a disgusted sound and waved his hand. "For God's sake, finish serving the damn meat before it's stone-cold," he snarled at the waiters. He turned to Drew. "You, come with me. I need to speak to you privately. Right now."

Drew let out a slow breath. He'd reached the end of the line.

In some ways, it was for the best. His bridges were burned, so he no longer had to torture himself with doubts or second thoughts. All he could do was move forward.

He should feel relieved, but as he looked into Jenna's worried eyes, he felt like something precious had been ripped from him. Something he'd just learned how to value.

He fixed Harold with a grim stare. "If you slime her again, I will flatten you."

"Come *now*!" his uncle snapped. "You're making a spectacle of yourself!"

"Yeah, that seems to be the general theme of my life lately." He leaned down and cupped Jenna's face. "I'm sorry," he whispered to her. "Goodbye."

He kissed Jenna, slowly and intensely, with all his pent-up desperation, ignoring the rising hum of excited chatter and his uncle's furious sputtering. Because what the hell.

He had nothing left to lose.

Fourteen

Jenna watched Drew follow his uncle out of the crowded room, head up and shoulders back, like a soldier on the march. Her fingers were pressed to her tingling, just-kissed lips. She was shocked speechless. On the verge of tears.

She jumped up to follow him, and found Harold's hot, damp fingers suddenly clamped around her wrist. "Jenna, no," he murmured. "Let them go. Sit down."

She jerked her wrist away. "With you? Why the hell should I do that?"

"Calm down," Harold said. "I am not the bad guy here."

She laughed right in his face. "You expect me to believe that?"

"This is old stuff, Jenna. Family stuff. A long time coming. Don't mix yourself up in it. You don't know the history."

She stared at Harold. "I don't think I need to. It's very clear to me."

And it was getting clearer all the time, like watching a photograph take form in a bath of darkroom chemicals. She thought of her first flash-assessment of Harold when she met him at the restaurant. Perfectly good-looking in his own right, but he suffered in comparison with Drew.

From what Ava had said, the same held true for Harold's professional life. He was competent and successful in his field, unless Drew was next to him with all of the medals and prizes and honors and high-profile projects. Next to Drew, Harold got bumped several notches down the scale, until he registered as barely higher than average.

She disliked the very thought in itself, because she did not believe in judging people in that way. But the rest of the world did.

Harold had spent his whole life in Drew's shadow and he was sick of it.

"You set him up," she said. "You sneaky bastard. You organized this whole thing."

Harold sipped his wine. "You'd like to have me be the villain so that your perfect, fantasy Drew can be innocent. News flash. He's not. Sorry to break it to you, honey."

"I am not your honey," she said. "You brought that woman up from San Francisco on purpose. I bet you told her to make that big scene as soon as Malcolm was in earshot."

"I didn't have to tell her a thing. Everything she said was literally true. Drew gets into trouble all by himself. He doesn't need help from me or anyone. Like that orgy at the Sobel party. He did that all by himself, and he does it often. That time, he just happened to get busted."

"He was lured into a trap," she said. "He was there to help a friend."

"That's what he told you?" Harold gave her a pitying look. "I checked the dates of your Women in STEM speech in San Francisco last year, when you and Drew hooked up. I know for a fact that Drew was screwing Lydia that whole time, and for months afterward. You were sharing him back then, Jenna. Knowing Drew, you're probably sharing him now. He's a star, and he never denies himself. I'm sorry to hurt you, but it's true. Think long and hard before you get in too deep with him."

Jenna stepped back, whipping her arm away before Harold could grab her wrist again. To hell with this guy. He wasn't worth another moment of her time.

And she had a few choice things she wanted to say to Malcolm Maddox.

She marched through the tables, chin high, ignoring the muttering and the stares, following the path Drew and his uncle had taken. Once outside the ballroom, she homed in on Malcolm's haranguing voice. It came from upstairs, so she followed it up, and down the wide hall until she came to the double doors of the Cedar Salon, a luxurious old-fashioned parlor.

As she threw the doors open, the old man's voice blared even louder.

"...sick of your depraved antics! After all Hendrick's complaining about your behavior, you decide to put on a floor show like that right in front of all of them?"

"Uncle, I didn't plan on that woman showing up to—"

"You think you dodged a bullet when you trotted out your perfect little Miss Butter-Wouldn't-Melt-In-Her-Mouth, eh? You think you can use her like some sort of goddamn human shield. But whatever you think you might have gained by that cheap trick, you just lost ten times over, and I for one am not fooled by your—"

"He is not using me!" Jenna yelled. "If anything, I'm the one using him!"

Malcolm's head whipped around, eyes shocked. "This is a private conversation, Miss Somers!"

"I don't care. If you're trash-talking me, I insist on participating. Miss Butter-Wouldn't-Melt-In-Her-Mouth, my ass! You should be ashamed of yourself!"

Malcolm Maddox stared at her for a moment, mouth open, and cleared his throat. "Well," he said gruffly. "That is a matter of opinion."

"So now you know my opinion!"

"Certainly. At that volume, the whole building knows your opinion."

"I'm fine with that," she said hotly. "I have nothing to hide. Nothing."

"That's not the case for him, unfortunately." Malcolm gestured at Drew. "You heard what that woman said. It's the story of his life! Is that what you want for yourself?"

"He was set up! He goes miles out of his way to help people, time and time again. He took a bullet in Iraq, risking his life for his country. Does none of that count for you?"

"Oh, God." Drew looked pained. "Jenna, I don't need for you to—"

"You just hush up!" She rounded on him furiously. "You've been doing a crap job at defending yourself lately, so step aside and let me handle it this time!"

"I appreciate your zeal, young lady," Malcolm said. "But you're sticking your nose into matters that aren't your business."

"Guilty as charged," she said. "I don't give a damn. Just don't expect me to smile and nod while someone I care about is being put down. I just…won't…do it. Period."

Malcolm Maddox frowned at her for a moment, then his gaze flicked to Drew. "Hmph," he grunted. "Played the wounded soldier card, eh?"

"I play the cards I have," Drew said.

"Don't blame you, to be honest." Malcolm looked her over, his eyes sharp and assessing. "She is something when she gets going, hmm?"

"That she is," Drew agreed.

"Do not talk about me as if I'm not here," Jenna snapped.

Malcolm laughed and gestured toward Jenna with his cane. "Hang on to this one if you can, boy," he said gruffly. "But you know damn well you don't deserve her. You're just a dog on the furniture. Pull yourself together. Try not to make spectacles of yourselves for the rest of the evening, if you can possibly manage it, eh? Both of you."

He turned his back and stumped out, hunched over his cane, still muttering.

Drew and Jenna looked at each other after the door fell to after him. Jenna shook her head, bewildered. "Um… What just happened?"

"Looks like you just charmed Uncle Malcolm," Drew said. "Congratulations."

She stared at him. "Charmed him? By scolding him? *That's* what charms him?"

"We're a contrary bunch." Drew's tone was almost apologetic. "And he favors strong women. With strong opinions."

"Oh, God." Jenna pressed both hands to her hot cheeks. "This is so crazy." She started digging in her evening bag for a tissue, sniffling into it.

"What's wrong?" Drew asked. "Why are you crying?"

"It happens when I lose my temper. Something shorts out in my brain. Don't be alarmed, you don't have to comfort me or anything like that. It'll pass quickly."

Drew still looked worried. "You're sure you're okay?"

"Fine," she assured him. "Really."

He just looked at her, hesitating. "Ah…thanks," he said, awkwardly.

"For what?"

"For coming out swinging like that. For having my back. I know that it was part of the whole being-engaged act, and I think we can hang that masquerade up at this point. But act or no act, it felt really good to hear."

She was horrified by a fresh wave of tears. "Oh, crap," she muttered. "That was not an act, Drew Maddox." There it was. The truth. She'd blurted it out at last.

His eyes sharpened. "Meaning what? You haven't been pretending?"

"Not at all," she admitted. "I've been a goner ever since I dumped that pitcher of sangria on you. I know I shouldn't tell you this, but that's the short circuit in my brain. I cry, and then

I blurt out stuff people don't necessarily want to hear. Anyhow. I've done enough damage tonight, so I think I'll just get my coat and get the hell out of—"

She let out a startled squeak as Drew pulled her against himself and kissed her.

It was electrifying. His breathless urgency. His hard body, muscles taut, shaking with emotion. The shining thrill racing through her, the ache of hunger in her body, always a constant smolder, but when he touched her, it flared into a bonfire.

Jenna wrapped her arms around his neck and melted into him. Kissed him back with everything she had. Ravenous for the delicious heat of his mouth as a new world of emotions and sensations opened up inside her.

Drew maneuvered them down onto an antique love seat, pulling her down onto his lap and kissing her bare shoulder with desperate tenderness. The beaded straps of the dress slid down, and the top of the lacy cups of her strapless bra were showing. Drew made a rough, tormented sound in his throat and pressed his face against them. Both of them moaned at the sweetness of it. The warm tenderness of his lips was an intoxicating sensation, kissing her, nuzzling her. His arms were so strong. Everywhere he touched her touched off a rush of delight. He stroked her back.

"Oh, God. So hot and soft," he murmured. "So smooth. You're killing me."

She settled right over that hard, unyielding bulge of his erection and leaned down to kiss him again. The bodice of the dress was slipping down but his hands stroking her bare back felt so good, and his hot kiss was so searching and seductive.

The doors squeaked, and a swell of noise behind them made them both freeze and turn. Drew's body went tense beneath her.

Uncle Malcolm, Hendrick, Bev, Harold, Ava, Ernest, eyes popping, mouths agape, and a dozen more people stood right behind them, pushing, craning. On tiptoe. A hum of shocked murmurs, embarrassed giggles.

"Oh, my God." Jenna struggled with her neckline, tugging it back up over the cups of her strapless bra before sliding off Drew's lap and onto her feet.

"Out! Everyone get out!" Uncle Malcolm shouted, but there was no possible retreat for the people in the doorway. The crush of gawkers pressing up behind them blocked their escape. Harold's face was a cold mask. Ava's smile was conspiratorial. Like she was in on the joke.

Except it wasn't a joke. It never really had been.

Bev smirked at her husband. "Well, Hendrick, that looks pretty sincere to me, wouldn't you say? I think I won this bet. Better get ready to pay up."

Hendrick just peered at them, his thick eyebrows knitted together like he just couldn't figure out what was going on.

Not that Jenna was doing much better, when it came right down to it.

"Get back!" Malcolm bawled. "All of you! Out! Damn it!"

Jenna finally got her dress straightened and slid her shoe back on. She scooped up her beaded evening bag from where it had fallen on the carpet. "That's my cue," she murmured to Drew. "Time to disappear."

"With me," Drew said swiftly. "Only with me."

She looked into his eyes, and promptly forgot that people were watching them. The longing in his eyes called out to her, a sweet pull so strong, not even public humiliation could quench it. It just raged on and on, wanting what it wanted.

"Yes," she said. "Let's disappear together."

His eyes flashed, and his warm hand closed around hers.

Malcolm overheard them. "That would be best, since neither one of you seems to be capable of any self-control," he snarled. "For the love of God, go! Let me try to salvage what's left of my company's image."

"Don't be grumpy, Uncle." Ava was still trying not to smile. "Everyone loves it, and you know it."

"Enough, Av," Drew said. "Dial it down to zero."

"Me?" Ava's chin rose. "I'm not dialing anything. I'm not doing a damn thing, bro. You two are doing it all on your own. But it would be a shame to stop now when everyone's having so much fun, don't you think?"

"We're out of here." Drew slid his arm around Jenna's waist and made for the crowd of people who blocked the doors. "Make way."

The steely quality in his voice made people actually shuffle backward. Jenna's face burned as they forced their way through, but Harold's cold eyes chilled her as she passed. She could feel the anger emanating from him.

People tried to speak to them, but she couldn't follow what they were saying. Drew ignored them, sweeping them both onward through the press of people and down the stairs, toward the coat check desk. He helped her slip her coat on. "You're shaking," he said as they made their way toward the exit. "Put on my coat. It's heavier."

"Not from the cold. I'm actually kind of hot," she said, as they went out the door.

The cold, damp night air felt good against her feverish face.

"Where's your car?" he asked.

"Didn't bring it," she told him, teeth still chattering. "I used a car service. Didn't want to be bothered with parking or driving."

"Good," he said, as the parking attendant pulled up in his silver Jag.

He opened the door for her, and she got in, waiting while he tipped the attendant and got in himself. Then they sat in stunned silence for a moment.

She laughed shakily. "Holy cow. What a circus."

"Yes it was." He started the engine and pulled out onto the street. "I'm sorry to put you through that."

"It wasn't your fault. I mouthed off to your uncle. I showed my strapless bra to the Board of Directors and God knows who all else. That's going to follow me around until I die."

He laughed. "At least the bra was still on."

"Well, thank God for that," she said. "I can't believe how I just behaved. I can't carry on in public like that. I'm going to lose all my professional credibility."

"I'm sorry if I put you in a compromising position," he said. "The last thing I want is to damage you professionally."

Jenna wound the beaded strap of her purse around her fingers. "I imagine that whole exhibition was kind of a buzzkill for you, right?"

"No." Drew reached across the console and grabbed her hand without taking his eyes off the road.

The contact with his hand flashed up her arm, then raced instantly to deeper, more secret places. "No?" She tried to keep her voice even, but it still quavered, betraying her. "You're not traumatized?"

"I barely noticed them," he admitted. "All I saw in that room was you. Nothing on earth could kill my buzz."

A glow of anticipation was filling her whole body.

"How about you?" he asked. "Are you still with me?"

She squeezed his hand. "Oh, yeah."

He squeezed back. "Can I take you to my house? It's closer. And I want you to see it."

"Yes, please. I'd like that."

Game on. She was done trying to control this.

Whatever he offered, she would take. If it was just his body, that was fine. Just a fling, fine. Just one night, also fine. She wanted this. She was grabbing it with both hands.

She could process the hurt later. There would be plenty of time for that.

Wow. Just look at her. After all her lofty notions and uppity attitude, she'd tumbled into Drew's honeyed trap after all.

She had just officially become a billionaire's plaything.

So be it. It was finally time to play.

Fifteen

Drew was tongue-tied the entire way home. Having Jenna in his car, taking her to his home—it was huge. It filled up his chest until he could barely breathe, let alone speak. He'd never felt this way, even when he was a teenager just learning about sex. He'd started out by faking it. Pretending to be cool and confident and smooth until that became the truth.

But it wasn't his truth anymore. Not with Jenna. He couldn't pretend. All bets were off with her. Nothing could be taken for granted. And the stakes were so damn high.

He kept his grip on her slim, cool hand, when he didn't need his own hand for driving. Whenever he had to let go of her, he promptly reached for her again. Assuring himself that she was real.

But she was also nervous. He could not screw this up.

He pulled into the driveway that led to his property on Lake Washington and parked the car in the garage.

"You designed this house," she said.

"How did you know that?"

"I've seen your buildings. I knew it was yours because it was so different from the lakeside McMansions we passed. Your designs don't fight with their environment. They're harmonious."

He was absurdly pleased that she got it, and that she liked the house he'd designed for himself. As well as embarrassed. He was showing off to impress her, like a little kid.

"Come on in." He took her hand to lead her down the flagstone path that wound through the trees and landscaped garden of the front lawn to the main entrance. When they went inside, Jenna stood in the middle of the entry hall with its row of skylights, and then strolled into the living room. A long wall of glass overlooked the lake, with lights from the other side of Lake Washington wavering on the water. French doors led out onto the patio. A wooden walkway wound through the grass and trees down to a floating dock, and his boat. Another thing he'd been too busy to use lately.

"I'll give you a tour tomorrow," he offered. "When we have some light."

But not now. I'm dying to touch you.

"Okay," she murmured.

Drew watched her as she wandered around his living room. He tried to remember what common courtesy demanded.

"Can I take your coat?" He slid open the panels in the wall in the entry hall, revealing the deep cedar-lined closet. She moved closer, turning to let him lift the coat from her shoulders. That released an intoxicating waft of sweet fragrance. Her hair had rebelled from its coif, her ringlets floating up free and dangling around her throat. Her skin was so fine. So soft. He wanted to bury his face against it.

He swallowed, hard. "Can I get you a drink? I have whiskey, brandy, or I could open a bottle of wine. Or mix you a drink from the bar. Anything you like."

She peeked over her shoulder, a seductive smile curving the corners of her luscious red lips. "Better not," she murmured. "I'm in an altered state already."

"Want me to build a fire?" he asked.

"When we're already so hot?"

Her light, teasing words made the heat roar through him. His hands flexed, clenched. "You have a point," he said, rigidly controlled.

"I'm too impatient for time-wasting moves like that," she told him. "After weeks of being constantly tantalized."

He let out a harsh crack of laughter. "Me, tantalizing you? Like hell! I've been stretched out at your feet ever since that very first day. I have held nothing back!"

"And this smooth seductive patter of yours? The drink, the fire?" She rolled her eyes at him. "Are you going to show me your etchings now? Your butterfly collection?"

Her voice was playful, but he was so attuned to her now, he could sense she was wound incredibly tight. Trying to keep him at arm's length with her teasing.

The first step was to unwind her. Very…slowly.

He didn't try to reply. Just came up behind her, and leaned down to kiss her shoulder, letting his lips trail up to the nape of her neck. No words. No seductive patter. Just his lips, moving over her skin. A slow, dragging caress, the rasp of his teeth. A delicate nip. Her hair was so soft and fragrant. So warm.

She tilted her head, allowing him more access.

He took advantage of it. Gave himself up to it. Oh, yeah. He could do this all night. Hot, hungry kisses, slowing down time. Exploring every inch of her throat, her shoulders. Getting her to relax and soften in his grasp. He wanted her helpless with pleasure. So aroused, she couldn't even stand up. That was the goal.

Her breath was uneven as he slid his arms around her waist from behind. One hand splayed over her belly, whisper-thin silk separating him from her warm skin. He loved the tremor in her body, the breathless sound in the back of her throat as he slid his hand up, feeling her rib cage. The soft weight of her breasts. The smoothness of her skin above the dress. Her racing pulse.

Jenna placed her hands over his. Not stopping them, just covering them. Pressing them closer to her. He leaned down, kissing her shoulders. Nudging the beaded strap of her gown until it fell off one shoulder. Then the other. He was slow. Persistent.

His pulsing erection was pressed up to her backside, and she leaned back against him, welcoming the contact. Inviting his touch, with that dreamy smile on her face.

It was getting more and more difficult to keep this slow. His hands shook, but he soldiered on. He found a stray hairpin trapped in one of her ringlets during his nuzzling kisses, so he took a moment to sort through her hair and pull out all the pins, setting that halo of wild ringlets loose. "I like it best when it's like this," he said. "Free and wild."

"Getting wilder by the second," she murmured. "The way you kiss me makes me crazy."

"That's how I want you to feel," he said. "I want you primed."

"That's how I want you, too."

"Not an issue. Done deal. I've been in that primed state pretty much since you first kissed me in the elevator."

She looked back at him, the mix of colors in her eyes hypnotically beautiful. Then she straightened up and turned around to face him, shrugging the bodice of her dress down until it was hanging off her hips.

She shook back her hair, holding his gaze with a blaze of sexy challenge in her eyes as she reached behind herself and undid the clasp of her bra.

She let it drop, and stood there, shoulders back. Displaying herself. The color in her cheeks was high. Her lips parted, breath coming fast. But her hands still shook.

Her breasts were so beautiful. High, full and soft, with tight dark pink nipples, and her skin was so fine-grained and smooth and perfect. The chill in his house had given her goose bumps but her chest had a pink blush that matched the one on her cheeks.

He wanted to lunge for her like a ravenous animal. *Easy does it.*

Drew placed his hands on her waist. A tremor went through

her at the contact, then another as his hands slid slowly upward, over her rib cage. Under her arms.

He cupped her breasts, almost reverently. "You are spectacular."

"I'm still waiting for the spectacle to begin. You certainly do keep a girl waiting."

"I'm trying not to rush it," he said. "We'll never get this first time back. I want the memory to be perfect."

Her smile sent fire shooting through every part of his body. "Really? Wow. I had no idea you were so sentimental."

"Neither did I," he admitted. "That thought has never passed through my mind before in my life. Only with you."

Her eyebrows went up. "Well, then," she murmured. "I am honored to be the one to have sparked an original thought in your head."

He gave her a narrow look. "I'm not sure quite how to take that."

She laughed at him. "You don't have to take it at all. I'm just messing with you." She reached up to deftly loosen his bow tie, then she started in on the buttons of his shirt, sliding her hand inside to caress his chest. "The way I feel right now, we couldn't make anything but amazing memories. Relax. Let yourself go. I trust you."

He knew she was just talking about sex, but the rush of emotion her words gave him made him throb and burn. Her hands moved over his chest.

"Just one quick thing first," she said hesitantly. "I don't carry condoms around in my evening bag, so…"

"I have some," he assured her.

"Good. That's a relief. But since we're on the subject, let's just power through this part all at once. I got myself tested for everything under the sun a few weeks ago, after I found out that Rupert was cheating on me. Thank God he didn't give me anything. I'm in the clear, just so you know."

"Thanks for bringing it up. Me, too. Just got tested myself, and I'm all good."

"Excellent," she said, undoing another button, and then another, spreading his shirt and murmuring in approval at what she found. "In that case. I have a contraceptive implant. So... We could just dispense with the latex. If you'd like."

Liked? The idea of no latex with Jenna made him dizzy. "Dream come true."

"Great," she murmured, leaning forward to kiss his chest. "So... Do you mean to do the deed right here in your foyer? I wouldn't mind, since it's all so beautiful—"

He scooped her up into his arms. She made a startled sound. "Whoa! The hell?"

He carried her down the long corridor, toward his bedroom. "My bedroom."

She wound her fingers into the fabric of his shirt collar and tugged it. "Wow," she whispered. "How masterful and ravishing of you."

"Do you go for that?"

"Sure, if it's you."

Good. He nudged the door to the master bedroom open with his foot. His bedroom was very large and sparsely furnished, everything in it subservient to the view. Two enormous windows looked out over Lake Washington, the waving trees and garden. The light filtering in from outside was just enough to make the bamboo floor planks gleam and dimly illuminate the low, enormous bed.

Drew carried Jenna over to the bed and laid her down, climbing on top of her. Covering her slender body with his own.

She said she trusted him to let himself go, and he was taking her at her word.

Sixteen

She felt like a live flame. Pure and essential, like everything superfluous had gone up in smoke. She barely recognized the woman moving beneath Drew, making those helpless gasping sounds. Enthralled by him, and yet more marvelously free than she'd ever felt.

She loved his heat, his lithe, solid body on top of her. His bare chest pressed to her breasts. Then he slid farther down, kissing her throat, then her collarbone.

When he got to her breasts, she floated up to a new level of shining hyperawareness. She clutched his head, fingers slipping through his short hair, thighs squeezing together, just trying to breathe. She wanted to wrap her legs around him, but her thighs were clamped between his, leaving her writhing, gasping, struggling instinctively toward release as her excitement crested to terrifying heights—and crashed down on her.

The climax pulsed through her body. Deep throbs of pleasure wiped her out.

When she opened her eyes, Drew was poised over her, his eyes hot and fascinated.

"I'd call that a good beginning," he said. "I love watching you come."

She wanted to laugh, but she was so limp, her chest barely lifted against his weight. But he still felt it, rolling off her and pulling her tight against him, so they were on their sides facing each other.

She plucked at his shirt. "Get that off," she said. "I want the full effect."

Drew sat up, shrugging off the tux jacket, wrenching off the shirt. He tossed it away, prying off shoes and socks while he was at it.

Jenna sat up, too, with some effort, as relaxed as she felt, and sat on the bed, struggling with the ridiculously tiny buckles on the ankle straps of her shoes. It was almost impossible, with fingers that were still shaking.

Drew sank down to his knees on the floor in front of her. His big, warm hands pushed hers away. "Let me."

He undid the buckles swiftly, tossing the shoes behind him, and looked into her eyes as he slid his big, warm hands up the outside of her legs, all the way up to the bands of stretchy lace that held up her thigh-high stockings, and then onto the warm, bare skin above them. He began exploring, with his usual hypnotically slow, magical caresses.

"The dress has got to go," he said. "But leave the stockings on."

She stood up, grabbing his shoulder to steady herself, and almost couldn't get a good grip, it was so thick with muscle. "I just got all that fancy beading repaired," she murmured. "Don't want to tear out the seams."

Drew tugged the crumpled pale green fabric gently down over her hips, until it fell to the floor. He made a low, grinding sound deep in his throat as he swayed forward, pressing his face to her belly.

His breath was so hot, so tender. His lips trailed over her

skin, and left a glowing trail of hyper-sensitized erogenous zone every place he touched.

She slid her fingers into his hair, caressing his ears, his cheekbone, his jaw. Savoring the texture of his faint rasp of beard shadow, squeezing the massive breadth of his powerful shoulders.

Drew hooked his thumbs into the pale lace of her panties and tugged them down. She shook them off her ankle, and sucked in a startled breath as he leaned to kiss her, his mouth moving skillfully over her sensitive flesh while his hands cupped her bottom. She vibrated like a plucked string.

"So good." Drew kissed his way around the swatch of hair adorning her mound.

Jenna wanted to respond somehow, but she was beyond words. She felt so vulnerable, so naked. Incredibly female. Tormented by longing as she wound her fingers into his hair, tugging wordlessly. Demanding more, more, more.

He responded eagerly, pressing his mouth to her, caressing her tender inner folds. He was bold and generous and tireless. So incredibly good at it. He went at her with ruthless skill until she was shaking wildly, head thrown back. Keening low in her throat, completely focused on the sensual swirl of his tongue, the delicate flick, the slow, suckling pull—and she came apart, as he unleashed another wave of shuddering pleasure.

Afterward, she found herself lying down with no clear memory of how she got there, but Drew was leaning over her, pulling the billowy, puffy comforter over her.

"Good?" he asked.

She licked her lips. "I never felt anything so fabulous in my life," she whispered.

"Excellent." She couldn't read his face in the dimness, but he sounded pleased.

She grabbed his belt. "The pants need to come off. I don't want to be naked alone."

"Oh, don't worry." He shucked his pants promptly. "I'll keep you company."

He worked his briefs down, and his erection sprang free. Jenna sat up with a murmur of approval. He was stiff, flushed, ready. She closed her hand around him, and Drew covered her hand with his own, moving it up and down his thick shaft. So hot and hard and sexy. Exciting her beyond belief. She stroked him, exploring him, teasing him, squeezing him. She loved making him shudder and gasp and moan.

Finally he stopped her hands, and stretched out next to her, sliding under the covers and into her arms.

The shock of contact with her whole body made her gasp. He was scorching hot. It was overwhelming. The buzz of intense awareness felt both brand-new and incredibly familiar, like she'd known him since eternity. Their connection was timeless, inevitable, in thrall to that kiss. Tongues dancing, arms clasping, legs twining. Struggling to get closer.

She didn't know what was up, what was down. He was her center of gravity, the only one that mattered. At some point, based on the fact that she was somewhat breathless, she realized that she was underneath, pinned by his solid weight. Her legs twined around his, pulling him closer. The heat of his erection throbbed against her belly.

"You ready?" he asked.

It was hard to respond, with her throat so soft and hot, her lips shaking. She nodded, pulling him closer. Insistently.

His grin flashed briefly in the dimness as he shifted on top of her, positioning himself as she arched and opened, stretching luxuriously.

"You're so soft," he murmured, parting her tender inner folds as he moved himself against her with small, teasing strokes.

She couldn't form words anymore, not in this state. She was stuck with nonverbal communication. She dug her nails into his chest and let out a low, breathless moan as he pushed himself slowly inside her exquisitely sensitized body. He filled her completely.

She could hardly move, but she was softer and slicker and hotter than she'd ever imagined being. They started slow, just rocking together, tiny surges, but soon it was just like all the other times he'd touched her. She felt possessed, out of control, writhing, making wild, demanding sounds, nails digging into his back. Demanding everything.

And he gave it to her. Deep, rhythmic thrusts that drove her wild, caressing all the new tender sweet spots that had suddenly come into being just for him. Every stroke was marvelous, perfect, poignant. She didn't want it to ever stop, but already the charge was building, bigger than ever before.

She had no idea what was on the other side of something so huge, just that it was unprecedented. She could burn to ash, disappear. But it didn't matter. There was no question of choice. She just let that wild power have its way. Like tumbling off a cliff.

And discovering, to her astonishment, that she could fly.

Drew lifted up onto his elbows, easing slowly and reluctantly out of her clinging depths. So hot and sweet. He hoped he'd read her cues right in his own frenzy, desperate for the next thrust before he finished the one he was doing. She was small and tight and perfect, and he hadn't kept it slow. The whole thing had gotten away from him.

He stretched out next to her, touching her body along its entire length, everywhere he could. Stroking her back and waiting. Holding his breath for the verdict.

He didn't have to wait long. Her beautiful eyes fluttered open, dazed and dilated. The smile she gave him was glowing. "Hey, you."

He pulled her hand up to his mouth, kissing her knuckles. "You good?"

"Great," she said. "I didn't know that was even possible."

"What?" He was cautiously hopeful. "Meaning...?"

"Feeling like that. Coming like that. It was... I never felt anything like it."

The tension inside him relented. "Ah. Okay. Good, then."

Her eyes went wide. "Wait," she said, rolling up to prop her head on her hand. "Were you actually worried?"

"Just wanted it to be perfect for you," he said, kissing her hand again.

"*Perfect* is the wrong word," she told him. "*Perfect* is careful and nervous and controlled. It wasn't like that. It was wild. Magic. But you know that. You were there."

He was grinning now, helplessly. "Still am. Not going anywhere."

He kissed her, and in a heartbeat, he was stone-hard again, as needy and aching as he was before.

Too soon. He had to hang back. Take it easy.

He rolled onto his belly, and tried to content himself by stroking her warm, lithe body under the covers. Studying the beautiful planes and curves and hollows of her face and throat in the shadowy dimness. So spectacularly pretty. So unique.

"I just don't get it," he said, almost to himself.

"What's that?"

"Your ex. I don't get how he could look at anyone else when he had you."

She snorted. "He didn't see me. He just expected to be the smack-dab center of my attention at all times. My job was to constantly make him feel a certain way about himself, and I couldn't keep up with it. It was exhausting."

"He works in your field, right?"

"He's an engineer, like me," she said. "He was on the team that developed the design for Cherise's arm. I'm not angry like I was before, though. Only my pride was hurt. Everything else is intact. All things considered, it was a near miss. He and Kayleigh did me a favor. A public, embarrassing, ego-crushing favor. Very generous of them. I'm grateful."

Drew shifted in the bed, rolling her over on top of him. "And I'm glad."

"About what?" Jenna positioned herself, and her sensual wiggling felt so good.

He adjusted their position so that she was settled right exactly where he needed her. She gasped as he pulsed his hips up against her. "I'm glad you're not hung up on him," he said. "Because I don't want to share."

She looked startled. "Um. Wow."

They stared at each other for a long moment, and Jenna's expression changed, as the ever-present heat between them surged.

She placed her hands against his chest and pushed herself until she was sitting up, straddling him. Tossing the cover back so it landed on his legs. Shoulders back. Eyes on his, full of fire. Full of invitation as she reached down, caressing his stiff, aching length.

She placed her other hand on his chest. "I can feel your heart. In both places."

Drew covered her hand with his own, pressing it. Then he seized her hips, lifting her up so he could position himself beneath her. She danced over him until they got the angle right, and she let out a low, wordless moan as she took him inside, sinking down with shivering slowness into her tight, clinging heat.

Together they found the perfect surging rhythm. He was desperate to explode inside her, and he also wanted this to last forever. Every point of contact was as sweet as a deliberate kiss. He went for all of them with deep, gliding strokes. Seeking out everything that made her melt and moan, the power building in her body.

She cried out, throwing her head back, convulsing over him, and just in time because his own climax was rumbling in his head, a landslide about to come down on him. Huge and inevitable.

It overtook him. Blotted out the world.

Some unmeasurable interval of time later, they drifted back to normal consciousness together. She was draped over his chest, kissing it.

"I knew it would be good with you," she murmured. "I just had no idea how good. My imagination didn't go that far."

"Same with me," he admitted.

He was taken aback when she looked up and laughed. "Oh, please," she said. "Seriously, Drew? With your history?"

"What history is that?"

"Come on," she scoffed. "With all the famous beauties that you swan around with on the red carpets and the luxurious yachts?"

He jerked up off the pillow. "What does that have to do with anything? A lot of women have been associated with me. That doesn't mean I had satisfying relationships with them. Or great sex. Or that I felt intimate with them. That's never come easy to me. Women complain that I can't open up. But with you, I can. It's different with you."

Jenna propped her head on her arms to study him. It was as if her beautiful eyes stared straight into his mind. All that sharp intelligence focused on him, trying to distinguish truth from bullshit. Trying to decide if he was for real. He was on trial.

He stared back. "I have never felt this way," he said. "Never. About anyone. That is not a slick, calculated line. I swear to God, I am being straight with you."

Jenna slowly reached out both hands, cupping his face, stroking it gently with her fingertips, from his cheekbones to his jaw. She gave him a misty smile, and nodded.

"Okay," she whispered. "I believe you."

It was as if the chains broke loose inside him, all at once. He pulled her close, and off they went again.

Like nothing on earth could hold them back.

Seventeen

Jenna drifted up from sleep, disoriented. She felt so good. Incredibly warm.

She opened her eyes. The two enormous windows showed the glow of sunrise on the lake and in the sky. Drew was behind her. One arm draped around her shoulders, the other curved around the pillow where she lay.

She stared at his powerful forearm, mere inches from her eyes, admiring the details. Trying to breathe. She couldn't believe this was real. It seemed like a dream, but her backside was pressed against his immense heat.

His bedroom was beautiful in the morning light. Soothing to the eye. Light reflected off the gleaming floorboards. Swaths of green and waving boughs set off the lake view. Mist rose in tendrils off the water. Tranquil and lovely.

Their hastily discarded clothing was strewn around the bed. She saw one of her shoes. Her dress, sadly crumpled. Sacrificed on the altar of lust, but she regretted nothing.

She really was here. Naked in Drew Maddox's bed. She'd

spent the night in his luxurious bachelor lair. She'd been well and truly seduced.

Last night had been a revelation. Some time ago, after a series of romantic disappointments, she'd come to the conclusion that she was just one of those people for whom sex was just never going to be a big priority. She just didn't get what the fuss was about. She was a busy person. Everyone had to decide where to put their energy and attention. A family would have been nice, but all those songs about passion and obsession and need... She just didn't get it.

Well, damn. She got it now, like a wrecking ball. Roddy's song flashed through her mind.

In your deep and honest eyes, I find my reason why. Her own eyes overflowed.

No, no, no. Cool your jets, girl. Too much, too soon. She had to keep this light. She appreciated Drew's pronouncements about how special their connection was—that was all very sweet and lovely, and she meant to enjoy it to the fullest—but she wasn't diving into this headfirst. She was going to tiptoe. Eyes wide open.

She peered over at the digital clock with eyes that burned and stung from sleeping in her contacts. She had an early lunch with Bev and her friends from the Bricker Foundation. She barely had time to organize for it. And Smudge would be so hurt at being abandoned all night, he probably wouldn't speak to her for days.

She slid out of Drew's arms, trying not to disturb him, and slipped off the bed, gathering those of her things that she could find. The bathroom was in disarray, water and towels on the floor. She'd come in at some point to wash up, but Drew had joined her and turned her shower into another delicious erotic interlude. The memory made her face go hot.

After a quickie rinse in the shower, she dried off and put on her clothes, insofar as she could. The stockings were lost in Drew's bed somewhere. Her hairpins were scattered all over his entry hall. Her bra was missing in action. She pulled on the dress without it, hoping that her landlady and the other tenants wouldn't see her waltzing up the steps to her house in the morning in rumpled evening wear. Her first official walk of shame, whoo-hoo. Better late than never.

The makeup smears were alarming. A dab of lotion she found on Drew's shelf got off the worst of it, but nothing would dim that wild feverish flush on her face.

Or the glow of terrified happiness in her eyes.

He was still asleep, stretched out on the rumpled bed, the coverlet draped across his waist, when she tiptoed out of the bathroom. She moved closer to admire, and saw the scars on his lower back that she hadn't noticed in the dark the night before. The ragged path the bullet had made as it tore through him. The more regular surgical scars that surrounded it. Her muscles tightened in cringing sympathy, imagining all that pain.

She needed to call for a ride home, and for that, she needed her phone. The evening bag was probably still in the foyer somewhere, so she tiptoed out there barefoot. There it was, on the dining room table. She scooped up as many hairpins as she could find, and shoved them into her bag. She needed to know where she was to call for a pickup, so she poked around until she found an architectural magazine with a mailing label. She made the call and was heading back for her shoes when she heard him.

"Jenna? You here?"

"I'm here," she called back. "Just getting myself together."

Drew was sitting up and leaning back against his hands, the cover draped across his lap, hiding all his excellent masculine bounty. Probably just as well. She had to avoid temptation this morning, considering her time crunch. But oh, he was so gorgeous.

He looked dismayed to see her dressed. "You're leaving already?"

"I'm so sorry, but I have to go," she said apologetically,

scooping up her shoes. She sat down on the bed next to him to put them on. "I have appointments today."

"Can't you reschedule? Say you're sick. Loll around naked in bed with me here all day. I'm no master chef, but I can handle bacon, eggs and toast just fine."

It sounded so wonderful. She struggled with the stupidly tiny shoe buckle, fighting the overwhelming urge to give in and stay with him. "I'm sorry," she repeated. "It sounds great, and I'd love to, really, but I just can't. Not this time."

"Then I'll drive you home. Let me throw on some clothes."

"Oh, no, no," she said quickly. "The car service is on its way."

A guarded look came over his face. "You're not panicking on me, are you?"

"No way." She finished with the last buckle, and leaned to give him a slow, lingering kiss. "I am not blowing you off. By no means. I promise. I loved every second of last night. It was incredible."

"Then have lunch with me," he said. "After your thing."

"Lunch *is* the thing, I'm afraid. An early one, with Bev and her lady friends from the Bricker Foundation. Some of whom may have seen me wrapped around you in my bra last night, so I think I should change my clothes and freshen my makeup before I face them. Plus, I am desperate to get these contacts out and put my glasses back on."

He grinned. "I love your glasses."

She kissed him again. "Good," she said. "That is extremely lucky for you."

"Dinner, then?" he asked hopefully.

She was floating now, and couldn't even control the smile that seemed wrapped all the way around her head. "Dinner," she agreed. "We're on. Text me the details."

"Will do." He tugged the comforter off his lap, displaying his erection, in all its glory. "All the details," he agreed. "For your viewing pleasure. Nothing held back."

She looked him over appreciatively, biting her lip. "You're making this really hard, Drew," she murmured.

"I think that's my line," he said, and then cut off her giggles with a kiss that sent a fresh jolt of aching sexual hunger through her body. In no time, she was stretched out on the bed, feet dangling off, arms wound around him. Oh, that seductive bastard. Out of nowhere, she was a breath away from pulling her clothes off and leaping on him again.

But she pulled back, breath hitching, face red. *Play it cool. Keep it light.*

"You're so bad," she said, her voice unsteady. "Enticing me."

"I can't help myself. How am I supposed to make myself respectable for work with a hard-on like this?"

She shrugged. "Don't know, but I just heard my phone beep with a message, so the car is probably waiting out there. You're on your own with that dilemma. Poor you. Maybe I can help you brainstorm possible solutions for that problem tonight at dinner. If you're good."

"Cruel, heartless Jenna. I promise, I'll be good."

The car service SUV was waiting in the driveway, and the driver had a long-suffering look on his face, as if he'd been there for a while. When she got in, her phone started beeping almost immediately. Messages coming in, one after the other.

She pulled her phone out of the evening bag. From Drew.

miss you already

can't wait for dinner tonight

wasn't ready for the night to be over

It was a painful inward struggle to keep herself from telling the driver to turn right around and take her back. She could not make a fool of herself and get all goofy about him. Just. Could. Not.

She tapped in same but then the emoji menu beckoned. Should she add a smiley face, a kissy face, heart eyes, a throbbing heart? Fruits and vegetables? Damn.

Keep it restrained, she reminded herself. Dignified. Not goofy.

She finally went with it was a wonderful night. No emojis.

my pillows smell like your perfume he responded.

Oh, God, he was killing her. She scrolled down the emoticon menu again. Picked out a single flower emoji, and sent it. Restraint. Restraint was everything.

Then she sat there, face red, heart thudding. Toes curling in her shoes. Waiting like a lovesick ninny for his response. It didn't take long.

aloof and mysterious as always

The driver gave her a doubtful look in the rearview as she laughed out loud.

hardly she replied, and then added three flame emojis and a lipstick kiss.

After a moment, going for a run to burn off excess energy. text you after.

She wished she could see Drew Maddox running. That big, sleek, stunning body in motion, bounding along, radiating heat, all flushed and sweatily gorgeous.

Mmm. Yes, please.

sounds good. enjoy yourself she tapped in.

Excess energy, ha. They'd made love five times, counting the shower time, and slept hardly at all. But she was buzzing with plenty of excess energy herself. She was restless and fidgety, and wanted to break into a song-and-dance routine on the street. But she contained herself, with some effort.

When she got to her apartment, she was relieved not to see her landlady or any of her neighbors. Smudge made his displeasure with her known the moment she walked in. She hastened to feed him and placate him, but he was having none of it, ignoring her frostily as he wolfed down his breakfast.

She plugged her phone in to charge and headed to the bedroom, picking out a burgundy wool dress suit with a short sixties-style skirt that made her feel like Audrey Hepburn. After a shower, she tried twisting her hair up into a tidy bun, but as usual, ended up looking like a burning bush. Sleek was just never going to be her thing.

As soon as she got her makeup on, she heard the rapid-fire beeping of text alerts. She lunged for the phone. It could be Drew.

It wasn't. Two missed calls from Ava, and a whole bunch of messages.

?? where are you?

didn't we have a coffee date at Ruby's to run over the Bricker Foundation stuff?

c'mon Jenna, I have things to tell you and a busy as hell day!

Oh, cripes. She'd asked Ava to give her feedback on the spiel she was going to give Bev's friends from the Bricker Foundation. All the drama had wiped that appointment completely out of her mind.

She tapped in a quick response.

sorry, running late. On my way. Hang tight.

A frowning emoji arrived and then, I'll order for you. cinnamon buns good today.

She gave Smudge an apologetic belly rub and got her thumb bitten, less gently than usual. Message received. She grabbed her car keys.

She got lucky with parking, and trotted into Ruby's panting

and red-faced. Ava sat in her usual booth with her laptop out and a pair of severe black reading glasses perched on her nose that somehow only managed to accentuate how ridiculously pretty she was. Her honey-blond hair was loose and swirling down over her black sweater. She looked up at Jenna, and her eyebrow climbed.

She lifted a cup. "Vanilla latte, triple shot," she said. "Because I am a good friend."

"Thanks." Jenna slid into the booth and took a grateful sip of the hot beverage.

"So before we take a quick look at the Bricker Foundation stuff for today, let me just show you these stats," she started briskly. "Ernest and I were talking about the big picture for Arm's Reach last night, and it's fantastic, the progress we've made."

"Um, about that," Jenna said. "I appreciate everything you've done, Av, but I need to back off for a little while."

"Back off?" Ava looked horrified. "That's insane. Your visibility is through the roof. You show up first on every search. You're trending everywhere. You've been telling a juicy story, and everyone's paying attention to it. You can't stop now!"

"But that's just the thing, Av. You're a storyteller. I'm not. I'm a scientist. I like facts. Hard data. Not stories."

"Sure, but this is all in the service of science, Jenn. Oh, hey. Speaking of facts and hard data, where in the hell were you this morning?"

Jenna choked on her coffee and sputtered into a napkin. "Excuse me?"

"I went to your apartment, since I was up early," Ava said. "You weren't there, but your car was, so I knew you hadn't gone to work. So what gives?"

Jenna almost blurted out the truth, but something stopped her. And she couldn't even lie and say she'd gone jogging, or to an early spin class. Her face got hotter. She couldn't meet Ava's eyes.

Ava took a bite of cinnamon bun, frowning in puzzlement. Then she stopped chewing, and just stared at Jenna's face, her eyes going wide.

"No way." Her voice was flat. "You didn't."

Jenna pressed her hands against her hot cheeks. She didn't bother to deny it. It seemed ridiculous to lie, after last night's huge, public scene. She tried to laugh it off. "It's so surprising to you? After what you saw last night?"

Ava swallowed her bite of pastry with evident difficulty. "I thought you were just, ah…you know. That it was all part of the, um…"

"Story? Good Lord, Ava, do you think I'd roll around half-dressed in front of the Board of Directors and your uncle just for a boost in my search engine optimization? How slutty and cynical do you think I am?"

"Not at all." Ava's voice was tight and colorless. "So you and Drew are…a thing now?"

Her friend sounded both incredulous and worried. Both reactions bugged the hell out of her. "It's so improbable to you?"

Ava didn't bother responding to that. "Since when has this been going on?"

"We've been circling around it since the very beginning," Jenna admitted. "But last night is the first time that we, uh…"

"Did the deed," Ava finished.

An appalled silence spread between them. The concerned look in Ava's eyes was driving Jenna nuts. "Don't look like that! Cripes, is it such a terrible development?"

Ava shook her head. "That's not it. I think you're wonderful. You know that. I just…it's just…" Ava's voice trailed off. She was uncharacteristically lost for words.

Icy clarity settled in, along with an ache of dread that threatened to completely dampen her buzz of excitement.

"You don't think I can hold his interest," she said flatly. "You don't think I can measure up to all his movie stars and models."

Ava dismissed the movie stars and models with a flap of her

hand. "Not at all," she said impatiently. "They were a bunch of airheads, mostly. He was with them because they were cute and right there in front of him, so why not. Besides, he never wants to risk actually caring about somebody with substance, so I never thought that he would actually…"

"So you don't think we're believable as a couple," Jenna said. "Believable for the Maddox Hill Board of Directors, and your uncle, maybe, because playacting is fine. But not for real."

"Don't be mad," Ava pleaded. "When I proposed this to him, I never in a million years thought that—"

"That he could actually be interested in someone like me," Jenna finished.

"Don't put words in my mouth," Ava snapped. "It never occurred to me that this could have, you know, consequences. That I could set you up for disappointment, or hurt. You've had enough already. I didn't think it through, that's all. And that…scares me."

Well, great. That made two of them.

Jenna got up and grabbed her coffee. "Thanks for the vote of confidence. If you'll excuse me, I have a busy day ahead, so have a good one."

"Don't forget that tomorrow morning, you and Drew have that interview with the—"

"No," Jenna broke in. "Cancel the interview. Cancel everything. Say I'm sick. Say anything you want. I can't handle any more PR events. I'm done playacting, I'm sick of being photographed. I appreciate your hard work and I think you're a genius, but the price is too high. As of today, Project Billionaire's Plaything is on indefinite hiatus."

"Jenn. Please." The tone in Ava's voice stopped her in her tracks. Her friend never sounded like that. Dead serious. Subdued.

"What?" she snapped.

"Just please. Be careful," Ava said.

That made her even more miserable. She'd spent weeks convinced that Drew could never be interested in her for real, and now look at her—all bent out of shape because Ava thought the exact same thing.

It was hypocritical and unfair.

She hurried toward her car. The text alert chirped as she got in. Then another. Two messages from Drew, responding to a picture she'd sent him of Smudge, glaring up at her over his chicken chunks.

Your cat fits my color scheme. He would look good in my living room.

Or I maybe I should say, my living room would look good on your cat.

Oh, man. Tears welled into her eyes.

All the feels. Floodgates open. His offhand remark unleashed wild fantasies of domestic bliss with Drew. Feeding chicken chunks to her kitty in his kitchen. Smudge curled up on his couch.

When he said things like that, how the hell was she supposed to stay careful?

Eighteen

The meeting about engineering problems in the Abu Dhabi project ran an extra hour over, but Drew was in too good a mood to be upset. Maybe he wasn't going to have to resign from his position after all. Which was a huge relief. Fingers crossed. For all of it, including Jenna.

He was on cloud nine after that night with her. He never allowed himself to look at his phone in meetings, but he could feel the phone vibrate in his pocket whenever she sent him a message. The constant buzz of anticipation kept his spirits sky-high, even with Harold giving him the fish-eye.

Eventually he was going to have to do something about his cousin's poisonous hostility, but today he couldn't be bothered to worry about it. He had better things to think about. Like Jenna's texts.

He usually felt annoyed and oppressed when his lovers texted him during a workday. He liked keeping things compartmentalized. Work was work, and he liked a hard focus.

Not an option with Jenna. She was interconnected with every thought in his head.

As they came out of the meeting, he already had his phone in his hand but was still talking to his VPs, including Harold. "Make sure you talk to Michaela and Loris about those budget details before you move forward," Drew said.

"Of course," his cousin drawled. "Look at you. In such a good mood today."

Drew gave him a wary look. "Why shouldn't I be?"

"I just expected you to look more hungover, considering the condition you were in last night," Harold said.

"I didn't drink last night," he said.

Harold snorted. "If you say so. Must be the health benefits of rolling around in bed with Jenna Somers. Guess I can't really blame you. She is red-hot."

Drew waited for a couple of breaths before he replied. "Don't say her name again," he said. "Don't even get near her. Or we will have a problem."

"Oh, yeah? You going to go all tough ex-Marine on me and rearrange my face?"

"If that's the only thing you understand," Drew replied. "Bring it."

"Break it up, boys." Ava's crisp voice came from behind them. "Harry, whatever your damn problem is, put it on ice and excuse us, please. I urgently need to speak to Drew. Alone."

Harold made a disgusted sound and stalked away.

Drew turned toward his sister. "Thanks for shutting him up. Uncle Malcolm wouldn't appreciate me breaking his jaw during working hours."

"Don't thank me yet," Ava said icily. "You're not going to be grateful when I'm done with you."

Tension gripped him. "Why? What have I done now?"

"Let's talk in your office, please."

Drew knew what this was about. He strode toward his office, Ava keeping pace beside him, and held the door for her. When the door closed behind them, he braced himself and turned. "Okay. Let me have it."

"What in holy hell do you think you're doing?" Ava burst out.

He sighed. "Help me out here, Av. Context, please."

"Don't you dare play dumb!" Ava said furiously. "I never meant for you to seduce her! That is self-indulgent and irresponsible!"

Drew let out a harsh laugh. "You threw her into my arms yourself."

"Is that what you think I did? That I just gave you license to amuse yourself?"

"Amuse myself?" Drew bristled. "What the hell, Av? She's a grown woman!"

"She's not like your usual type. You know. All the Lydia clones."

"Lydia is not my type," he snarled.

"Well, if Lydia herself was ever confused about that, I wouldn't blame her," Ava said. "I thought you understood. This was a little bit of theater to help you over a bad spot, and goose the stats for Jenna's company, and now you decide to have a taste? Of my best friend? What the hell were you thinking?"

Drew spoke through his teeth. "You're pissing me off."

"Yeah? Well, the feeling is mutual." Ava's voice was low and furious. "I love Jenna. And I mean, for real love her, get me? She's the kindest, most selfless, principled person I know. She is not a disposable squeeze toy for you to play around with!"

"What makes you think I'm playing?"

His sister laughed harshly. "Oh, I don't know." Her voice was heavy with irony. "Your track record? You bore easily, big brother. Don't think I or the rest of the world hasn't noticed. You've left a trail of high-profile, royally pissed-off women in your wake. If you do that to my girl Jenna, I will rip your head right off your neck."

"It's not that I bore easily," Drew said. "I've just been choosing badly."

"Seriously?" Ava shook her head in disbelief. "You just now realized, at the ripe old age of thirty-four, that you should maybe take something other than a pretty face and a hot body into consideration when choosing a lover? Wow, Drew! Boom! Blinding insight, huh? Congratulations! Better late than never, I guess!"

He turned his back on her and stared out at the view. "I don't get this," he said. "If you think she's so fabulous, what made you think I wouldn't notice?"

Ava made a frustrated sound. "I don't know. I just didn't think it through. I never would have imagined the two of you together, because you..." Her voice trailed off.

Drew stared her down. "You think I'm not good enough for her," he said.

Ava bit her lip. Her angry flush had faded. "No. I didn't say that."

But she'd hesitated too long for her denial to be convincing.

They were locked in an awful silence, unable to look away from each other.

Finally Ava shook it off. "Damn it, Drew. Just don't lead her on, okay? I don't want to be responsible for that. It would suck if she got hurt and it was all my fault."

He walked over to the door. "Get out." He opened it for her.

The crowd of people gathered outside suddenly turned away and wandered off with extreme nonchalance. Damn. So they'd been yelling loud enough to be heard through the expensively sealed soundproofed door. Ava stalked out, chin high, lips tight.

Drew closed the door after her, leaning against it. Stung.

He wondered if Jenna felt like Ava did. That he was faithless and irresponsible. Good for nothing but sex. A dog on the furniture, like his uncle said. He wondered if she was just amusing herself while keeping her shields up and her heart fully armored.

It didn't feel like that was the case, but it would serve him right if it was.

Ava and all the rest of them could all go to hell. He'd make this work. He could be a better man for her. He'd show her. If it took years. A lifetime.

This was the first time that the concept of spending a lifetime with one woman made sense to him.

Roddy's song ran through his head, along with a powerful sense memory of that soul-melding kiss they'd shared at the Wild Side. Roddy had nailed it with those lyrics.

He'd found his reason why. He was all hers. It was a done deal. On his part, at least.

All that was left was to convince her that he was for real.

"So, Jenna. Enough business. Let's dish a little. We're all so excited about your upcoming wedding!" Helen Sanderson said. "Give us some juicy details!"

Jenna looked around the table at the older ladies, all Bev's philanthropist friends from the Bricker Foundation, who were smiling at her expectantly.

"Um, we don't actually have firm plans yet," she hedged.

"Well, we certainly can help with that," Jayne Braithwaite said eagerly. "We have experience in these kinds of things. All of us have helped our kids get married."

"It was such a shock to hear that Drew Maddox finally got lassoed," Margot Kristoff confided. "That boy always was way too handsome. It's so satisfying when one of those types finally figures out what's good for him."

"Hendrick was like that, years ago," Bev mused with a nostalgic air.

The other ladies all chuckled. "He figured out what side his bread was buttered on quick enough," Helen said.

"Exactly," Bev said. "And that's what I hope for you, honey."

Jenna forced herself to smile. "Me, too."

"Did you ever see Drew in his dress uniform?" Gwen Hoyt asked, miming fanning herself. "Oh me, oh my."

"Only pictures, I'm afraid," she said. "I wish. I'm sure he looks stunning."

"My husband was in the air force, see," Gwen confided. "And

that uniform just did something to me. I just love to see a man in a dress uniform."

"So, sweetie," Jayne said briskly. "The Wexler Prize Awards Banquet is coming up in just a few weeks. Are you shopping for the ultimate dress and writing your acceptance speech?"

"Oh, it's by no means a sure thing," Jenna said. "There are many excellent candidates. They're all fabulous projects."

"True, but I put my money on you," Bev said. "In any case, everyone wants to put money on you right now. The Maddox Hill Foundation is interested in partnering with Arm's Reach, and so is the Bricker Foundation. There's so much buzz about you! Seems like you can't turn around without seeing another photo of you and Drew, or hearing something about Arm's Reach. You're on everyone's lips!"

Jenna felt freshly guilty for being so angry with Ava at the coffee shop. "That's completely Ava's doing," she said. "She's a marketing genius."

"That she is," Bev agreed. "That girl is a live wire. But the magic was there to begin with, honey. She just shone a brighter light on it so everyone could see."

"Thank you." Jenna's face went hot.

Helen reached out and grabbed her hand. "So, you haven't set a date yet?"

"Not really," Jenna said. "We've just been kicking ideas around."

"If you're getting married close to home, your best bet is May through September," Gayle advised. "But always with an indoor option."

"My brother-in-law runs a gorgeous resort on the coast," Margot told her. "It's called Paradise Point. It's on this spit of land that juts out on the coast. Sea cliffs, beaches below, fields of wildflowers, crashing waves, stunning views. There's even a lighthouse and rock monoliths on the beach. And the resort itself is a gem. Drew designed the building, you know."

"No, I, uh, didn't know that."

"Here, look at this." Margot leaned over the table, showing Jenna her phone. "These are some of the pictures I took of my niece Brooke's wedding at Paradise Point last year. Enchanting place. And would you believe, it drizzled the whole time, but because of the way the building was designed, we never felt like we were trapped indoors. That's what I love about Drew's designs."

"Agreed," Jenna said. "His house is like that, too. It feels so soothing."

The older ladies exchanged delighted glances that she pretended not to see as she swiped through Margot's photos. "Isn't that just sweet?" Bev murmured. "He talks that way about her work, too. They're so proud of each other. I just love that."

"So next summer, then?" Jayne prompted. "Or did you want spring flowers?"

"Oh, good, I finally found it," Margot said, holding up her phone again. "This is my favorite. This is Brooke and her new husband, Matthias, the moment that the rain stopped and the sun came through. Look, how the photographer actually caught them framed in a rainbow. Isn't that just precious?"

Jenna looked at the picture. A pretty blonde held up the muddied hem of her wedding dress, gazing adoringly up into the face of a stocky, beaming young black-haired man. All around them, sunlight had broken through the clouds, highlighting the flowers.

And a rainbow arched over them. It was unbearably perfect. The couple looked so happy.

The feelings came over her too fast to fend off. She dove for a tissue. Margot pushed one into her hand before she found them. The older women clustered around murmuring in consternation.

Bev grabbed her hand. "Sweetie, are you okay?"

"I'm fine," she said. "These photos are so beautiful, and I'm just so damn emotional right now. Everything sets me off."

Bev pressed her hand. "You sure you're fine?"

Jenna dabbed carefully under her eyes. "I'm great. It's just that it's too new to talk about wedding venues. Seeing the pictures of Brooke and her husband—it's just too much. I'm so happy right now, but I'm still afraid of jinxing myself. Sorry."

"Don't apologize," Margot said gently. "That picture makes me cry, too, and I've been married for forty-two years. We're all just so happy for you. Sorry we pushed you, honey."

"We all know how risky it is," Bev said. "Loving someone, marrying him. You just have to cross your fingers and hope to God you don't crash and burn."

Jayne squeezed her shoulder. "We're rooting for you. You seem like a lovely girl."

Jenna looked around at their kindly faces, and her eyes got misty again. She wanted so badly for this relationship to be real, and worthy of all this benevolent well-wishing. But she wasn't even convinced herself yet. It was premature, to talk about wedding venues.

Too much, too soon. It was a recipe for disaster.

Nineteen

"Drew, will you do up these hooks for me?"

Drew finished buttoning his tux shirt and came up behind Jenna, who stood in front of the big standing mirror he'd gotten a couple of weeks ago for his bedroom. He'd never felt the need for one before, but now he had Jenna in his space, dressing for work, putting on her makeup, doing her hair. A beautiful woman like her needed a full-length mirror to put herself together.

He paused for a moment to admire her. The low-cut, midnight blue taffeta evening dress consisted of a tight-fitting strapless boned bodice of textured taffeta that showcased her elegant curves and narrow waist, billowing out into a big, full, rustling skirt.

The bodice was open over her back, showing the long, graceful curve of her spine and the delicate shadow of her shoulder blades, her fine-grained, flawless skin. The enticing shadow of her cleavage. Lust stabbed into him, predictably enough.

Jenna shot him a glance as he placed his hands on her waist

and slid them up until he was cupping her breasts. "So fine." His voice was a sexy rasp.

She fluttered her lashes at him seductively. "Be that as it may, we can't be late. Don't be bad."

Her voice had that breathless catch that it got when he succeeded in tempting her.

"They'll wait for us." He bent down to press a hot kiss against the back of her neck, making a delicious shiver of sensual awareness vibrate through her body.

"Oh, no you don't," she murmured. "Don't make me all sweaty and damp and have to fix my makeup all over again."

"I'll make it worth your while," he coaxed.

"Save it," she said sternly. "You'll get what you want…but later."

He bowed to the inevitable, but took his own sweet time with the tiny hooks, relishing the opportunity to touch her hot, petal-smooth skin as he fastened them up. Admiring all the details. The shape of her spine, her elegant posture, the shape of her shoulder blades.

He'd liked the way his life felt, these last weeks. Liked it so much, it scared him.

Ava had eased off on the punishing PR schedule, thank God, so he and Jenna had been able to spend some free time together. He was greedy for all of it, so bit by bit, she'd started spending most of the time at his house—along with her cat.

Smudge wasn't quite sure about Drew yet. He kept trying to establish dominance. But even that couldn't put a damper on how much Drew loved having Jenna in his living space.

"One moment, for the full effect," she murmured, adjusting the cups of the bodice. Afterwards, her perfect high breasts spilled out of the top of the cups just enough to make Drew slightly uncomfortable.

"I could have adjusted that for you, too," he told her.

"And then we would have ended up being late. I know you." Her mouth was stern, but her eyes smiled.

"You look fantastic," he told her.

It was the stark truth. He couldn't stop staring. The deep blue made her skin glow like it was lit from inside. The design hugged her stunning figure. Her blue satin spike-heeled shoes had delicate, glittering ankle straps. He ached to touch her.

"Which glasses today?" he asked. "The blue ones?"

"Contacts, for special occasions. The announcement of the Wexler Prize is a special occasion. I'm not wearing workaday specs for that."

"You know that your specs make me hot," he told her.

"No, Drew, you just exist in a generally overheated state, and the specs are incidental. Not that I'm complaining. I like having you perpetually ready for action."

"Always," he promised. "The dress looks great on you."

"It ought to, considering what it cost," she said, fastening her little diamond drop earrings into her ears with a secret smile. "I still think it was extravagant of you. My other dress would have been fine."

"I wanted you to get this dress because it looks good with this other thing I got you," he told her.

Her eyes filled with alarm. "Drew. We talked about this. Remember?"

"Yes, yes. I know. No billionaire's-plaything scenarios. Not even as fun, lighthearted bed-play. We're just two people enjoying each other's company. No mind games. No power plays. No expensive gifts. All of this is forbidden. Rules are rules."

"Good," she said cautiously. "Then... What did you do?"

"This." He pulled a teardrop sapphire pendant, ringed with smaller diamonds, out of his pocket and held it up in front of her. It settled right at the hollow of her throat as he fastened the clasp of the delicate, glittering white gold chain.

Jenna gasped. "Oh, my God, Drew. I can't accept this."

"I found it a couple weeks ago. I thought it would look perfect with the ring. That was why I pushed for blue, even though the other dresses looked great on you, too."

"But… It's against the rules." Her hand went up to touch it delicately.

"Sometimes rules have to be broken. That nugget of wisdom brought to you by Michael Wu, who has finally kicked my underperforming ass up to level eight. He advised me to be bolder and risk harder, or else I'll just keep running around in the same circles."

She gazed at herself in the mirror, wide-eyed. "Very smooth," he said. "Video game wisdom, to manipulate me. You know that Michael is my soft spot."

"I love manipulating your soft spots," he whispered into her ear. "I'll use whatever works. But Michael's logic makes sense to me. Because I think we're ready."

She turned to look up at him. "For what?"

"The next level," he said.

They just gazed at each other. The air hummed with emotion. Endless possibilities.

He took her hand, and kept kissing it until he felt that subtle shift of energy, like the wind ruffling the grass. They were so attuned to each other. God, how he loved that.

Her eyes dropped. "This isn't a conversation to have when we're late to an important function," she said. "Let's, um, hit Pause. Pick this up later."

He let out a sigh. At least it wasn't a flat-out no. But he wanted so badly to nail this down and close the deal. "You will wear the necklace, though, right?" he wheedled.

She narrowed her eyes at him, fingering the pendant. "You are sneaky."

"Always," he assured her.

"Hmmph. This time," she conceded. "I have to go find my evening bag. I think I left it in the studio."

The skirt swooshed and rustled past his legs as she swept out, leaving him alone and secretly exulting. It was a huge deal that she was wearing jewelry he'd gotten her. She was so prickly about the billionaire-plaything vibe. Every little silly detail made her twitchy.

He looked around for his tux jacket and found it on the bed, with Smudge curled up on top of it, purring loudly.

As Drew approached, Smudge rolled onto his back and stretched luxuriously, flopping this way and that, making sure to cover the entire jacket. Then he flipped over and began digging his claws into the shiny black lapels, kneading them. His golden eyes fixed on Drew's face, waiting to see how he took it.

Drew sighed. "I need my tux jacket, cat."

He picked the cat up and dropped him on the floor. Smudge hissed and stalked away with his tail high to plot his next move.

The jacket was hot, creased and crumpled and covered with a layer of downy gray fluff. Drew got the lint roller, an item that now hung on the closet door for easy and constant access, and rolled the cat fluff carefully off from his jacket.

This was next-level stuff for sure.

The first part of the evening passed in a daze for Jenna. She had to hope that her mind was functioning on autopilot during the mix-and-mingle part of the evening, because she'd talked with what felt like hundreds of people and had not the slightest memory of what she'd said to them. She just kept touching the pendant at her throat and trying to keep herself from dancing with excitement.

Next level? What exactly did that mean, other than the screamingly obvious? She didn't dare get it wrong. Could she have misunderstood, projected, overshot his intentions? She was head over heels in love, and he kept luring her deeper into his life.

And it was so much fun. She slept at his house every night. Weekend mornings were coffee and sex and brunch, then more sex. Evenings they cooked dinner together, cuddled on the couch or on his terrace on the lake, sipping a glass of brandy under a cashmere blanket, legs wound together on the hassock. He'd dedicated a studio for her so she could work weekends from his house. He'd installed a cat door in his kitchen for Smudge. He'd designated a huge closet for her, as if she had a wardrobe vast enough to fill it.

And then, relentlessly, he was filling it. Like this gown, for instance. It was stunning, but it was total billionaire-plaything nonsense, the very kind she'd forbidden from the very beginning. Now the sapphire pendant, for God's sake. To match the ring.

He was getting bolder.

She wondered if she'd be required to spend obscene amounts of his money on dressing herself at the next level. Hmm.

She'd cross that bridge when she came to it.

At some point in the evening, Bev and her friends and colleagues from the Bricker Foundation ganged up on her and towed her away from Drew to introduce her to someone, and she quickly got embroiled in a lively discussion about partnership possibilities with a charity that helped the victims of land mines. Afterward, she strolled through the ballroom, scanning for Drew. It seldom took long to find him, even in a big crowd, he was so tall. And no one filled out a tux like that man.

"Jenna," said a familiar voice from behind her.

She spun around with a gasp and beheld Rupert, all dressed up in a tuxedo.

"What in the hell are you doing here?" she demanded.

"Way to make a guy feel welcome." Rupert sounded a little hurt.

Like he had any right to expect a welcome from her. But she suppressed a tart reply. There were people all around and she was tired of being the floor show.

"What are you doing here, Rupert?" she asked again.

"I was invited," he said huffily. "You do remember that I worked on these projects, right? The Wexler Foundation sent the invitation to the whole team." He tossed back the rest of his champagne and smacked it down with far too much force on the tray of a passing server, causing all the champagne flutes on the tray to totter and sway. By some miracle of coordination, the server managed not to drop them all, but Rupert didn't even notice.

"I knew they sent an invitation to the team, but I didn't expect to see you come," Jenna said. "I thought you were in Bali. Where's Kayleigh? Didn't she come with you?"

Rupert's face tightened. "Ah. Well, no. About that. It's over with Kayleigh. I came back early from Bali."

"It's over? You mean…"

"Finished," Rupert said glumly. "We broke up."

Jenna realized that her mouth was hanging open, and closed it. "Oh. That was quick."

He shrugged. "Can I speak with you?"

"You're speaking with me now, aren't you?"

"I mean in private. Please."

Jenna glanced around at the murmuring crowd filling the ballroom of the stunning Crane Convention Center, one of Maddox Hill's newest projects. "Rupert, I'm really busy tonight, and this isn't the time or place."

"Please," he urged. "Just a word. It won't take long. You owe me that."

Actually, she didn't owe him a damn thing. But she didn't want to make a scene and she also wanted to be done with this, whatever it was. That way, she didn't have to schedule another encounter. Things were always better dealt with hot and on the spot.

She sighed silently, and gestured for him to follow her. She led the way out of the ballroom and swiftly up the sweeping double staircase, to the luxury suite that Maddox Hill reserved for its own use. In this case, it had served as a headquarters for the event planners. It was deserted now, since all the event coordinators were downstairs, on the job.

"Okay, Rupert," she said crisply. "Dinner's about to be

served. After that, they're going to award the Wexler Prize, and I'm really hoping to win it. So please, make it snappy."

"I see you're as career oriented as you ever were," he commented.

That got her goat, but she didn't rise to the bait. "You better believe it," she agreed, noting his peeling sunburn from too much beach in Bali and his affected little goatee. And the smug, superior expression on his face. Thank God, she'd stopped short of marrying that. She was so grateful. "Tell me."

"I'm not sure just how to say this to you, Jenna—"

"Figure it out fast."

He looked hurt. "You're being sharp."

She gave him a look. "Do you blame me?"

His expression softened. "No," he said earnestly. "I truly do not. Jenna, I've learned so much about myself in the past few weeks. That's what I wanted to tell you."

She stifled a groan. Just what her evening lacked. To hear what Rupert had learned about himself. "It's not a good time," she repeated, through her teeth.

"It was a mistake," Rupert said. "Getting involved with Kayleigh, I mean. I got carried away. It was an illusion. All lust and hormones. I just didn't realize who she really was."

It took all her self-control not to roll her eyes. "Really? What tipped you off?"

She immediately regretted the question, because Rupert didn't get the irony. "She had an affair," he said, his voice cracking with emotion. "Just days after our wedding. With the yoga instructor. At the honeymoon resort."

Jenna managed somehow not to laugh and tell him that karma was a bitch. "That's awful," she said. "How disappointing."

"I knew you'd understand." Rupert's eyes were soulful. "I have no right to say this, after what happened, but you are just… radiant tonight. I've never seen you look so beautiful."

Compliments from Rupert made her uneasy. She shifted back a step. "Um. Thanks."

"It's so strange. Almost as if it took that stupid, squalid adventure with Kayleigh to actually be able to see you clearly, for what you are. The contrast between you and her, you know? It's like, I never saw you... And now I'm dazzled. A veil has been lifted."

Jenna was horrified. "Rupert, don't."

"Please, let me finish. You're the only one for me. I'm sorry it took me so long to figure that out. I'm so sorry I ever let you down."

Jenna backed away from him. "I don't know if you've been paying attention, but I'm involved with someone else right now," she said cautiously. "I mean, seriously involved."

"Yes, and that's another thing." Rupert's voice took on that maddening tone it got when he decided to school her about something. "I know you might be dazzled by Drew Maddox. He's rich and famous, and all that. But I've heard stories—"

"Hold it right there. I'm not interested in hearing sleazy gossip about my boyfriend, and from you, of all people. Just don't."

"He'll be unfaithful to you," Rupert informed her.

Amazing, that he could say it with a straight face. "Are you listening to yourself?"

"Of course I am," he said huffily.

She realized, with a flash of understanding, that had been the problem all along. He listened to himself only. That was the difference between him and Drew. One of the many. Drew actually heard what she said. Rupert never had.

"You cheated on me with Kayleigh, and you dare to preach to me?" she said.

"I learned from my mistakes," Rupert said loftily. "And I suffered for them. I doubt very much that Drew Maddox will. From what I read, he's not even capable of—"

"Shut up, Rupert," she said. "I don't want to hear about your mistakes, or your suffering. And don't say a word about Drew."

"I'm sorry to distress you, but you have to face the facts," Rupert said, in lofty tones. "Truth hurts, Jenna."

"So does a broken jaw."

Drew's voice sounded from behind them, low and soft with controlled rage.

Twenty

Jenna spun around, horrified. "Drew?"

Drew studied that son of a bitch looming over Jenna through a haze of red. His hands clenched. "What are you doing up here alone with this loser?"

"He wanted a word with me," Jenna said tartly. "And I didn't want to have an audience for this conversation. I'm tired of my life being public performance art."

Rupert shrank back as Drew strode over to stand behind Jenna, giving the man a stare that was calculated to make him squirm and sweat.

"Would you excuse us, Jenna?" he said. "I'd like to talk to this guy in private."

Rupert was now edging along the wall toward the door. *Good. Be afraid, jerkwad.*

"Why?" Jenna demanded. "You have nothing to say to him."

"I have plenty to say to a guy who's trying to move in on my fiancée." Drew kept his eyes fixed on the guy, tracking his every move. Rupert's forehead was getting shiny.

"The answer is no," Jenna said sharply. "I'm not going anywhere while you have that look on your face."

Rupert was almost at the door, still sliding along with his back to the wallpaper. "Come with me, Jenna!" he begged, holding out his hand to her as if to a drowning person. "We belong together! You deserve better than a...a degenerate playboy!"

Jenna sighed heavily. "Rupert, go. And I mean, right now. Leave the building."

"You had your chance, and you blew it." Drew's voice was low and menacing. "Stay the hell away from her. Or I will destroy you."

Rupert stumbled out the door and disappeared.

After a moment's stunned silence, Jenna turned to Drew, her eyes bright with outrage. "You'll destroy him? Did I really hear you say that?"

"I meant every word," Drew said. "That son of a bitch was making a move on you. Am I supposed to pretend I don't notice?"

"No!" she said sharply. "You're supposed to actually not notice! Rupert doesn't count! He's not your rival, he's just a silly, self-involved jerk. Nothing he says should be taken seriously!"

It took Drew a moment to work up the nerve to say it. "What about me?" he asked. "Do you take me seriously?"

Jenna looked startled at the question. She gazed at him for a moment.

"Yes," she said finally. "I do, absolutely. There is no comparison between you and him."

A sigh of relief came out of him. "So you don't still have feelings for him?"

She let out an incredulous laugh. "For Rupert? Oh, God, no. You were jealous?"

"Yes," he admitted. "I wanted to kill the guy."

"Oh, please. I never did have feelings for him, not really. I just convinced myself that I did, because I had nothing to compare it to."

"Meaning that now you do?"

Her face flushed. "Well, yes. As I'm sure you can guess."

"I could guess," he said. "But I don't want to. Not anymore. Spell it out for me."

Jenna let out a long, shaky breath. "I never felt for him what I feel for you."

He just kept on waiting. "So far, so good, but I'm still in suspense. What do you feel for me?"

She let out a shaky laugh. "Wow, you're relentless tonight."

"I just walked in here and found another man trying to steal my lady," Drew said. "I need some reassurance. So sue me."

"How's this for reassurance?" Jenna wound her arms around his neck and kissed him.

Reality shifted on its axis, like it always did when they touched. Desire flared up, hot and immediate. She wrapped her leg around his legs and braced herself, her breasts pressing against his tux shirt. Melting for him, straining to get closer. Locked in a breathless kiss.

Jenna lifted her head when she felt cool air on her bare back. He'd undone some of the hooks of her dress. She pulled away, laughing and shaking her head. "Oh, no you don't! You're not getting my clothes off any place where people could burst in on us. Never again. I haven't even processed the trauma from the last time."

He looked around, and pulled her into the bathroom, flipping the door lock and switching on the light. Two soft-focus lights from wall sconces lit the flesh-toned marble of the bathroom. She was so beautiful, her eyes dazed, cheeks pink, red lips softly parted as he hoisted her up onto the wide sink, pushing up the big, rustling armfuls of midnight blue taffeta until he found her hot, smooth skin above the thigh-high stockings.

He slid his hands higher, to the tender, secret flesh. Stroking her with teasing fingertips, making her melt and writhe and press his hand against herself, demanding more.

He sank down to his knees, pushing taffeta out of his way

and tugging her small blue satin thong panties down. He pressed his mouth to her tender secret folds.

Her hot, sweet taste was intoxicating. He could never get enough. The way she opened to him like a flower, and then melted into shivering pleasure, coming for him. A long, strong, lingering climax that made him feel like a god.

He held her there for a few minutes until the aftershocks gave way to the shimmering glow, and that was as much as he could stand. He needed her…right…now.

He rose up, unfastening his pants, and scooped up her legs, draping them over his arms. Her hands clutched at his shoulders, fingernails digging in as he eased himself slowly, insistently inside her.

She was exquisitely ready. She took him so deep. Every liquid, sliding stroke was unbearably perfect. She'd forgotten the rest of the world existed, and he was glad, because he loved those breathless whimpering sounds she made, until that deep, sensual pulsing rhythm of his thrusts made them shake apart.

He pulled slowly, reluctantly out of her, leaning his damp forehead against hers. Awestruck, like always.

He set her gently on the floor before he tucked his shirt back into his pants.

"Staking your claim much?" she asked shakily. But there was breathless laughter in her voice.

Drew took his time in responding, washing his face in the sink. "If that's what I was doing, expect me to keep doing it. I'll stake my claim every chance I get."

His phone buzzed in his pocket. A text from Zack.

Someone threw a rock through a window in the Azalea Room while they were setting up the dessert buffet. They're moving the buffet to the Rose Room.

"There's a situation downstairs," he said. "I need to check it out."

"I'll take a minute to put myself together," Jenna said. "See you back in the ballroom?"

"Yeah." He gave her a long, possessive kiss, then stepped back to watch as she smoothed and shook down her skirt. She started fixing her makeup. She was so damn gorgeous. It blew his mind.

Jenna slanted him an amused look. "Didn't you have someplace to be?"

Damn. "Yeah, guess so." He forced himself to back out. Closed the door after himself.

Kissing her had knocked Zack's message right out of his mind.

Being in love made it hard to concentrate.

Twenty-One

Jenna remained in the private suite for at least ten minutes before she could stand without wobbling. She washed up, freshened her makeup, adjusted her hair. She'd put her whole heart on the table for him. It made her giddy and scared.

She was as decent as she could make herself by the time she ventured out of that room, but her hot pink flush just wouldn't fade.

It would be all too easy to guess what she and Drew had been up to. All they had to do was look at her eyes, her cheeks, her hair. She was so sick of having her private life be everybody's entertainment.

"Jenna! I thought I might find you here."

She spun around with a squeak of alarm as a hand clamped her wrist. "Harold? What on earth—you scared me!"

"Just wanted a word." His eyes raked her up and down.

"Yeah, you and everyone else. Not now." She tugged at her wrist.

He didn't let go. "I just need a minute of your time. Could we slip into the suite to have a private—"

"Absolutely not," she said forcefully.

Harold shrugged. "Fine, but I have something to tell you and it's in your best interests to hear it behind closed doors. Trust me on this."

Trust him? *Ha.* "Right here is just fine," she said. "Make it quick."

Harold's eyes lingered on her flushed face, the smudges of makeup below her eyes, her cleavage. "I saw Drew strutting down the stairs like the cock of the walk," he said. "I can imagine what the two of you were up to in there. Fun, huh?"

"Get lost, Harold." She yanked again.

Harold held on, his fingers digging into her skin. "I'm trying to do you a favor."

"I'm doing just fine without any favors from you."

"Believe me, you'll be grateful." He held up his phone. "Have you seen this?"

Her eyes went to the screen, in spite of herself—and stiffened at what she saw.

The screen showed a photo of Drew, stretched out naked in a huge bed, apparently sleeping, and surrounded by naked women. And there was more—much more. Many women. The pictures flashed by, one after the other.

In all of them, Drew appeared to be unconscious.

Harold just watched her face avidly as she stared down at his screen. "Where did you get these photos?" she asked. "Who gave them to you?"

"Just what did Drew tell you about Sobel's party?" Harold asked.

"None of your business, Harold," she said.

"I know what he told my uncle," Harold said. "They knocked him down onto that couch and took compromising photos of him. Right? And that was all. He didn't tell you that he slunk out of that place the next morning after rolling around all night with a bunch of call girls. There's timed security footage of him walking out of that place at ten thirty-five. Word is, there are videos of the fun and games that happened during the night, too. Imagine how you'll feel when those videos drop."

She tried not to imagine it. There was a painful rock in her throat. "We are not having this conversation," she said. "Get the hell away from me."

"He's a liar, Jenna. Don't fall for it. You're smarter than that."

Jenna seized Harold's fingers, still clamped around her wrist, and pried them loose. She stepped back, rubbing her sore arm. There was a cold, sick weight in her belly. "I don't believe you," she said.

Harold's expression didn't change. "Those pictures don't care what you believe. Neither will anyone else who sees them. And they will see. They're viral already."

"All I saw was an unconscious man with some woman draped over him in bed," she said. "He told me he was ambushed. This doesn't disprove that."

Harold shook his head. "You are so far gone," he said, in a pitying tone. "What's it going to take to disillusion you?"

"A lot more than you've got," she told him.

Harold shrugged. "Your blind faith is touching but pathetic. Let Drew sort out his own garbage. You have a career and reputation to protect. The more distance you get from him, the better off you'll be. Believe me. I'm trying to help."

"No, you're not," she said. "I've had people help me before. It doesn't feel like this."

Harold walked away, and Jenna stood like she'd been turned to stone. Her euphoria had been transformed into a gut-churning cold sweat. If those pictures really were doing the rounds on the internet, then things were going to get ugly for Drew in a big, public way. Tonight. She had to warn him.

At the same time, she was furious at him. Had he been making a fool of her, telling her it had just been photos that evening at Sobel's party? He'd said nothing to her about staying the night in a bed full of naked women and leaving the next morning.

Not that it was any of her business. It all happened before

she'd gotten involved with him at all, to be absolutely fair. Still, if they'd videotaped him in that state, his goose was cooked. At least at Maddox Hill.

Was that what she had to look forward to? Her lover's sex tapes, doled out online one by one, with lots of buzz and buildup to a gleeful, greedy viewing public? It would be so awful.

She stopped next to the window overlooking the garden, pressing her forehead against the cold glass. God, what was it about her and men? Was she destined for this? Did she have a sign on her back? Gullible Nitwit. Please Lie to Me.

In any case, she didn't want him taken by surprise. She texted him. where r u?

She hurried down the stairs and caught sight of Vann, Drew's CFO, muttering into a phone. He closed the call when he saw her.

"Vann, have you seen Drew?" she asked.

"Last I saw, he was heading over to the security station with Zack."

"Thanks." She stared down at her phone. Still nothing from Drew. She texted ?? and started trotting in that direction, tottering on those ridiculous heels. Then she stopped, and with a muttered obscenity, plucked the shoes off. She gathered up big armfuls of that huge skirt and ran in her stocking feet.

Zack gave her an odd look when she skidded into the security center sideways, pink and out of breath. "Jenna? What's up? Everything okay?"

"Fine," she said, panting. "But I need to find Drew. He's not answering my texts."

"I saw him heading back toward the ballroom a few minutes ago," Zack told her. He gestured toward the bank of security monitors. "Check those out. You might see him."

Jenna leaned over, peering at the images on various screens, one after the other. Drew didn't show up in any of them. Damn.

She turned to hurry out, but something on the last screen caught her eye. She turned back, leaning closer. That camera showed part of the grounds and the parking lot, and a tall man walking toward...*wait.*

Was that Harold? What...?

A car pulled up, and a woman was getting out of the back seat. She was tall and slim with a big cloud of curly blond hair. In the orange-tinted gloom of the parking lot, her eyes were smudgy pools of shadow. Harold took her arm, and she stumbled back against the car.

Harold pulled the tottering woman sharply after him and out of the camera's range. They looked like they were heading toward the side lobby, which was currently not in use.

Harold was up to something. She had to find out what it was. She didn't need any more damn surprises tonight, thank you very much.

Jenna ignored the security staff's puzzled looks as she took off once again, shoes swinging by their straps as she ran to the side lobby. No time to explain anything to anyone.

The eastern lobby was deserted. It had a large number of large, bushy plants in the vaulted atrium around a decorative waterfall that wasn't in use yet.

The big revolving door was shut, but someone had propped open the door beside it. Jenna slunk back against the wall behind the bushiest foliage as Harold and the woman with him appeared through the glass door.

They burst through it, arguing. Jenna slid back along the wall and into the recessed entry to the women's bathroom, gathering her skirt into a tight bundle to keep it quiet.

"You had one job, Tina. One. I said not to be late. Timing is everything tonight."

"I told you! I had a problem with Lauretta's bonehead boyfriend, and he—"

"I don't want to hear about it," Harold snarled. "Hurry!"

"I gotta stop at the bathroom," Tina said, her voice sulky. "When you're pregnant, you gotta pee all the time. I came all the way from Lauretta's house and it's, like, an hour and a half from here. So I—"

"We don't have time!" Harold urged.

Jenna's heart thudded as she slunk backward through the bathroom door, hoping it wouldn't creak. She dived into one of the stalls, locking it and climbing up onto the toilet, her skirt wound into a ball in her lap. Her phone chirped with an incoming message. Oh, no, no, no… Drew was finally responding to her texts. Freaking spectacular timing.

Jenna jerked the phone out of her evening bag with trembling hands, silenced it, then clicked open the audio recording app. She crouched there, balanced on her toes. Afraid to move or breathe as she heard Tina's shoes clicking against the bathroom floor.

Harold followed her in, still scolding. "Hurry up! We're missing it!"

Tina banged open the door of one of the stalls. "Why do you have to be so mean?"

"Why do you have to be so dumb?" Harold shot back. "And speaking of dumb, did you check the bathroom stalls?"

"No," Tina said, her voice sulky.

Jenna's teeth clenched as Harold swept the line of stalls, peering under the doors for feet. He didn't try to open any of the doors, to her intense relief.

"I don't deserve to be treated like crap," Tina said.

"I paid you." Harold's voice was icy cold. "We had an agreement."

"Yeah, well we also have a baby," Tina said, sniffling.

Harold made an impatient sound. "You signed the documents. You took the money. Do what I ask and don't give me trouble. Have the baby or don't, whatever you want, just don't involve me. He'll give you more money not to bust his balls, or else my uncle will. So shut up and be grateful."

"Why do I always get sucked into your schemes?" Tina complained. The toilet flushed loudly. "It's gross," she went on, when the noise abated. "Having me spray ketamine in your cousin's face was a real psycho move, Harry, and it was a monster dose, too. Poor guy was sick as a dog. You coulda killed him. And now I gotta go in front of all those people and tell them he got me pregnant? Why do you hate this dude so much? Did he, like, kill your puppy?"

"Hurry up, Tina. It's too late for a crisis of conscience."

She banged the stall door open again. Her heels clicked on her way to the sink. "I don't see why you even have to be this big-shot CEO at all." The water hissed as she washed her hands. "You're doin' fine. I've seen your house, your car. You got money. More'n I ever had, that's for sure. Can't we just be happy? With the baby?"

"You really think that scenario could ever make me happy, Tina? Wake up."

Tina turned the water off, sniffling loudly.

"Oh, for God's sake, don't start crying," Harold said impatiently. "We don't have time for this. Put your lipstick on. Come on, hurry!"

The door sighed closed after them, and clicked shut. Their squabbling voices faded away.

Jenna finally dared to exhale, teetering. She caught herself on the side of the bathroom stall, stepped down onto the bathroom floor. Her legs felt like jelly.

She ran the recording back, with ice-cold, clammy fingers, and clicked Play.

...we're missing it.

Why do you have to be so mean?

Why do you have to be so dumb? And speaking of dumb, did you check the bathroom stalls?

The voices were faint, but clear, and turning the volume up made Harold's nasal, drawling voice perfectly recognizable. Thank God.

She'd gotten it all, from the very beginning. But it wasn't going to do Drew a damn bit of good unless everyone heard it all at once, at the right moment, and before Harold's big fabricated bombshell.

Jenna edged out of the women's room and looked up the hall. Tina and Harold were just turning the corner, still snarking at each other as he dragged her along toward the ballroom. She couldn't go that way without overtaking them, and she wanted to get there first, without them knowing that she'd copped to their game.

The fastest alternative way back to the ballroom was outside, along the walkway skirting the building and back through the front entrance.

Jenna hurried out, barely feeling the frigid wind or the wooden planks beneath her feet as she ran. She hiked her skirt up and held her shoes with the other hand. They bounced against her leg with each step.

She stopped outside the lobby and stepped back into her shoes. A swift peek at her own reflection in the glass made her realize that at this point, there was just no way to salvage the up-do. Her hair needed to come down, once and for all. She plucked out the pins and shook her mane loose over her shoulders, finger-combing it as she hurried inside. She was flushed and her chest was heaving, but she was presentable.

She pushed through the double doors into the dimmed ballroom. All lights were trained on the dais where the master of ceremonies stood, about to award the Wexler Prize.

Vann stepped out of the shadows, looking alarmed. "Jenna? What's going on? They're announcing the prize! Get over there with your team, quick!"

Jenna grabbed his arm. "Vann, I need your help. Can you run an audio recording that's on my phone onto the sound system of this room, right now? It's for Drew. To save his bacon. Please, please, please help me. Time is of the essence."

Vann's eyes widened. "Yes," he said swiftly. "Of course. Where is it?"

She pulled up the file and handed him her phone. "Listen

for my cue," she said. "It was recorded in a bathroom stall, so crank up the volume to the max."

"...and this year's Wexler Prize for Excellence in Biomedical Engineering is awarded to...the Arm's Reach Foundation!"

The room erupted in thunderous applause.

"Go!" Vann whispered into her ear. "I got this."

Her team, gathered at the table that had been assigned to them, had risen to their feet and were scanning the room for her with desperate eyes.

She waved at them and hurried up to the front of the room, hoping her hair wasn't too wild. She'd just throw her shoulders back, tilt up her chin, and act like she'd meant it all along. It was the only way to go.

Applause swelled as she climbed up onto the stage and joined her team. The master of ceremonies went on with his spiel. "We've just in the past few months had the immense pleasure of learning about the work of Jenna Somers and her amazing team at Arm's Reach. Now let's watch a video tribute to their passion and dedication that the talented Ava Maddox has prepared for us! Ladies and gentlemen...enjoy!"

The lights went down, the screen lit up and the video began to play.

Twenty-Two

Something was extremely wrong. Drew had been continually texting back to Jenna's frantic message, and she wasn't responding. She wasn't at her place for the dinner either, nor was she at the Arm's Reach table, and now everyone was giving him strange looks, as if they knew something that he didn't.

What the hell? The Wexler Prize was about to be presented, and Jenna was nowhere to be found. Screw this stupid ceremony. He was about to march up on the stage, grab the mic and tell everyone to leave what they were doing and start looking for Jenna when an excited murmur swept over the place.

There. It was her. A flash of light from the brighter corridor outside had spilled into the candlelit ballroom, lighting her up from behind. She'd let her hair down. It was a halo, rimmed with light from the door behind her like a cloud with the sun behind it. She looked wild and gorgeous and sexy. A celestial sky-being. The queen of the night. So damn hot.

Thank God she was okay. Now he could breathe.

She grabbed Vann by the arm, whispered something to him,

pressing something into his hand. The murmuring of the crowd got louder.

"...Wexler Prize for Excellence in Biomedical Engineering is awarded to...the Arm's Reach Foundation!"

Drew pushed his way through the ballroom toward her, but Jenna didn't see him. On her trajectory, he wouldn't be able to intercept her before she got up to the dais.

Now she was up on stage with her team. She looked amazing. Her color was high and her eyes sparkled as she scanned the crowd.

The MC carried on with his presentation as Drew forced his way closer to the dais.

"...watch a video tribute to their passion and dedication that the talented Ava Maddox has prepared for us! Ladies and gentlemen...enjoy!"

The lights on the podium dimmed and the screen lit up, but it wasn't the montage of highlights that Ava had compiled from her video series that started to play.

It was a series of photos of him from Arnold Sobel's party. What the *hell*...?

There were gasps all around him. Drew fought the sinking feeling. Cold sweat broke out on his back. He suddenly had the stench of perfume in his nose. The pain of his throbbing head. He looked up at Jenna on the dais.

She wasn't even looking at the photos on the screen behind her. She was looking straight at him. There was no anger or blame or even surprise in her eyes, just a piercing urgency, as if she wanted him to do something, understand something.

He had no idea what, but he was horrified. Whoever was trying to mess with him had chosen the most public moment possible, and was humiliating Jenna in the process. This was her big night to be celebrated for all of her accomplishments, and somehow, Drew had managed to burn it to the ground.

Uncle Malcolm was yelling at him, of course, but Drew

couldn't bring himself to listen. He just stared up at the woman he loved, feeling it all slip away.

Uncle Malcolm's words started sinking in. "...turn that thing off, for the love of God! Turn it off!"

"I'm trying to, sir, but I don't know—"

There was a crash, followed by shrieking. Drew looked around. Uncle Malcolm had hurled the laptop down onto the marble tiles. Glass from the screen and letters from the keyboard were scattered all around.

"I've had enough!" his uncle roared. "No more!"

There was another flash of light from the back of the room, and another woman ran into the room, tottering on her high heels. She threw herself at Drew.

"You got me pregnant!" she shrieked.

She was close enough now for him to recognize her. It was the blond woman who had been pictured with him in the tabloid photos, and the ones he'd just seen. The same puffy lips, the same black-rimmed blue eyes, the same streams of mascara running down both her cheeks.

It was the perfume-squirting girl from Arnold Sobel's party.

Pandemonium. Everyone in the room was talking or yelling. Uncle Malcolm could be heard howling above them all. Jenna tried to catch Drew's eye, but now Tina was pounding her fists on Drew's chest. Drew caught her hands and immobilized them, leaning close to speak to her urgently. Whatever he said made her face crumple, and she started to ugly-cry, her mascara cascading down even faster.

"Get out!" Malcolm yelled. "Get this creature out of my sight! And you!" He rounded on Drew, pounding his cane on the floor, his face a dangerously dark red. "You think you can make a fool of me again? I am through with you! You are *done*!"

Drew didn't even respond to his uncle. He just turned his back, looking up at Jenna with a question in his eyes. She could tell that he thought he already knew the answer.

Jenna pulled the mic from the MC'S hand. The man was too startled to yank it back. "It's not his child, Malcolm," Jenna said into the mic. "She was paid to say that."

Malcolm swung around, eyes bulging. "Of course you would cover for him!" he sputtered. "You're in love with him, God help you."

"I have proof." Her voice rang out. "And I want you all to hear it."

Malcolm went still. He slowly turned toward her, his eyes sharpening. The room started quieting down. "What proof are you talking about?" he demanded.

"Vann?" Jenna called out. "Hit it."

There was a buzzy, staticky squeal in the speakers, and the recording began to play. Harold's voice blared out, grinding and nasal.

...we're missing it.

Why do you have to be so mean? Tina's voice, gratingly loud.

The room went silent to listen. The people in that room hung on every word of the bathroom conversation. Tina put her hands on her face, sobbing and shaking her head *no*.

Drew looked up at her, shaking his head. *How?* he mouthed.

Jenna shrugged, which was a very bad idea, considering the precarious state of her décolletage. She grabbed her bodice before it slid down to do a nip slip worthy of a Super Bowl half-time show, and tugged it up, willing it to stay put.

...put your lipstick on! Come on, hurry!"

The click of the bathroom door closing ended the recording. The crowd let out a collective sigh of wonder, and the excited conversation swelled again.

Jenna and Drew couldn't look away from each other. The MC was yelling at her excitedly but Jenna couldn't understand a word the man was saying.

"Harold?" Malcolm roared. "That was Harold on that tape?"

"Yes, it was Harold," Jenna said into the mic. "There he is, slithering away out the southeast door right now! Don't run off, Harold! Some people want a word with you!"

"Stop him!" Malcolm hollered. "That lying bastard has to answer to me!"

Once again, the room erupted into noisy madness. Jenna handed the mic back to the MC. Fortunately, the guy was an old pro, and good at crowd control. He got to work on trying to get the evening somehow back on track, but Jenna couldn't follow his patter. Not with Drew walking toward the dais, gazing up at her. His whole soul shining out of his eyes.

"...Ms. Somers? Ms. Somers?" The MC again.

"Jenna!" Charles, her team leader, stage-whispered from the back of the dais. "Hey! Jenna, he's calling you! Come and get the prize!"

Somehow, she got herself functioning again. She pasted on a big smile as she went over to receive the prize plaque, and held it up to thunderous applause.

It felt surreal. Far away, like a dream. She made some kind of an acceptance speech. God knows what she said, but the crowd seemed to love it.

So...great. She'd done it. Arm's Reach had the Wexler Prize, in spite of everything. She should feel triumphant, but she couldn't seem to breathe.

In front of the stage, Tina had crumpled to the floor in a dead faint. Pregnancy hormones, guilt, theatrics, who knew. Not Jenna's problem. All she cared about right now was Drew and the dazzled look in his eyes as he gazed up at her.

Afterwards, the rest of the team went back to their table, but she didn't follow. She walked over to the edge of the dais where Drew stood.

He reached up, clasping her waist. She laid both hands on his shoulders as he lifted her and let her slide down his body into a tight, hot embrace. His arms tightened around her, and he put his mouth to her ear.

"That was incredible," he murmured. "Are you okay?"

"Fine," she murmured. "You?"

"Never mind me. I'm so sorry, Jenna. This was your moment to shine. And it got steamrolled."

She shrugged. "I'm fine. I got the prize, right? That's the important thing. And I kicked Harold's ass, which is very satisfying. So it's all good."

He shook his head, wonderingly. "How in holy hell did you pull that off?"

She wound her arms around him and squeezed. "I got lucky," she said. "Right time, right place."

Drew hugged her back, putting his mouth to her ear. "I want you to know this," he said quietly. "The only reason I was in that bed with those women was because I was drugged. That's not who I am."

She nodded. "Yes," she replied. "I know that."

He let out a sigh of relief. "Thanks," he whispered. "For believing in me."

They just swayed together like a single being, shaking with the intensity of their embrace. Drew looked up. "You know what this means, don't you?"

"It means a whole lot of things," she observed. "Where to even begin?"

"My uncle just fired me," he said. "And I'm fine with that. Finally, things between us are simple, like they should have been from the start. No putting on a show, ever again. I don't need you to save my reputation. I don't want anything except to love you. I don't have anything to offer you but myself."

She pressed her hand to her shaking mouth. "Drew," she whispered.

"Marry me," he said. "For real."

Jenna looked around them, at the crowd of people watching. She laughed out loud.

"You're proposing to me here? In front of everyone?"

Drew's laughter was so happy, she started laughing, too.

"Sorry," he said. "I got overexcited and completely forgot they were there. You just have that effect on me."

Jenna wiped her eyes. "I…wow," she whispered.

"Take your time," he said. "As long as you need. I'm not going anywhere, Jenna. I want you to marry me, and I'll spend the rest of my life making damn sure you don't regret it."

"Oh, God, Drew."

Drew glanced around, as if suddenly noticing the ring of people around them, avidly listening. "Maybe some privacy, to talk it over?" he suggested. "We could skip town for a while. I'm a free man now, and your team can cover for you at Arm's Reach for a little while, right? We could blast out of here tonight."

"What?" Uncle Malcolm's voice cut through the murmuring buzz of voices around them. "Who said you were a free man? Who said you could blast out of town?"

"You just banished me, Uncle," Drew pointed out. "I think that means I can go."

"Oh, don't be childish," Malcolm said gruffly. "I wasn't myself. You're not going anywhere. You're my CEO!"

"Actually, you weren't invited into this conversation at all," Drew told him.

Ava stepped forward. She blew Jenna a kiss, her eyes shining, and then murmured into her uncle's ear in low, soothing tones, leading him firmly away.

Drew turned back to her, and when their eyes met, that magical bubble reformed around them. They were surrounded by people, but they might as well have been alone.

Drew rested his forehead against hers. "Now, from the top," he said. "Shall we go find someplace private so I can try this whole marriage proposal thing again?"

Jenna laughed through her tears. "How about if I just save us some time and say hell yes right now, so we can skip ahead to the good part?"

His reply was a kiss of such molten intensity, neither of them even heard the appreciative roar of applause that shook the room. It could have been miles away.

All that mattered was the two of them together. The road ahead, to parts unknown.

And the love, lighting their way.

* * * * *

Corner Office Secrets

Dear Reader,

We can all probably agree that letting someone get close is dangerous. It takes heroic courage to allow it. And to do it with a stranger is terrifying.

I love stories about children being reunited decades later with their birth parents. It's a huge risk with an uncertain reward. Those stories make me feel like I have electricity buzzing through me. Primordial emotions. Fears and longings and hopes that move us in ways we can't imagine. Those are the stakes for my heroine, Sophie Valente, in *Corner Office Secrets*.

Sophie has come to Maddox Hill with a huge secret. She's the biological daughter of the company founder, famous architect Malcolm Maddox. Sophie's mother's last wish was that Sophie find her father, so she's giving it a shot...but very carefully. Trying to make sure she won't get hurt. And having tall, dark and dreamy CFO Vann Acosta smoldering mysteriously at her while she does it...oh, Lord. Too much to take.

I hope you like this second installment of the Men of Maddox Hill series! Be sure to check out book one, Drew Maddox and Jenna Somers's story, *His Perfect Fake Engagement*, where you'll be introduced to Malcolm. Stay tuned for the next installment, Drew's little sister Ava's story!

Be sure to follow me to stay up-to-date on future books! Look for contact links to my socials and my newsletter on my website, shannonmckenna.com.

Happy reading! And please, let me know what you think!

Warmest wishes,

Shannon McKenna

One

Vann Acosta stared at the screen, his jaw aching. "Play it again," he said.

Zack Austin, Maddox Hill Architecture's chief security officer, let out a sigh. "We've seen it ten times, Vann. There's not much to unpack in the video itself. Just Sophie Valente, taking pictures of a computer screen. Let's move on to the next step."

"It's not time for that yet," Vann said. "Play it again."

"As many times as you need." Tim Bryce, Maddox Hill's chief technology operator, put his hand on the mouse. "But nothing's going to change. So there's hardly any point."

Vann gave Bryce a cold look. He was not going to let himself be rushed. As chief financial officer of Maddox Hill, he owed it to his employees to get all the facts, and to study them for as long as it took to get clarity.

"I'll make that call," he said.

"Where the hell did you put that camera?" Zack asked. "It looks like it was recorded from directly behind your desk."

"It was." Bryce looked pleased with himself. "The camera is in a picture frame above the desk. I bought it from a spy gadget website. It has photos of my sons in it. Looks perfectly innocent, but it got the job done."

"Don't get ahead of yourself," Vann said. "Sophie Valente's been personally developing our own data loss protection software. She's teaching our IT department to prevent exactly this kind of data leak, right? It's her specialty." He looked at Zack. "Wasn't that the point of hiring her in the first place?"

"Yes, it was," Zack admitted. "And yes, it seems strange."

"Very strange," Vann said. "If she wanted to steal Maddox Hill project specs, she wouldn't fish for them on Tim's desktop computer where she could be seen by anyone. She's smarter than that. It's far more likely she was conducting a random spot test."

Bryce's eyebrows climbed. "On my computer, at twelve thirty on a Friday night? I doubt it. I made a point of talking about the Takata Complex project in front of her last week, and letting her see the documents on my screen. She knew those files weren't watermarked yet. Drew and his team are still fine-tuning them. I just wanted to see if she'd bite, and she did. The files were copies of old, outdated specs, so she got zip. But I nabbed her. Maybe she can wipe herself off our log files, but she can't wipe herself off my video camera."

The smugness in Bryce's voice bothered Vann. This was not a kid's schoolyard game. There were no winners here, only losers. "Play it again," he repeated.

"Be my guest." Bryce set the clip to Play. It was time- and date-stamped 12:33 a.m. from four days before. For twenty seconds all they saw was a dimly lit office.

Then Sophie Valente, Maddox Hill's new director of information security, appeared in the camera's view frame. The light from the monitor brightened, illuminating her face as she typed into the keyboard. The camera was recording her from behind the screen and slightly to one side. She wore a high-necked white blouse with a row of little buttons on the side of her neck. Vann had memorized every detail of that shirt. The silk fabric was tucked loosely into her dress pants, lapping over the wide leather belt she wore with it. Her hair was wound into its usual thick braid, hanging over her shoulder.

She lifted a cell phone and began taking pictures of the screen. Her hand moved quickly and smoothly between keyboard and phone as if she'd done it many times before.

But her face looked so focused and serene. That was not the nervous look of a person doing something shady after midnight. She was not shifty-eyed, or looking over her shoulder, or jumping at shadows.

On the contrary. Sophie Valente was in a state of total, blissful concentration.

"Who logged into your computer at that time?" Vann asked.

"Me," Bryce said. "But I wasn't here. I was home watching TV with my wife and son."

Vann stared at the screen. "It doesn't make sense," he said again.

"Facts don't lie." Bryce's voice had a lecturing tone. "I don't say this with a light heart, but Valente is responsible for our data breaches. She knew the documents weren't watermarked. She's avoiding a log trail by taking photos of the screen. What's not to understand? If you're confused, we can go over my data—"

"I understood it the first time around." Vann tried to control his tone, but the look on Maddox Hill's CTO's face set his teeth on edge.

Bryce did not look as sorry as he professed to be. In fact, he looked gleeful.

Still. The man had been at the architecture firm for over twenty years, working his way up the ranks. More than twice as long as Vann had worked there. He'd never been Vann's favorite person, but his opinions had weight.

"What is it that doesn't convince you?" Bryce sounded exasperated.

"Every piece of evidence could be coincidental," Vann said. "We all use multiple computers. She's often here at night. She's responsible for information security. She was thoroughly vetted by the HR department before the hire, and she checked out. We already gave her the keys to the kingdom. Hell, we hired her to code the keys to the kingdom for us. She should be allowed to explain what she was doing before you accuse her."

"Yes, but she—"

"Corporate espionage is a serious charge. We cannot be wrong about this. I won't trash a woman's professional reputation unless we're one hundred percent sure."

"But I am sure!" Bryce insisted. "The data breaches started a month after Valente was hired to head up Information Security. She's fluent in Mandarin. She went to school in Singapore. She has contacts all over Asia, and at least two of the stolen project specs were tracked to an engineering firm in Shenzhen. On top of it all, she's overqualified for her job here. With her credentials, she could make twice as much if she took a job at a multinational bank or a security firm. She had a specific reason to come here, and I think I've figured out what it is. Have you even looked at her file?"

Vann glanced at Sophie Valente's open personnel file, and looked away just as quickly. Yeah, he'd looked at that file. For longer than he'd ever dare to admit.

It was the photo that got to him. It captured her essence as photos rarely did, and it was just an overexposed, throwaway shot, destined for a personnel file or a lanyard.

Sophie Valente's face was striking. High cheekbones, bold dark eyebrows, a straight, narrow nose. Her mouth was somber, unsmiling, but her lips had a uniquely sensual shape that kept drawing his eye back to them. Her thick chestnut hair was twisted into her trademark braid, with shorter locks swaying around the sharp point of her jaw. Large, intense, deep-set topaz-gold eyes with thick, long black lashes gazed straight at the viewer, daring him not to blink.

Or maybe that was just a trick of the light. The effect of the proud angle of her chin. And the picture didn't even showcase her figure, which was tall, toned. Stacked.

Sophie Valente didn't look like a shifty, dishonest person. On the contrary, she gave the impression of being a disarmingly honest one.

His instincts had never led him astray before. Then again, he'd never gotten a stupid crush on an employee before. Hormone overload could make him blind and thick.

He would not let himself fall into that hole. Oh, hell, no.

"The evidence you've shown me doesn't constitute proof," Vann said. "Not yet."

Zack crossed his arms over his burly chest and gave him a level look. Zack knew him too well. They'd served together in Iraq, and worked together at Maddox Hill for almost a decade. His friend sensed that Vann's interest in Sophie Valente went beyond the strictly professional, and Zack's level gaze made him want to squirm.

"We need more information," Zack said. "I'll talk to the forensic accounting firm I usually use. Meantime, this matter stays strictly between the three of us."

"Of course," Vann said.

"We don't know much about her, beyond the background checks," Zack went on. "Just that she's smart and doesn't miss much, so investigating without her noticing is going to be a challenge. She doesn't fit the profile of a corporate spy. She's not a disgruntled employee with a score to settle, she's not recently divorced, she doesn't have debts, or a drug habit. She doesn't appear to live beyond her means, and she doesn't have a motive to seek revenge. At least, not that we know of."

"How about old-fashioned greed?" Bryce offered. "Those engineering specs are worth millions to outside firms. We should alert Drew and Malcolm and Hendrick. Now."

"I'll handle that when the time is right," Vann said. "When we're sure."

Bryce made an impatient sound. "The time is now, and we *are* sure. I'm not talking about hauling her off in cuffs in front of everyone, Vann. I'm just talking a discreet warning to the bosses. Who will not thank us for keeping them in the dark."

"Malcolm and Hendrick are both in San Francisco for the meeting with the Zhang Wei Group," Vann said. "I'm joining them tomorrow, and Drew's wedding is afterward, at Paradise Point this weekend. Let it wait, Tim. At least until next week, after the wedding. And leave Drew alone. He's busy and distracted right now."

Massive understatement. Drew Maddox was the firm's CEO, but at the moment, he was so wildly in love with Jenna, his bride-to-be, that he was useless for all practical purposes. It was going to be a genuine relief when the guy took off for his honeymoon and got out of everyone's way for a while. At least until he drifted back down to earth.

But Vann couldn't knock his friend. It was great that Drew had found true love. No man alive deserved happiness more. They'd been friends ever since they met in their marine battalion in Fallujah, Iraq, many years before, where Drew, Zack and Vann had shared a platoon. He loved and trusted Drew Maddox.

Still, the upcoming wedding had changed things. Drew had moved into a new phase in his life when he got engaged to Jenna. Vann still belonged to the old phase. It felt lonely and flat back there.

But hey. People grew. People changed. Whining was for losers.

He had nothing to complain about. He liked his job as chief financial officer of an architecture firm that spanned the globe and employed over three thousand people. He hadn't set out to achieve that title. He just did things intensely if he did them at all. An ex-lover once told him he was so laser-focused it bordered on the freakish.

Too freakish for her evidently. That relationship had fizzled fast.

"So how do you intend to investigate her? Is there some way

to get her out of the way?" Bryce demanded. "We'll bleed out if we drag our feet on this."

Vann leafed through her file, thinking fast. "You said she speaks Mandarin?"

"Fluently," Bryce said.

"That's perfect," Vann said. "We just found out that they need a last-minute interpreter for tomorrow's meeting in San Francisco with Zhang Wei. Hsu Li just had a family emergency, and Collette is our usual backup, but she's out on maternity leave. If Sophie speaks Mandarin, I could ask her to fill in for Hsu. That way, we get an interpreter, and she'll be out of the investigators' hair. Sophie will be too busy to notice what's going on up here. You know how Malcolm is. He'll keep her running until she drops."

Zack's eyebrow went up. "And have her listen in on all the private details of Malcolm and Hendrick's negotiations with Zhang Wei? You sure that's a good idea?"

"We're not going to negotiate the nuts-and-bolts details of the specs in San Francisco," Vann said. "That's not in the scope of this meeting. It'll be about money and timing, nothing all that useful to an IP thief. It's not ideal, but I think it's worth it, to get her out of the way for your forensic team to do their work. It also gives me a chance to get a sense of who she is."

"Well, they say to keep your friends close and your enemies closer." Bryce chuckled. "Should be no hardship to keep close to that, I'm guessing, eh? Whatever else you could say about the woman, she sure is easy on the eyes."

Vann ground his teeth at the comment. "I'm not yet assuming that she's my enemy," he said. "None of us should be assuming that."

"Uh, no," Bryce amended quickly. "Of course we shouldn't."

Zack nodded. "Okay, then. That's the plan. Keep her busy. Keep your eyes on her."

Like Vann had any choice. Vann glanced back at the computer screen. Sophie Valente's face was frozen in the video clip, her big, clear golden eyes lit by the bluish squares of the reflected computer screen. She seemed to be looking straight at him. It was uncanny.

Bryce got up and marched out of Vann's office, muttering under his breath, but Zack lingered on, frowning as he studied his friend.

"You're tiptoeing around here," he said. "I agree that it's appropriate to be careful. You don't want to ruin her career. Just make sure you're holding back for the right reasons."

"Meaning what exactly?"

"You tell me," Zack said. "Are you involved with her?"

Vann was stung. "No way! I've barely even spoken to the woman!"

"Good," Zack soothed. "Calm down, okay? I had to ask."

"I am calm," he growled.

His friend didn't need to say a word, but after a few moments of Zack's unwavering X-ray stare, Vann had reached his limit. He got to his feet. "I'll go to her now," he said. "I have to tell her we need her for the meeting down in San Francisco."

"You do that," Zack said. "Just watch yourself. Please."

"I always do," Vann snarled as he marched out the door.

Zack was just being thorough. Careful. That was what made him a good chief security officer. But it pissed Vann off to have his professionalism questioned, even by a friend.

Particularly when he was questioning it himself.

He was careful not to catch anyone's eye as he strode through the halls of Maddox Hill. He needed every neuron buzzing at full capacity to interact with that woman, considering how sweaty and awkward she made him feel.

Sophie Valente stood in her big office near a window that overlooked downtown Seattle. The door was open, and she was talking on the phone. Her voice was low and clear and musical, and she was speaking...what the hell was that? Oh, yeah. Italian.

Vann was competent in Spanish, and Italian was just similar enough to be intensely frustrating to listen to. His father had been second-generation Italian, but food words, body parts and curses were all that he'd picked up from Dad.

Frustrating or not, Italian sounded great coming out of Sophie Valente's mouth.

She sensed his presence and turned, concluding her conversation with a brisk I'll-get-back-to-you-later tone.

She looked hot. Sleek, professional. Her braid was twisted into a thick bun at the nape of her neck today, and slim-cut black pants hugged her long legs and world-class backside. A rust-colored, loosely draped silk shirt was tucked into it. She was already tall, but spike-heeled dress boots made it so that she was just a few inches short of his own six-foot-three frame. Her clothes didn't hide her shape, but they didn't flaunt it, either.

There was no need to flaunt. Her body effortlessly spoke for itself. He had to constantly course-correct the urge to stare.

She laid her phone down. "Mr. Acosta. Can I help you with something?"

"I hope so," he said. "I hear you speak fluent Mandarin. Is that true?"

"Among other things," she said.

"Was that Italian I just heard?"

"Yes. I was talking to the IT department in the Milan office."

Then she just waited. No greasing the conversational wheels with friendly chitchat. That wasn't Sophie Valente's style. She just stood there, calmly waiting for him to cough up whatever the hell he wanted from her.

Most of which was unspeakable. And extremely distracting.

Vann wrenched his mind back to the matter at hand. It took huge effort to keep his gaze from roving down over her body. "I'm going to San Francisco for the negotiations for the Nairobi Towers project," he explained. "Our Mandarin interpreter had a family emergency and we need someone last-minute. I was wondering if you could help us out."

Sophie's straight black brows drew together. "I am fluent in Mandarin, yes. But simultaneous or consecutive interpreting is not my professional specialty. I do know several top-notch specialists in Seattle and the Bay Area, however. It's last-minute, but I could put you in touch. Or call them myself on your behalf."

"I appreciate the offer, but both Malcolm and Hendrick prefer to use in-house interpreters," he told her. "The interpreting doesn't have to be perfect, just serviceable. And it's just Mandarin to English, not English to Mandarin. Zhang Wei will have his own interpreter. His grandson will be with him, too, and the young Zhang Wei speaks fluent English. We'd rather have you do it rather than call someone external."

"If that's their preference, I'm happy to help," she said. "But it will slow down the work we're doing on the watermarking, as well as my plans to implement the new three-step biometric authentication process. I had sessions scheduled all week with the coding team, and the project can't go forward without me. That'll be delayed."

"It's worth it to facilitate Malcolm and Hendrick's meeting with the Zhang Wei Group," Vann told her. "I'll make sure everyone is on board with the new timetable."

She nodded. "Okay. Will we fly down with Malcolm and Hendrick tomorrow?"

"They're already in San Francisco, at Magnolia Plaza," he told her. "Be prepared for an intense couple of days. Hendrick, Malcolm, Drew and I have back-to-back meetings scheduled with Zhang Wei and his people all through Thursday and Friday."

Sophie's mouth curved in a slight smile. "I'm no stranger to hard work or long days."

"Of course not." Vann felt awkward and flustered, his mind wiped blank by that secret smile and what it did to her full lower lip. "My executive assistant, Belinda, has the briefing paper she was going to give to Hsu Li. She'll arrange for a car to pick you up tomorrow morning. Talk to her about the travel details, and I'll see you on the plane."

"Great," she said. "Until tomorrow, then."

He turned and walked away, appalled at himself for feeling so sweaty and rattled. It already felt sleazy to gather information on a colleague without her knowledge.

It would be even worse if he got all hot and bothered while doing it.

But there was no question of getting sexually involved with her. He never got involved with coworkers, much less subordinates. That was begging for disaster.

Vann ran his sex life with the same detachment he used for his professional life. His hookups were organized to never inconvenience him. He never brought his lovers to his own home, and was equally reluctant to go to theirs.

He favored hotels. Neutral ground, where he could make some excuse after he was done and just go, with no drama. And he was careful to sever the connection before his lovers got too attached.

He was a numbers guy. He liked control. He kept his guard up. That made him a good CFO, and it had made him a good soldier, too. He was chill under fire. He'd learned from the best.

Sex was fun, and giving satisfaction to his lovers was a point of honor, but emotionally, it ended right where it started for him. It never went anywhere.

Which worked for him. He was fine right where he was.

He had no playbook for coping with feelings like this. He didn't even recognize himself. Muddled and speechless. Distracted with sexual fantasies and embarrassing urges.

He had to stay sharp and analytical. Vann didn't buy Tim Bryce's accusation. It just didn't fit with his impression of Sophie Valente.

He needed to find out more about her to defend her innocence effectively, but that was going to be a hell of a challenge, if just listening to that woman speak Italian on the phone reduced him into stammering and staring.

Not a great beginning.

Two

Good thing Sophie's chair was right behind her when Vann Acosta walked out. The adrenaline-fueled starch went right out of Sophie's knees the second he cleared the door and she plopped down onto the seat. Breathless.

Going to San Francisco with Vann Acosta? Hoo boy.

Please. It was ridiculous to get all fluttery. This was a business trip. She was just a resource to be exploited. Besides, she was almost thirty, wise in the ways of the world and thoroughly disillusioned about men. They were more trouble than they were worth, and they always had some fatal flaw or other. In her experience, the more attractive the man, the more fatal the flaw.

If that rule applied to Vann, then his fatal flaw had to be one colossal humdinger.

Still, even if he miraculously had no flaws, he was a C-suite executive at Maddox Hill, which was a flaw itself, for all intents and purposes. She was walking a fine line already, juggling a demanding job with her own secret agenda. The firm's chief financial officer was sexually off-limits. A thousand times over.

But Vann Acosta fascinated her. He was the youngest CFO

that Maddox Hill had ever had, and he'd held that title for almost five years now. Company gossip painted him as a numbers god. He could have made far more money than he made at Maddox Hill if he'd gone to work for a hedge fund or opened his own.

If watercooler gossip was to be believed, he stayed out of loyalty to Drew Maddox. They'd been comrades in arms in Iraq, along with Zack Austin, who was in charge of Maddox Hill's security. Both of whom, coincidentally enough, were dreamboat hotties in their own right. The Maddox Hill Heartthrobs, they were called. Every straight woman who worked at Maddox Hill had her favorite of the trio, but from day one, it was Vann Acosta who commanded all of Sophie's attention.

It was late, and she had to scramble to reorganize her week, so she set off, stopping here and there to reschedule meetings and tweak deadlines. In the months that she'd been here, she'd found Maddox Hill a good place to work. She hadn't made close friends yet, since she took her own sweet time with that, but she had lots of pleasant acquaintances.

She leaned into Tim Bryce's office, tapping on the open door. "Hi, Tim."

Surprised, Tim spilled coffee on his hand and cursed, flapping his fingers in the air.

"Oh, no!" she exclaimed. "I'm so sorry. I didn't mean to startle you."

"Not your fault," Tim said tightly. "Just clumsy today."

"I came by to let you know that we have to reschedule the team meetings for tomorrow and Friday," she told him. "I'm going down to San Francisco to fill in for Hsu Li. They need an interpreter for the Zhang Wei negotiations. I'll see you on Monday."

"Tuesday actually. I'll be coming back from the wedding on Monday. I won't be in to work that day." Tim pulled some tissues from a pack on his desk and dabbed at the coffee stain on his sleeve. "I'll have Weston email out a memo and reschedule the team meeting. Tuesday afternoon work for you?"

"Tuesday sounds great. Thanks. Have a great week."

"You, too," he said, rubbing at his sleeve. "We'll miss you. But we all must bow to the will of the masters."

She hesitated. "Tim? Is everything okay? Other than scalding yourself, I mean?"

"Fine," he said emphatically. "Everything's fine."

"I'm glad. Later, then."

Sophie made her way into the open plan area, admiring the walls of glass, the towering ceilings and the lofted walkway that led to the corporate offices above. She liked working in beautiful places. Life was too short to hang out in ugly ones.

Drew Maddox strode by. The Maddox Hill CEO was surrounded by his usual entourage, and all the women in the room tracked his progress hungrily with their eyes. She hardly blamed them. Maddox was gorgeous, as well as rich, famous and talented. He'd designed the building she was standing in, the firm's Seattle headquarters. The striking skyscraper was constructed out of eco-sustainable wood products, and the lattice of red-tinted beams overhead was made of cross-laminated timber, as strong as concrete and steel, but much more beautiful.

Drew Maddox had been the first of the Heartthrob trio to fall, after his highly publicized romance with Jenna Somers. His wedding was this weekend, and scores of female employees were mourning their dashed hopes.

But all was not yet lost. They still had Vann Acosta and Zack Austin to cling to.

Sophie was surprised to be on Acosta's radar at all. She'd been introduced to him, but he'd barely seemed to notice.

Better not to be noticed, she reminded herself. She was keeping a low profile while awaiting her chance to make contact with Malcolm Maddox, the company founder. Malcolm was semiretired, leaving most of the decision-making to his nephew, Drew. He spent most of his time in his luxury home on Vashon Island.

Approaching a reclusive, elderly, world-famous architect who seldom ventured from his island home was easier said than done. And Malcolm Maddox was a grumpy, curmudgeonly old man who, famously, did not suffer fools gladly.

Damn good thing she was nobody's fool.

The assignment this weekend was a perfect opportunity to encounter Malcolm, but it came with a hitch—Vann Acosta looming over her, watching her with his smoldering eyes. Distracting her from her mission while she most needed to keep her wits together.

Laser-sharp focus, please. No forbidden lust allowed.

But damn, it was hard. She was a tall woman, at five-foot-nine, but Vann Acosta made her feel like a little slip of a thing, towering over her at six-foot-three. And those thick shoulders? Mmm. She wanted to sink her fingers into his solid bulk and just squeeze.

She loved his rangy build. All lean, taut muscle and bone, with those huge, big-knuckled hands that looked so capable. Those wide shoulders. Pure, raw physical power vibrated right through his perfectly tailored suit and blazed out of his eyes. It made her nervous, in a restless, ticklish, delicious sort of way. She could get addicted to the feeling.

His face was angular; his nose had a bump on it. He had a strong jaw, and his mouth managed to be both grim and sensual. She loved the dark slashing line of his eyebrows. The glossy texture of his thick dark hair.

She couldn't help but imagine how it would feel to wind her fingers into it…and yank him toward her. *Get over here, you.*

Stop it right now. Not the time or place.

Vann had a huge corner office, and his executive assistant, Belinda Vasquez, guarded it jealously. She was a square-built lady in her late fifties with jet-black hair, and she eyeballed Sophie as she approached, her red mouth puckering in anticipatory disapproval. "Can I help you?"

"I'm Sophie Valente," Sophie said. "I'll be filling in for Hsu Li as translator in San Francisco. Mr. Acosta said to speak to you about the briefing paper and the travel arrangements."

"Ah, yes. He mentioned that. I have that briefing paper for you right here." Belinda reached down into a drawer and pulled out a thick folder with Confidential written across the corner. She pushed it across the desk. "That's for you." She pushed a notepad and pen after it. "And write down your address and cell phone number for me to give to the driver, please. He'll be there to pick you up at 3:45 a.m."

Sophie put the folder under her arm, taken aback. "Wow. That's early."

Belinda smirked. "I know, right? Malcolm and Hendrick like to get an early start. Oh, and clothes. It's regular business wear for the meetings, but there's almost always a reception at the end of the second day, so be sure to bring a nice cocktail dress."

"Will do," Sophie said. "Thanks for the heads-up."

"Ah, there you are!" Belinda's face lit up as she looked at someone over Sophie's shoulder. "I was just squaring away the travel details with Sophie."

"Excellent." Vann's deep, resonant voice sent a ripple of emotion rushing up from someplace deep inside her. She braced herself and turned toward him.

"I was about to tell her to hide some energy bars and Red Bull in her purse," Belinda said. "Collette and Hsu Li tell me horror stories about those interpreting sessions."

Sophie met Vann's eyes with some effort. "Horror stories?"

"Oh, those architects just never stop blabbering." Belinda chuckled, shaking her head. "You'll be at it from morning till night, hon. They'll squeeze you dry like a lemon."

"I can take it," she said. "Let 'em squeeze."

Yikes. That had sounded so terribly suggestive. The nervous silence that followed didn't help. Her face went hot.

Belinda cleared her throat with a prim cough. "Well, good, then. As long as you're psychologically prepared for a grind. That's all from my end. Your hotel room is all set."

"I'll fill you in on any last-minute details on the plane," Vann said.

"Great," Sophie said, backing away. "I'll go get organized. See you at dawn."

She'd never seen his smile before. It was more devastating than she'd imagined. She set off, trying not to bump into walls and hoping that no one was watching.

But she had to stay focused. Her secret agenda was top priority, and now she was closer than ever to accomplishing her mission: to obtain a specimen of Malcolm Maddox's DNA for the genetics lab. Not that she doubted her mother's word, but Mom was gone now, and couldn't provide the proof Sophie needed. She was all alone with this.

She had proof already, by virtue of the DNA sample she'd gotten from Malcolm's niece, Ava, some weeks before. The lab techs had assured her that the results were conclusive, so getting a sample from Malcolm was overkill at this point.

Still, it was overkill she felt she needed. She wanted a sheaf of hard scientific evidence in her hand before she looked Malcolm Maddox in the eye and told him that she was his biological daughter.

Three

Vann felt his tension rise when the attendant showed Sophie Valente to her seat, across the aisle, in the small private plane. He hadn't slept well. He kept dreaming of Sophie, and waking up agitated and sweaty, heart thudding.

He was accustomed to being in control. He managed his staff smoothly, pulling just the right strings to get what he wanted out of people. And all that hard-won managerial skill went up in smoke whenever this woman walked into a room.

Sophie gave him a cool and distant smile. "Good morning."

A curt answering nod was all he could manage. He tried to focus on the financials on his laptop screen but he couldn't concentrate. His senses were overwhelmed.

Not that she was showing off. If anything, she'd dressed down today. She wore a white silk blouse, a tan pencil skirt and a tailored jacket. Her hair was wound tightly into a sleek updo. Little tasteful swirls of gold rested on her well-shaped earlobes. She wore elegant brown suede pumps on her slender feet.

No stockings. The skin on her calves was bare. Golden,

even-toned, fine-grained. It looked like it would be beautifully smooth to the touch.

The ultraprofessional, understated vibe just highlighted her sensual beauty. He could catch an elusive hint of faint, sweet perfume as she took her seat across the aisle. He wanted to lean closer, take a deeper whiff.

He didn't do it. He wasn't a goddamned animal. *Get a grip.*

The plane took off, and when they'd reached cruising altitude, the attendant came out to offer them coffee and tea. Sophie gazed out the window at the dawn-tinted pink clouds as she sipped her coffee, lost in her own thoughts. Serenely ignoring him.

This would be the perfect time to start a conversation and start learning more about her, but Vann was stuck in a strange paralysis. It felt all too similar to adolescent shyness. Ridiculous, for a grown man. After a long, silent interval, the flight attendant came out to offer them some breakfast, which Sophie declined.

That gave him an opening, which he gratefully seized upon.

"Now would be the time to fuel up," he suggested. "When we touch down, we'll hit the ground running. There won't be any opportunity later."

Her smile was wry. "Thanks, but my stomach isn't awake at this hour," she said. "It wouldn't know what to do with food."

"You changed your hair," he blurted, instantly regretting it. Too personal.

"From the braid, you mean?" She brushed back the loose locks that dangled around her jaw, looking self-conscious. "The braid needs to be periodically refreshed during the course of the day, or it gets frowsy. An updo is lower maintenance. If it holds. Fingers crossed."

"It looks great," he said. "So does the braid, of course."

"It's my go-to," she admitted. "I finish my morning kung fu class before work, and it's the quickest style if I need to hustle to get to the office."

"Kung fu?" he asked. "Every morning?"

"Oh, yes. It's my happy place. A kung fu teacher came to my high school once to give us a self-defense workshop, and I fell in love with it. It keeps me chill."

"Agreed," he said.

"You practice it, too?"

"Not specifically. I studied a very mixed bag of martial arts. I leaned from my dad. He was a marine sergeant, and a combat veteran, and he borrowed from every discipline, from boxing to jujitsu. He even saw American football as a martial arts discipline. Good training in learning to run toward pain and conflict, not away. So I did football, too."

She gave him a quick, assessing glance. "I can see why your high school would have wanted you on their football team."

"I guess," he muttered, wishing he hadn't started a line of conversation that focused on his body. He was far too conscious of both hers and his own right now.

"Lucky you, to learn to fight from your own dad," she said.

He grunted. "*Nice* isn't the word I'd choose. My father was a hard man. I got my ass kicked on a regular basis. But I learned."

The piercing look she gave him felt like she was peering inside his head with a high-powered flashlight. God forbid she thought he was asking her to feel sorry for him.

"How about you?" he asked, just to change the subject. "I bet your father was glad you learned kung fu."

Her eyebrow tilted up. "Why would you think that?"

"The world is full of sleazeball predators and ass-grabbing idiots. If I had a daughter, I'd want her trained to sucker punch and crotch-kick at a moment's notice."

She nodded agreement. "Me, too. But my dad was never in the picture."

He winced inside. *Damn.* "I'm sorry."

"It's okay," she said. "My mother, on the other hand, didn't know what to think of the kung fu. It's not that she disapproved.

She just wasn't the warrior type. Her idea of heaven was a hot bath, a silk shirt and a glass of cold Prosecco."

"They don't cancel each other out," he said. "A person can have both."

"Who has the time? My life doesn't allow for hot baths. Lightning-fast showers are the order of the day."

"Me, too," he said. "When I was in the service, we only had a couple of minutes in the water. You learn to make them count."

Damn. From bodies to baths and showers, which was even worse. Time for a radical subject pivot. "Have you met Malcolm and Hendrick yet?"

"I've seen them in passing, but I've never been introduced. What are they like?"

Vann chose his words carefully. "Hendrick will never acknowledge your existence except to lean closer with his good ear to hear you better. But if you're female, he won't look you in the eye."

"Which ear is his good ear?"

"The left one. Hendrick is extremely shy around women. Any woman who isn't his wife, that is. He worships his wife, Bev. So don't take it personally."

She nodded. "Understood. How about Malcolm?"

"Malcolm is tougher. He's moody, and quick to criticize. He thinks that you should just toughen up and learn to take it."

"Take what?"

He shrugged. "Whatever needs to be taken. So don't expect to be pampered. In fact, don't even expect common courtesy. You won't get it."

She nodded thoughtfully. "Understood. I don't need to be pampered."

"Then you'll be fine. With Malcolm, you're guilty until proven innocent. He'll just assume that you're an incompetent idiot who is actively trying to waste his time and money. Until you prove to him that you're not."

"Wow," she said. "That's good to know in advance. Thanks for the heads-up."

"That said, I genuinely do respect the guy. He has incredible talent. Vision, drive, energy. We get along."

"So you passed his test evidently," she said.

He shrugged. "I must have."

She got that flashlight-shining-into-the-dark look in her eyes again. "Of course you did," she said. "You spent your childhood training for exactly that, right? Getting your ass kicked. Learning to run toward pain, instead of away. It doesn't scare you."

He couldn't think of a response to that, but fortunately, just then, the attendant came through for their coffee cups and told them to prepare for landing.

He shut down his laptop, appalled at himself. What a mess he'd made of that conversation. The idea had been to gain her trust, get her to open up. And without ever meaning to, he'd revealed more about himself than he had learned about her.

And now he had those images in his head. Sophie, hot and sweaty from her kung fu class, stripping off her practice gear and stepping into the shower. Steaming water spraying down on her perfect skin. Suds sliding over her strong, sexy curves.

The harder he tried not to see it, the more detailed the image became.

Soon he had to cross his leg and lay his suit coat over his lap.

Four

Sophie sat next to Vann in the limo as it crawled through rush-hour traffic, trying to breathe deeply. Now she was all wound up with anxiety. She had no doubts about her ability to do the job, but damn, she hadn't counted on being hazed by a bad-tempered old tycoon while she was doing it.

And in front of Vann, too. He just stirred her up.

She'd worked hard on her professional demeanor. Steely control and calm competence were the vibe she always went for. And Vann Acosta just decimated it.

She was spellbound by his dark eyes that never flinched away. Her own directness and focus didn't intimidate him at all.

It felt as if they were communicating for real. On a deeper level.

Please. Stop. She had a crush on the man. She was projecting her own feverish fantasies onto him, that was all. Snap out of it already.

She was here to do a spectacular job, earn Malcolm Maddox's good opinion and get a viable DNA sample while she was at it. But the last part might be tough, with Vann Acosta watching her every move. It would be awkward if he saw her slipping Malcolm's salad fork into her purse.

She also had to find the time to monitor the traps she'd set for the IP thief at Maddox Hill. Depending on what kind of intellectual property made the corporate spy rise to the bait, she'd be able to interpolate if it was an inside job, or an outside entity.

She'd discovered the data breach within weeks of starting the job, but she was so new here, with no idea who she could trust. Until she had more definitive data, she'd decided to stay quiet about her investigation. Her best-case scenario was to be able to offer the thief up to Malcolm Maddox on a silver platter, kind of like a hostess gift. To set the tone, before she delivered her bombshell about being his biological daughter.

She wanted to make it crystal clear that she had skills and talents and resources of her own to offer. She was not here to mooch.

Vann was speaking into the phone in a soothing tone. "I know, but the traffic is crazy, and we can't control that. Tell him to calm down... Fine, don't tell him... I know, I know... Yeah, you bet. See you there."

He put his phone in his pocket, looking resigned. "Charles will let us out at the North Tower of Magnolia Plaza and take our bags on to the hotel for us," he said. "We're already late, and Malcolm is having a tantrum."

"Oh, dear," she murmured. "A bad beginning."

"You'll make up for it by being awesome," he told her.

She laughed. "Aw! You sound awfully confident about that."

"I am," he replied.

"How so?" she demanded. "You've never seen me in action."

"I'm a good judge of character," he said. "You're tough and calm, and you don't get rattled. Malcolm likes that. He'll be eating out of your hand by Friday."

"We'll see," she said. "Let's hope."

"This is us," Vann said as the limo pulled up to the curb.

Vann held the car door open for her. He led them through

the lobby, and then down a long breezeway across the plaza under an enormous glass dome, all the way to the second tower.

"Is this building one of Maddox Hill's designs?" she asked.

"Yes. It was finished last year. Zhang Wei, the man we're meeting, is the owner." Vann pushed the door open and beckoned her inside, waving at a security guard who waved back with a smile. "They want us to design another property in Nairobi, similar to the Triple Towers in Canberra that we did two years ago. That's what we're negotiating today."

"Yes, all that was in the briefing paper," she said. "I read it last night."

"Malcolm and Hendrick and Drew are upstairs with Zhang Wei's team, waiting for us."

"Drew Maddox is here?" She was surprised. "Isn't he getting married this weekend?"

"Sunday. After this meeting, he heads to Paradise Point, and the party begins."

"I've heard about Paradise Point," Sophie said. "That's the new resort on the coast, right? I hope I get a chance to see it sometime."

"Yes, it's a beautiful property," Vann said. "That's one of Drew's first lead architect projects. He made a big splash with it. Got a lot of attention."

The elevator doors hummed open. A woman with curly gray hair and round gold-rimmed glasses hurried toward them, her eyebrows in an anxious knot. "Thank God!"

"Sylvia, this is Sophie Valente, our interpreter," Vann said. "Sophie, this is Sylvia Gregory, Malcolm's executive assistant."

Sylvia shook Sophie's hand and then grabbed it, pulling Sophie along after her.

"Come on now, both of you!" she said. "He's just beside himself. Hurry!"

"He'll live, Sylvia," Vann said wryly.

"Easy for you to say," Sylvia fussed. "I wish you two had gotten here in time to have some coffee or tea or a pastry from the breakfast buffet, but it's too late now. We just can't keep him waiting any longer. Come on now, pick up the pace, both of you!"

Sophie glanced at her watch. Not even 8:20 yet. The guy was hard-core.

Sylvia pointed at two doors as she hustled them down the corridor. "See those two offices? Take note of the numbers—2406 and 2408. The Zhang Wei Group has made them available to Mr. Maddox and Mr. Hill for the duration. If you're ever called upon to interpret for a private meeting, you'll meet in one of those offices."

Sylvia ushered them into a large conference room with an elegant, minimalist design and a wall of windows. The hum of conversation and clink of china stopped as they entered. On one side of the table was a group of Chinese men. The man seated in the center was very old. Those ranged around him were younger.

There was staff from the Maddox Hill legal department there, as well, but Sophie focused on the three men in the center. She saw Drew Maddox and Hendrick Hill, Malcolm's cofounder. Tall and bald and bony, he gave them a tight-lipped frown.

Then Malcolm Maddox stood up and turned to them.

She'd seen Malcolm in passing, and she'd seen photographs of him online. But this was the first time she'd seen him up close and in the flesh. She finally got why her mother had fallen so hard all those years ago. He was seamed and grizzled now, but still good-looking, with a shock of white hair and deep-set, intense gray eyes. Bold eyebrows, chiseled cheekbones. He would have been tall, if the arthritis hadn't bent him over, and he was trim and wiry for a man with his health problems.

Her mother had fallen for him so hard she'd never recovered. She'd been on a team of interior designers on a project in New York thirty years ago. A luminously pretty, naive twenty-six-year-old with a mane of blond curls and head full of romantic notions.

Malcolm had been over forty. He'd been lead architect on

the Phelps Pavilion. Charismatic, seductive, brilliant, charming. Intense.

They'd had a brief, hot affair, and then he'd left, returning to the West Coast.

When Vicky Valente found that she was pregnant, she'd gone to look for him. His wife, Helen, had opened the door when Sophie's mom knocked on it. She'd left without ever making contact with Malcolm. Mortified. Heartbroken.

Malcolm glowered at them, clutching his cane with a hand gnarled from arthritis. "So," he growled. "Finally deigned to make an appearance, eh? Mr. Zhang, I believe you met Vann Acosta at our last meeting, correct?"

"Yes, we did meet," Vann said, nodding in Zhang Wei's direction. "I'm sorry to have kept you waiting, sir."

"You should be," Malcolm barked. "I don't have time to waste. Neither do Mr. Zhang and his team."

Sophie set her purse down and promptly situated her chair behind and between Hendrick's and Malcolm's chairs. "Whenever you're ready, sir." Her voice was calm.

Hendrick's eyes slid over her and skittered away, but Malcolm's eyes bored into her with unfriendly intensity for a moment.

The meeting got under way with some formal speechifying about mutual friendship and regard and Mr. Zhang's best wishes for prosperity for all in their shared undertaking, etc., etc. Sophie interpreted whenever Zhang or one of the others paused for breath, in a clear, carrying voice. After a certain point, Malcolm's patience began to fray. She could tell from how he clicked the top of his ballpoint pen, a rapid tappety-tap-tap.

Funny. She did that herself when she was nervous. In fact, she'd stopped using ballpoint pens because of that particular nervous habit. She couldn't seem to stop doing it.

Mr. Zhang's speech finally wound up with a flowery expression of best wishes on behalf of the entire Zhang Wei Group for Drew Maddox's upcoming nuptials, and best wishes for the future and wonderful prospects for the happy young couple.

Drew responded with grace, echoing the older man's formal language as he thanked Zhang Wei for his kindness. Finally that part was over, and they got down to business.

It was fortunate that her mind was occupied so completely with translating while she was just inches away from her biological father. Close enough to smell his aftershave, to compare the shape of his ears and his fingernails with her own. His hands were bent by arthritis, so their original shape was impossible to determine, but he had the same broad, square fingernails that she had. The same high cheekbones. Drew had them, too, as well as Malcolm's coloring.

Her intense focus altered her perception of time. She was surprised when they finally broke for lunch. Sylvia approached her as they exited the conference room. "You do know that you'll be interpreting for Mr. Hill and Mr. Maddox during lunch, as well?" she asked, her eyes daring Sophie to say no.

"Of course," Sophie said. "Whenever I'm needed."

"You'll want to arrive before Malcolm and Hendrick get there. I'll show you where to go. Right this way, please."

Sylvia led her onto the elevator and up to the restaurant on the penthouse floor.

When the rest of the party came into the private dining room, Sophie took her place behind Malcolm and Hendrick and interpreted their conversation with Zhang Wei as they ate lunch. She must have done it competently enough, because no one complained, but very little of what they said penetrated her conscious mind. Her stomach had woken up, and the *fettucine ai limone* and stuffed lobster smelled freaking divine.

No pampering. Belinda had warned her to stuff her purse with protein bars. Vann had advised her to grab breakfast. But she'd been all a-flutter to meet Malcolm up close. And in a tizzy from gawking at Vann Acosta's ridiculous hotness. It was her own damn fault.

As if there'd been so much as a single free moment to gnaw a protein bar today, anyhow.

Lunch dragged on. Dessert, then coffee and still more talk. Global international trade, geo-politics, pictures of Zhang Wei's twin great-grandsons, which had to be admired and chatted about. Still more coffee.

On the way back to the conference room, Sophie trailed Malcolm and Zhang Wei and interpreted as they walked. Mr. Zhang waxed eloquent about the poetic significance of empty space in architecture.

All she got was a pit stop in the ladies' room where she splashed her hands and face in the sink before the afternoon session began. It was twice as long as the morning one, and more technical. This involved Zhang Wei and his lawyers facing off with Maddox Hill's legal department. They got deep into the weeds and stayed there for hours.

At some point in the afternoon, her voice got thick and cracked. Malcolm whipped his head around to glare at her as she coughed to clear her throat.

Then a shadow fell over her. She heard a popping sound and turned to find Vann next to her, twisting off the top of a bottle of chilled water. Everyone watched in silence as she took a quick, grateful sip. That was all she dared to take the time for.

The sky was a blaze of pink before they wrapped up the meeting. Dinner plans were announced, this time at the restaurant at the top of the South Tower, on the other end of Magnolia Plaza. Sophie was unsurprised when she walked out to see Sylvia approach her with that now-familiar look on her face.

"Same song and dance for dinner," Sylvia said. "Head over there before Mr. Zhang, Mr. Maddox or Mr. Hill arrive. You don't want them standing around before dinner trying to making small talk with no interpreter to help. Mr. Maddox hates that."

Sophie let out a silent sigh. "Of course."

"Are you familiar with the Magnolia Plaza complex? I'll give you a map if—"

"I know it." It was Vann's deep voice behind her. "I'll make sure she gets there."

Sophie followed Vann into the elevator, too tired to feel self-conscious. Her eyes stung, and her throat was sore. She uncapped the water he'd given her earlier and drank deep. "Wow," she remarked. "Those guys have stamina."

"So do you," Vann said.

Sophie slanted him a wry look as she drained her bottle.

"It's true," he said. "Don't think Malcolm didn't notice."

"Oh, please," she said. "He didn't look at me once the whole day. Except to glare at me for being late this morning. And for coughing. Thanks for the water, by the way."

"That's exactly what I mean," Vann said. "Malcolm doesn't reward perfection. He expects it as his due. He doesn't appear to notice if things go smoothly, but if something doesn't measure up to his high standards, by God you'll hear about it."

"So being ignored by Malcolm Maddox all day is a good sign?"

"Very good," he said. "You're excellent. You never missed a beat. I don't speak Mandarin, so I can't vouch for your language skills, but there was good flow all day long. We got more accomplished than any of us expected. Because of you."

"Hmph." She tucked the bottle back into her purse. "It's kind of you to say so. Is Malcolm always like that?"

"Workaholic, hyperfocused, obsessive? Yes. And he expects the same maniacal focus from everyone who works for him. Which makes for some guaranteed drama."

"I was told he was a hard boss to work for," Sophie said.

"He's infamous," Vann said. "You have to be like him to earn his approval. Drew is, at least before he fell in love. His niece, Ava, is, too, in her own way. So are you."

"Me, like him? An alarming prospect." She said it with a light tone, but Vann's words made her hairs prickle with a shiver of undefinable emotion.

Like him? Maybe they did have some subtle, mysterious genetic similarities. But be that as it may, she couldn't be seduced by the idea of getting to know her birth father. When her mother had learned about her stage IV pancreatic cancer, she'd been so afraid at the thought of Sophie being alone in the world. She'd pressed her daughter very hard for a promise that Sophie would approach Malcolm and his niece and nephew once she was gone.

She'd slipped away so fast. Just a few weeks afterward.

Sophie still remembered Mom's chilly, wasted hand clutching Sophie's fingers. *You have more to give them than you have to gain from them. They'd be lucky to know you. I know I was. My darling girl.*

The memory brought a sharp, tight lump to her throat.

She appreciated Mom's effort. It was a sweet thought. But Malcolm Maddox was famously difficult. Even unlikable, by some accounts. The chance that they would truly connect was small. She couldn't let her own loneliness set her up for almost certain disappointment. She'd just fulfill her promise to Mom, and move on.

Vann was talking again. She forced herself to tune back in. "...are kind of like him," he was saying. "I've seen the hours you put in at work. You stay late every night."

"That's more a function of not having a social life than being dedicated to my job," she said without thinking. "I stay late because why not, if I'm on a roll. There's no one at home competing for my attention."

"So you're unattached?"

Heat rushed into her face "I'm new in town," she said. "I just got to Seattle a few months ago. I'm still finding my feet."

The elevator door rolled open, a welcome distraction from her embarrassment. They walked in silence on the cool breezeway beneath the great dome between the two towers, which was nearly deserted at this hour.

"I'm sorry you didn't get any lunch," he said.

"I'm fine," she assured him. "No pampering, right?"

He grunted under his breath as the glass elevator in the South Tower arrived and the door opened.

They got in, and the elevator zoomed up the side of the building. The top-floor restaurant had walls of floor-to-ceiling glass. The ambience was hushed and elegant, and the aromas from the kitchen made Sophie's mouth water.

The host led them to a large private dining room bathed in the fading rusty glow of sunset. A long candlelit table was set for sixteen.

But there was no seat for her. She asked the waitstaff for another chair to be brought in, and was positioning it behind two chairs near the head of the table when they heard Malcolm's deep voice outside the door. He was arguing with someone. The door opened, and that someone proved to be Drew Maddox, looking frustrated.

"...don't see why you should be so concerned," Malcolm snapped. "She doesn't strike me as a type who needs coddling. And these young skinny females never eat nowadays, anyway. No fat, no carbs, no this, no that. Ridiculous creatures."

He and Drew caught sight of Sophie at the same moment. Malcolm harrumphed, and made his way to the table with his cane, muttering under his breath. Drew cast her an apologetic look as she took her place behind Malcolm.

The rest of the party lost no time in sitting down to eat. Vann's encouraging compliments had bolstered Sophie quite a bit, but it was harder this time to concentrate on the conversation without gazing with longing at the artichoke tarts, the succulent entrecôte, seared to perfection and cut into juicy pink slices with slivers of Grana Padano, the gemlike cherry tomatoes and scattered arugula leaves, the rosemary-thyme oven-roasted potatoes and the deep red Primitivo wine.

The aromas were dizzying.

Of course, it would be too late for her to order from room service once she got to the room. It would be peanuts from the minibar if she was lucky. Cue the violins. She hoped the clink of cutlery and the hum of conversation would cover the grumbling of her stomach. Suck it up, buttercup.

At long last, the men from the Zhang Wei Group made their farewells and took their leave. Now it was just the executives from Maddox Hill, and Sophie.

Malcolm drained his wine, and turned to give Sophie an assessing look. "Make sure this one is on call for all future meetings that require Mandarin," he said, directing his words to Drew and Vann. "I don't want anyone else from here on out."

"Actually, she's our information security director," Vann informed his boss. "She's just filling in for Hsu Li and Collette. She usually directs the team on cyber—"

"She's a better interpreter than Hsu Li or Collette. Much better." Malcolm turned his scowl directly on Sophie. "What other languages do you speak?"

"Ah…fluently enough to interpret professionally, only Italian," she told him. "But I'm not actually specialized in—"

"Then it's settled. Whenever we require Italian or Mandarin, you're up."

"Ah…but I—"

"Get some sleep. Tomorrow's another long day. Not as long as I expected, though. We're ahead of schedule." Malcolm frowned, as if fishing in his mind for something to complain about, and then threw up his hands with a grunt of disgust when he couldn't think of anything. "Well, then. Whatever. Good night."

He hobbled out, cane clicking. Drew hurried after to help him to the elevator.

Sophie felt her body sag. She turned to Vann. "How far away is the hotel?"

"Not far," Vann told her. "We're in it already. The first six floors of this building is the Berenson Suites Hotel. Come with me. I'll show you where your room is located."

"Don't we need to go down to the desk? We never checked in."

"Sylvia took care of it. Your bags have been brought up.

You're in room 3006, and I've asked for a hotel employee to meet you at your door with a key card."

She gave him a teasing smile as their elevator plunged downward. "What's this I sense? Is this…dare I say it…pampering?"

"It's been a long day," he replied, grinning back at her. "I'd call it survival."

The doors opened onto the third floor and Vann strolled with her down the hall. They turned the corner, and there was room 3006, with a uniformed young man standing by the door, holding an envelope with a key card to her. "Your luggage is inside, miss."

"Thanks so much." She took the envelope and fished out the card.

"And here's your meal," the man said, gesturing at the rolling cart full of silver-topped dishes. "May I take it inside?"

"Meal?" she said blankly. "Ah…no. You must have mixed me up with someone else. I didn't order a meal."

"No, it's not a mistake," Vann said. "I ordered the food."

"You?" Bewildered, she looked at the cart, and then at him.

"From the look on your face in the restaurant, I assumed that tonight's menu would be agreeable," he said. "So I ordered you the same meal. I hope that's okay."

"Oh, dear. Was it so obvious?"

"Only if you were paying attention," he said.

The fraught silence following his reply made her face heat up. She turned away and inserted her key card in the door, opening it and stepping back to let the hotel attendant wheel the cart inside. "I'm ravenous, yes," she admitted. "A hot meal sounds great. But this definitely qualifies as pampering."

"This is just smart management of human capital," he said. "It's stupid to misuse a vital resource just because you always have in the past. Tradition is not a good enough reason to be rude. It's bad business. But Malcolm doesn't listen to me. Not about this, anyway. So this is my imperfect solution."

"Very kind of you," she said. "I like to be considered a vital resource."

"Malcolm certainly thinks that you are."

The hotel employee said good-night and departed, leaving them standing there in awkward silence.

"Well, then," Vann said. "I'll say good-night. Enjoy your meal." He turned to walk away.

"Wait!"

The word flew out of Sophie's mouth against her better judgment.

Too late now. Vann had already turned around, eyebrows up.

"Would you come in and help me eat it?" she asked. "It's a ridiculous amount of food for just one person."

"I had plenty at dinner," he told her. "You've been fasting all day."

"Just have a glass of wine, then," she said. "There's a whole bottle. It's wasted on me alone."

He hesitated, and turned back. "All right. A quick glass of wine."

She had a frantic moment as he followed her in. What had she just implied? Would he misinterpret it? The room was airy and luxurious, with a king-size bed dominating it, but Vann's presence made the place feel breathlessly small.

"Would you excuse me for a moment?" she asked. "I need to pop into the bathroom."

"Of course," he said. "I'll pour the wine in the meantime."

Once she shut the bathroom door behind her, her breath emerged in an explosive rush. She lunged at the mirror over the sink, gasping at the undereye smudges, the worn-off lipstick, the loose wisps around her face and neck. They had gone well beyond the romantically tousled look, and were now officially a straggly mess.

She still had her purse, which was a damn good thing, since it had her makeup wipes and some lip gloss and mascara. But, oh, the hair, the hair. She pulled out all the pins and unwound the coil. The effect, after a day of the tight twist, was wild waves every which way. The quickest solution was a tight over-the-shoulder braid, but she had nothing to fasten the end. The ties were packed in her toiletries case, which was zipped up in the luggage outside. She could put her hair back up, but that would take time. Her hands were cold and shaking. And he was waiting for her out there.

Damn. She'd finger-comb it, shake it out and act like that had been the plan all along.

Sophie fixed her face with the wipes and a little fresh mascara. She put the hotel's courtesy toothpaste and toothbrush to good use and brushed her teeth before putting on a final slick of colorless lip gloss. It was the best she could do under these conditions.

Toothpaste and red wine, yikes. It was an unholy combination, but hey.

A girl had to do what a girl had to do.

Five

Vann poured out two glasses of wine and strolled over to stare out the window at the city lights. No big deal, he kept repeating. Just a quick drink with a colleague to unwind after a high-pressure day, and then he was out of here, leaving her to her well-deserved rest. No weirdness, no agenda, other than learning more about her and keeping her too busy to notice the forensic investigation under way back at headquarters. God knows when it came to that, Malcolm was keeping her busy enough without Vann's help.

Her stamina was incredible. She was classy and tough. Elegant, composed, pulled-together. That voice, wow. It was a problem for him. Constant, relentless sexual stimulation every time she spoke. Like he was being stroked by a seductive invisible hand.

It kept his blood continually racing. He needed to shut. That. Down.

Sophie Valente couldn't be Bryce's IP thief. A woman as accomplished as she was wouldn't waste her time and energy stealing the fruits of other people's labors. She had plenty of fruits to offer herself. She had that rare quality he'd seen in only a few people, his friends Zack and Drew among them. Ava, too, Drew's sister, and Jenna, Drew's soon-to-be wife. They knew who they were and what they were meant to do on this earth, and they just got on with it, no bullshit.

People like that didn't cheat and steal. Entirely aside from their morals and principles, it would just never occur to them to do so. It would bore them.

Insecure, jealous, damaged people cheated and stole. That wasn't Sophie Valente.

The bathroom door opened. The light and fan flicked off. He turned to speak, and forgot whatever he had meant to say.

She hadn't changed. It was the same silky white blouse over the tan pencil skirt. But she'd kicked off her heels and let down her hair. Her bare feet were slender and beautiful. High arches. Nails painted gold. That flirtatious glint on her toenails made the sweat break out on his back.

Her hair was a wild mass of waves swirling down over her shoulders. Her lips gleamed. Her skin looked dewy and soft. Fresh. Kissable.

"Excuse me," she said, her voice uncertain. "Sorry to keep you waiting."

"No, no. Take your time. It's been a hell of a day." He picked up her full wineglass and presented it to her.

She took it and sipped. "Mmm, thank you," she said. "It's very nice."

He gestured toward the table. "Waste no time," he urged her.

"Don't mind if I do," she said, taking her seat.

He sat down across from her as she loaded up her plate and forked up her first bite. "Oh, happy me. Are you sure you don't want some? I'll never manage to eat it all."

"Positive," he assured her. "Am I making you self-conscious?"

"Maybe a bit," she said, popping a cherry tomato into her mouth.

"I could just go," he offered. "And leave you to it."

"Oh, stop." She grabbed a dinner roll and tore a piece off. "This steak is delicious."

"Glad you like it. Drew and I both complained to Malcolm about not giving you a lunch break. But he's got this hazing mentality baked into his system. Everyone has to run the gauntlet and get clobbered to prove their worth. Classic Malcolm for you."

"You shouldn't have said anything. I can take whatever he dishes out."

"Yeah," he said. "We noticed."

Her eyes dropped. "I heard that you met Drew when you two were in the military together. Is that true?"

"Marines," he said. "*Semper Fi.* Two tours in Iraq. Fallujah, the Anbar Province."

She nodded. "And you've been with the firm for how long?"

"I've worked here for over eleven years," he replied. "Since I was twenty-three."

"And you're already the CFO? Of a big global company like Maddox Hill, at age thirty-four? That's really something."

"I started on the bottom," he said. "After I mustered out of the marines, I was at loose ends. So Drew suggested that I take a job at his uncle's architecture firm. He knew I was good with computers. I thought, what the hell? It might keep me out of trouble."

Her eyes smiled over her wineglass. "Did it?"

"More or less," he said. "I started out as an assistant general gofer and computer guy in the accounting department, and they busted my ass down there. Then the finance manager, Chuck Morrissey, took an interest in me. Fast-forward a couple of years, and he arranged for Maddox Hill to pay for me to get a degree in accounting and get myself certified. After that I was off and running. I got an MBA a few years later. Chuck encouraged that, too."

"No college after high school, then?"

He shook his head. "Almost. I was offered a football scholarship my senior year, but then my dad died. My grades tanked and I lost the scholarship. I couldn't afford college without it, and nobody was hiring where I lived. Central Washington is mostly rural. Sagebrush, wheat fields. So I joined the marines."

"A self-made man," she said.

He shrugged. "Not entirely. Chuck mentored me. When he got promoted to CFO, he made me his finance manager. Malcolm and Hendrick took chances on me over and over again. And Drew went to bat for me every single time I was up for a promotion. I wouldn't be where I am now if they hadn't helped."

"Their investment in you paid off a hundredfold. Out of curiosity, why the marines?"

He sipped his wine, considering the question. "It was a way to test myself, I guess," he said finally. "And learn some new skills."

"And did you?"

"Oh, yeah. I even thought about making a career out of it. But Fallujah and the Anbar Province changed my mind. Then Drew got wounded, and they sent him home. After that, it was pretty rough. I lost some good friends there."

Sophie sipped her wine and waited for more, but he couldn't keep up this line of conversation. The more painful details of his time in Iraq were too heavy, and the atmosphere between them was already charged.

"You said that your dad was a marine," she said. "A combat veteran. Did you join up because you wanted to understand his demons better? You followed in his footsteps so you could make some sense out of it all, right?"

He stared into her clear, searching eyes, speechless. Almost hypnotized.

"Did you find out what you needed to know?" she prompted. "Was it worth it?"

The question reverberated inside him. He'd never articulated that wordless impulse she had described, but the insight rang so true.

His eyes dropped. He took another sip of wine, stalling. Unable to speak.

Sophie put down her knife and fork. "I'm sorry," she said quietly. "That was invasive and presumptuous. Please forget I said it."

"Not at all," he said. "It just took me a while to process it. The answer is yes. That's probably what I was doing, but I didn't know it at the time. And yes, I think it was worth it."

She looked cautiously relieved. "I'll stop making big pronouncements about things that are none of my damn business."

"Don't stop," he urged her. "Make all the pronouncements you want. That way I don't have to rack my brains for small talk. I prefer the crossbow bolts of truth, straight to the chest."

She laughed as she forked up another chunk of her steak. Licked a drop of meat juice off her fingers. As her full, smiling lips closed around it, his whole body tightened and started to thrum. His face felt hot. His back getting damp with sweat.

He had to look away for a second and breathe.

"Your turn," she offered. "You're authorized to ask me any embarrassing question you like. Within the limits of decency, of course."

The limits of decency were feeling about as tight as his pants right now. Vann crossed his leg to protect his male dignity. "Give me a second to think up a good one," he said. "It's a big opportunity. I have to make it count."

She laughed. "Don't think too hard," she said. "It doesn't have to be a zinger."

"Okay, how about this? You talked about being a self-made man. How about you? Are you a self-made woman? How did you come to be so accomplished?"

She nibbled on a roasted potato. "I certainly had financial help," she said. "My mother's parents were well-to-do, and she earned well in her own right, so no expense was spared in my education. But they just assumed I'd do great things as a matter of course. 'From those to whom much is given, much is expected.' That was the general attitude."

"So you're a pathological high achiever," he said.

She snorted into her wine. "I wouldn't go that far. But I ask a lot of myself, I guess. Just like you."

"Do I get a bonus question?" he asked. "Now I'm warmed up. The questions are starting to come thick and fast."

"Go for it," she said. "Ask away."

"Okay. Going back to fathers, what happened to yours? Did he leave?"

Sophie's smile froze and Vann felt a stab of alarm. He'd taken her at her word, and still he'd overstepped. He studied her whiskey-gold eyes, barely breathing.

"He never knew I existed," she said finally. "I can't blame him for being absent."

"His loss."

"I like to think so," she said.

"So it was just you and your mom?"

Sophie's face softened. "Mom was great. I was lucky to have her. She was a brilliant artist. A bright, wonderful person. She was a textile designer, very much in demand. She worked all over the world, but by the time I finished middle school, she'd pretty much settled in Singapore."

"Is she still there?"

Sophie shook her head. "I lost her last year. Pancreatic cancer."

"Oh. I'm so sorry to hear that."

She nodded. "It happened so fast. It took us both by surprise."

"I lost my mom, too," he said. "When I was in Iraq. She had one of those sneaky heart attacks. The kind that seems like an upset stomach. She went to bed to sleep it off and never woke up."

"So you didn't even get to say goodbye," she said. "Oh, Vann. That's awful."

He nodded. "It was hard to find my place again when I came home. Civilian life seemed strange, and I had no one left to care about. So when Drew suggested coming to work here, I thought, what else have I got to do? At least I'd be close to a good friend."

"And the rest is history," she said.

"I guess so. Anyhow, that's my story. What brought you to Maddox Hill?"

Her eyes slid away. "More or less the same thing as you, I guess," she said. "After Mom died, I was out of reference points. I needed new horizons. Fresh things to look at."

"You lived in Singapore before?"

"Mostly. I studied there. Software design. Then a friend of mine who was a biologist had all her research for her doctorate stolen. I was so indignant for her I started learning about computer security and IP theft, and I eventually ended up specializing in it. I learned Mandarin in Singapore."

"How about the Italian?"

"My mom was Italian," she said. "Italian American, rather. Your people must have been Italian, too, with a name like Acosta. I take it Vann is short for Giovanni?"

"You nailed it," he said. "Calabrese. Third generation."

"My grandparents moved from Florence to New York in the seventies, when Mom was in her early teens. She spoke English with no accent, but we spoke Italian at home with my grandparents. I lived with them for half of my childhood. My mom would jet off to do her design jobs, and I'd stay in New York with my *nonno* and *nonna*. My grandfather had a company that shipped marble from Italy. ItalMarble. A lot of the big buildings on the East Coast are made of the stone he imported."

He was startled. "ItalMarble belonged to your grandfather? Really?"

"You know it?" she asked.

"Of course I know it," he said. "We're up on all the providers of high-end building materials. The company changed hands a few years ago, right?"

"Yes, that was when Nonno retired. He died shortly after that."

"I'm sorry to hear that," he said.

She nodded in acknowledgment. "When I was eleven, I persuaded my mom to rescue me. Take me with her the next time she left."

"Rescue you? From your grandparents? Why? Were they hard on you?"

She twirled some feathery arugula fronds up off the plate with her fork. "The opposite actually. They were very sweet to me. But suffocatingly overprotective."

"Yeah? Were they old-fashioned?"

"Very," she said. "But it was mostly because of my health."

He was taken aback. "Your health? Were you not well?"

"I had a heart condition when I was a toddler," she explained. "I almost died a few times. I had to have open-heart surgery. I spent the better part of two years recuperating. After that my grandparents always treated me like I was fragile, and I couldn't stand it."

Vann gazed at the glowing, vital woman across the table from him, tucking away her roasted potatoes with gusto. He couldn't imagine her having ever been ill.

"You don't seem fragile," he said. "Not with the crack-of-dawn kung fu classes, the high-octane male-dominated career and the killer heels."

"I may have overcompensated a little," she admitted. "I push myself. But I never want to feel weak or helpless ever again."

He lifted his wineglass in a toast. "You've succeeded in your goal."

"Have I?" she said. "A person has to climb that mountain from the bottom every single day, forever. You can't just sit back and rest on your past achievements."

"Wow, what a rigorous mindset," he commented. "Don't you get tired?"

"Sometimes," she admitted. "But you know what? It's a lot easier to have a rigorous mindset when you have a big steak dinner inside of you. It was wonderful. Thanks for thinking of me. I can't believe I ate so much."

"Don't mention it. You up for dessert?"

Her whiskey-colored eyes widened. "Dessert?"

"There was a choice of four different desserts. I went with chocolate cheesecake."

"Ooh. I love cheesecake."

Vann retrieved the plate from the tray and placed it in front of her, removing the cover with a flourish. *"Voilà."*

Sophie admired the generous slab, with multiple gooey layers on a chocolate cookie-crumb crust, swirled with drizzles of raspberry syrup. Fruit was artfully arranged next to it: watermelon, pineapple, kiwi, a cluster of shining red jewellike currants, a succulent strawberry and velvety raspberries.

"You have to help me out," she informed him, popping a raspberry into her mouth. "It's too gorgeous to waste, but if I eat it all, I'll hurt myself."

"Try it," he urged. "You go first."

She scooped up the point of the cheesecake slice and lifted it to her lips.

It was agonizing, watching her pink tongue dart out to catch a buttery chocolate crumb. Seeing the pleasure in her heavy-lidded eyes. He fidgeted on his chair.

"Now you." She fished for another spoon and prepared a generous bite for him.

He leaned forward and opened his mouth. That rush of creamy sweetness nudged him right past all his careful walls and limits and rules. He was so turned on it scared him.

He chewed, swallowed. "Wow," he said hoarsely, trying to recall all the bullet points in his lecture-to-self.

Bryce had accused her of spying. Zack was investigating her. She was an employee. A key employee. He was her superior. He never got involved with coworkers. Especially subordinates. Cardinal rule.

He couldn't remember why that was relevant when he wanted

this so badly. He stared hungrily as she took another bite of her dessert.

So. Damn. Beautiful.

"Want another bite?" she was saying.

He dragged his eyes away. "I should go. Tomorrow will be another long day."

Sophie's smile faded. "Thanks again. The meal was lovely."

He was supposed to say something polite, something automatic that he shouldn't even have to think about, but the mechanism wasn't working. In any case, he didn't trust his voice. Or any other part of himself. He had to get the hell out of this room.

Before he said or did something he could never take back.

Six

Sophie preceded him to the door, glad to have her back to him for once. She felt so exposed. All that blushing and giggling and babbling. Things she'd never told anyone. And the inappropriate personal questions she'd asked him? What had come over her?

And was he flirting, or just being gracious? She couldn't work it out.

She usually beat down attempts at flirting with a sledgehammer. But she couldn't treat Vann Acosta that way. Nor could she quite tell if it was happening or not.

Ordering her a fabulous meal was a seductive move, but he hadn't tried to capitalize on it. She had invited him in and insisted on sharing the wine. He'd made no sexy comments or innuendos; he'd given her no compliments.

At least, other than for her work ethic and professional focus.

But that conversation had gone beyond flirtation. She had such a strange, electric feeling inside. Like they were connecting on a deeper level.

Soul to soul. The intimacy was jarring. And arousing.

It wound her up. Her toes were shaking, clenched in the carpet fibers. Her chest felt tight; she was afraid to breathe. She was acutely aware of him, and of her own body. Her clothes felt heavy on her sensitized skin. Her thighs were clenched. Her heart thudded heavily.

She reached for the door handle—and Vann's hand came to rest on top of hers.

The shock of connection flashed through her. Her heartbeat roared in her ears. It felt like a sultry fog of heat had surrounded her head.

She was drunk with his nearness. Conscious of every delicious detail of him. His scent, his height. The way his clothes fit on his big, muscular body. The ridiculous breadth of his shoulders, blocking the light from the room behind them.

His eyes locked on hers. A muscle pulsed in his jaw.

She had no more doubt. This wasn't a lighthearted *"How 'bout it, babe?"*

This was raw, stark desire.

She glanced down. His desire was visible to the naked eye. He reached up and wound a lock of her hair around his forefinger, tugging it delicately.

She swayed forward, drawn helplessly by his pull. He was so tall. Her neck ached from staring up at him. Then her head fell into the cradle of his warm hand. His heat surrounded her. The scent of his shirt, his cologne, was intoxicating. Just a little closer and their bodies would touch—and she would be lost to all reason.

His hunger called to her own. She craved it. A big, strong, gorgeous guy who was smart and classy and thoughtful and attentive, a man who wasn't afraid to be real with her, a man who rang all her bells like a church on Easter Sunday. Hell, yeah. Give her some of that. Give her a massive double helping, and keep it coming. She wanted to pull him toward her and wrap herself around him like a scarf. The yearning made her ache.

Then she thought of Mom. Her life blighted by one ill-considered affair with her boss. It was swiftly over, and she was quickly forgotten—by him. But Mom hadn't forgotten.

Sophie saw her mother in her mind's eye, sitting on the terrace of the Singapore apartment with a glass of wine and a cigarette. Every evening, quietly watching the sun set on another day, with that remote, dreamy sadness on her face.

Vicky Valente had never recovered from Malcolm. She'd never bonded with any other man. She'd gone on a few dates, had the occasional brief hookup, but the men always drifted away once she started comparing them to Malcolm.

No one else ever measured up, and she could not settle for less.

That affair had marked her forever.

Sophie sensed the same potential for destruction right now. She was so drawn to Vann. More than she'd ever been to anyone. This could leave a scar just like the one Malcolm had left on her mother. A life-altering wound.

She took a step back, bracing herself against the wall. "You're my boss." Her voice was unsteady. "This could blow up in our faces."

Vann let go of her hair, and let his hand drop. He started to speak, then stopped himself. "It probably would," he said. "I'm sorry. Good night."

He pulled the door open and left without another word.

Sophie watched as the door swung shut on its own. She felt like yelling in a rebellious rage. Kicking and screaming. What a goddamn waste. Not…freaking…fair.

But the cosmic timing sucked. She was in a state of overload. On the one hand, she was trying to get a DNA sample to verify if Malcolm really was her father. On the other, she was trying to demonstrate to him that she'd be worth having as a daughter.

No one should have to scramble to prove her right to exist. Yet here she was, scrambling for Malcolm's notice and approval and respect. Terrified of not being found worthy. She didn't want to feel that way, but still, she did.

It made her so vulnerable. And that was enough vulnerability for the time being.

She did not need to fish for more.

Seven

Sophie looked as fine today as she had the day before, Vann reflected. She wore closed-toe shoes, but he knew the sexy secret of those gold toenails. She'd left her hair down today, which was a dirty trick. Those heavy locks had slid through his hands like—

Thud. A kick to the side of his foot jolted Vann out of his reverie. He looked around to find Malcolm glaring at him. His boss's gaze flicked to Sophie, who was leaning forward and speaking in a low, clear voice directly into Hendrick's good ear.

Down, boy, Malcolm mouthed.

Nothing slipped past the old man. *Damn.*

Sophie had sensed the interchange, too, and she flashed them a swift, puzzled look while never missing a beat with her interpreting. Thank God they were wrapping it up. They were at the stage of congratulating each other for reaching a mutually satisfactory accord. Zhang Wei had been at it for forty minutes now.

An hour after the meeting concluded they met again for the reception on the observation deck, where the restaurant had laid out a buffet. Sophie was already there when Vann arrived.

He stood next to Drew, making conversation with Zhang Wei's grandson while trying not to stare at her. She was dramatically silhouetted against a sky streaked with sunset colors, translating for Hendrick and the elder Zhang Wei. He loved the flounced ivory silk skirt. How it hugged her shape.

Look away from the woman. Damn it.

The atmosphere was finally relaxed. The food and wine were good. After they'd eaten, the younger Zhang Wei was congratulating Drew on his upcoming wedding when Malcolm interrupted, beckoning to both of them imperiously. "Vann! Drew! Come here! I have an idea!"

Vann followed Drew over, careful not to meet Sophie's eyes.

"Mr. Zhang should come to the wedding along with his grandson," Malcolm announced. "They'll both be in the States until the middle of next week, so why not?"

Drew smiled in cheerful resignation. "Great idea, Uncle. The more, the merrier." He gave the elder Mr. Zhang a short bow. "I'd be honored to have you there, sir."

"Damn straight," Malcolm said. "You already have over two hundred and fifty people coming. What are two more? I'll tell Sylvia to arrange a suite. Sophie, too. Mr. Zhang will need to have an interpreter on hand." He turned on Sophie. "You'll make yourself available this weekend? You can go back to the city on Monday."

"Ah...yes, of course," she said after a startled pause. "I'll let them know back at the office."

"Excellent," Malcolm said. "Vann, you didn't have a plus-one for this weekend's extravaganza, right? I remember Ava complaining about it. Now you have one, so it's a win-win for everyone, eh?"

The younger Zhang murmured in his grandfather's ear. "Grandfather is tired," he told them with a smile. "I will escort him to his room." He turned to Drew. "Will you meet me downstairs at the bar later? I must drink to your last days as an unmarried man."

"With pleasure." Drew turned to Vann. "Join us there?"

"Sure," Vann said.

After the Zhangs made their way out, Sophie spoke up. "Since Mr. Zhang no longer needs me, would you gentlemen excuse me?"

"What for?" Malcolm demanded. "Where are you going?"

Sophie's smile was utterly serene. "The call of nature, sir."

Malcolm harrumphed. "Oh, fine. Off you go."

Malcolm, Drew and the others kept talking after Sophie left, but Vann couldn't follow what they said. His entire attention was on Sophie as she retrieved her purse.

She left the room, and after a decent interval, he excused himself and grabbed his jacket from the chair where he'd left it. He slipped out the door just in time to see Sophie at the end of the corridor, turning the corner.

He followed, peering around the corner when he reached it. She'd gone right past the ladies' room and was approaching the office suite that had been assigned to Malcolm.

She started to look back to see if anyone was watching. Instinctively, Vann jerked back behind the corner.

When he peered around it again, Sophie was gone, and the door to Malcolm's office was closing behind her.

Vann's stomach plummeted into a cold, dark place. He strode after her, wondering if Malcolm had left his laptop in there, unprotected. The old man couldn't quite wrap his mind around the realities of modern corporate security.

Various other Maddox Hill project specs were on it, brought along to illustrate possibilities for the Nairobi Towers project for Zhang Wei and his team. That data could be of great value to an IP thief.

He was almost running. Running toward pain, like Dad had coached him to do in his football days. He pushed open the door of the office, looking wildly around.

The room was dark and empty. Malcolm's laptop sat undisturbed.

Water rushed in the sink in the suite's bathroom. Sophie was in there.

Vann let the door fall shut behind him. He felt almost dizzy with relief. Sophie hadn't opened the computer. She couldn't have, in the little time it took him to sprint down the hall. She might have planned to do so after emerging from the bathroom, but a smart spy would take her opportunities fast. She wouldn't dawdle for one...two...three minutes in a bathroom. Almost five minutes now. He waited until the water stopped running.

Light blazed out as the bathroom door opened.

Sophie's fingers shook as she tucked the fork she'd seen Malcolm use to eat fruit trifle that afternoon into the plastic bag and shoved it in her purse. It had been hard to interpret Malcolm's and Zhang's conversation while simultaneously following Malcolm's fork with her eyes, memorizing exactly where it ended up on the tray when he was done using it. Hoping desperately that it would still be there, untouched, when she had a chance to get back in here and swipe it. He'd left it laying crosswise over his dessert plate, while the other forks lay scattered around on the tray.

And they were all still that way, thank God. The cleaning staff hadn't taken anything away yet. A stroke of pure luck.

She tucked the plastic bag down into her purse and headed for the bathroom, setting the water running as soon as she locked the door. No toothbrush or razor in here. She'd only find those items in Malcolm's hotel room, and she couldn't risk trying to get in. She simply didn't have the nerve. But she'd seen him take his blood pressure meds and wash the pills down with a glass that he left in the bathroom. That would work.

Two DNA samples ought to do the job. In truth, it was all unnecessary. She'd already tested Ava's DNA from a champagne glass at the company-wide reception celebrating Drew's engagement. The test had demonstrated an overwhelming probability that they were cousins. The geneticist assured her that the test was conclusive.

But even that wasn't strictly necessary. Her mother had no reason to lie to her. Not on her deathbed. She'd always refused to talk about Sophie's parentage. It was one of the few things they had argued about.

Mom had never given in. Not until the very end.

But it wasn't about doubting Mom's word. Sophie needed objective proof for the Maddoxes that she wasn't an opportunistic scammer.

Sophie snapped her purse shut, washed her hands and unlocked the door.

"What are you doing in here?" It was Vann's voice.

Sophie shrieked and jerked back, heart pounding. "Oh, my God! You scared me!"

He just stood by the door, his dark eyes gleaming. The only light in the room came from the bathroom, and the city lights outdoors.

"Why are you here?" he asked again.

"I came in to use the bathroom," she said. "Given a choice between a public bathroom and a private one, I'll always choose the private one."

"This is Malcolm's office," he said.

Sophie felt defensive. "I was in and out of here all afternoon, and I watched people from our team come and go the whole time. I was under the impression that the office was available to all of us. But if it makes you uncomfortable, I'll leave. Excuse me."

She strode past him, chin up.

Vann reached out and gripped her wrist. "Sophie."

It was happening again. The slightest touch of his big hand released that feverish swell of heat, the roar in her ears. That clutch in her chest of wild excitement. "What do you want?" She tried to keep her voice from shaking.

"I didn't mean to offend you. I was surprised, that's all."

"Were you following me?"

He just stood there silently, not admitting it, not denying it. She tugged at her wrist, but he wouldn't let go. "Answer me, Vann."

"Yes, I was following you," he admitted.

"What for?" she demanded.

No part of her could resist as his arm slid around her waist. As his hand came to rest at the small of her back. The heat of it burned through the fabric.

"For this," he said as his lips came down on hers.

Eight

Sophie had spent two nights imagining how it would be to kiss that man. Her imagination hadn't come close to reality.

Her body lit up. A blaze of raw power rushed up from her depths, blindingly intense. His lips coaxed her, drawing her deeper into the seductive spell of his kiss. His fingers twisted into her hair. Her arms wound around her neck. Her heart thudded frantically. She came up from the desperate tenderness of that wild, sensual kiss for a quick, whimpering gasp of air, and then she went right back for more.

The world rocked, shifted. She felt a hard surface under her bottom. He'd lifted her up onto the mahogany desk. One of her shoes dangled off her toe. She kicked it off, then the other one, and wrapped her legs around his. He cupped her bottom, pressing her against the stiff bulge of his erection.

She twined around him, bracing her legs around his as their tongues touched. She loved his taste. The hot, sinuous dance of lips and tongue that promised every possible pleasure, multiplied infinitely. She'd never responded to a man this way. She forgot where she was, who she was, what she was doing, what was at stake. All she felt was him.

The door flew open. The light flicked on. Sophie blinked over Vann's shoulder.

Malcolm Maddox stood in the doorway. He looked horrified.

Damn. Vann felt Sophie go rigid and shrink away.

"What in God's name is going on in here?" Malcolm sounded furious. "Vann? What's the meaning of this?"

Vann pulled away from Sophie's warmth, and turned around to face his boss.

Sophie slid off the desk, shaking her skirt down. She knelt to retrieve her shoes, slid her feet back into them and picked up her purse from the floor, shaking her hair defiantly. "Good night, Vann," she said.

She paused near the doorway, waiting for Malcolm to step aside to let her pass.

"My apologies for the spectacle, Mr. Maddox," she said when he didn't move. "We shouldn't have been in here. But I'd like to go now."

"For damn sure you shouldn't have been in here," Malcolm said. "After two days of watching you work, I expected better judgment from you, Ms. Valente."

Her lips tightened. "Agreed," she said. "Excuse me. I'd like to go."

Malcolm stepped aside to let her pass, then closed the door behind her sharply.

Vann braced himself. This was going to hurt.

"And just what the hell do you have to say for yourself?" Malcolm demanded.

"Nothing," Vann said. "I apologize that it happened here. For the record, I initiated what you saw, not her. She never behaved unprofessionally. That's on me."

Malcolm let out a dubious grunt. "Gallant words, but that looked like equal opportunity bad judgment to me. She should have slapped your face and told you to take a cold shower and grow up. You are her superior. This kind of thing is messy and stupid."

"I understand," Vann said stiffly.

"Only when it's convenient for you," Malcolm snapped. "I never expected you to live like a monk, but think long and hard before you indulge with my key employees. Because it will not play out well for you."

"Yes, sir, I understand," he repeated.

"I doubt it," Malcolm said. "You could hurt her, you know. And when it comes to that, she could hurt you, too. There are very few possible happy endings to a story like this. And all of the unhappy ones reflect badly on my company."

That was true, but Vann didn't want to dwell on it. "I understand," he repeated. "Can I go?"

"That girl," Malcolm said slowly. "She reminds me of someone I knew long ago. Decades ago. Mistakes I made that I still regret."

Vann felt trapped. "Sir, I'm really not sure what that has to do with me."

"I hurt someone back then," Malcolm went on. "I was a selfish dog, thinking of my own enjoyment. I paid the price. I didn't appreciate something special when I found it, and then it was gone. I don't even know why I'm saying this. But I don't want you to make the same...oh, hell. Never mind. Forget I said it."

"If you say so, sir," Vann said.

Malcolm laid his hand on Vann's shoulder. He stared into Vann's eyes with unnerving intensity. "Don't be like me," he said roughly. "Be better than that. You'll thank yourself later."

"Okay," Vann said, bemused. He'd never seen that look in Malcolm's eyes, or ever imagined his boss displaying pain or vulnerability. It was painful to witness. "I will, sir."

Malcolm broke eye contact with a snort. "No, you won't. You'll do as you damn well please. I know it, and you know it."

Vann sidled past him. "Good night, Mr. Maddox."

"Behave yourself," the old man snarled. "Get out of here."

Vann wasted no time in doing so.

Nine

Sophie was surprised at herself. She wasn't in the habit of shedding tears, but getting scolded by Malcolm Maddox when her guard was down—it shook her to her core, and now here she was, blubbering in the shower.

God knows Malcolm was in no position to judge her. But men held women to different standards. Even women they cared about. And she was not in that category.

Nor would she ever be, at this rate. He'd probably written her off already. Decided she was a silly piece of man-crazy fluff who would just wind up embarrassing him.

And that kiss, oh, God. She'd gone molten with desire. She was still dizzy, even after the humiliation of the scene with Malcolm.

What a mess. And she'd thought she was being so slick, whisking away DNA samples. She'd dropped her purse when Vann kissed her. Ker-plop, down it went on the floor with a glass tumbler inside it. Would have served her right if the glass had shattered.

Sophie toweled off, shook her hair down from its damp top-knot and wrapped herself in the terry-cloth robe that the hotel had provided. She brushed her hair and teeth, wondering if she should check on the honeypots, traps and snares she had laid out for the corporate spy. She'd been too busy and exhausted yesterday to monitor them. She was too tired tonight, too.

She'd nab that thieving son of a bitch eventually, but it looked like her fond fantasy of impressing Malcolm with her smarts and her skills had just gone up in smoke.

In her own defense, it wasn't a fair fight. Vann Acosta was so gorgeous no one could blame her for getting swept away.

The low knock on the door made excitement flash through her like lightning.

Calm down. Could be housekeeping, bringing fresh wash-cloths and body soap. For God's sake, breathe.

The knock sounded again.

"Who is it?" she asked.

"It's Vann."

The seconds that followed were charged with uncertainty. Images, sensations and memories swirled through her. She felt Vann's big, hot body pressed against hers. His lips, demanding sensual surrender. That vortex of need pulling her down.

If she gave in, it would pull her in so deep and fast she might never get out.

She opened her mouth to ask what he wanted, and then closed it. There was no point in playing dumb. She either wanted this, with all the risks and potential consequences, or she didn't. She wasn't going to make herself decent. That would be silly.

Vann hadn't come here to see her decent. He came here to get her naked.

She opened the door.

Vann just looked at her. She was acutely conscious of how unprepared she was for this moment. Naked under the robe. Hair damp, flowing loose and wild over the bathrobe. Flushed from the shower. Her face bare of makeup.

No need to state his purpose. She'd stated her own by opening the door. Sophie stepped backward without a word, making room for him to enter.

Vann walked in and turned to face her. "I'm sorry about what happened."

"It wasn't completely your fault," she said. "I didn't exactly shove you away."

"That's why I'm here," he said. "To see if you want this. Because I do. If I read you wrong, or if you've changed your mind, just tell me."

She couldn't speak. Words just wouldn't form in her throat.

"Say something," he insisted. "Please. Tell me where we are with this."

She licked her lips. "It's…a little soon," she said. "Hookups with virtual strangers…it's not my style. I barely know you."

Vann let out a jerky sigh. "I understand." He turned to the door. "I'll go."

"Don't!" she blurted.

He turned back. They gazed at each other in the yawning silence.

There were so many ways to start this. Her breath came quick and shallow, and the air between them felt thick. Time slowed down.

Vann drifted closer. He reached out, touching her lower lip with his forefinger. Stroking it. She vibrated like a plucked string as he slid his hand downward, tugging at the tie of her bathrobe. It came loose and the bathrobe fell open, revealing just a shadowed, vertical stripe of her naked body. Her centerline. Throat, chest, belly, mound.

He had made his move, and now he was waiting for her countermove. Now would be the perfect time for her to say something provocative. To grab his tie, yank him closer. To throw off her robe with a flourish. Ta-da. Take that.

His finger trailed downward. Chin, jaw, throat. He stayed in that strip of space between her robe as he traced the rough, puckered surgical scar on her breastbone, then slid his hand inside her robe to press his palm over her frantically beating heart.

She quivered as his caresses began again. The tender stroke of his fingertips felt so aware, so switched on, so deliberate. Every faint touch felt like a kiss.

Over her belly button. Lower. He brushed the trimmed swatch of dark hair on her mound, then lower, stroking sensitive, hidden folds between. Taking his time. Slow, teasing. He leaned over her shoulder, kissing her throat, his breath warm against her neck. His fingers delved into her secret heat. Petting and probing. Driving her nuts.

She gripped his shoulders to brace herself as she moved against his skillful hand. He coaxed her arousal higher and higher—until the wave crested, and broke.

Pleasure wrenched through her. A torrent of chaotic, beautiful energy. Deep, pulsing throbs, expanding wider and wider, filling her entire consciousness.

Vann's murmur of satisfaction rumbled against her throat.

Sophie felt wide open to the sky. As soft as starlight. She shrugged the robe back and let it fall. No attitude. No bow-down-before-my-celestial-beauty vibe. She just wanted to be seen by him, known by him.

Vann hid his face against her hair. "Sophie," he whispered. "You're perfect."

She leaned against him, shivering with laughter. "Hardly. With my battle scars."

"Your scar is beautiful. It's the reason you're still here. It represents triumph over death. All the effort it took to make yourself whole and strong."

Her throat tightened. "That's a poetic spin on a big old surgical scar. Nicely done."

"I swear, I could not blow smoke at you if I wanted to. You're taking me apart."

"Me? You're the guy with the magic hands." She looked him over, eyes lingering on the bulge in his pants. "What other secrets have you got hidden away in that bespoke suit of yours? I showed you mine. Now show me yours."

His big grin carved sexy grooves in his lean cheeks as he shrugged out of his suit jacket. He jerked the tie loose, kicked off the shoes, tugged the shirt out of his pants, while Sophie attacked his belt buckle.

He pulled a strip of condoms out of his pocket, and tossed them onto the bed, and then flung his clothing onto the chair. Pants, briefs and socks, whipped off in a few quick gestures.

His naked body exceeded her expectations. She'd seen how tall and broad and solid he was, and she'd felt the intense physical energy he generated. But she hadn't dreamed of the effect his nakedness would have on her. His body was thick-muscled, sinewy and taut and defined. Dark hair arrowed down to his groin. He was beautiful there, too. Stiff, substantial and ready for action. She seized his penis, enjoying the taut firmness, the throbbing pulse, in her palm. The gasp of pleasure he made as she stroked him.

He clamped her hand and held it still. "Stop," he told her, breath hitching. "Let me save it for later. Keep that up and I'll go off like a grenade."

"Sounds exciting," she murmured.

"Oh, it would be, for me. But it's too soon, and I don't want to lead with that."

"No? How do you want to lead?"

His eyes held hers. "Just in case that's a trick question, I don't have to take the lead at all."

"Trick question?" She laughed. "Please. Do I really seem so treacherous?"

"If you'd rather call the shots, just tell me. My master plan is to make you come until you're too exhausted to roll over. The details don't matter to me. Got me?"

She squeezed his stiff, pulsing hardness once again. "Oh, yes. I've got you," she murmured, delighted at the shudder that racked him. "Right in the palm of my hand. It all sounds great.

I don't have any sort of master plan, so I'll just enjoy yours. Carry on."

His grin flashed again, and he turned her to face the mirror, holding her gaze as his hand slid up to cup her breast. Stroking the undercurve. Teasing her nipple.

She sagged back against him with a whimpering gasp. The tip of her breast was a glowing point of concentrated pleasure, and every slow caress racked her with fresh shivers of need. Her thighs clenched as his hand crept lower. His lips were hot against her neck, giving her lazy, seductive kisses that slowed down time. She felt suspended, breathless, as he gripped her hips, caressing her bottom.

She struck a provocative pose, leaning over. "Do you want to do it from behind?"

"Of course," he said. "But not the first time, or maybe even the second time. It's too soon to mess around and be playful. The first time should be...worshipful."

"Oh. So that's what this is? Wow. Being worshipped works for me."

"That's good, because that's what's happening." He pulled the bed covers down and pushed her until she sprawled on her back in the bed. Scooping her hair up, he arrayed it on the pillow, burying his face in it with a wordless groan.

Then he slid down over her body, trailing kisses to the scar on her chest.

She vibrated with emotion as he lingered there, kissing right over her frantically beating heart. Any place he touched began to glow and melt into something shining and liquid. His touch was magic. Transforming her.

After a sweet, languorous eternity of kisses, he trailed them down over her breasts, then her belly. Farther, and then farther down, kissing and licking and nuzzling, until he settled between her thighs and put his mouth to her most sensitive flesh.

And she could do nothing but shiver and gasp.

Ten

Worshipful.

It wasn't a tactic, or a choice. It was a stark truth, a physical necessity, like breathing. His body worshiped hers. Some part inside him bowed before her, dazzled by her beauty. Humbled by the privilege of touching her, pleasing her. Tasting her.

She was so sweet. He'd never imagined anything as exciting as caressing her secret female flesh with his tongue, taking his time. Making it last. Making her wait. The longer he made this last, the bigger the payoff.

Finally, she exploded in another shattering orgasm. He savored it, and kissed his way back up her body, settling himself over her. "You're good?" he asked.

Sophie smiled as her eyes fluttered open. "You couldn't tell?"

"I take nothing for granted with you," he said. "It's too important."

"It's wonderful," she whispered. "It's superdeluxe. Please, proceed with your master plan. As a matter of fact…" She grabbed the pack of condoms that he'd tossed on the bed and opened one. She put the little circle of latex in his hand, and slid her fingers into his chest hair, gripping until he felt the bite of her nails. "Don't make me wait."

Vann was teetering on a tightrope of self-control. He got the condom on with no fumbling. Then she pulled him into her arms, wiggling until she had him right where she wanted him... slowly easing deeper into her tight, clinging heat.

Then the deliberate, rocking surges, jaw clenched, panting for control as he fought the urge to go crazy. Lose control.

No. He was sticking to the plan. Oh-so-slow. Until it was too slow for Sophie, and she was winding her legs around his and insisting with her body. Her nails dug into him. She made those whimpering sounds that made him want to explode... but he hung back. Just a little longer...until her felt her climax start to overtake her.

Then he was lost. The power crashed through him, obliterating thought.

Afterward, he felt her lips against his cheekbone. Her chest jerked and heaved.

Still inside her, he rolled off to let her breathe. He was amazed by her beauty. He could hardly believe she was real. He drew away with extreme reluctance. "I have to get rid of the condom," he said. "Don't go anywhere. Please."

"Don't worry," she murmured. "I can't move."

He slid off the bed and went into the bathroom to take care of it, then slid right back into bed with her, tugging the sheet up over the two of them. Hungry for contact. She was so long and lithe and exquisitely smooth. Her soft curves. Those high, full breasts.

She snuggled up close, and her pink tongue licked his collarbone, making his body instantly stir. "You taste good," she whispered. "So salty."

"You, too," he told her. "You're so sweet. Can't get enough of you."

Her full lips curved in that seductive smile. "Awww." Sophie slid her fingers through his sweat-dampened hair, exploring him. Neck, shoulder. Squeezing and murmuring her approval. "This is going to get us into so much trouble."

"Is it?" he said.

"You saw how Malcolm reacted. He's angry. And disgusted."

"He has the wrong idea about us."

"How so?"

He pulled her closer, wrapping his leg around her body. "He thinks I'm just serving myself. Using you. That's not what's happening here."

She laughed. "If you are using me, then you're doing a damn good job of it."

"All jokes aside, it was never about that," he told her. "This is like nothing I've ever felt before."

"I'm glad. Because honestly? I do not feel used right now."

"What do you feel?" He blurted out the question without considering whether he was ready to hear the answer.

She considered the question for a moment. "Hmm, let me think," she said. "Sexually satisfied. Flattered. Delighted. Infinitely pleasured. And definitely pampered."

"That's a good starting place," he said, relieved.

"Also worried," she added. "About the fallout."

"We'll get through it," he said. "We'll look back on this and laugh."

She gave him a dubious look. "I'm not sure what that means. But it sounds hopeful."

"It is hopeful," he said forcefully. "As a matter of fact, I haven't felt this hopeful in…well, hell. I don't know. Ever, maybe."

Her eyes widened. "Vann. Put the brakes on. We hardly know each other."

"We can fix that," he suggested. "This weekend is the perfect opportunity. We'll accelerate the process. We can work at it every waking moment. I want to learn all your secrets. I want to know everything about you. Hopes, dreams, fears, nightmares."

To his dismay, Sophie pulled away. She sat up, tossing her

hair back over her shoulder. "Okay," she said, her voice guarded. "But let's take it easy."

"Easy how?" he demanded. "What does that even mean?"

"I'm not an invited guest, Vann," she reminded him. "I'm hired help, remember? I'm a convenience for Zhang Wei. I'll be at his beck and call, not yours. You won't have a chance to learn my secrets while I'm following Zhang around. And Malcolm will definitely be watching us like a hawk after tonight."

"I don't care." He realized, as the words came out, that they were literally true.

"Well, I still do," she said. "So don't rush me."

Sophie slid off the bed, giving him the opportunity for a long, appreciative look at her backside, that mass of dark hair swinging against her back, the perfect curves of her bottom. The pearl-like luster of her skin. Those long, shapely legs.

She uncorked the wine he'd ordered the night before, and took the paper caps off the two water tumblers that were on the tray, pouring out two glasses. Then she sauntered back, aware of his gaze. Taking her time. Letting him look.

She handed him a glass. "One step at a time," she said. "Let's not get ahead of ourselves."

"Why not?" he demanded, rebellious.

"It's not smart to push our luck."

He shrugged. "I have never felt so lucky in my life."

She sipped her wine as she studied him, gorgeous and enigmatic in the darkness. He suddenly thought of Tim Bryce and his accusations.

They seemed even more ridiculous now. He'd met liars and cheats. Some were attractive, smart, charming, but none of them shone like Sophie. Strength and toughness radiated out of her, impossible to mistake.

Sophie was for real. He'd bet everything he had on that.

"It doesn't scare you?" she asked him. "Feeling so lucky?"

He shrugged. "Sure, it scares me. So what? I'll be brave."

She came closer, placing her glass on the bedside table, and clambered onto the bed, flinging her leg over his thighs. "Okay," she said softly. "Let's be brave. Careful…but brave." She kissed his chest, her gaze flicking up at him with a teasing smile as her kisses trailed lower.

"Whoa," Vann said. "What are you doing?"

"Getting to know you," she said. "Didn't you say you wanted to accelerate the process?"

"Of course. But…ah… I thought you wanted to slow down."

She pressed a kiss to his thigh, her hand caressing his shaft. "But then we decided to be brave, right?"

"Uh…yeah," Vann choked out as she took him in her mouth. And that was the end of any words.

Sophie floated in bliss. Her body was lapped by it, caressed and cradled and rocked by waves of pleasure as she drifted up, closer to waking consciousness—

Just in time for the explosive burst of release. It welled up from some mysterious source inside her, radiating out into the universe like the sunrise.

Her eyes fluttered open as pleasure echoed through her. She looked down, gasping for breath. Vann lay between her legs, kissing the side of her thigh, petting her tenderly with his fingertips. Smiling at her as he wiped his mouth.

"Couldn't resist," he said. "Thought it might be a good way to start the day."

Wow. She could not voice the word. She just formed it with her lips.

Vann rose up, a condom ready in his hand. "Am I overdoing it?"

She shook her head and held out her arms, and Vann rolled the latex swiftly over his impressive erection. He covered her with his warmth, resting on his elbows. Her body's response was instinctive, immediate. She arched and opened as he pressed slowly inside her.

Their breath was ragged, eyes locked with each slow, surging thrust. Each stroke a caress, a sweet lick of pure delight.

It was harder to look into his eyes in the light of dawn, with the day ahead of them, with all its dangers and uncertainties. The night they'd passed was a wild erotic dream of sensual delights. She'd been so wanton, surrendering to pleasure, over and over again.

He'd awakened a need that got bigger, hotter and wilder every time.

They moved frantically against each other, desperate for release…and came to pieces together.

Vann rolled to the side, breathing raggedly. They lay there, stroking each other's damp skin. Speechless with emotion. He seized her hand, and kissed it.

"You remember that we have a plane to catch this morning, right?" she asked.

He nodded, still kissing her knuckles. "There's still time."

"There's always less than you think," she said. "And remember. Be discreet."

"If you want."

"You don't want? You want to throw caution to the wind? Already?"

He shrugged. "I'm not ashamed," he said.

"Well, I'm not ashamed, either. But for now, I don't want anyone else to know about what's between us. It's new and fresh. Let's protect it from the outside world for a while."

"That's fair."

She laughed at him. "And to that end, you should get back to your room before anybody sees you wandering the halls with bedhead and lipstick stains."

"Do I have lipstick stains?" His eyes widened. "Cool. Where?"

She swung a pillow at him, laughing. "Oh, get out."

"I'm dismissed? Already?" he asked, crestfallen.

"Just for now," she said demurely. "Later, we'll see. Don't you need to pack?"

Vann headed into the bathroom with a long-suffering look. He emerged a few minutes later, hair damp, and pulled on his clothes. "See you downstairs."

"Downstairs," she echoed.

The door shut behind him, and the room felt unbearably empty and quiet.

Sophie rolled over, pressing her face against the pillow to bury a scream of pure emotional overload. Excitement, terror, shock, joy.

And hope. This had been beyond anything she'd ever imagined. She was head over heels in lust. She'd fallen into bed with a guy she hardly knew. She'd given him everything she had to give.

And now all she could do was count the hours until she could do it again.

Eleven

Sophie was good at playing it cool. She greeted Vann at the coffee bar in the hotel restaurant with the same crisp friendliness with which she greeted Drew and the others. No one would have known they had passed a night of searing passion.

Except Drew, who knew him well. As soon as Sophie went to the buffet for some scrambled eggs and fruit, he spoke up.

"Zhang and I missed you last night at the bar," he said. "I thought you said you'd meet us. We waited for you for quite some time."

"Oh. Ah, yeah." Vann had completely forgotten. "Sorry. I ended up getting involved in some work stuff in my room."

"Yeah? I texted you. Several times." Drew's voice was carefully nonchalant.

"Sorry I missed it."

"Came by your room, too, on my way to bed. Knocked on your door. Pretty loudly. Guess you must have crashed hard. Long day yesterday, hmm?"

"I was wearing headphones," Vann said through his teeth.

"I blast heavy metal when I'm looking at numbers. It keeps me focused."

"Oh. I see." Drew's eyes flicked over to Sophie, and then back to Vann. "Well, good luck with those numbers. I hope they all add up for you."

Vann's phone chimed. When he got it out he saw the four messages from Drew from the night before. And one from Bryce that had just arrived.

Learn anything about SV?

Tension gripped him. It offended him that Bryce was so convinced that Sophie was the spy. As if Bryce had accused Vann himself.

Nothing, he texted back. Not her. One hundred percent sure of that.

He could feel Bryce's irritation in the quickness of the man's response.

Didn't try too hard, did you?

Vann texted back rapidly. Malcolm invited her to the wedding to interpret for the Zhangs. Suspend everything. You're barking up the wrong tree. Look elsewhere.

Wrong tree, my ass, Bryce texted back. SV at P Point this weekend is perfect. We'll settle this. I'll call a meeting with Malcolm, Hendrick, Drew and SV when you get to P Point. Do not tip her off.

Don't do this, Vann texted. Not at the wedding. Not the place or time.

Bryce did not respond. *Shit.*

"Vann?"

He looked up at the sound of Sophie's voice, and thumbed the app closed. "Yes?"

"The others are waiting in the car," she said. "Time to go."

"On my way." He slid his phone into his pocket and followed her.

Sylvia was in the lobby, looking harassed as always. "There you are! I had them go ahead and load your luggage. Malcolm is getting agitated!"

Vann suppressed a rude suggestion about what Malcolm could do with his agitation. "Thanks, Sylvia," he said. "I appreciate your help."

"Thank God someone does," Sylvia snapped.

The one free spot in the limo was right next to Sophie. Her sweet scent was dangerously overstimulating. Drew sat in the front, while Hendrick, the Zhangs and Malcolm were in the other car.

"They don't need me to interpret over there?" Sophie asked.

"Zhang's grandson can manage," Drew said. "At the wedding he'll probably do most of the interpreting for his grandfather, anyway. You won't have to work like you did these last couple days. You'll be able to relax and enjoy yourself."

Sophie looked doubtful. "Ah. Well, in that case, should I even go at all?"

"Yes, by all means," Drew urged. "For backup. Just in case. At this point, my uncle would pitch a fit if you pulled out. You can be Vann's plus-one. He's always throwing off the seating arrangements by refusing to bring a date."

Sophie gave Vann a quick, teasing glance and patted his knee. That tiny brush of contact made his heart race and his face flush.

Bryce could not be allowed to mess with her. He'd never met anyone so clear and honest and real, and he was going to make damn sure all the people who counted knew it.

But it made his guts chill to think how Sophie would feel if she knew that doubts had been cast on her character. She'd feel mortified and betrayed.

If he could shield her from that, he would. If he was careful, she might never even know.

* * *

They were picked up at the Sea-Tac Airport by another pair of limos, and they set off straight to Paradise Point. As they drove, Sophie pondered the relative merits of the two cocktail dresses she'd brought, longing for fresh wardrobe options. Neither dress was perfect for the occasion, but that was just too damn bad. She'd probably go with the dusty-pink one with the chiffon wrap.

Her phone beeped, and she checked it. It was a message from Tim Bryce.

Heard you were going to be at Paradise Point. Calling a quick emergency meeting this morning before the rehearsal dinner. See you there. Tim.

She looked at Vann. "No rest for the wicked, I'm afraid. Tim called a meeting. Five o'clock. What could possibly be so urgent, I wonder."

"Count me out," Drew said. "I've been waiting to see Jenna for days. The minute I get to Paradise Point, I'm officially unavailable until after the honeymoon."

"Right," Vann said. "The rest of us grunts can pick up the slack."

"Don't even try to guilt me." Drew grinned widely over his shoulder. "Wasted effort. I'm too buzzed to notice or care."

The car had turned onto a long driveway through a blaze of spectacular spring wildflowers. Evening sunshine slanted through them, lighting up the blossoms like stained glass, glinting around the edges of the clouds over the ocean.

The entrance to the Paradise Point Resort was a glassed-in reception hall with a wooden roof made of big interlocking geometric triangles. A wall of glass at the end of the building looked out on a terrace, the grounds and the ocean cliffs.

Malcolm turned to them. "I've been told that Tim Bryce just called a meeting, God knows why. The resort has kindly made the southwest conference room available to us. The rehearsal dinner begins in less than two hours, so let's get this dealt with."

Tim Bryce was waiting in the conference room. He jumped up as they came in.

"Congratulations, sir," he said to Malcolm. "I heard the negotiations went well."

"They were fine," Malcolm snapped. "So what in God's name is so important that it can't wait until next week?"

"Ah, well, sir, when I learned that Mr. Zhang was here, it occurred to me that now was the best opportunity to show him the latest eco-engineering that Drew's team developed for the Johannesburg project," Tim said. "There's a lot of overlap. We've been keeping them in the vault until the new security technology is in place, but being able to show them to Mr. Zhang was worth the risk." He indicated the laptop on the table. "So here they are."

"And this couldn't have waited until after the rehearsal dinner?"

"I thought it was better to know right away, so that you could schedule—"

"Thanks, Tim." Malcolm snatched up the laptop. "I'll take this for safekeeping." He looked at Sophie. "Our interpreter will make herself available to discuss these plans with Mr. Zhang whenever we can carve out a free hour."

"Of course, sir," she assured him.

"Excellent. Sylvia has your number. She'll let you know when we need you." He clapped his hands. "So! We're done, correct? Or is there more?"

"That was the main issue, but I also—"

"Good. Then let's get ready for this rehearsal dinner." Malcolm squinted at Sophie. "You come, too. You're Vann's plus-one."

"Me?" she said, alarmed. "Why? Do I need to interpret? Will Mr. Zhang be there?"

"No, he'll be resting," Malcolm said. "Come to the dinner, anyway."

"But I barely know the groom, and I've never even met the bride!"

"You're Vann's plus-one, and I want you there," Malcolm said testily. "Don't be late." He stomped out, the laptop clutched under his arm.

Sophie turned to Vann. "This is awkward. A rehearsal dinner is an intimate gathering. It's already strange that I'm at this wedding at all."

"Don't bother arguing," Vann advised. "You'll only hurt yourself. And don't worry about the crowd. They're all nice people, and they understand how Malcolm is. You'll like them."

"I'd better go make myself decent," Sophie said.

"I'll be waiting for you in the front hall at eight thirty," he told her.

She gave him a grateful smile and set off, consulting the map of the grounds the reception staff had given her. She was in number 82, the Fireweed Cabin. Wooden walkways led out from the main reception hall like the branches of a tree out from the trunk, each winding branch leading to a cluster of individualized cabins.

It was a beautiful walk. The wooden pathway led around jagged rock formations, ferns sprouting below the walkway, vines and flowers sprawling over the wooden boards. Flowers were everywhere. Much of the walkway was shaded with huge, fragrant pines and firs, and stunted, wind-twisted madrone trees. The sinking sun outlined the clouds with shining gold, and the sea's constant roar in the distance filled her ear.

She found the Fireweed Cabin, unlocked the door—and jerked back with a gasp.

Someone was already inside.

The woman shrieked, dropping something on the floor. "Oh, God! You scared me half to death!"

Sophie looked at the number written on her card. "Excuse

me, but my card envelope says 82. Am I in the wrong room? This is 82, right? Fireweed Cabin?"

"Yes, it is, and no, you are not in the wrong room." The woman was young and rosy-cheeked with a high, bouncing blond ponytail. "I'm resort staff."

Sophie registered the maroon jacket and black pants, as well as the name tag on the woman's ample chest. "Oh. I see. I'm sorry I startled you."

"Not at all," the woman said. "I gave you a scare, too, I imagine. I was just bringing your bags to your room from the reception hall."

Sophie realized belatedly that the stuff spread over the bed were her own clothes. "Why are my things out on the bed?"

"Oh, I'm so sorry about that." The woman gave her an anxious smile. "Your garment bag slid off the luggage cart and fell into one of the swampy bits. It rained last night, see, and there's some bits that don't drain very well. Your bag got mud on it, so I was just getting your things out and making sure they were okay before water seeped through and stained them. I know it's kind of strange, but I figured, if it was me, I'd prefer having my stuff rescued than finding a wardrobe crisis on my hands."

"I see." The woman's name tag read "Julie," she saw as she came inside. She leaned to touch the garment bag, unzipped on the floor. It was sodden, as Julie had said.

"I took a washrag and sponged off the mud," Julie explained. "I'm so sorry this happened. I hope you don't mind me taking the liberty of trying to save your clothes."

"No, I guess I appreciate the effort," she said. "Did anything get ruined?"

"No, thank God." Julie's toothy smile blazed at full wattage. "Everything seems just fine! Shall I hang your clothes up for you?"

"No, thanks," Sophie said. "I'll take it from here. Have a nice evening."

"You, too!" Julie crouched down and grabbed a smartphone

up off the floor, slipping it into her pants pocket. "Sorry. I was so startled I dropped it when you came in."

Sophie watched the woman leave with mixed feelings. She didn't care for having her private things handled by a stranger, but in Julie's position, she might have made the same call, even if it was an invasion of privacy.

Sophie draped the sodden garment bag over the luggage rack to dry and hung her clothes up. She'd thought she was overdoing it when she packed three days ago. Now she wished she'd brought a much wider selection.

She took a quick shower, then let her hair down and shook it loose. The tight twist gave it enough curl and movement so that it looked quasi-styled. She put on the bronze knit top and white flounced silk skirt that she'd worn yesterday. Drew, Malcolm and Vann had already seen it, but if she wanted a fresh dress for the wedding, she had to recycle this one tonight.

After freshening up her makeup, dabbing on perfume and sliding on her heels, she was ready. Malcolm had insisted, so there was no help for it.

Time to crash her long-lost cousin's wedding.

Twelve

Vann lingered by the entrance to the dining room, keeping his eyes trained on the walkway outside. Sophie was already at a disadvantage tonight. He wasn't letting her walk into a room full of strangers all alone.

Tim Bryce strolled in, caught sight of Vann and started toward him.

Hmm. This might get interesting.

The other man stopped at a safe distance. "You're not doing yourself any favors, you know."

"What the hell is that supposed to mean?" Vann asked.

Bryce smiled thinly. "You know exactly what I'm talking about."

Vann's hands had balled into fists. He forced them to relax. "What you're doing is a pointless waste of time and resources. I've already told you it's not her. This is supposed to be a celebration. Do not mess it up."

"I won't ruin Drew's precious wedding," Bryce said. "I'll be discreet. The fallout can wait." He gave Vann a meaningful look. "Unless you tip her off, that is."

Rage made the hair prickle on his neck. "What are you implying?"

Bryce shrugged. "It just seems strange. You've been her biggest champion, from the very start. You really, really don't want it to be her. And anyone with half a brain could figure out why. That makes your judgment suspect."

"She doesn't need a champion," Vann said through his teeth.

"Well, be that as it may. You'd better not say anything to her. Because she's the one, Vann. There's no doubt in my mind. The truth will come out, and when it does, you'll be implicated. And it will not go well for you."

Vann's jaw ached. "Whatever you're plotting, she won't take the bait."

"Shhh." Bryce's gaze fixed over Vann's shoulder, at someone behind him.

"Good evening, gentlemen." It was Sophie's voice, coming up behind him.

Vann turned around. The sight of her was like a punch to the chest. Her gold-kissed skin, her luxurious hair swirling loose, those let-me-fall-into-your-infinitely-deep eyes. She wore the same outfit as yesterday, and he liked it even better tonight. Her smiling lips shone with a shimmery, gold-toned lipstick. She looked like a goddess.

He caught the expression on Bryce's face as the man looked away. That knowing smirk, like Bryce had something over him. *Bastard.*

"Hey, Tim," Sophie said. "Are you coming to the rehearsal dinner, too?"

"No, not me," Bryce replied. "I'm just out here waiting for my son Richard. He drove up from LA, and should be arriving soon. He and I are having dinner later on."

"Oh. So your son knows Drew?" she asked.

"They went to high school together," Bryce told her. "Now Richard works on CGI for a movie studio down in Hollywood."

"That's wonderful," Sophie said. "I look forward to meeting him tomorrow."

Bryce turned a meaningful gaze on Vann. "Have a good time at the rehearsal dinner. Remember what I said. Not one word." He nodded at Sophie, and walked away.

Sophie gazed after him, puzzled. "What was that about?"

Vann shook his head. "Nothing," he muttered. "Just some accounting stuff. Shall we go on in?" He offered her his arm.

She took it, smiling. "Thanks for waiting for me."

Vann introduced her to people as they circled the table. Bev, Hendrick's wife. Jenna, the bride. Then Ava, Drew's sister, and Cherise, one of Jenna's bridesmaids.

Sophie was seated between Vann and Cherise. Today Cherise was sporting a bright purple and crimson forelock that dangled playfully between her eyes. She had a mechanical arm decorated with flashing accent lights, and it seemed to do anything she wanted it to do. Cherise had gotten her bionic arm from Jenna's foundation, Arm's Reach. She'd since become one of Jenna's closest friends. Several other people Vann had met from Jenna's foundation were also at the table.

"Nice work, Vann," Cherise said, eyeing Sophie with approval. "She's a hottie. Let me load you guys up with some of this fabulous bubbly." She poured everyone champagne, demonstrating total mastery of her state-of-the-art prosthetic. Sophie couldn't help but be in awe.

His friends toasted Cherise's progress while giving him and Sophie that considering look. Drew must have said something to Jenna about them and God only knew what Jenna had said, and to whom.

Fortunately, Cherise kept Sophie too busy to notice the speculative glances.

By the end of the meal, after numerous touching speeches, toasts and roasts, everyone in the room was buzzed on excellent food and fine wine, and Sophie was talking and laughing with his friends as if she'd known them for years. He'd never seen her this way before. He'd only ever seen her in work mode, cool and focused, or else alone with him.

He could just stare for hours, but people would notice. Hell, they already had.

Sophie looked as if she belonged in the wedding party. He wished he could enjoy himself as much as she seemed to, but Bryce's scheming made him tense.

He felt cheated. He was in a beautiful place, surrounded by the people he loved most in the world, in the company of the most sexy, fascinating woman he'd ever encountered.

It would have been perfect, if someone hadn't been trying to prove that his new lover was a liar, a thief and a spy. And warning her about it would only make it worse.

No matter how he sliced it, it felt like betrayal.

Sophie was surprised at how much fun she was having. This was her first real opportunity to observe Ava and Drew Maddox at close range, and she liked them. Ava and Jenna made a big effort to draw her out, and she let them do it.

Everyone was so warm and welcoming. They really seemed to care about each other. And she had more in common with her cousins than she'd thought. They were all orphans, since Drew and Ava had lost their parents in a plane crash when they were in their teens. But Malcolm had looked after them, in his gruff, clumsy way, and they had turned out fine. It seemed like a wonderful family to belong to.

She wondered if that would change if she came forward with her claim. If they would close ranks against her. It was a painful thought and hard to imagine now, with everyone so relaxed and happy because of the wedding.

Except for Vann, for some reason. Vann was unusually quiet, and his expression was grim. As the dinner began to wind down, and people started pushing their chairs back to leave, Drew stood up.

"Public service announcement, everyone," he said. "Jenna

and I arranged for perfect weather for you all. The moon's almost full, there's no rain and not much wind. Perfect night for a walk on the beach. That's where we'll be. You're welcome."

Jenna stood, and the two of them came together in a swift, intense kiss. Then they waved at the crowd and strolled together, arms around each other's waists, out the dining room exit onto the terrace outside.

Sophie caught that tormented look on Vann's face again. "Everything okay?"

"Sure," he replied. "Why wouldn't it be?"

"You tell me," she said. "You seem off tonight. Too quiet. And tense."

Vann drained his wineglass. "It's been a long day," he said tersely.

"Understood," Sophie said, standing up. "Go rest, then. See you in the morning."

He caught her wrist as she started to leave the table. "Wait. Where are you going?"

"To the beach. I've never walked on a beach on this side of the Pacific before."

"Not alone," he said.

"Oh, please," she said. "I bet almost everyone at this table apart from Malcolm will end up out there on the beach. It's perfectly safe. Go to bed. Don't trouble yourself."

"Hell, no," he said. "I'm going with you."

She rolled her eyes. "Fine, then. Suit yourself."

The terrace outside segued into a walkway leading to an observation deck that overlooked the sea cliffs. A staircase to the beach below was bolted to the cliff face. The gleaming expanse of wet sand was lapped by the wide, foamy waves, and broken at intervals by jagged humps and spires of black volcanic rock. There was a bright, eerie glow on the water as the almost full moon lit up the night.

Vann led her to the head of the stairway. "There's a wooden shelf here where you can leave your shoes," he said.

Sweet relief, to slip off her heels. Vann took off his own shoes, and they made their way down the sandy staircase, zigging and zagging until they reached the bottom.

Their feet sank into the cool, dry sand as they slowly worked their way over to the water. The foam was icy cold when it first rushed over Sophie's feet, and she gasped and laughed. Vann stopped to roll up the legs of his pants.

At some point, she stumbled on a rock that poked up out of the sand. Vann caught her arm to steady her, and his hand slipped down to clasp her fingers, squeezing them as the cold water had numbed away the pain of her stubbed toes.

The contact made the memories of their passionate night flare through her body, making her weak with fresh yearning. She tugged her hand free. "We can't."

"Why not?"

"Don't you dare play dumb," she said. "We've been through this. Your best friend is getting married. His uncle is your boss. Let's nix any potential drama and concentrate on what's important here, which is Drew's wedding."

"There's nothing shocking or dramatic about holding hands on a moonlit beach."

Sophie took a step away from him. "Depends on the context. And the audience."

They looked around. As Sophie had predicted, several people had taken Drew and Jenna's suggestion. The happy couple were a tiny bit farther up on the beach. They were madly kissing each other, not caring who saw.

Lucky them.

"What would it take to get us to the point where we could hold hands on a beach?" Vann demanded. He sounded almost angry.

Sophie's chin went up. "We'd have to do the work," she said. "It's not instant. It's not automatic. You know, the way sex can be sometimes. Maybe that was a mistake."

"No," he said. "That was the farthest thing from a mistake I ever felt."

"Nice to hear, but even so," Sophie said. "We'd need transformation before hand-holding on a beach could happen. We'd have to make some big choices. Come to some conclusions about things. Otherwise, nothing. So stop it. You're bugging me tonight."

"I didn't mean to piss you off," Vann said.

"It's fine." She turned her back on him and walked away.

Vann trailed along behind her for a while before catching up and walking next to her again. The silence was starting to weigh on her, so she threw out a conversation opener as a peace offering.

"Your friends seem wonderful," she commented. "What a fun group of people."

"Yes, they are. I'm lucky. Drew and Zack are like brothers to me. Not that I had brothers as a kid, but I like to imagine it would be like my relationship with them."

"I have good friends like that, but they're scattered all over the world," she said. "One's still in Singapore, one is in Hong Kong, one got married to a guy from Sydney. A couple of them are in Europe. I never see them all together. And I hardly ever see any of them face-to-face. Just phone calls, or Skype."

"That's tough," he said. "It must be lonely."

Sophie didn't reply. For a moment, she couldn't trust her own voice. Her throat felt hot and soft. Admitting to loneliness was taking this instant intimacy a little too far. She didn't want him to feel sorry for her.

She turned away from him, staring out at the streak of moonlight on the sea and the surges of surf. They'd almost reached the end of this expanse of beach, and were coming to a more jagged, rocky place full of tide pools. Without a word, they turned and started back the way they came. They were quiet this time, but she was intensely aware of Vann's tall, brooding presence.

The water boiled and frothed around her toes and ankles. The salty breeze whipped her skirt and lifted her hair like a banner.

His spell was working on her again. Being out in the infinite hugeness of this beautiful place…it fed that part of her that yearned for freedom, wildness. The same part of her that hungered for Vann. His power, his energy. His sexual generosity.

Sophie climbed back up the many long flights of steps that hugged the cliff side. Her shoes had gone clammy and sticky in the humid sea air, so she didn't bother putting them back on her sandy feet, but just walked down the wooden walkway barefoot.

Vann walked her to the door of her cabin. "Wait," he said as she reached for her key card.

"What?"

"Look at this. For sandy feet." Vann stepped on a small wooden pallet placed near the stepstone, and grabbed a small, retractable spray hose coiled up there.

He rinsed the sand off his own feet, and then gestured for her to step on the pallet.

Once she did so, Vann aimed the stream of cool water over her feet.

It was yet another one of his seductive tricks. The rush of cool water was soothing. He brushed the sticky sand off, caressing her feet with his hands.

The contact made her speechless and flustered. She fumbled for her key card. Fumbled again as she tried to find the switch that turned on the lights. Vann waited silently outside the door.

She turned around and beckoned impatiently for him to enter. "Oh, just get in here before someone sees you lurking."

He came inside and shut the door, but didn't walk into the room. "You're still mad at me," he said.

"Yes," she said. "Because you're still sulking. And you won't tell me why."

"Do you want me to leave?" he asked.

"No," she said. "I want to know what the hell your problem is. So I can understand if it's fixable or not."

"I'm not sure what you mean." His voice was guarded.

She flapped her hand at him angrily. "You're different tonight. All wound up. Negative. You weren't like that last night, so what's changed?"

He shook his head. "I don't know. I'm sorry if I'm pissing you off."

She waited for more, then shook her head in frustration. "You can't say what's wrong?"

"No," he said. "Sorry. I don't know what else to say."

She tried to read his face, but it was an impenetrable mask. "Did I say or do something that bothered you?"

"Not at all," he said. "You're perfect."

She snorted. "Hardly that. Then what is it?"

He turned toward the door. "I think I'd better go."

"Stop it," she snapped. "I already told you to come in. I want you here, but not the whole night. I don't want people seeing you leave in the morning, and have to deal with the snickering and the side-eye. I'm at a disadvantage here as it is. Understand?"

He set his shoes down. "As you command."

She gave him a narrow look. "Are you making fun of me?"

"Hell, no," he said. "I wouldn't dare."

Sophie put her hands on her hips. "Before anything else happens," she said. "Let's discuss a couple logistical details. We got carried away last night, and we never talked about safe sex. I trust you have more condoms with you?"

"Only one. I didn't have a chance to buy more. But I'll make that one count."

"You'd better," she said. "But while we're talking about this, I'll take this opportunity to tell you that I haven't been with anyone for a long time, and I've had bloodwork done since then. I'm disease free. Just so you know."

"Thanks for bringing it up, and so am I," he told her. "I always use condoms. I get tested regularly, and I've been tested since the last time I was involved with someone."

Sophie bit her lip thoughtfully as she weighed the risks and temptations. He did not strike her as dishonest. By no means. Moody, yes. Mysterious, yes. But not a liar.

"In that case, shall we dispense with the latex?" she said, her voice tentative. "I have a contraceptive implant, and it's good for another year or so."

Vann's throat worked. "Whoa," he muttered. "That would be…incredible. I would love it. I'm honored that you trust me that much."

"I haven't done that with anyone, ever," she told him. "I never wanted to risk it before. But tonight, for some reason, I do."

"Thank you," he said.

They gazed at each other in a moment of confused shyness.

Sophie shook it off with some difficulty. "So, Vann," she said. "Since yesterday's adventure started with me naked and you fully clothed, let's switch it up. Your turn, buddy. Strip. Let's see your stuff."

Vann's lips twitched, but he undressed quickly. Shirt, belt, pants. In moments, he stood there, stark naked, and ready to play from the looks of his stiff erection.

He reached out, sliding the silk jacket off her shoulders. "Your turn," he said.

He took his time with peeling off the close-fitting knit top. He explored the contours of the balcony-lace demi bra that propped up her bosom, his thumb sliding across her nipple, taut and dark against the lace. He slid his hands to her waist and sank down to his knees, pressing his face against her belly. The warmth of his breath heated the chiffon fabric of her skirt. He stroked his big, hot hands slowly up her legs beneath her skirt. Hooking her panties, he eased them down.

She stepped out of them, gasping as he pushed the front of her skirt up and pressed his face against her. Kissing, caressing, opening her with lips and tongue.

She watched the shockingly intimate scene in the mirror. Her in just her skirt and bra, him naked on his knees, her skirt bunched up at her belly as he pleasured her. The back view of him would have taken her breath away if she had any breath to take.

She clutched his shoulders, swaying on her feet, panting with shocked delight at the tender swirl and flick of his tongue against her most sensitive flesh. She wound her fingers into his warm hair as the wild sensations lifted her—and then sent her flying.

Vann was on his feet, holding her steady. She barely noticed as he peeled the rest of her clothes off. She just felt gravity shifting and was aware of being lifted. Then cool sheets pressed against her back, and his scorching heat came down next to her.

"Wait," she said.

He went still, eyes narrowed. "Yeah? What for?"

"You lie down on your back," she said. "I want to look at you."

He rolled over, head propped on the pillow. She feasted her eyes on that gorgeously strong male body, draped lazily across the bed. He held his stiff erection in his hand. He stroked it slowly as he smiled, his dark, sultry bedroom eyes saying, *Come and get it. If you dare.*

His self-assurance aroused her. Without ever seeming arrogant, he had complete confidence that he could please her. He instinctively knew how.

It switched her on like nothing ever had.

Sophie clambered over him, swinging her leg over his until she had him right where she needed him. She slowly took him inside...undulating, rising and falling, until the pleasure surged up, hot and sweet and wrenching.

When she came back up for air, Vann had rolled her over onto her back, folding her legs high. He propped himself up on his elbows as he once again pushed inside her clinging warmth and began to move. Surging, rocking. She was so primed, after what had come before. Slick and soft and sensitized. Every slow, gliding thrust made her whimper with delight.

The bed shook as their rhythm quickened. Sophie writhed,

digging her nails into him, goading him on. That hugeness was opening up in her mind again, the endless space and power that she'd felt on the beach with the stars and the sky and the sea. Wild magic, wild mystery. Pleasure exploding, flinging them into that enormous nowhere together.

Sophie floated in the glow of residual pleasure. When she opened her eyes, she turned to look at Vann with a lazy, satiated smile.

He didn't smile back.

He almost looked like he was bracing himself.

A chill settled into her, someplace very deep.

She tried to breathe down the hurt, but she had no barriers right now. Her walls were down, but he'd kept his own walls as high as ever. That hurt.

Be a grown-up, she lectured herself. He'd made no promises to her. This was just a fun, hot thing for him. Women must throw themselves at him all the time.

She was the one making it stupid by getting all emotional. Like a shivering virgin falling like a ton of bricks for the first guy who ever touched her.

She was careful to keep her tone light. "There you go again. All down in the mouth. What is it with you tonight, Vann?"

Vann shook his head, but he didn't deny it. "I can't seem to shake it."

Sophie rolled onto her back and stared at the ceiling. "If what just happened can't make you feel better, nothing will," she said. "If you're so miserable, why are you here?"

"Because I'm starving for more," he said. "Because I never want it to stop."

She was taken aback by his stark intensity. And confused. "You just got more," she said slowly. "A lot more. And you've still got that sad look on your face."

Vann clapped his hand over his eyes. "I'm sorry," he ground out. "There's nothing I can do about it. I can't control the way I feel. It just happens."

"I understand." Sophie slid off the bed. "That settles it. Go sulk in your own room. That was hot and fabulous, but we're done, Vann. Like always, it's been real."

"Sophie—"

"I'm getting into the shower. When I'm out, I want the room to myself."

"I didn't mean to make you angry."

"You say you can't control the way you feel. Well, neither can I. Good night."

She made it into the bathroom just in time and set the shower running, hand pressed to her quivering lips. She welcomed the hot spray coming down on her face.

She wished she could wash away those inconvenient feelings. Be empty and free of them. Then the shower door creaked. A rush of cool air kissed her skin.

Vann stepped inside with her. His big body took up all the space, making the huge shower stall suddenly feel cramped. She dashed water from her face, and opened her mouth to tell him to back the hell off—and then she saw his eyes. Pain he couldn't express.

She recognized that nameless pain. She'd felt it herself. "Vann—"

He cut her off with a kiss. It was too sweet and too hot to resist.

Vann hit the faucet to switch the shower off. In the steamy, dripping quiet she could hear her own heart thudding in her ears, her own breathless, helpless whimpering gasps. The sounds of absolute sensual surrender.

He spun her around, placing her hands flat against the wall, and then pulled her hips back and nudged her feet apart. She opened to him, arching her back as he reached around with his hand to expertly caress her as he sank his thick shaft slowly inside her.

She rocked back, trying to take him deeper, but he kept his surging rhythm slow and relentless. The heavy, gliding thrusts were delicious, each one stoking her excitement until she wanted to claw and scream at him.

He finally gave in to her demands and moved faster, harder, rising to meet the power building up inside her.

She cried out as the intense sensations raging through her body wiped her out.

Vann stayed inside her afterward, his face pressed to her neck. He bit her shoulder gently, then tenderly licked the spot. "I know I was supposed to go," he said. "I just can't seem to pry myself away."

"You are the master of mixed signals, you know that?"

"I know," he said. "I'm sorry."

"I'm sick of your apologizing," she said. "Go back to your room now."

"Do I have to?"

"Yes," she said. "There are some definitions to get straight. There's scenario A, a secret workplace affair. That's a specific set of rules and expectations. Then there's scenario B, a boyfriend. Totally different rules and expectations. You're mixing them up. You're not my boyfriend. Don't act like you are. That's a whole other level of intimacy."

"This feels pretty intimate to me," he said.

She squirmed out of his grip, and turned the water back on, soaping herself up without looking at him. "My job is important to me," she said. "Don't threaten it."

"I never meant to," he said.

She met his eyes. "You're pushing too hard. I need a break. I'll see you at breakfast. Good night, Vann. Off you go."

Vann didn't look at her as he toweled off and left the bathroom. Something inside her snapped when she heard the cabin door close a couple of minutes later. Alone at last, just like she'd insisted.

She promptly fell to pieces.

Thirteen

Vann had to stop himself from jumping up to get Sophie's attention at breakfast. He had to abide by the rules. But the rules felt like a jacket that was two sizes too small.

"Sophie! There you are!" Jenna called out. "I was wondering where you were."

Sophie gave Jenna a smile as she approached the table where Vann sat with Ava, Drew, Zack and the bride-to-be. She looked amazing, in a stretchy sunshine-yellow top that wrapped smoothly over her breasts and showed off her narrow waist, and wide-legged white linen pants. Her hair was still down. He could smell her fresh scent from across the table.

A stern glance from Sophie told him he was staring. He looked away.

"Good morning," Sophie said, smiling at Drew and Jenna. "I see the weather is holding for you. My phone told me it's going to be sunny and warm this afternoon."

"I know, right? And the beach last night was wonderful," Ava said. Her curious gaze flicked from Sophie to Vann, but thankfully, Sophie didn't seem to notice as she sat down. "Did you sleep in?"

"No, I've just been running around, getting organized," Sophie said. "I went to see when Mr. Zhang might need me. His grandson tells me that Malcolm and Hendrick have the conference room scheduled for eleven. That gives me plenty of time for breakfast."

"Good," Ava said. "Relax and enjoy. I hear Uncle Malcolm was doing his best Dickensian supervillain routine down in San Francisco. He's so annoying when he does that."

She shrugged. "It wasn't that bad. I lived."

"We're glad you did," Jenna told her. "Fuel up. We've got a long day of celebrating ahead of us."

"Hey, Richard," said Ava with a bright smile. "How nice to see you again!"

Vann glanced up and saw Richard Bryce standing there. He'd met Tim's son a couple of other times over the years. Richard was a tall, good-looking man with a buzz cut and a neatly trimmed beard. From the way Richard looked at Sophie, Vann suspected that Bryce had already shared his suspicions about her with his son.

Then again, any guy could be excused for staring at Sophie.

But then Richard slid into the seat opposite Sophie and proceeded to talk her ear off as she ate her breakfast, trying to impress her with his clout as a budding Hollywood mogul. As the minutes passed, all desire to be charitable and understanding with Richard Bryce swirled down the drain.

"Yeah, it's intense," Rich was saying to Ava. "There are always at least a hundred people ready to stab me in the back so they can take my job. I have to stay on my toes."

"Hmm," Sophie murmured. "Sounds stressful. Do you like the work at least?"

"God, yes," Rich said. "It's what I was born for." As Rich spoke, his eyes drifted down to Sophie's chest. "I've won six awards in the last two years. I get offers from headhunters every day. People try to poach me all the time."

"That's great, Rich," Ava said. "I'm so glad it's working out for you."

Rich turned his attention to Sophie. "Everyone in this crowd is in the wedding party except for you and me," he said. "Let's leave them to it and go down to the beach until it's time for the ceremony. There are some amazing tide pools I'd love to show you."

"She's working," Vann said. "Interpreting for Malcolm and Hendrick."

Rich blinked at him, as if startled to realize that Vann existed. His smile widened. "Ah! Dude, I get it. My apologies. I didn't mean to move in on your territory."

"Not at all," Sophie said. "No territory here. And I can speak for myself." She gave Vann a sharp look. "But it's true," she said to Rich. "I'm busy this morning."

"Well, all right. Looks like you all have lots to do, so I'll just get out of your hair." Rich got up. "See you at the ceremony."

After Rich was halfway across the room, Ava smacked her forehead with the heel of her hand and glared at Drew. "Remind me why you invited him?"

Drew shrugged. "Uncle Malcolm insisted. To make Tim Bryce happy, I guess? Tim is convinced that Rich and I were the best of friends all through our tender boyhood. You know. Childhood memories, summers on the lake and all that?"

Ava snorted. "Yeah, him constantly trying to undo the strings of my bikini top," she said. "He was a bra-snapping dweeb back then, and surprise, surprise, he still is."

"Ignore him," Drew said. "We've all got better things to think about."

"We certainly do." Ava turned a misty look on Jenna. "I still can't believe it. My two favorite people in the world, coming together. It's a dream come true."

Ava and Jenna dissolved into tears and wrapped each other

in a big, sniffling hug. Sophie caught Vann's eye. "I should go get ready for Malcolm and Mr. Zhang," she said.

"I'll walk you to the conference room," Vann said.

"You're drawing attention to us," Sophie said as they walked through the dining room.

"I'm just walking beside you," he said under his breath. "I'm not touching you. Surely that's not suspicious. We're colleagues, right?"

"And fending off that guy at the breakfast table? What was that all about?"

He shrugged defensively. "He pissed me off. Tide pools, my ass."

"I don't need protection," Sophie told him. "I'm capable of decimating any man who gives me unwanted attention with no help from you. You're acting like a jealous boyfriend, and it's visible from miles away. Please, stop it."

Vann stopped in the corridor. "I can't get anything right with you."

"Not if you draw attention to us in public like that," she said crisply. "I know the way to the conference room. I'll take it from here. Later, Vann."

As Sophie walked away, he stood there, stung.

Banished to the doghouse.

Malcolm, Hendrick and Zhang discussed the Nairobi Towers project for well over two hours before a knock finally sounded on the door.

Ava poked her head in, giving the men a brilliant smile. "I hate to interrupt you gentlemen, but just a heads-up. The ceremony is in two hours, and Bev sent me to nudge you." She winked at Hendrick. "So blame her and not me. She wants everything to run on time."

"Bev is, as always, the ultimate authority," Malcolm said, his voice surprisingly jovial as he snapped the laptop shut. "We can continue tomorrow, I suppose. Don't keep your wife waiting, Hendrick."

After the men left the conference room, Sophie hurried back to her room to look through her much depleted wardrobe. The choice was clear. The last dress standing.

She slipped on the dusty-rose dress. It was bias-cut silk chiffon with a long, filmy wrap. The underdress faded from dark on the clinging bodice to light at the skirt, and the wrap was a couple of shades lighter, with a loose, floppy chiffon rose at the hooked closure. She put on her spike-heeled strappy sandals made of black velvet, and freshened her makeup. Then she transferred phone, tissues and room card to her beaded evening bag with a chiffon rose that matched the wrap.

And that was it. She'd done all she could.

At least the bride and groom in question were incredibly sweet about her crashing their wedding. She hoped that someday she'd be able to claim those people as friends. Maybe even family. A girl could hope, but hope was a risky enterprise. The chance of this going sour was very high.

With Vann. With the Maddoxes. She had to stay chill, or she could hurt herself.

She'd tried to tame her hair with the blow dryer and the curling iron, but the minute she stepped outside, the wind whipped it around madly. The wedding was to be held out on a relatively sheltered swath of lawn in the lee of a big rocky outcropping near the reception hall of the resort. Beyond the lawn, the turf segued into waist-deep fields of wildflowers that covered the rest of the countryside.

Once she got there, the worst of the wind would be blocked, but her hair was already a casualty.

The day was warm for spring on the coast. She was fine in the clingy sleeveless dress and the filmy chiffon wrap. As she drew near to the main building, a woman came out, dressed in the tailored maroon jacket and black trousers of the resort staff.

It was Julie, she realized. The woman spotted her and hurried in her direction, her ponytail bobbing wildly.

"Ms. Valente! I'm so glad I caught you!" she called out. "I called your room, but you must have just left!"

"You're looking for me?" Sophie asked. "Why?"

"Mr. Maddox needs you urgently, for a quick interpretation job," Julie said. "You're supposed to go to his room immediately."

"Now?" Sophie glanced at her watch. "But…the wedding's about to begin."

"I know! Which is why you have to hurry! The room number is 156, the Madrone Suite." Julie held out a brochure with a map. She'd scribbled with a ballpoint pen to mark the way, and circled cabin 156. "See? It's this big one, at the end of the main walkway."

Sophie took the brochure, still perplexed. "Are you sure—"

"Absolutely! You'd better hurry. You don't want to hold them up."

"Okay. Thanks for telling me."

Sophie was tempted to take off her shoes to run back to Malcolm's cabin. She'd certainly make better time. But she didn't want to spend the day with sand between her toes.

The walkways were deserted. The timing was strange but Malcolm Maddox was the boss. Maybe he was so eccentric and egoistic he figured everyone and everything could wait upon his pleasure. Including his nephew's wedding.

Still, what on earth could be urgent enough for such a delay?

Whatever. It was not her call, nor was it her problem. She was just a lackey, so she'd do her job and shut up about it. But damn, the wind was tossing her hair around. She was going to look like she'd been flying through a storm on a broomstick by the time she got back to the ceremony. She spotted the cabin up ahead, peeked at her watch and half ran on the balls of her feet to the door. She knocked.

She waited for a moment for a response, then knocked again. "Mr. Maddox?" she called. "Are you in there?"

No response. The seconds ticked by. She tried again, knocking for the third time, loudly enough so that it might seem rude to anyone inside. He was an old man, but she hadn't gotten the impression that he was hard of hearing. "Mr. Maddox?" she yelled. "Are you in there?"

Could he be in the bathroom? Or, God forbid, having some kind of health emergency? But she had no way to go inside and check on him.

The best thing would be to run like hell back to the main hall and let someone else know that Malcolm was in his room, but not responding. So he could get help.

She checked her watch again, shoving her hair back impatiently, and trotted back the way she came as quickly as she could. Hoping that everything was okay with Malcolm.

When she got to the main building, she was in a cold sweat, scared for him.

She could see the crush of the wedding party through the picture window at the end of the building, the tents and streamers.

Then she saw Malcolm there, clutching his cane. Jenna was on his arm. He was starting up the grassy aisle with slow, halting steps. Giving away the bride.

He'd never been in his room at all. What the *hell*? So this Julie character had sent her on a fool's errand. The directions were too specific to be a mistake. Was it some sort of lame prank?

She turned around, fuming, and went to the front desk. "Excuse me," she said to the woman behind the desk. "Could you put me in touch with your colleague Julie?"

The woman gave her a blank look. "Um, who?"

Sophie's patience was at the breaking point. Her voice got louder. "Julie? Short, blond ponytail? She just sent me off to my boss's room and told me he was waiting for me there. But he wasn't, because he's outside right now, giving away the bride. I really need to talk to her and find out what the hell just happened."

The woman, whose name tag read "Debra," looked frightened. "Ah, ma'am… I'm supersorry, but I don't know what you mean. We don't have a Julie on our staff."

Sophie stared at her, mouth open. "Excuse me?"

"We have a Gina and a Jennifer," Debra said. "And a Julian, on the maintenance staff, but he's a man in his sixties."

"But I saw…but she had a name tag like yours," Sophie said blankly. "She wore the uniform. She knew my name, and that I worked for Mr. Maddox. How is that possible?"

"I have no idea, ma'am. I promise you, I have absolutely no idea," Debra said. "I've never met a Julie since I've been here, and this is my third year. Do you want me to call the general manager? Maybe she can tell you something more."

Sophie was opening her mouth to say yes, by all means, do call the general manager, when a voice from behind made her jump.

"Sophie! What are you doing here? The ceremony's already begun!" It was Rich Bryce, poking his head inside the door. "Aren't you coming out?"

"Ah…sure. I'm just confused. Someone told me to meet Mr. Maddox in his room just now. But when I got there—"

"Meet Malcolm? Any fool knew that he'd be here, giving away the bride."

"I know," Sophie said through her teeth. "But—"

"It must have been some kind of mix-up. Come on, or we'll miss the whole thing."

Sophie glanced back at the wide-eyed Debra. "After the wedding, I would like to speak to your general manager. Would you let her know I want a meeting?"

"Of course! I'll let her know right away," Debra assured her. "I'm so sorry!"

Rich took her by the arm, pulling her so abruptly she tottered on her heels. Sophie jerked her arm back. "I'll walk at my own pace, thanks," she said frostily.

Rich lifted his hands with an apologetic grin. "Sorry. It's just that you're late."

"Don't concern yourself," she said. "It's my problem, not yours."

But Rich wasn't easy to shake. He followed on her heels as she made her way across the wide swath of green lawn to the crowd.

Rich took her arm as she stepped onto the grass. She snatched it away again. She was forced to pull so hard the gesture was evident to everyone around them.

Sophie joined the edge of the big crowd and Rich took up a position uncomfortably close to her, the front of his body touching the back of hers, forcing her to inch forward again and again. Their position suggested that they were together.

As-freaking-if. She edged away. He oozed after her. This was all her reputation needed, now that people had noticed the energy between her and Vann. Showing up late for the wedding trailing yet another man in her wake? Just call her the Harlot of Maddox Hill.

And, of course, Vann's gaze locked on to her the second she was in his line of vision. He had a perfect view up there on the raised dais, flanking Drew along with Zack, and looking absolutely smashing in his tux. Malcolm had brought Jenna up the aisle, and had gone back to the front row to sit down next to Bev and Hendrick.

Jenna and her bridesmaids took their places. The bride looked stunning in her white lace and long train, holding a bouquet of wildflowers, her hair a curly strawberry blond cloud crowned with yet more flowers. She was followed by Ava and Cherise, both looking great in clinging midnight-blue wrap dresses. Cherise's bionic arm was decorated with blinking lights of every shade of blue. The ring bearer, a preteen Arm's Reach client

Sophie had met at the dinner last night, was holding a pillow with two rings pinned to it, a big smile on his face.

Sophie slid between two of the other guests to put space between herself and Rich, but it didn't work. Rich just shamelessly elbowed them out of the way to reclaim his place beside her, to the accompaniment of hissing and muttered complaints.

The only way to get away from him was to be harsh, bitchy and loud. To make a big, unattractive spectacle of herself and risk marring the wedding.

What a way to endear herself to her new cousins.

Fourteen

Zack nudged Vann's arm. He'd zoned out during his best friend's wedding, first wondering where the hell Sophie was, then wondering why in holy hell she'd ended up coming out so late, and in the company of that asshat Rich Bryce.

He dragged his attention back to the celebrant, who was saying something sentimental about mutual trust. Jenna and Drew had that drunk-on-happiness look that used to make him nervous and uncomfortable, and now just made him envious.

Nervous and uncomfortable had been preferable.

He was going to schedule a meeting with Hendrick and Malcolm as soon as possible when they were back in Seattle on Tuesday. Lay it all out for them. He wanted to take this relationship with Sophie to the next level.

And he wasn't going to let Bryce's bullshit hold him back.

The crowd erupted in cheers and applause. Drew and Jenna were kissing passionately. When they came up for air, they beamed at each other.

Zack nudged him again. Time to process out after the new

bride and groom. They'd practiced the choreography after breakfast, but it was all gone from his head.

Zack and Ava went first, and then Cherise took the lead, grabbing his arm and towing him along after them.

Sophie looked at him intently as he passed, as if she were trying to tell him something with her eyes, but he couldn't grasp what it was, not with Rich Bryce hanging over her with that self-satisfied look on his face, like he'd gotten away with something.

Postwedding chaos followed. Tears, showers of flower petals and eco-friendly bird feed over the bride. A crush of wedding guests descended on the receiving line.

He couldn't find Sophie in all the hubbub afterward, but he kept looking.

He finally found her on one of the cliff overlooks. She'd gotten a glass of champagne, and was gazing out on the surf as she sipped it.

Vann grabbed a glass from a passing waiter's tray and joined her. "There you are."

She gave him a guarded smile and lifted her glass. "Well, they did it. Beautiful ceremony."

"It was," he said, clinking it with his own. "To Jenna and Drew."

They drank, and leaned their elbows on the railing, gazing out at the sea together.

"Where were you when the ceremony started?" he asked.

Sophie shook her head. "It was the strangest thing," she said. "I was on my way there, but right when I got to the door of the reception hall, this woman dressed like hotel staff told me that Malcolm urgently needed me in his hotel room."

"What?"

"I know, right? She said he needed me to interpret. The timing seemed bizarre, but she was very insistent, so I just high-tailed it up there and knocked on his door. But he wasn't there. Of course, because he was here all along. Obviously. The wedding was about to start. Which means that someone was jerking me around. So I hurried back, and asked at the desk to speak to the person who's sent me on this fool's errand—Julie's her name. And the woman tells me there is no Julie on the resort staff. Never has been in the three years she's worked here."

"That is bizarre," Vann said.

"I know," Sophie agreed fervently. "And it's not the first time I saw her. She was in my room last night when we got here. She'd delivered my bags while we were in that meeting with Tim. She said she dropped my garment bag and got it wet, so she was laying my clothes out on the bed. Now they tell me this person I've interacted with twice never worked here? It gives me the shivers."

Vann shook his head. "I don't like the sound of it."

"Me, neither. I'm hesitant to talk to the general manager about it now. Out of embarrassment. It sounds…weird. Like I'm delusional. Or seeing ghosts."

"You're as solid as a rock," he assured her. "Trust yourself. I certainly do."

She gave him a grateful smile. "Thanks. I appreciate your faith in my sanity."

"So, ah…" he said after a moment's silence. "How is it that you ended up arriving at the ceremony with Rich Bryce?"

Vann had kept his voice neutral, but Sophie still gave him a withering look. "For real, you are asking me that?"

"Just wondering," he said innocently.

"I ran across him in the resort lobby when I was asking about this mysterious Julie, if you must know," she said. "He attached himself to me like a leech. I literally had to pry him loose a couple times. So don't waste my time being jealous about that guy. I have far more urgent problems. He does not even make the cut. Clear?"

Vann felt his chest relax. "Crystal clear. Shall I kick his ass?"

"Not funny," she said. "I want no more drama. Spectral hotel staff are more than enough stress for me to deal with."

"Oh, so that's where you two are hiding!" Ava broke in after bursting out the door of the reception hall. Her blond hair was tousled around her flushed, beautiful face. "Come back in! Bev and Malcolm are about to start speechifying. You guys can whisper and canoodle later."

Busted. He shot Sophie a guilty glance, but she ignored him as she followed Ava inside, her skirt fluttering in the breeze.

It was strange. In spite of all her issues, plus the mysterious, disappearing Julie, Sophie was actually having a good time. The happiness around her was infectious. Drew and Jenna were ecstatic to be married to each other, and everyone else basked in the reflected glory.

The party had a natural momentum. Everything was beautiful. The surroundings were gorgeous, the food was fabulous and abundant, the wine was excellent and the music was amazing. The band played three long and very danceable sets, and the music was a perfect blend of high-energy pieces to get everyone dancing and heart-melting romantic ballads.

Sophie didn't usually dance, but she couldn't say no when Ava dragged her out onto the floor to be part of a chorus line. It left her breathless and damp and pink, and intensely aware of Vann watching from the table where he sat with Zack.

"Single ladies, single ladies! All the single ladies gather around!"

Oh, no, no, no. Bev Hill was on the warpath. Hendrick's wife was the honorary benevolent matriarch of this event, since both Drew's and Jenna's mothers were gone. She was hustling around, rousting out the unmarried women and herding them into the center of the room. No way was Sophie getting roped into the bouquet toss.

Sophie tried to melt out of sight, but Bev swung around and pointed an accusing finger at her. "And just where do you think you're going, young lady?"

"Oh, no. Not me," Sophie protested. "I'm only here in a professional capacity. I wasn't even invited to this wedding. So I certainly shouldn't participate in the—"

"Nonsense. You just get your patootie right out here with the other girls," Bev directed. "This only counts if everybody plays along. Come on, now!"

So it was that Sophie found herself in the midst of twenty sweaty, giggling young woman, all high on dancing and champagne. They were herded into a tight formation, she and Ava shooting each other commiserating glances as Bev jockeyed Jenna into position.

The rest of the crowd ringed the group, laughing and cheering them on as Jenna positioned herself, turned around...and flung her bouquet high into the air.

It arced, turning and spinning...right toward Sophie's head.

She put up her hand to shield her face. It bounced off her fingers like a volleyball, and then thudded down onto her chest, where she caught it instinctively. Oh, God. No.

The room erupted in riotous cheers.

"Woo-hoo! You're next," Ava shouted over the din. "Good luck with that!"

Sophie couldn't reply, being thronged with hugs and squeals and teasing best wishes.

Vann kept his distance during the ordeal, thank God, but he'd watched the whole thing. She was too self-conscious to go near where he was sitting, so she let Bev lead her over to a table where Ava and Jenna were resting their feet.

She sat down gratefully. There was a steep price to be paid for dancing in high-heeled sandals. She needed a break from the implacable force of gravity right about now.

Bev pulled a bottle of champagne out of the ice bucket and poured them all fresh chilled glasses. "Drink up, hon! Fate has chosen you to be next."

Sophie couldn't hold back the snort. "Fate may have a rude surprise in store," she said. "I'm a tough nut to crack."

"Nonsense." Bev patted her hand. "A gorgeous young thing like you must have the suitors lined up out the door."

"It's never easy, Bev," Jenna reminded her.

"I suppose you're right," Bev admitted. "My romance with Hendrick was rather rocky at first. He was quite the bad boy, back in the day."

"Hendrick?" Sophie repeated, disbelieving. "A bad boy?"

Bev, Ava and Jenna burst out laughing at the tone of her voice.

"Yes!" Bev said. "Believe it or not, Hendrick was quite the player. I had to treat him very, very badly for a while. But I got him in line. Elaine helped me with that. Drew and Ava's mother. She was the one who got us together, forty-six years ago. She's been gone for over eighteen years now, and I still miss her so much."

Sophie looked from the rounded little lady with her white pixie cut, eyes dreamy behind her rimless glasses, over to the bald, tight-lipped Hendrick, sitting at a table with Malcolm, the elder Mr. Zhang and his grandson. Hendrick was leaning his good ear to hear young Zhang's interpretation, scowling in concentration. It was hard to imagine him as a focus of romance, but Bev's eyes were misty with sentimental memories.

"Congratulations," Sophie said. "On forty-six years of happiness." She looked over at Jenna, and lifted her glass. "May you be just as lucky."

They drank, and Bev pulled out a tissue and dabbed at the tears leaking from below her glasses. She grabbed Jenna's hand. "This was Elaine's engagement ring," she told Sophie, lifting Jenna's hand. "Doesn't it just look perfect on her?"

Sophie admired the night-blue sapphire, nested in a cluster of small diamonds, that adorned Jenna's slender hand. "It is lovely."

"I can just feel Elaine's presence here tonight." Bev's voice was tear-choked. "She would have been so happy to see Drew with you. She was so proud of her children."

Ava dug into her purse for a tissue and mopped up her own

eyes. "I should have worn waterproof mascara. What was I thinking?"

"Oh, honey, I didn't mean to make you cry."

"It's okay, Bev," Ava said. "It's just that I actually felt her, you know? Just a flash of her. It's been such a long time. I was afraid that I'd forgotten the way she made me feel forever. But I haven't. And you helped me remember."

Bev scooted closer and grabbed Ava in a tight hug.

Then they all broke down in tears. Sophie's eyes stung, and her throat was so tight it ached.

She missed Mom so badly. Mom would have known just what to say to transform all the tears into cathartic laughter, but Sophie hadn't inherited that gift.

"Was Malcolm ever married?" Sophie asked after Bev had wiped her eyes and blown her nose.

"Briefly," Ava said. "To Aunt Helen. It only lasted a few years. She got bored easily, if you know what I mean. Though Uncle Malcolm is anything but boring."

"No one really liked her." Bev's voice hardened. "We all knew it was a mistake. Sure enough, she ended up running off." She turned to Ava. "That was before you were born. Drew was just a toddler."

"And he never married again?" Sophie asked.

"He never wanted to risk it," Bev said sadly. "In spite of all the choices he had. And he could have had his pick. Oh, he had his adventures. Nothing serious, though. He left a trail of broken hearts in his wake. But all that's long past now."

Sophie looked over at Malcolm. She thought about Bev, and her forty-six-year marriage with Hendrick. Of her own mother, staring at the sunset on the terrace with her glass of wine, and her regrets.

Vicky Valente had been a one-man woman, just like Bev. She should have had what Bev had. Weddings and births and graduations and funerals and all the messy, complicated business in between. But fate had not been kind.

Sophie pushed her chair back and got up, babbling something incoherent to Ava, Jenna and Bev. They looked up, blinking back tears, calling after her as she left.

She didn't register what they said. They were probably asking if she was okay, or if there was anything they could do. But she wasn't okay. And there was nothing anyone could do.

She just had to get someplace private, before she disgraced herself.

Fifteen

Where the hell had Sophie run off to?

Vann excused himself and headed toward the door he'd seen her leave through. Once outside on the walkways, he caught a flutter of her dark pink skirt before the path turned and the foliage hid her from view.

People on the walkway stared as he ran by. A big guy in a tux sprinting down the wooden walkway at top speed must look strange.

He hit the branch in the path. One way led to Malcolm's room, and Bryce's baited trap, whatever it might be. The other way led to Sophie's cabin. He turned in that direction, only slowing down when he got there. He tried to get his breathing calmed down before he knocked.

"No housekeeping, please," Sophie called from inside.

Vann was so relieved he practically floated off the ground. "Sophie? It's Vann."

There was a long pause. "It's not a great time."

"Are you okay?"

"I'm fine. I just need to be alone. I'll catch up with you later."

"Please," he insisted. "Let me talk to you. Just for a minute."

The silence was endless. Finally, to his huge relief, the door opened a crack.

He pushed it open and went inside. Sophie was in there, standing with her back to him. "What's so important that it can't wait a few hours?" she asked.

He shut the door. "What's wrong?"

"Oh. That's why you're invading my privacy? Because you're curious?"

"Just concerned," he said.

She blew her nose loudly. "I didn't ask for your concern."

"Too bad," Vann said. "You're getting it, anyway. Please tell me what's wrong."

She turned to face him. Her wet topaz eyes blazed. "Fine," she said. "Here it is, Vann. The shocking truth. I miss my mom."

He had no idea how to respond to that. "Ah…"

"Yes, I know," she said. "And that's the sum total of what's going on in here. Happy now?"

"I wouldn't say happy," he said carefully. "What brought that on?"

Sophie fished another tissue out of the pack. "It was a sneak attack," she said, blowing her nose. "Bev was going on about how sad it was that Drew's mom couldn't be here for the wedding. Ava started to cry, then Jenna piled on, then Bev, too, and the whole thing just got out of hand. But I'm not part of their club, and I didn't feel comfortable indulging in a cry with them. So I bailed. My clever plan was to have my sobfest in the privacy of my own room, where nobody could see me or judge me or, God forbid, feel sorry for me. But no, it was not to be. I have to do it in front of you."

"Not part of the club?" he asked. "What club?"

"Oh, you know," she said impatiently. "The inner sanctum. The family circle. I'm just hired help. It didn't seem appropriate. But I just miss her so much…" Sophie pressed her hand to her mouth.

"I'm so sorry you can't have what you want," he said. "I wish I could change that."

"Me, too," she whispered. "Thanks for wanting to."

He had hesitated to touch her—she seemed so raw and charged with electricity—but the impulse was too strong now. He pulled her into his arms, and waited until the tension vibrating through her relaxed, and her soft weight settled against his chest.

After a few moments, she rubbed her eyes. "I'll ruin your shirt."

"I don't care," he said.

"Wow," she whispered. "That just blindsided me. It was so hard last year, losing her. It happened so fast. I thought I was handling it, and suddenly, kaboom. I fall to pieces."

"I think it's normal," he said. "Family gatherings, holidays, weddings. They can really slip past your guard."

"Exactly," Sophie said. "My guard is usually miles high. It's the organizing principle of my professional life, you know? That's what I do. I help people keep up their guard. But the last few days, my guard has been like Swiss cheese. And my mom is the biggest hole of all. She's the reason I'm here."

Vann waited for more, but Sophie stopped speaking.

She pulled away with an incoherent apology, and went into the bathroom and bent over the sink, splashing her face.

He followed her and slid his arms around her waist from behind as she straightened up, dabbing at her face with the towel.

"What does that mean? That your mom is the reason you're here?" he asked.

She wouldn't meet his eyes. "I told you, remember? That's why I moved to Seattle. I needed a fresh start after she was gone."

Vann waited for more. Sophie finally met his eyes in the mirror.

"What?" she demanded, almost angrily.

"You're always straight with me, so I have a good baseline

reading on you for honesty," he said. "And this doesn't ring true. What is it about your mom?"

She made a frustrated sound. "You are all up in my face to-night, Vann."

"Yes," he said. "And I'm not backing down."

Sophie let out a sharp sigh. Her eyes looked almost defiant. "All right," she said. "Here goes nothing. If I tell you a secret, will you promise not to tell a soul?"

Vann felt himself go ice cold inside. He couldn't think of what to say. "Ah…"

Sophie laughed out loud. "Oh, my God, your face," she said. "Relax, Vann. I'm not confessing to murder or anything shocking."

"Even so, I can't make that promise blind," he said carefully. "How do I know what you'll say?"

Sophie sighed. "How about if I promise in advance that my secret will not compromise you morally? It will not sully your honor to keep my promise. It's just private, that's all."

He nodded. "I see."

"So? Do you promise?"

Vann let out a slow breath, and braced himself. "I promise."

Sophie spun inside the circle of his arms, and placed both her hands on his chest. She looked like she was working up her courage.

"Is this about your mother?" he prompted.

Sophie nodded. "She was the one who wanted me to go to Seattle," she said. "It was her dying wish for me to come here."

Vann waited for the rest, unable to breathe. "And why is that?"

Sophie raised her eyes to his. "Because Malcolm Maddox is my father."

Vann looked blank. Stunned. But not dismayed, which was heartening.

"Whoa," he whispered at last. "No way. For real?"

"Absolutely for real," she said. "I didn't even know myself until right before Mom died. She always put me off when I asked about my father. It was the one thing we ever fought about. But when she got her terminal diagnosis, she changed her mind."

"So, it's a sure thing? You know this for a fact?"

Sophie nodded. "Mom had an affair with Malcolm thirty years ago, in New York. It happened while he was working on the Phelps Pavilion. My mother was on the team working on the interiors. They had a wild affair, for just a couple of weeks. She fell madly in love with him."

"And she never told him about you?"

"She tried," Sophie said. "She went to his house in Seattle. His wife, Helen, met her at the door. She was mortified. She left, and she never came back."

Vann stared at her, fascinated. "Yeah. I can see the family resemblance, now that I'm looking for it. To Ava, to Drew, to Malcolm. It's in the shape of the eyes, the eyebrows. It's so obvious. I can't believe I didn't notice it before."

"So you believe me? You don't think I'm some grifter trying to con them?"

He looked shocked. "Hell, no. Why would you lie about a thing like this?"

She laughed at him. "Oh, come on, Vann. Malcolm is rich and famous in his field, and he was known to get around in his wild youth. He probably has paternity suit insurance, for God's sake. Not that it's in any way relevant. I'm not after his money, or any sort of notoriety. On the contrary."

"It would never occur to me that you were after Malcolm's money," Vann said. "If you wanted money, you'd go make it yourself. You have the skills."

"Well, thank you," Sophie said. "That's a lovely compliment. To tell you another secret, I actually inherited quite a considerable sum of money from my grandparents. ItalMarble made my grandfather a very rich man. So I would never need to bother Malcolm at all if money was all that I cared about."

"What do you care about?"

"It's hard to put my finger on," she said. "It was important to Mom. Fulfilling my promise made me feel closer to her. My grandparents died several years ago, and my mother was an only child, like me. And there's no one else in my family. So she was worried. Poor little Sophie, all alone in the world. She thought maybe Malcolm could at least offer me fellowship and family."

"So you're sure that it's him? There's no doubt in your mind?"

"I don't think Mom would have led me astray about something like that on her deathbed," Sophie said. "But I still tested Ava's DNA. I swiped a champagne glass at the reception announcing their engagement. She's definitely my cousin. This trip to San Francisco was my first chance to get close enough to Malcolm to get a sample from him."

"And did you?"

She gave him a sheepish smile. "I did, actually. The other night, when you found me in his office? I was in the bathroom, stealing his water glass. I'd already swiped his dessert fork. They're wrapped up in bubble wrap, packed in my suitcase. So if it looked like I was sneaking around in there, I guess I was. Stealing flatware and glassware."

"Wow," he murmured.

"I needed hard objective proof," she explained. "I didn't want to have to defend my mom's truthfulness, of my own. So I'm covering all my bases. But truthfully? I don't know if I can stand to wait any longer. It took almost four weeks to get results that last time, for Ava's DNA."

"No, don't wait any longer," Vann said. "Just do it."

"I've been taking my time, just watching them," Sophie said. "Some families are poisonous. But from the looks of this wedding, the Maddoxes aren't."

"No, they are not," Vann said. "They're solid. Not perfect, but solid."

Sophie crossed her arms over her chest. She felt vulnerable…

but hopeful. "You know these people well. So you don't think they'd ride me out of town on a rail if I come forward with this?"

"By no means," he said. "I think you'd be a great addition to their family. You'd fit right in. You're smart, tough, talented, accomplished, gorgeous. You'd just be another jewel in their crown."

"Oh, please," she scoffed.

"It's the objective truth," Vann said. "As far as looks are concerned, they've got great genes going for them, and you are no exception to that rule."

Sophie walked out of the bathroom, sat down on the bed and unbuckled the ankle strap on her sandal. "I know that Malcolm raised Ava and Drew after their parents were killed," she said. "I was afraid that if I came out of nowhere and claimed to be Malcolm's daughter, they might get jealous and possessive. Protective, even. He's like their dad, in every way that counts. I'd understand if they did."

Vann shrugged. "Who can say how they'll feel? People are complicated. But they'll get over it because they're not stupid or spiteful. And they'll do the right thing because that's who they are. In the end, they'll be glad they did."

Sophie was so relieved at Vann's reaction her eyes were fogging again. She wiped away the tears, laughing. "Wow. That's an extremely positive spin on this whole situation."

"That's how I see it," he said. "Drew's my best friend. I trust him. I respect Malcolm. I don't know Ava as well, but I like her, and Drew worships his baby sister. I know you. You're amazing. What's not to be positive about? It's a win/win for everyone."

"That's sweet, Vann, but it would be silly to think there's no downside."

"I don't see it," he said. "Having you in their lives is like finding buried treasure."

"Aww! Don't go overboard," she warned him. "I'm already overwhelmed from the party. Thinking about how it might have been if Mom had been a part of the Maddox family. And me, for that matter. I could have been one of them. It just got to me somehow. All the lost chances. Brothers or sisters I might have had. It's silly, I know."

"It's not silly at all." Vann sat down on the bed and clasped her hand.

"I know that the past is gone," she said. "The mistakes are over and done with. There's no point in thinking about them."

"Except to learn from them," he said. "To not repeat them."

She gave him a wry look. "I'm not having an affair with a married man, Vann. Nor will I find myself with a surprise pregnancy."

"Actually, I was thinking about my own father," he said. "He never let down his guard. Not with my mom and not with me. It was probably his PTSD, but it marked him forever. Maybe it was that way for your mom, too. And Malcolm."

Sophie nodded. "Mom never let down her guard, either," she said quietly. "She had the occasional date now and again, but she couldn't let herself care that much about anyone again. Except for me."

"That won't be us." Vann pressed his lips to her hand.

Sophie let out a shaky laugh. "It's so strange," she said. "But I just can't keep up my guard with you. No matter how I try."

Vann shook his head, gazing into her eyes. "So don't try."

The moment was so fragile. Delicate. A rainbow-tinted bubble, made of longing and possibility. With feelings so powerful she could barely stand their charge.

They made her shake with fear. And hope.

She stroked Vann's face, memorizing every tiny detail. He moved her, excited her. So beautiful, with those serious dark eyes.

He reached out slowly to unfasten her dress, working loose the hook she'd sewn under the fabric rose. He opened it and pushed the light, sheer wrap off.

Sophie tossed her hair back, but couldn't help a self-conscious glance down at the frilly neckline of the under-dress, dipping low to show the entire length of the scar on her chest. Her hand drifted up to cover it.

Vann's hand covered it first. Her heart felt like it was thudding against her ribs.

"Beautiful," he whispered.

"What?" she asked.

"Your heart," he said. "It's been through so much, but it's so strong."

She smiled at him. "It's galloping like a racehorse." She tugged the soft fabric of her bodice, peeling it down over her breasts, freeing her arms.

"Mine, too," he said hoarsely. He slid his hands down from her shoulders to cup her breasts.

Her hunger was too urgent to put up with teasing games. She reached back and unhooked the bra, tossing it aside.

He got up and stripped off his tux, tossing item after item in the general direction of the chair. Some hit, some missed. He didn't seem to care. Sophie pushed the covers down and then took off her dress and panties. Soon he was pressing her into the sheets.

Oh, *yes*. The heat of his big body was a shock to her system. He tasted so good. Like whiskey and coffee. Hot and wet. She gasped with pleasure as he situated himself over her. The length of his hot, stiff shaft rested against her most sensitive folds without entering her. Just slowly caressing her. Sliding and teasing. Driving her mad as he ravaged her mouth with those frantic kisses.

Sophie moved against him, sensually at first, but it soon turned to moaning desperation, fighting to get him where she needed him—deep inside her.

"Take it easy," he murmured. "The longer you wait, the better it will be."

She laughed with what breath she could. "Please don't tease."

"Not tonight." Vann shifted his weight, nudging himself inside her.

They sighed in agonized delight as he slowly pushed inside. Every moment of it was an exquisite, shuddering bliss. Every part of her so sensitive, alive to sensation. As if she were being painted with light, and every stroke made her glow brighter.

Every deep, surging stroke made her crazy for the next one. A frenzy of need. An explosion of bliss. She lost herself in it.

As she came back to earth, she was afraid to open her eyes. That it would be like the night before. She'd be floating on air, and he would have those grim shadows in his eyes.

But he didn't. He was smiling.

"Hey," he said. "There you are at last. I was about to send out a search party."

She felt almost weak with relief. "I was destroyed. Beautifully destroyed."

"Same." He stroked his hand slowly over her hip. "Incredible."

"So, ah…what's different tonight?"

His hands stopped. "Meaning?"

"For you," she specified. "Yesterday the sex was amazing, but you weren't happy. What changed for you?"

His grin dug gorgeous, sexy grooves into his cheeks. "Maybe I'm letting my guard down, too."

"You seem relieved," she said.

A puzzled line formed between his brows. "In what way?"

"I think I scared you, asking you to keep my deep dark secret," she said. "What on earth where you afraid I was going to say?"

"In my experience, long-kept secrets usually aren't happy things," Vann said. "Otherwise, why would they be secret?"

"Like our hot affair?" She batted her eyes at him teasingly.

"I can't keep that a secret anymore," he said. "I'm sorry, but I just can't."

She gave him a stern look. "You will not add to my burden right now."

"But I want to stay here all night," he said. "I want to walk out with you in the morning and go to breakfast. Brazenly. Holding hands."

"In your tux?" she teased. "You naughty boy."

He laughed. "Fine, so I'll get a change of clothes. But that's not the point. I want to sit with you at the breakfast table. Pour your champagne. Peel your grapes."

She laughed at him. "Whoa! Serious stuff!"

"Remember what you said on the beach? When I asked what it would take to be able to hold your hand?"

"I remember," she said.

"I'm ready," he said. "I want to do the work. Whatever needs to be done so I have the right to hold your hand on the beach, or hover over you at the breakfast buffet, or be stuck to you, any damn place we want."

"Slow down," she said gently.

"Why?" he demanded. "Why waste time? I want to show you off. You're a prize. I want to flaunt you to the world. I can't play it cool. I want to court you."

"I like being courted," she said, her hand trailing down over his belly until it reached his erection. "I suggest that you start by demonstrating exactly what I stand to gain from your offer."

"You got it," he said as he covered her mouth with his.

Sixteen

"Noon would be fine," Vann told the employee at the car rental employee. He finished his business, closed the call and pushed the bathroom door open.

Sophie was awake and smiling at him. Morning sunlight spilled through the lofted skylight. The light showed the deep red highlights in her glossy brown hair. She stretched luxuriously, and the movement made the sheet twist and tighten around her gorgeous body. "Who are you talking to?" she asked.

"Sorry I woke you," he said.

She saw the clock and jerked up with a gasp. "Oh, God. The limo! We're so late!"

"No, we're not," Vann said.

"It's supposed to leave in fifteen minutes, and I'm not even packed!"

"You don't have to take the limo," he told her. "I just rented a car. A convertible. I got online this morning, while you were still asleep. They're driving it over for me. I figured, no one expects us at work today, and the weather's holding, so maybe we could spend the day exploring the coast together. We can make our way back to Seattle this evening." He paused, and added delicately, "Or not. If you're in a hurry to get back."

A belated smile broke out all over her face. "That sounds like a blast."

"Great," he said. "They're dropping it off at noon. That gives us time for breakfast."

"Time for the walk of shame, eh?" she teased. "Back to change the tux?"

"I'll live," he said, but flushed as memories of last night's erotic play flashed through his mind.

"Well, then." She stretched, letting the sheet drop to her waist. "Why don't you go get dressed and get your suitcase ready, and I'll do the same. Then come on back, and we'll go in to breakfast together."

He grinned as he buttoned his shirt. "Do I get to hold your hand as we go in?"

She tilted her head to the side, considering her answer carefully. "If you like," she conceded. "But you're not peeling my grapes. A girl's got to draw the line somewhere."

"No grapes," he agreed swiftly.

She got up, sauntered over to him naked and kissed him.

"You're making it hard for me to leave," he murmured, his voice thick.

"Your problem," she whispered. "Not mine."

He seized her. "Aw, hell. The walk of shame can wait."

The breakfast crowd had thinned out by the time they finally got to the dining room. Many of the wedding guests had left already but there were more than enough people still there to notice the grand entrance. Holding hands, at Vann's insistence. It made her face hot, but it was a symbolic thing. A milestone.

Drew and Jenna noticed immediately. Drew grinned, Jenna looked delighted and Ava fluttered her fingers and winked. Even Bev, sitting with Hendrick in the corner, blew Sophie a benevolent kiss.

Tim Bryce was there, with Rich. Both men gave her a cold stare. She wasn't too surprised. She'd been curt with Rich the day before. She didn't regret it.

"It looks like Malcolm's gone back," she said. "He must have caught the limo. I was going to ask if I could schedule a meeting for tomorrow. I'm going to take your advice, and meet with him now. The testing can wait. If he needs proof."

"There's Sylvia, having breakfast," Vann said. "Have her set up a meeting. He would have told you to talk to her, anyway. Let's ask her right now."

Wow, this was all getting very real, very fast. She felt rushed, but there was no reason she could think of to put it off, so they walked over to Sylvia's table.

Sylvia's eyes had a speculative twinkle over the rim of her coffee cup as they approached.

"Good morning, Vann," she said. "Looks like you've been busy."

"Always am, Syl. Sophie needs to schedule a meeting with Malcolm as soon as possible," Vann said. "Will he be in the office tomorrow?"

Sylvia pulled a tablet out of her bag, opened a scheduling app and flicked through it. "You're in luck," she said. "Usually he doesn't come in on Tuesdays, but he's playing catch-up after the wedding and San Francisco. I could put you in for ten thirty."

"That's great," Sophie said faintly.

"Done." Sylvia tapped the keypad with a stylus. "See you tomorrow."

They seated themselves near the window. Vann studied Sophie's face as they waited for the waiter to bring coffee. "You look nervous," he observed. "Don't be."

"It just hit me," she said. "I wasn't expecting things to move this fast. The documentation phase was easier. Guess I'm more chicken than I knew. I almost regret not waiting for another test."

"Do you want me to be there tomorrow?" he offered.

Sophie smiled at him. "Thanks, but this should be just between me and him."

"In any case, let's meet for lunch after," Vann said. "That way you can debrief me."

Sophie gladly agreed to that. Their eggs Benedict arrived, and they took their time with their breakfast before getting on their way.

The day that followed was perfect in every way. Not just because of the sexy little car, the beautiful weather, the stunning scenery.

It was the way she felt. The melting warmth all through her body. The company of this man made her tingle and glow and laugh constantly. They had long, winding conversations about everything that popped into their minds. There were no awkward pauses. Even the pauses seemed right and natural, full of their own proper significance.

The sky was cloudy, but there was no rain, just stunning moments when sun burst through the clouds, illuminating the sea. They stopped at every scenic vantage point, strolled barefoot on every beach. When they got hungry, they picked up some fish and chips and cold beers at a boardwalk restaurant and ate on the sand on a beach blanket that Vann had bought at the first tourist shop they came across.

That was followed by double-decker ice-cream cones, and a lively difference of opinion about the relative merits of milk chocolate versus dark chocolate. The dispute was never resolved, but the argument required multiple taste tests, which soon turned into chilled, chocolatey kisses. After a few minutes of that, someone drove past them and yelled, "Get a room!"

Vann pulled away with some difficulty. "We could," he murmured.

"Get a room, you mean?"

"In a heartbeat," he said.

"I'd love it," she said. "But tomorrow is a big day for me, and I don't want to get back to the city late."

"I guess we should hit the road, then. As it is, we'll reach Seattle after dark."

"I hate to go," she said. "Hey, watch out. Ice cream is dripping on your shoes."

They set out again. With the top down, it was too noisy for conversation, but Vann held her hand whenever he didn't need it on the gearshift or the wheel. The feeling that hummed between them transcended words.

The occasional glance or smile was enough. No barriers.

Vann turned to her when they got close to the city. "I'll take you home if you want," he said. "But my house is close. On Lake Washington."

She hesitated, thinking about tomorrow's meeting. But being with Vann made her feel brave and fearless, and naturally lovable. She could use every last drop of that feeling. It would give her courage. "I have one last outfit in my bag that would be acceptable in a work setting," she said.

"Do you need to get any lab documentation from home?" he asked. "Like the test on Ava's DNA?"

"I have the documents on my computer at home, but I also have them on my tablet, right here in my bag," she told him. "I'm all set for this meeting."

"So you'll stay with me? Can I take you home?"

After a single suspended breath, she smiled at him.

"Yes," she said softly. "Take me home."

Seventeen

Vann's house didn't seem big from the road that circled the lake, but on the other side, it opened up and revealed itself to be larger than it seemed, with a terrace looking out over the water. The entrance led to the upper floor, and corridors led to bedrooms on either side. Then a wide, shallow staircase in the foyer under a big skylight led down to a huge central space that opened off into a dining room, living room and kitchen, all with spectacular walls of glass to showcase the view.

"What a beautiful place," Sophie murmured.

"I can't take credit for it," he said. "Drew designed it. I told him in broad strokes what I wanted, and he made it happen. Better than my wildest dreams. One of the perks of having a best buddy who's a world-class architect."

He hung up her coat and turned the lights on in the kitchen. "I'm too distracted to cook," he said. "But I've got some take-out favorites I can recommend. A Thai place, a Japanese place, a Middle Eastern restaurant, Indian. And some really excellent Italian."

"I'm fussy about Italian, since it's my heritage," she teased. "Excellent?"

"You won't know until you try," he said.

"Then I opt for the Italian," she said.

Vann picked out a menu from the bundle in his drawer. "Want to take a look?"

"You know their dishes," she said. "You pick this time."

He grabbed his smartphone and dialed as he uncorked a bottle of red wine. "Hello?... Yes, this is Vann Acosta. I'd like an order delivered to the usual address. Let's start with the smoked salmon. Fresh artichoke salad, stuffed mushroom, batter-fried spring vegetables, the half-moon smoked cheese ravioli with butter and sage. Fresh greens with orange and fennel. Grilled cacciatore sausage. Panna cotta with blackberry topping for dessert. All of this is for two... Excellent... Yes. Put it on the usual card."

Sophie gave him a shocked look. "That's a lot of food. Overdoing it much?"

He poured the wine. His hungry, lingering glance made her nipples tighten. "I'm burning off the calories just looking at you." He held out the glass. "Come on back to the lake."

She followed him out into the water-scented air on the terrace, listening in the stillness for the hollow sound of water slapping the pebbles on the beach. City lights gleamed on the dark ripples. Wind ruffled the water's surface like a stroking hand.

"It's beautiful," she murmured. "So peaceful."

"I was actually the first one to buy waterfront property here," he said. "Then Drew decided he liked the lake, too, and he found another piece of land. So he's my neighbor, just mile or so up that way." He pointed.

"How wonderful, to have a friend nearby. Do you guys hang out on weekends?"

He snorted. "What weekends? We see each other mostly at work. At least until he met Jenna, at which point I basically stopped seeing him at all. Not that I begrudge him his happiness." Vann smiled at her. "Now less than ever."

Sophie raised her glass. "To Drew and Jenna. May their love endure forever."

"To Drew and Jenna," Vann echoed.

They clinked glasses, and drank. He reached out to stroke the side of her cheek with his knuckle. "So soft," he said. "It's amazing how soft your skin is."

"Usually I feel as hard as glass," she said. "You make me feel soft."

He reached down to grab her hand. "We have to stay close enough to the house to hear the doorbell," he told her. "They usually don't make me wait very long for the food."

They'd only just finished their first glass of wine when the delivery arrived. Vann brought in the food and set the table, dragging out some candles and candleholders.

They spread the containers out, and feasted by candlelight.

At a certain point, the conversation wound down into long, speaking silences. They gazed at each other, feeling the sweet, delicious anticipation build.

This looked and felt so…well…real. This fantasy of happiness, pleasure and love. It felt like a future. A family. Something she'd never quite been able to envision for herself.

Against all odds, this actually seemed to be real.

Vann stood up and held out his hand. "Are you ready to go upstairs?"

She got up and took his hand. "Lead the way," she said.

The night was a feverish erotic fantasy. After the first few wild, frenzied times they made love, they slowed down, dozing from time to time, tightly twined together.

Vann was too happy to sleep. He just stroked Sophie's hair, his throat too tight to speak, his chest bursting with emotion. He craved more of her. Now and forever.

Dawn was lightening the sky outside. Tendrils of mist rose

off the lake, creating an ethereal, otherworldly realm where nothing could intrude on their love. They gazed at each other until gazing wasn't enough, and it turned to kissing, tasting, stroking. She caressed him boldly, guiding him into her tight, slick warmth. They rocked together in a surging dance of pleasure that crested into yet another explosion of delight.

They lay together afterward, lost in each other's eyes. Sophie's hands moving over his chest, fingertips sliding through the hair that arrowed down from his chest to his belly.

"It's such a strange feeling," she said.

"Which one?" he asked. "I'm fielding a lot of them."

"Being so open," she admitted. "I let my guard down so far, I don't even know where I left it."

"Me, too," he admitted.

"Does it feel good?" she asked hesitantly.

"Great," he assured her. "Let's never put our guard back up. Not with each other."

Sophie put his hand to her lips, kissing his knuckles. "It's a deal," she whispered.

He felt like his heart was too big for his chest as the meaning of her whispered words sank in. They were taking a step into something so rare and pure and precious. He was humbled, dazzled to realize it. She trusted him. It was such a gift.

He wanted to be a better man. To fully deserve that trust.

"What time is it?" she asked.

"Really early," he said. "But I'm too jacked up to sleep any longer. It's a big day. I'll make you a good breakfast."

He bounded out of bed, threw on a pair of sweatpants and went down to get to work.

The dining room was a mess from last night's feast, but the breakfast nook was still pristine, so he set up there. By the time Sophie came down, swathed in his blue terry-cloth bathrobe, her hair a mass of damp waves, he had breakfast sausages, English muffins, OJ and coffee on the table, and was tipping a panful of eggs, two for her, four for him, onto the plates. He hadn't felt this hungry since he was a teenager.

"Wow," she said, impressed. "Look at you, pampering me. Don't tell anyone."

He poured her coffee. "I don't care who sees me," he said. "I'll do it out in front of God and everyone."

"Whew." She sank into her chair and sipped her coffee, smiling. "Scandal."

"Bring it on," he said. "I'm so wound up. I'll try to chill."

"No, don't. I like you like this. It excites me."

Their eyes locked. The air ignited.

Sophie looked away first, laughing. "Not now, for God's sake! There's no time!"

"Soon," he promised. "I'll pamper you again. Until you can't even see straight."

"Mmm, something to look forward to."

He realized, over halfway through the meal, that having breakfast with a lover was a first for him. He never stayed with anyone all through the night. Never wanted to.

But everything about Sophie was different. New.

After breakfast they got dressed. Sophie was as stunning as ever when she was all put together, in a silver-gray linen tunic over matching wide-legged trousers and gray suede pumps. Her hair was loose, styled in long waves and curls. Her lips were a glossy red, and her whiskey-colored eyes were full of mystery as she looked him over. "Nice suit," she said. "I think we're both presentable."

"Should we take the convertible to go to work?"

"I wish." She shook her head with a regretful smile. "I'd ruin my hair. Not today."

"No problem," he assured her. "We can take my Jag."

Morning traffic was what it always was in Seattle, but he was too euphoric to be frustrated today. It meant more time with Sophie. And as early as they'd risen, they got there with time to spare.

"Can you let me out at the front entrance?" Sophie asked as they got closer to the downtown office. "I need to take care of some things before the rest of the staff gets in."

He pulled over in front of the building. "I'll be at your office at 12:15."

She had a shadow of lingering doubt on her face. "Shouldn't we just meet at the restaurant? For now, anyway?"

He shook his head, resolute. "We're through with that now. Onward."

She gave him a smile that made his body tingle. "You are just on fire today, Vann."

"You lit the flame," he said.

Her laughter sounded happy. "Okay, fine. My office, then. Later."

"Good luck with the meeting," he called. "I know it'll be fine. He's a lucky man."

Her smile left him just staring helplessly after her until the cars started beeping impatiently behind him.

Vann floated through the morning in a haze. Then Zack leaned inside his office.

"Hey," he said. "Do you have a quick debrief for me before I go to Malcolm's office?"

Vann looked at him blankly. "Debrief about what?"

Zack frowned. "Your info-gathering project? Sophie Valente? The IP theft?"

"Oh, that. I'll give you the short version. Not her. Look elsewhere."

Zack's face froze. Then he stepped inside and closed the door behind him. "You're sure of this?" he said. "You have proof?"

"You need to prove guilt, not innocence," Vann said. "I know her now."

"What, in the biblical sense?"

Vann stood up. "What the hell is that supposed to mean?"

"Sorry," Zack said. "I guess that wasn't appropriate."

"No, it wasn't," Vann said through his teeth. "What I meant

was, I know exactly what Sophie Valente is after here at Maddox Hill. And it's not money."

"So what is it?"

Vann hesitated. "I'll leave that for her to reveal. It's not my place to tell."

"She'd better hurry up about it," Zack said. "And she better be prepared to defend herself. From what I heard Bryce say, he's got her in the bag."

A chill seized him. "Bryce is full of shit."

"I won't say you're wrong, but if he has the ironclad proof he says he has, Sophie's in trouble."

"Bryce can't have proof," Vann said. "He's going down a dead end."

"Be that as it may, he's meeting with Malcolm now," Zack told him. "Explaining his discoveries."

"But Sophie was supposed to meet with him. In just a few minutes, in fact. We were supposed to talk with Malcolm and Bryce about all this tomorrow."

"Malcolm got in early," Zack said. "I heard him complaining about Sylvia scheduling back-to-back meetings this morning. Evidently Bryce couldn't wait until tomorrow. He looked buzzed. I was just going there, but I wanted to check in with you first."

"He can't be showing Malcolm what he discovered," Vann repeated. "There's nothing to discover! I'll go and tell Malcolm myself."

"Steady, now," Zack cautioned. "You're not currently in the best position to come to Sophie Valente's defense. Keep that in mind."

"Because I'm in love with her, you mean?" Vann said. "I'm not ashamed of it."

Zack winced. "This is worse than I thought."

Vann was already out the door. Zack caught up and kept pace with him as he made his way to Malcolm's office. Sylvia gave him a disapproving look as he approached.

"I'm going in to see Malcolm," he said.

"And a pleasant good morning to you, too, Vann. I'm sorry, but you can't quite go in yet! Tim Bryce is in there with him. Vann...hey! Vann, he's in a meeting!"

Malcolm's office door flew open. Malcolm poked his head out. "Sylvia!" he bawled. "Get Zack and Vann in here right— oh, there you are. Get your butts in here this instant."

Vann and Zack filed past Sylvia. She leaned in the door. "Do you gentlemen need coffee or—"

"They can drink coffee on their own damn time," Malcolm snarled. "Leave us."

Sylvia quickly closed the door. Malcolm's face was splotchy with anger as he rounded on them. "You two have been keeping secrets from me, eh?"

"No, we haven't," Zack said evenly. "We've been taking care of business, just like we always do."

Malcolm gestured at Vann. "I've seen some of his business lately. I'm not impressed."

"You've got it wrong, Malcolm," Vann said.

"No, he doesn't," Bryce said. "On the contrary, I think he's nailed it. Quite literally." Bryce chortled at his own joke, but the snickering died out as Vann fixed his icy gaze on him. "It's her," he said, his voice triumphant. "What I just showed Malcolm is airtight."

Vann breathed down the urge to punch that smug, self-satisfied look right off Bryce's smirking face. "What do you think you've got on her?"

"I don't think it, I know it. Look for yourself. I have a video of Sophie Valente stealing documents out of Malcolm's laptop."

"That's impossible," Vann said.

"It's a fact," Malcolm said heavily. "I saw it. The video is time-stamped. She's in the dress she wore at the wedding. I recognize my hotel room. There's no mistaking her. To think I invited a lying thief to my own nephew's wedding and let her mix with all the people I care most about. And the sensitive information she heard in the Zhang Wei meetings, God help us."

"I thought Vann's plan was to get more information before we went any further with our investigation." Bryce's voice was oily with insinuation. "Looks like he took the job more literally than we ever dreamed."

Zack blew out a sharp breath. "I want to see that video, right now."

They circled the desk and gathered around the monitor. Bryce edged closer but kept the length of the desk between himself and Vann. "I rigged cameras on the walkway leading to your room at Paradise Point," Bryce began.

"I doubt that's legal," Zack said. "Privacy laws—"

"Shut up and watch," Malcolm said. "Show them the clip from the walkway."

Bryce tapped the mouse and set the video clip to play. The camera was trained on one of the wooden walkways at Paradise Point, the rhododendron branches swaying gently and casting shadows on the weathered planks.

Sophie appeared, walking briskly and purposefully. She paused, frowning, and lifted her arm to check the time on her glittering gold wristwatch. She moved swiftly out of the camera's frame.

"You will all agree that's Sophie Valente. Correct?" Bryce said.

Vann ignored the question. "What time was it?"

"The video clock shows that it was 3:51," Bryce replied. "The ceremony began less than ten minutes later. She picked her time carefully. Everyone was already assembled on the lawn for the wedding. Now look at this." He fast-forwarded until there was another flash of pink, then ran the video back and set it to Play.

It was Sophie again, coming back the other way. Still frowning. The wind tossed her hair over her face. This time, she was almost running.

"Four minutes and twenty-five seconds," Bryce said. "Just a

couple of minutes after that, Rich saw her in the entrance hall and told her she was late for the ceremony. The two of them came in together, as I'm sure you noticed."

Vann looked into Bryce's face, his gaze unwavering. "Sophie told me that a woman who claimed to be on the resort staff told her to go to Malcolm's suite right before the wedding was scheduled to begin."

Malcolm made a derisive sound. "My suite? Right before the ceremony? What for? That's absurd!"

"She thought so, too," Vann said. "This mystery person told her that you were there and that you needed her to interpret something. Obviously, she found no one in the room. She said she knocked, waited for a couple of minutes—"

"Four minutes and twenty-five seconds, to be exact," Bryce said. "That's how long she was inside his suite."

"She never went inside," Vann said. "She and I discussed it. And they told her at the front desk that the woman who sent her to Malcolm's room had never worked there."

"Well now," Malcolm said. "Isn't that convenient."

"Are you interested in seeing what happened in Malcolm's room during that interval, or not?" Bryce asked.

"For God's sake, Tim, just play the damn thing," Malcolm growled. "Gloating is in poor taste, and I'm not in the mood."

Bryce tapped on the keyboard for a moment. "I'm emailing a courtesy copy of these clips to both of you," he said. "Review them at your leisure." He shot a sly glance at Vann. "Something to remember her by?"

"Tim!" Malcolm barked. "What did I just say?"

"Sorry." Bryce hit Play and stepped back. "Enjoy."

The video was shot from the wall behind the desk. The room was dimly lit. At 4:34, they saw a dark silhouette position herself on the desk chair in front of the open laptop.

The figure reached out to hit the mouse, and the computer came to life, flooding the figure in the chair with cool blue light.

It was Sophie, in that same silk chiffon thing she'd worn at the wedding. She stared into the screen, seeming serene and absorbed, typed rapidly for a moment and then lifted her phone, as she'd done in the video Bryce had shown them the previous week, before the San Francisco trip. She was taking pictures of the screen.

"I loaded the laptop with dummy files," Bryce said. "Just for her. They look very convincing, but all the details and calculations have been scrambled. Her buyer is going to be very angry. I'm afraid our bad little girl is in for quite a spanking."

"Don't talk about her that way," Vann growled.

"Not another word out of you," Malcolm said. "You're in no position to criticize."

The video continued. Just Sophie looking calmly into the screen. She would lift the phone, focus, snap the picture. Lift, focus, snap. Her long hair hung over her shoulders, the waves and curls smoothly arranged.

At a certain point, she dropped her phone into her beaded bag and put the computer to sleep. A blurry shifting of shadows in the dark, a brightening as she opened the door to leave— and it was over.

Vann felt rooted to the ground. His brain seemed frozen. It wouldn't process this information. The woman he knew, the woman he was in love with—she could not have done this. It just…wasn't…possible.

"Well?" Bryce said. "Does that satisfy you?"

"*Satisfy* is not the word I'd use," Malcolm said slowly. "But it's certainly damning evidence. I don't think I need anything more to be convinced of her guilt. Not much more to say about it, eh, Vann?"

"You have to let her defend herself," Vann said. "She may have an explanation. Something we don't know about. Something we've overlooked."

"What explanation can she have for being inside my private room?" Malcolm demanded. "Now that I think about it, she turned up in my guest office in the San Francisco meeting, too.

Remember? That's where I found the two of you, as I recall. Did she go in before you went in, Vann?"

Vann had to force himself to speak. "Yes. A couple of minutes before me. I saw her heading in there, and chased after her to see if she was up to anything. She wasn't."

"So she hadn't told you to meet her there," Malcolm persisted.

"No," Vann admitted reluctantly. "I surprised her."

"And she distracted you by coming on to you," Bryce said, smirking. "Well, that's a classic move. Nothing like sex to distract a man. I hardly blame you. Except that I do."

"Shut up, Tim," Malcolm said. "There is nothing amusing about this situation. So she might have been snooping around on my computer in there, too."

"No," Vann said. "She didn't go near your computer. She was in the bathroom."

"Really?" Malcolm grunted. "Public ladies' room not good enough for her, then?"

Vann didn't answer. His face felt numb.

"Well, Vann?" Malcolm said. "You've got your work cut out for you."

Vann looked at him, baffled. "Come again? What work?"

"You're the one who has to do it," Malcolm went on. "You know her best."

"Do what?"

Malcolm made an impatient sound. "Stop playing dumb. Get her to come clean about everything she's done up to now. Every detail, every dollar. Do it, if you care about her at all. Persuade her to cooperate. I'll be as lenient as I possibly can if she does."

His mouth was bone-dry. He forced out a rasping croak. "I can't."

"It has to be you," Malcolm said. "Would you rather she spend the best years of her life in jail? Don't make me be the bad guy here, Vann. Help me out. Help her out."

The intercom buzzed. "Mr. Maddox?" Sylvia said. "Ms. Valente is here for your ten-thirty meeting. Shall I have her wait until you gentlemen have finished, or shall I reschedule her for later on?"

"No, Sylvia, send her on in," Malcolm said.

"Are you sure?" Sylvia sounded baffled. "With everyone still there?"

"Exactly." Malcolm glared around at each of them. "Why drag this out?"

The worst-case scenario was unfolding before Vann's eyes with terrifying speed. His belly clenched with dread. Then the door opened and Sophie walked in.

Suddenly, all at once, Vann remembered the powerful rationale he'd always instinctively understood for keeping up one's guard. Love had made him forget that basic, elemental rule of nature.

You kept up your guard to not get annihilated.

Eighteen

Sophie stopped the minute she entered Malcolm's office, startled to see so many people there. Including Vann.

He didn't smile. In fact, his face was a blank, tight mask. It reminded her of something sad, something painful. It came to her after a split second.

Mom's face, that last, terrible week before she died. It was the bloodless tension in a person's expression when they were trying not to show intense pain. She almost asked Vann if he was okay, but then Malcolm spoke.

"Good morning, Ms. Valente."

She turned back to Malcolm, who was behind his desk with Zack Austin and Tim Bryce, of all people. "Sorry to interrupt," she said. "I can find a better time if—"

"Not at all," Malcolm said. "Go on. Say whatever you need to say."

Sophie was taken aback. Something was off, and she was smack-dab in the middle of it, with no clue. "Are you sure—"

"I am. Please, just say it, whatever it is. Out with it."

Oh-kayyyy…fine. She took a careful, calming breath. "Actually, what I wanted to discuss with you is of a private nature. I'd prefer to speak with you alone."

Malcolm studied her from under heavy, furrowed eyebrows. "I think not," he said. "Anything you have to say can certainly be said in front of these people."

This was all wrong, and it gave her chills. But it wasn't like she could retreat in confusion. That would look mealy-mouthed and cowardly and just...well, weird. As if she were somehow in the wrong. Trying to hide something, trying to pull something.

What the hell. She'd do this for Mom. If this bombed, she'd just leave this place forever and start fresh elsewhere. She gave Vann another swift glance, hoping for a smile, a signal. Any sign of solidarity.

He wasn't even looking at her. It was starting to scare her.

"I came in to see you because I have something important and very personal to tell you," she said. "It involves us both."

"Tell it," Malcolm said. But he did not beckon for her to move closer to his desk, nor did he offer her a chair.

Tim grabbed a chair and sat down, looking at her like she was the main attraction. What on earth?

"Bryce," Zack said under his breath. "Do not start."

"I didn't say a word," Tim said. "Don't mind me. I'm just watching the show."

That pissed her off too much to keep silent. "I didn't come in here to put on a show for you, Tim."

"I guess that remains to be seen, hmm?"

Sophie turned her attention from him and approached Malcolm's desk despite his marked lack of an invitation. She'd be damned if she was going to cower by the door, ready to bolt like a scared little bunny.

She squared her shoulders. "I asked for this meeting because I have decided to tell you that I am your biological daughter," she announced.

Malcolm's face was absolutely blank as seconds of painful silence ticked by.

She wanted to break the silence, but it was his place to make the next move. Tim's mouth hung open. Zack looked startled. The only one who didn't look shocked was Vann—but he still looked like he was hiding mortal agony behind a mask.

She looked back at Malcolm. His eyes were downcast now. "I see. So… Vicky," he said hoarsely. He coughed to clear his throat. "You're Vicky Valente's daughter, correct? You look like her. I noticed your surname when you were introduced. It's not an uncommon name, so I never dreamed you might be related to her."

And to you. "So you remember her?"

He put his hand up to his eyes. "Of course I remember Vicky. How is she?"

"She died, not long ago," Sophie said. "April of last year. Pancreatic cancer."

Malcolm covered his eyes again. Almost a minute went by before he cleared his throat with a sharp cough. "I'm very sorry to hear that," he said. "You have my sincere condolences."

"Thank you," Sophie said, bemused. And then she just stood there, in the awkward silence. Waiting.

This was so weird. The hard part was done. He hadn't thrown her out, or yelled at her, or laughed in her face, or called her a liar. He hadn't denied ever knowing her mother. Those were the outcomes she had feared, and none of them had come to pass.

So why did the air still feel so thick in here? And why did Vann and Zack look like they were being forced to witness an execution?

Tim, on the other hand, looked like he should be munching buttered popcorn.

"So you believe my claim?" she asked. "I was born in New York City, nine months after you and she worked together on the Phelps Pavilion."

"I do not disbelieve it." Malcolm's voice was expressionless.

Sophie pulled her tablet out of her bag, opening the files. "This is my birth certificate. I got a sample of Ava's DNA several weeks ago. I had it analyzed by a local genetics lab, and these are the results. As you can see, there's an overwhelming probability that she's my close relative. At least a cousin."

"I see." Malcolm didn't even lean forward to look at the birth certificate or the genetics lab test results. Which was not promising.

"I also took the opportunity to get a sample of your DNA when we were in San Francisco," she said. "Not because of any doubts I had, since I believe what Mom told me, but just because I wanted objective proof, for your sake. I took a fork and a water glass from your office in San Francisco. But then I decided I couldn't wait to have the results analyzed to speak to you. The stress of keeping this secret was getting to me."

"This explains a lot," Tim said.

"Your contribution was not requested, Tim," Malcolm said.

Tim made a lip-zipping gesture. Sophie looked around at all the men present in the room and threw up her hands. "This explains what?" she demanded.

But no one answered. "Come on, people!" she said. "What the hell is going on in here? What aren't you telling me?"

"One thing at a time," Malcolm said. "Why didn't you tell me immediately? You've been working here for months. Why not come to me before?"

"I wanted to line up objective, scientific proof," Sophie said. "Plus, I had to work up the nerve. I couldn't just pop out of nowhere with an announcement like that."

"I see," he said. "And what exactly did you hope to gain from this revelation?"

Sophie flinched inwardly. It wasn't a surprise, of course, but it still hurt, that he would automatically assume that her motives were just money-grubbing avarice.

"Nothing financial, if that's what you're wondering," she said. "I have many hard-won and highly marketable professional skills. I could make an excellent living anywhere in the world that I chose to go. I also have inherited a considerable amount of money and property from my mother's side of the family. I own homes in Singapore, New York City, the Catskills, Florence and Positano. I don't need one penny from you. I wouldn't even need to work, strictly speaking, but I wasn't cut out to be a bored socialite. I need challenge in my life."

Malcolm cleared his throat. "It's a lot to take in all at once. So if you are independently wealthy as you say, then what do want from me, Ms. Valente?"

Damn. It was a bad sign if he had to ask.

"Please, call me Sophie," she said stiffly. "My mother asked me to come to you. It was a deathbed request. She wanted us to know each other. She was worried about the fact that I have no living family left. It's mostly for her sake that I'm here. I promised her I'd come and tell you about myself."

She and Malcolm stared at each other. Her heart sank. Malcolm didn't look angry, or defensive, or even suspicious. Just sad.

"I would be satisfied just to be known to you," she said hesitantly. "And acknowledged by you. I would be open to us getting to know each other as people, if that interests you. I've enjoyed my time working here, and I've done my best for the company. I'd also like to get acquainted with my cousins. Ava and Drew seem well worth knowing."

"That they are," he said.

Sophie tapped on the tablet, opening the file of photographs. "I have pictures of my mother and me over the years, if you'd care to take a look."

For this, Malcolm did lean forward. He swiped through more than fifty pictures, studying each one for many long moments. Finally, he closed the file, pushing the tablet sharply away. "You can take that back."

She slid the device back into her bag, chilled. "So where do we go from here?"

Malcolm wrapped his arms over his chest. "That depends entirely upon you."

"Me?" She shook her head, confused. "Not at all, Mr. Maddox. I've made my move. It's your turn, to either respond to it or not. As you prefer."

Once again, that cool stare, like he was waiting for something more from her.

Something that he thought he was owed.

Which seemed backward. She'd given him everything she had to offer. She'd displayed her most intimate memories, for God's sake. Showing him that file was like pulling a piece of her heart out of her chest and handing it over to a stranger. Not knowing if it would be flung back into her face or not.

Malcolm made an impatient huffing sound. "Come on now, Ms. Valente. Is there anything else important that you need to tell us today?"

She was confused. "Excuse me? Does this issue not seem important enough to warrant a private meeting with you?"

"Skip the snark, please. Do you have anything else to say, beyond your genetic revelation?"

Sophie studied each of the people in the room in turn. She had the uncomfortable feeling that some inexplicable trap was about to spring shut on her.

She shook her head. "Nothing," she said. "This was the sum total of my agenda for today."

"Oh, enough of your bullshit." Malcolm slapped his hand down on the desk, making everything on it rattle.

Sophie jerked back, startled. "What on earth? What bullshit?"

"Come on, girl! For your mother's sake, and for everything that I should have done for you while you were growing up, I'll give you a pass. But you've got to come clean!"

"Come clean about what? A pass on what? Explain yourself, for God's sake!"

Malcolm shook his head. "Don't play dumb with me. I'll go

easy on you, on the condition that you cooperate completely with our internal investigative team, and then swear never to contact me or my family ever again. But for that, you have to confess."

"But…what are you suggesting that I—"

"God knows, I'd want to get back at me, too, if I were you," he said.

"Get back at you? Hold on." Sophie sucked in a shocked breath. "Oh, my God. You think I'm the one who's been selling Maddox Hill proprietary IP to China?"

"Oh, so you know about that!" Malcolm's voice rang out in challenge.

"Of course I know! I found out right after I got here. But I didn't know who I could trust here, so my plan was to unearth the thief myself and serve you his head on a plate before I even told you we were related. But it turned out to be a slower business than I anticipated."

Tim shook his head in disbelief. "Can you believe this?" he said. "She's still playing the innocent. She waltzes in here, gets a job on false pretenses—"

"I never misrepresented myself!" she said sharply. "I gave one hundred percent to my work here!"

Tim snorted. "A little more than a hundred percent, from what I can tell."

"Shut up, Bryce," Vann said. "You don't know what you're talking about."

Malcolm turned his fulminating glare on Vann. "You shut up. You've mishandled this from the start. You took advantage of not just my trust but also hers, which was truly despicable, whether she deserved it or not. It was very badly done, and I'm disgusted. Clear out your desk. Right now. I don't want to see your face around here any longer."

With those words, the bottom fell out of Sophie's whole world.

She turned to stare at Vann, horrified.

"You knew," she said, her voice hollow. "Even before San Francisco. You knew they thought I was the thief. You were setting a trap the whole time."

"No!" he said swiftly. "I was defending you! I never for one second believed that you could—"

"Do not hammer away at this false narrative, either one of you," Malcolm said. "We're not stupid, Ms. Valente. We have you red-handed. Video footage of you sneaking into my room at Paradise Point, taking photos of documents from my laptop."

"I was never in your room!" Sophie said curtly. "I was sent to your suite by a woman who claimed to be on the hotel staff. I was standing outside that door, knocking and yelling for you like an idiot, but I never went inside. Why would I?"

"Please." Malcolm put his hand to his head as if it hurt him. "Please, Sophie. We saw you on the video. Inside my room. Sitting at my computer. Please, just stop this."

"You may have seen something, Mr. Maddox, but you did not see me, because I was never...freaking...*there*!" Her voice rose in pitch and volume no matter how hard she tried to control it. "As if I would need to break into your hotel room to steal from you. Hah! I could reach into your system and pull out all your deepest, darkest secrets in no time, from anywhere in the world, without leaving a trail. But I didn't, because I'm not a thief, or a spy! I have no reason to be one!" She rounded on Malcolm. "You really think this is about money?"

"In my experience, it usually is," Malcolm said. "And it looks like you got your pound of flesh, so keep it. Just take it, with my apologies. My blessing, even. Consider it your inheritance, your back child support, your payoff, however you want to label it, as long as you never show your face around here again. Do not come anywhere near me and my family. If you do, I will come after you with the full force of the law."

Sophie had to take a moment to control her expression. Tears welled up in her eyes. Anger, hurt, confusion rampaged through her. There were too many things that were breaking her heart and outraging her pride right now. She was overloaded.

She slung her purse over her shoulder and straightened up. "I'm not your thief," she said. "But I doubt anyone here has the brains to figure that out. I hope that bastard bleeds you dry. It's what you deserve."

"Goodbye, Ms. Valente," Malcolm said. "We're done here."

She turned, tear-blinded, and marched in the general direction of the door. Zack opened it for her. She was grateful not to be forced to fumble and grope for the handle. Once outside, she dug in her purse for tissues.

Sylvia called after her. "Ms. Valente? Are you all right?"

She waved her hand, shaking her head as she hurried away. No point in saying anything to the other woman. Sylvia would know soon enough. Everyone would know.

Her reputation would be trashed in this firm in a matter of minutes. And the news would spread like wildfire. She would never work in her chosen field again.

But that was something to mourn at another moment. One damn thing at a time.

"Sophie." It was Vann's voice behind her. He put his hand on her shoulder.

She didn't think or reason, just spun around and slapped him in the face with all the force in her arm.

He didn't block her, or even flinch. "Sophie, please listen—"

"You lying scumbag!" she hissed.

He reached out to her. "I swear to God, I never—"

"Do not touch me! You *bastard*!"

Their audience was growing by the second. All chatter subsided. Heads popped up to peep over cubicles.

"I never believed it was you," Vann insisted. "Never for a second, and I still don't. From the very start."

"You set me up! Deliberately! What kind of monster would do that to somebody? Why, Vann? What have I ever done to you?"

"Sophie, I didn't do that! I never—"

"You maneuvered me into a firing squad! Knowing that they'd pinned the IP theft on me. You never warned me. Oh, yes, go tell Malcolm, you said. He'll welcome you with open arms. It'll be all flowers and rainbows. You set me up to get emotionally destroyed. Deliberately. That's a special kind of evil."

"I swear, I never—"

"You thought I was a liar and a thief, but you seduced me, anyway, because you could. So why not just squeeze the situation for everything you could get out of it, right?"

"No! I never thought you were a—"

"If you'd trusted me, you would have warned me!" she yelled.

"I didn't know Tim had that video, or that he was going to show it to Malcolm before he saw you. We were supposed to meet about that tomorrow, and I was going to explain that you couldn't possibly be—"

"Stop!" She backed away from him. "Just stop. I don't want to hear it. If your master plan was to inflict maximum pain and humiliation on me, then congratulations, it was executed perfectly. Quickly, too. What did that take, ten minutes? You couldn't have done any more concentrated personal harm unless you'd hired a hit man and had me shot. Next time, maybe. Practice makes perfect, right?"

"Sophie, please," he begged. "You have to listen to me."

"No, Vann." She backed away. "I don't have to do a damn thing for you."

"Please," he said roughly. "I believe in you. I'll do anything on earth to help untangle this for you. If you would just tell me what in God's name you were doing in Malcolm's hotel room at Paradise Point. I'm not saying you're a thief. I just need to understand why you were there, so I can organize your defense. I'm on your side, I swear. Just please. Make me understand. Spell it out for me. Why were you in there?"

Sophie backed away, wiping her stinging eyes. "I wasn't," she whispered. "I was never there."

His face contracted. "Oh, God. Sophie. Please. Help me out here."

She shook her head. "Burn in hell," she whispered as she turned and fled.

Nineteen

Vann stared after Sophie. Her gleaming hair swung as she walked. The no-nonsense click of her heels faded away as she turned the corner and was lost to his sight.

People began to murmur and stir as they realized the show was over. Those nearest him, who had been frozen in fear, began sidling discreetly away.

He had to get to his office. Tell his personal staff. Make them understand what had happened. Not that he understood it himself.

He couldn't seem to move. It was as if moving would propel him into this new, awful future where Sophie had lied, cheated, stolen. Connived to cheat his employer. Used him to cover her misdeeds. A future where Sophie had been banished and disgraced, and he'd been part of it. Participating in it.

Moving, taking any kind of step...it would make this awful future real somehow.

So would standing still. Time ground forward with or without his participation.

It wasn't true. His gut, his instincts, his heart, they all refused this new data utterly.

Vann lurched forward. Left foot, right foot. The truth didn't care if he accepted it or not. He moved down the corridor toward his office. Belinda was already on her phone, eyes wide and horrified. She'd heard.

She laid her phone down. "Oh, Vann." Her voice was thin. "I'm so sorry."

"Me, too," he said dully.

"This is just…it's insane."

"I'll tell Zack and Drew to look out for your job," he said. "They'd be stupid to lose you."

Belinda sank down into her chair and burst into tears. "I don't understand it! How can he fire you? You're the best thing that ever happened to this place. Just because some thieving little slut decided to use you for her—"

"She's not a thief, or a slut," he said sharply. "She's innocent."

Belinda clapped a tissue to her reddened nose and gave him a look that was hard to misunderstand, even with her eyes overflowing with tears. It was pity.

He turned away without a word and went into his office.

He took in the floor-to-ceiling window, the deluxe furniture, the fancy decorating. This office signaled that he'd moved up the ladder in life. That he'd achieved something.

It was all gone now. The office, the job, his whole life. Up in flames, along with his love for Sophie. Everything was burning in hell, just like she'd invited him to do.

The dissonance paralyzed him, the gap between the Sophie he knew and the conniving creature that Tim had painted her to be. And Tim had somehow painted Vann to be just as bad. A lying user, out for what he could get. Capable of getting a woman's trust, using her sexually and then stabbing her through the heart.

The videos literally hurt his head, as if someone had wrung

out his brain like a wet towel. What was up with that? How could it be?

The thought of watching them again made his stomach heave, but he turned grimly to his computer. Following his dad's stern training. Run straight toward pain. Like he had at high school football practice. Like when he'd been out on patrol in Fallujah.

Same thing now. He had to run straight toward the pain and the fear. Not away.

He opened his email program. The last highlighted, unopened email in his list, the one from Bryce, had two video attachments. His jaw ached from being clenched so hard.

He played the first one.

It was Sophie on the walkway outside Malcolm's room, her luxuriant hair tossed back by the wind. He fast-forwarded all the way through the hotly disputed four minute and twenty-five second window when she was in the room, and then watched Sophie come back the other way. Her hair was now tossed forward over her face by the wind. She brushed it back and took off, moving as fast as heels like hers would permit. Definitely Sophie.

Then Vann set the other clip to Play. He watched the dark, shadowy figure come into the room, sit down and wake the computer up.

In this video, she seemed different. It was Sophie's face, yes, but her expression was out of sync with the video he'd seen of her outside. Outside, she had looked worried, agitated, angry. In this video, she looked calm and unhurried. It was the look of a person in the blissful zone of pure concentration. Not looking at her watch, no shifty eyes or nervous gestures, no lip-biting or shoving her hair from her forehead. No hint of urgency or stress. Or guilt.

Of course she wouldn't be looking at her watch. There was a clock on the computer screen. But her hair? It didn't look windtousled at all. It was smoothed over her shoulders in perfect, freshly styled ringlets arranged decorously over her shoulders.

He'd just seen her finger-comb them back off her face moments before.

This was all wrong. The look on her face. The calmness, the unhurried air. Her hair, unruffled by wind or fingers, curling over her chest.

Which was on full display. Luscious cleavage popped up over the neckline of the crinkly edge of the chiffon bodice. The fabric encased her breasts like flower petals.

He didn't remember admiring Sophie's cleavage during the party. It was the type of sexy detail that would burn itself permanently into the long-term memory of any straight man with a pulse. But it hadn't registered on his.

His hand shook as he guided the mouse to click back on the previous video of Sophie outside the room.

No cleavage here. Because the floppy pink chiffon rosette was positioned right at the level of her breasts. Not below.

He observed the indoor clip again. In this image, the rosette was much lower. Hooked loosely closed at waist level, leaving her chest uncovered.

It wasn't adding up.

But something told him that drawing Malcolm's attention to Sophie's luscious cleavage was not going to earn him any points. He'd just look like the balls-for-brains idiot that he was, wildly in love with the woman that he'd just stabbed through the heart. That wasn't going help her cause, if he—

Wait.

Stabbed. Through the heart.

Oh, God. Sophie's *heart*.

His own heart started thudding so loudly he had to bend over for a moment. The searing flash of emotion almost wiped him out for a second. Then he was out the door. Belinda leaped to her feet as he raced past.

"Vann!" she called. "What is it? Did anything happen? Can I help?"

He turned, still moving. "Yes! Tell them all that it's not Sophie. Tell everyone. It's not her, and I know it for a goddamn fact. I have hard proof!"

"Um… Vann, slow down! I'm not sure it's a good idea to rush back into—"

"I have proof," he repeated. "The video they're using was a fake. And I know who did it, too. He framed her, and he defamed her. And now he is going down."

Belinda hurried after him, panting. "But…but where are you going?"

"To beat that lying bastard to a pulp," Vann said.

Rage bore him along like jet fuel, all the way back to Malcolm's office. He heard Sylvia's squeak of protest behind him as he burst through the door.

Malcolm's face darkened. "What are you doing back here? I already dismissed you! Get gone!"

"Not until I'm done," Vann said. "I have something to say to all of you."

Zack stepped in front of Malcolm. "Calm down, Vann," he said.

"Sophie is not your thief," Vann announced.

Malcolm grunted. "For God's sake, stop letting your little head do your thinking for you. She's been exposed. Lying won't help her now. Don't embarrass yourself."

"I don't have to lie," Vann said. "I'm in love with her, yes. I'm crazy about her, and I'm not embarrassed to admit it. But it's not necessary to lie for her. The woman in the video taken inside your hotel room is not Sophie. The outdoor images are genuine, and they dovetail with Sophie's account of what happened on the day of the wedding. She was set up. This whole operation was carefully planned. But the woman at the computer? Not Sophie."

"Vann." Malcolm's voice was pained. "Don't insult my intelligence. I saw her with my own eyes. It's very clearly Sophie Valente."

"You saw a doctored video," Vann said.

"Vann, please," Bryce scoffed. "Don't do this. You saw her come to the ceremony twelve minutes after it started. You saw the videos. She has no alibi, because we were all at the wedding. It's a slam dunk. I'm sad, too, but it's time to accept it and move on."

Vann lunged before Bryce had finished talking.

Crack. His fist connected with Bryce's jaw. The other man careened backward, arms flailing as he hit Malcolm's antique Persian rug with a heavy thud.

Malcolm stared in shock. "Vann!" he barked. "How dare you?"

Zack grabbed him from behind before he could do any more damage. "Easy now," his friend muttered into his ear. "Stop it right now. Not the place or time."

Vann went still, breathing hard. He jerked his chin in Bryce's direction. "It was him, Malcolm," Vann said. "Bryce doctored the video. It's a deepfake."

"That's a lie!" Bryce blustered, dabbing at the blood from his split lip. He cowered back as Vann jerked toward him, but Vann was still restrained by Zack's hard grip.

"Keep that thug away from me!" Bryce said, his voice high and shaky. "He's gone nuts!"

"It's not a lie," Vann said. "The woman in that video was dressed like Sophie, and she'd styled her hair like Sophie's, but she is not Sophie."

"Don't try to confuse me, boy," Malcolm said. "What the hell are you saying?"

"It's a video of another woman, with old footage of Sophie's face incorporated into it," Vann said. "It's called deepfake technology. It's done with artificial intelligence. It's hard to spot. But that's what happened here."

"You're grasping at straws, Vann," Malcolm told him. "Why should you conclude that the woman in the video is not Sophie? She's in the same clothes."

"The woman in the video has no scar," Vann said.

Malcolm's eyes narrowed. "Excuse me?"

"Sophie had open-heart surgery when she was a toddler," Vann said. "She has an eight-inch surgical star over her sternum. That's why you've never seen her wear anything low-cut. If you look at the outdoor video, you can see that the fabric rose is holding the wrap closed right at the level of her chest. But whoever played Sophie's body double in the video had her wrap closed at the waist. And there's no scar to be seen. It's not Sophie. It's not even necessary to investigate the video itself, but if you did slow it down, you'd find the splices. It's a fake." He glared at Bryce. "His son, the one who was looking for Sophie before the wedding. Isn't he a CGI expert? He doctored that video. Bryce is your thief, Malcolm. Not Sophie."

Malcolm leaned heavily on his cane, looking appalled. "My God," he said, his voice hollow. "Tim. Is this true?"

Tim's face tightened, and it took him a long time to answer. "I… I'm sorry."

Malcolm shoulders slumped. He sank down into the chair. "Oh, Tim. What in God's name have you done?"

"I'm sorry," Tim repeated brokenly. "I had no choice. It was Richie. He got into drugs down there in LA. He got into trouble with his dealers. He owed them money. Mobster types. A whole lot of money. They were going to hurt him."

"And instead of coming to me and asking for my help, after twenty-five years of working together, you decide to steal from me," Malcolm said. "And to set up an innocent woman to take the fall. For the love of God, Tim. How could you do that to her?"

"You sleazebag liar," Vann said. "Sophie could have gone to prison for years."

"I had to keep them from going after Richie." Bryce pushed himself up onto his elbow. "Try to understand, Malcolm. Those men who were after him—"

"Get back down on the floor," Vann snarled. "If you get up, I'll hit you again."

Bryce looked up at Zack, who deliberately lifted his arms, freeing Vann. "I won't stop him," Zack said coldly. "You're on your own, Bryce."

Bryce's face crumpled, and he collapsed back onto the carpet. "I was afraid they would kill Richie," he said thickly. "I knew it was wrong, and of course I was sorry to do that to her, but imagine yourself in my place. Would you rather see some random woman spending a few years in a medium-security prison for a white-collar crime, or see your son tortured or murdered?"

Vann's fists shook. He looked over at Zack. "Please, get this piece of garbage out of my sight. For his own safety."

Zack nodded. "On your feet, Tim," he said. "Let's go get this thing started."

Tim struggled upright, swaying on his feet. Vann and Malcolm watched Zack lead the shambling, slump-shouldered man out of Malcolm's office.

The door fell shut behind him. The two men gazed at each other.

"So, then," Vann said flatly. "That's settled. I'll be on my way."

"I take it you're going to follow her?" Malcolm asked.

"Of course I am," Vann said. "Not that it's your business. She's already told me to burn in hell. She thinks I set her up for this horror show. I have you to thank for that."

"Me? Hah!" Malcolm snorted. "I didn't do a damn thing! You were the one who misbehaved and got caught with your hand in the cookie jar, so watch your mouth!"

"I don't see why I should," Vann replied. "You fired my ass, Malcolm. There's no reason for me to watch my mouth with you any longer."

"Don't be such a drama queen," Malcolm scoffed. "I was overwrought. Things are not what they seemed a short while ago. You may now consider yourself officially unfired. For now at least. If you behave."

Vann shook his head. "I'm not in the mood to behave, or to

be unfired. I have more important things to do right now than work for you, and I don't know how long they're going to take. Go ahead and hire someone to replace me. Screw this job."

"Don't be a fool, Vann," Malcolm blustered.

"I love that woman, you know that?" Vann said forcefully. "I want her to be my wife. The mother of my children. Till death do us part. You and Bryce killed that."

"Well, guess what, boy? You're not the only one who lost something today," Malcolm said. "Sophie came to me in good faith, and I attacked her, brutally. I destroyed my chance to makes things right with her. Vicky's girl. My own flesh and blood."

"I sure do hope that you're not asking me to feel sorry for you," Vann said. "Because you caught me on a bad day for that."

"Oh, shut up," Malcolm snapped. "Take your smart ass and your superior attitude and get out of my face. Go get her. And good luck with it."

Vann headed for the door.

"Vann!" Malcolm called as he pulled it open. "When you find her, please tell her that I hope she'll give me another chance."

Vann turned to look at the older man. "Hunt her down and tell her yourself if you give a damn," he said. "It'll mean more to her if you do. I'm not your errand boy."

"Out!" Malcolm roared. "I've had enough of your lip! Get gone!"

Vann did exactly that, his pace quickening with every step he took. By the time he reached the parking lot, he was running as if his life depended on it.

Twenty

Sophie jerked out of the nightmare, a scream caught in her throat.

God. Every time she drifted off, she had the same ugly dream. She was naked in a cage and people filed by, peering through the bars like she was an animal on display. She huddled, hiding her nakedness under her tangled, matted hair.

Then she saw Vann, standing beyond the crowd. Their eyes met. He shook his head slowly, then turned his back and walked away.

Every time, she leaped up and rattled the bars, screaming his name. But Vann never turned around. He didn't seem to hear her.

Her own scream woke her every time, and she was freshly furious at herself for being so vulnerable, even in a dream. He wasn't worth her tears, damn it.

She swung her legs over the lounge chair and sat up. She'd fallen asleep reading an article on becoming a security consultant while lying under a canopy of drooping wisteria blossoms, and the afternoon light sifted through them, bathing her in a luminous lavender-tinted glow. Every puff of the scented breeze showered her with flower petals. A fountain gurgled in the courtyard.

She got up, stretched and climbed up to the terrace that over-looked the sea. The breeze blew her hair back and fluttered her crumpled linen dress. The ancient villa was built right on the edge of a sea cliff that overlooked the colorful, gorgeous scenic town of Positano, which clung to the side of the stunning Amalfi Coast. The sea was an endless, aching blue. Puffy clouds floated in the afternoon sky. Behind her, the courtyard was a mass of lemon and orange trees, their tender, pale new leaves fluttering in the breeze.

It should be easier to breathe here. Her happiest memories were in this place. But she'd had fantasies of showing this place to Vann. A lovers' paradise.

That was uniquely depressing right now.

To think that she'd come to Positano to cheer herself up. The Palazzo Valente in Florence was magnificent and beautiful, but too grand in scale for a single woman to rattle around in. It was made for a dynasty. She should probably sell it to some big sprawling family. Being alone in it felt like a personal failure.

But one thing at a time. There was so much to stress about. Her broken heart, her hurt pride, her damaged dignity, her trashed career, her crushed hopes. Whether anyone on earth would ever want to hire her again. She could take her pick of disasters.

But right now, her main challenge was just remembering how to breathe.

She hadn't known how attached to the family fantasy she'd actually become. Initially she'd done it for Mom, of course. Asking Sophie to approach Malcolm had been Mom's final attempt to heal that ancient wound. Sophie respected that, and had wanted to honor it.

But it had backfired in such a spectacular way. She'd been publicly rejected, in every way. By her father, her lover, even her workplace. Humiliated, disgraced, banished.

It had been too much to hope for. The family she'd hoped to join. The man she'd hoped to marry. She'd fallen like overripe fruit for the happy daydream of Sophie and Vann, blissful together. Sprinkle on some more fantasy ingredients: Malcolm welcoming her, wanting to know her. Cousins Drew and Ava drawing her into their inner circle. The noise and laughter of a big extended family. Love and sex and babies. Life's adventures and milestones, all faced together with a partner. Growing old together, hand in hand.

Right. She'd abandoned Rule Number One. She'd known it back in her smarter days, but love had made her willfully forget it. The more attractive the man, the more fatal the flaw. And setting her up to get destroyed by Malcolm—hell, damn.

A flaw just couldn't get more fatal than that.

She'd blocked all her Maddox Hill contacts on social media, and changed her phone number. This increased her isolation, but seeing online gossip about her professional reputation was more than she could bear right now.

Staring at the beautiful sunsets over the sea just reminded her of Mom, on the terrace every evening, pining for Malcolm. Letting all of her other chances at love and marriage pass her by, one after the other.

And here she was, Vicky Valente's luckless daughter, staring dolefully at the sunset all alone. History was repeating itself.

But no. Screw those bastards. She wouldn't give into it. They could sit on it and spin. The whole stupid pack of them. Fate, destiny and all the rest.

She was changing this story, and she'd start by taking better care of herself. Buying some decent food, cooking it with care. Treating herself more tenderly. She'd give a damn about Sophie Valente, even if no one else did.

She collected her canvas shopping bags, slipped on her sneakers and headed out to pick up some basic ingredients for quick, tasty, extremely easy meals. Three stops would do the job— the fruit and veggie place, the deli for cheese, cured meats and a bottle of wine, and the butcher's shop. Operation Self Care had begun.

Usually when she was in Italy, she loved the intimacy of shopping in places where she was recognized by all the shopkeepers. Today, it was salt in the wound. Three different worried old ladies fussed over her and tried to tempt her with samples of this or that. Signora Ippolita, the butcher's wife, even insisted on wrapping up a thick Florentine steak for her, despite her protests that it was too much for a single person to eat.

She stopped for a moment outside, to rearrange the contents of her bags. When she looked up, she saw Vann across the road.

She dropped the bags. The wine bottle clanked on the cobblestones, and began rolling noisily downhill. Vann was still there. He was not a dream, or an apparition.

Vann intercepted the wine bottle before it could roll any farther. He picked it up and brushed it off as he walked toward her. "Sophie," he said quietly.

"What are you doing here?" she demanded. "How did you find me?"

"I had to see you," he said. "I've been looking for you for weeks."

"*Ehi!* Onofrio!" Ippolita poked her head out the door and bawled for her husband. "Get out here! There's a man bothering Signorina Sofia!"

"*Che cosa?*" Onofrio, a tall, burly guy with a blood-smeared apron stretched over his large belly, stepped out onto the street, holding a huge meat cleaver in his hand. "Signorina Sofia, *va tutto bene*? Is this idiot bothering you?"

Sophie gave the older couple a reassuring smile. "Don't worry," she soothed. "He isn't a problem for me."

"I could chase him away," Onofrio offered. "Put the fear of God into him."

"Or chop a few parts off," Ippolita offered. "If he's the one who made you look so sad."

"I'm fine," she assured. "It won't be necessary to chop anything off." She held out her hand for the wine bottle. "I'll take that back now."

Vann gave it to her. She tucked it into a shopping bag and picked them up.

"Can I carry those for you?" he asked.

"No, thank you." She turned back to wave at the butcher and his wife.

"Everything's fine," she reassured them with another smile. "Really. *Buona sera.*"

He fell into step beside her as she walked up into the big wooden door that opened into the villa. She glanced back, and noticed that Onofrio and Ippolita were still standing on the street outside their shop, watching her anxiously. Three or four other people in the square had also taken notice.

She cursed under her breath, held out the bags. "Hold these while I get my keys."

He silently did so. When the door swung open, she gestured impatiently for him to enter.

She pulled the door shut behind them.

"Thanks for letting me come in," Vann said. "I think the butcher wanted to hack me into stewing chunks."

"You're only in here because I don't want an audience," Sophie said. "It's not for your sake, that's for sure."

She led the way through the shadowy stone arch and out into the center courtyard. Vann followed, and set the grocery bags down on the pavement next to the burbling fountain.

It was unfair, how good Vann looked in those slouchy tan cargo pants and a crumpled white linen shirt that set off his tan. His dark eyes were full of emotion that bewildered and infuriated her. After what he had done, he had no right to look at her that way.

"You're not welcome here," she told him.

"I know," he said. "Please hear me out. That's all I ask."

"I don't remember ever telling you about this place. Or giving anyone the address."

Vann's big shoulders lifted. "You told us that last day, in Malcolm's office. That you had property in Singapore, New York City, the Catskills, Florence and Positano. That, and the name Valente, was all I needed."

"And you figured I'd come here? Good guess."

"I've been to all of your houses," he said. "Staking them out. Watching for you."

That startled her. "All? You mean, you've been flying all over the world? What about your job?"

He shook his head. "That's over," he said. "I'm between jobs right now."

"So he really did fire you," she said. "Seems like your time would be better served job hunting than chasing around after me. I'm sure you wouldn't want my criminal taint to wear off onto you. Hardened felon that I am."

"No," he said. "Malcolm knows it wasn't you."

She froze in place. Any news that good had to be a trap. Some fresh new cruelty.

"How on earth could that be?" she asked. "They were so sure."

"Your name has been cleared. I wanted you to hear it from me. I also thought you should know that Malcolm feels guilty as hell about what he said to you."

She crossed her arms over her chest. "So he should. How did all this come about?" She kept her voice cool and remote.

"It was the videos," he explained. "That girl who sent you to Malcolm's room? She was on their team. The thieves' team, I mean. Tim and Rich Bryce hired her. Bryce was selling the IP, and setting you up to take the fall. The girl you saw had to get you into position outside Malcolm's room at that exact time. Inside the room was another woman, already dressed up like you. They deepfaked your face onto that woman's image. Rich is a special-effects guy. But I don't think it's that hard to do anymore, even for laymen."

"Ah," she said slowly. "So when I found Julie in my room

that first night, she was checking out my wardrobe. I remember that she dropped her phone when I came in. She must have been taking pictures of all my stuff."

"Yes," Vann said. "After you left, I studied the videos until I finally saw it. The body double's boobs were spilling out of her dress. Her wrap closed at her waist."

"I see," Sophie said slowly, putting her hand over her heart. "So. Saved by the scar. Again."

"Yes," he said. "Malcolm was mortified."

"Good," she said crisply. "Rightly so."

In the silence, the birds twittered madly in the lemon and orange trees. Swallows swooped and darted. She had a hot lump in her throat. She coughed to clear it.

"So, Vann," she said in a formal tone. "I'm glad to know that my reputation is intact, and that I don't need to change careers. I appreciate you telling me. But it would have been cheaper and simpler for you to send a letter to my lawyer."

"I needed to see you," he said.

She shrugged. "The feeling is not mutual." She couldn't bear to look into his eyes.

"We have something between us," he persisted.

"We did have something," she corrected. "Then you ran over it with a truck."

"Please, let me finish," he said. "I never thought you were the thief. The more time I spent with you, the more convinced I was. You would never take a sleazy shortcut. You don't have weak spots and fault lines and holes inside you. You're complete. Sure of your own inner power. You know who you are and what you can do. People like that don't lie, cheat and steal. They can't be bothered."

She let out a bark of bitter laughter. "I hate to disappoint you, but I'm not exactly a poster child for inner power and self-confidence right now."

"I told Bryce that I knew it wasn't you when we got to Paradise Point," Vann went on. "But I never imagined he was framing you for theft. I just thought, if it's not you, then you're safe. I figured, let Bryce bait all the traps he wants. You'd never take the bait. So when I told you to go to Malcolm and tell him you were his daughter, I swear, I had no idea you were in danger. By the time I knew what was going on, Malcolm had already called you into his office."

She let out a shaky breath. "Did you ever believe it was me?" she asked. "When you saw that doctored video, I mean?"

He shook his head. "Never," he said. "I was confused, but I never thought you were the thief. But I hate that I didn't come to your defense fast enough. If I'd been smarter and quicker, if I'd caught the detail of the scar in time, I could have spared you all that pain. I'm so sorry, Sophie. Please forgive me."

Oh, no. Not again. The slightest little thing and down came the tears.

"Damn it, Vann," she snapped. "This isn't fair."

"No, it wasn't. None of it. You were treated so badly. And it just kills me."

"Well." She sniffed back her tears with a sharp laugh. "Please, don't die. God only knows what they'd accuse me of then."

A smile flashed across his face, but he just stood there with that look on his face. Like she was supposed to pass judgment, make some sort of declaration to him.

"I don't know what you want me to say," she said. "I accept your apology. Satisfied?"

He was silent for a long moment. "No," he said.

Tension buzzed between them. He was doing it again. Playing her, with his seductive energy. After everything, he still had the nerve. It made her furious.

"I hope that doesn't mean you're hoping to get your sexual privileges reinstated," she said. "Because you'll be very disappointed."

"I want more than that," he said.

She stared at him, her heart racing. "Um…"

"What would it take to make you trust me again?" he asked.

Sophie pressed her hand to her shaking mouth. "I have no idea. I've never been hurt this badly. It's uncharted ground."

"Then let's start the journey of exploration." He sank down onto one knee. "Sophie Valente, I love you. I want to be your man. I want to marry you, have children with you, explore the world with you, grow old with you. You're the most beautiful, fascinating, desirable woman I have ever known. You excite me on every level of my being. Please be my bride, and I promise, I will try to be worthy of your trust until the day I die."

Her mouth was a helpless O of shock.

"Wait," he said, digging into his pocket. "Damn. Important detail." He pulled out a small, flat box covered with gray silk and tied with a gray silk bow. He pulled the bow loose, and opened it. "Here."

It was a stunning square-cut emerald ring, in a classic, gorgeous design, flanked by pearls and tiny diamonds, fit for a duchess or a queen.

"Oh, God, Vann," she whispered.

"I remember you saying something on the beach, about making choices, coming to conclusions," he said. "I've made my choice. I'm sure. I want you."

"But I…" Her voice trailed off. She pressed her hand over her shaking mouth.

"After I finished in New York and Singapore, I headed to Florence and staked out the Palazzo Valente for about a week," he said. "So I was walking over the Ponte Vecchio with all its jewelry shops twice a day, going to and from my *pensione*. All those jewelers on the bridge knew me by first name by the end of that week. I know it's risky, buying something so personal without getting your input, but I felt like I couldn't come here without a ring in my hand. I had to demonstrate commitment on every level. We could always get you something else if you prefer a different style or stone."

"It's…it's incredibly beautiful," she whispered. "But… I just can't…"

"Can't what? Can't trust me?" He grabbed her hand and kissed it. "Then I'll be patient. And persistent. I'll just hang around until you can. Years, if that's what it takes."

Her face crumpled.

Vann placed a tissue in her hand, but he stayed on his knees, patiently waiting. This was embarrassing. She needed so badly to be tough, and here she was, melting down.

"I'm a mass of bruises inside," she said. "I just…don't know if I can."

"I'll wait as long as it takes," he said. "My mind's made up. You're the only one for me. You're everything I could ever need or want. I'm a goner."

She laughed through her tears and tugged on his hand. "Get up, you. It makes me nervous, having you down there."

Vann rose to his feet, and without thinking, she was suddenly touching him. His arms wrapped around her, and, oh, God, it felt wonderful. A flash flood of feelings, tearing through her. It was so intense it hurt. In a good way.

After a while, she leaned against his chest, which by now was rather soggy. She felt emptied out, but not embarrassed anymore. If Vann was going to make all those fancy promises about forever, he could start proving himself by seeing her when she ugly-cried.

When the tears eased off, she felt so soft inside. Buoyant. Like she could waft up into the sky like one of those floating lanterns. Lit up, lighter than air.

She wiped her eyes again. "Got another tissue?"

Vann whipped out the pack. "As many as you need."

"Big talk, mister," she said, mopping up the mess. "I hate crying in front of people. Now you've seen me lose it, what, three times now? A record only my mom could beat."

"It's a privilege," he said solemnly. "An honor. I'll try to be worthy."

Her face crumpled again, and she covered it with the tissue. "Oh, damn."

"What? What is it?" he asked.

"Mentioning my mom," she said. "It set me off. I've been thinking so much about how she must have felt after Malcolm left her. But she had to raise a kid alone on top of it, while feeling all of that. It must have been so hard. She had to be so strong for me."

"I'm so sorry, baby." He kissed her hand again.

She blew her nose. "That day in Malcolm's office, I thought it was like a curse, and I got caught in it somehow."

"Malcolm did, too," he said. "So did I. But we broke the spell. I've been thinking about my father these last weeks. He was so defensive he alienated his wife and kid. He died like that. Cold, hard and alone. I want better than that for myself. I'll do whatever it takes. I'll learn, I'll grow. Whatever I need to do."

"Hmph." She mopped away her tears, and looked up. "Well. That's lovely to hear. I'm glad for you. I want to grow, too. But I'm not sure I'm ready to forgive Malcolm yet."

"Never mind Malcolm," Vann said. "How about me?"

She straightened up, gazing straight into his eyes. "Swear to me," she said. "Never, ever leave me in the dark about something important. Ever again. Not to protect my feelings, or to spare me hurt, or pain, or embarrassment, or fear. Not to avoid a fight. Not for any reason. You have to promise to be brave. Swear to me. On your honor."

His eyes burned with intensity. "I swear it," he said. "I'll be brave for you. But you have to swear the same thing right back to me. We'll learn to be brave for each other."

She nodded. "I swear."

Vann pulled the ring out of the box. "So you'll wear my ring? You'll marry me?"

She tried to speak, but her voice broke. She just nodded.

He slid the ring onto her finger. It fit perfectly. He kissed her hand, his lips lingering, reverent. "My love," he whispered. "My bride. Damn, Sophie. I'm so happy right now I'm scared. I mean, out of my mind scared. Like this can't possibly be true, and I'm going to wake up."

She laughed through her tears. "Aw. Do you want me to pinch you?"

The wind gusted, and wisteria blossoms swirled around them in a pale purple cloud, fluttering gently down to kiss the pavement stones around them.

"Oh, please," Vann said. "Just stop it. A shower of flower petals? That's total overkill, and it's not helping me believe that this is not a dream."

She laughed. "You have no idea what you're in for, Vann. Wait until I get you up to the bedroom with the Juliet balconies overlooking the sea and the vaulted ceilings frescoed with naked pink cherubs and chubby shepherdesses. I will show you overkill like you never imagined. Get ready, big guy."

His grin was radiant. "Cherubs, shepherdesses, angels, rainbows, unicorns, I don't care. Bring 'em on. Have at it."

"Ah...you mean now?"

He shrugged. "Anytime, anywhere. I'm all yours. Lead the way."

"Well. In that case..." She took his hand and tugged him toward the wide marble staircase that led to the upper floors. "Follow me."

"To the ends of the earth," he told her.

"How about just my bed for now? The ends of the earth can wait."

Their time in the bedroom left them exhausted and famished, which turned Sophie's thoughts to the goodies she'd procured on her shopping trip.

Delicious tender mozzarella knots. A wedge of aged pecorino cheese. Salt-cured smoked ham. Spicy olives. Delicious crusty bread. Ripe plum tomatoes still on the vine. Freshly grilled artichokes drenched in lemon and olive oil. Cherries, those fat shiny deep red ones. A bottle of good red wine. And Signora Ippolita's thick Florentine beef steak.

By the time the wine was poured and the table laden with the rest of their meal, Vann had finished grilling the steak. It was resting on a platter, seared to perfection. Vann served them each a big, juicy pink-tinged chunk of it, and they fell to. Food had never tasted so wonderful.

They were just starting to slow down when she heard a rhythmic buzzing sound. A text message notification. Not her phone. It came from under the table.

Vann fished his phone out from the pocket of his cargo pants. "Sorry, I'll turn it off. Just let me see if—whoa, wait. It's Malcolm."

Sophie was startled. "But didn't he fire you? Why is he texting you?"

"He did fire me, but he…wait. Hold on." He read the text. "Oh, God, he's here."

"Here meaning…where?"

"In Italy," Vann said glumly. "On his way down from Rome to Positano right now. To see you."

"Me?" Her voice broke off into a squeak.

"Yes. Evidently Drew and Zack have been passing along my progress reports. I can hardly blame the old man for wanting to see you, but his timing sucks. I wanted you all to myself for a while."

Sophie wiped her mouth, her heart thudding. "What does he say?"

"Oh, he's just busting my balls." He held his phone out. "Here, read it. Be entertained."

Sophie scrolled through the long message.

Vann. Twelve hours of silence means one of two things. A) You found Sophie, she spit in your eye and you have thrown yourself off the sea cliff in despair, or B) You found Sophie, she fell prey to your slick line and you are taking advantage of the situation like the dirty dog that you are. Ava and I will soon arrive in Positano. In the case of option A, we will make arrangements for your broken body to be sent home for burial. Otherwise, you and Sophie will join us for dinner tomorrow at eight, at Buca di Bacco.

I await confirmation.

Sophie blew out a sharp breath. "Oh, my God."

"And so it begins," Vann grumbled. "Ball-breaking of monumental proportions. My own fault for losing my temper. He asked me to tell you that he hoped you'd give him a second chance, but I was so pissed I told him I wasn't his errand boy and he could tell you himself. So that's exactly what he did. Now here he is."

She couldn't help laughing at the chagrin on Vann's face. "Well, wow," she murmured. "I'm touched that he cared enough to come all this way."

"Oh, yes," Vann said. "He cares. But he used me first. Shamelessly. He bided his time and monitored my progress while I hauled ass all over the globe, the sneaky old bastard. You wanted family? You've got it now, by the truckload. You will now have the unique pleasure of Malcolm's advice, opinions and judgment about every single aspect of your life going forward. Lucky, lucky you." Then his eyes widened.

"What?" she demanded. "What's that face all about? Is something wrong?"

"It just hit me," he said, his voice hollow. "Malcolm Maddox is going to be my father-in-law. God give me strength."

"Oh, you poor thing. How will you manage, I wonder." She set down her wineglass and selected a plump, gleaming cherry. He watched, fascinated, as she slowly ate it.

"Sophie Valente, you are a dangerous woman," he said, his voice a sensual rasp.

"Probably," she said. "But if you're afraid…if you just can't face it…it's not too late to reconsider."

He shook his head. "You're wrong," he said. "It was too late from the first moment I saw you. My fate was sealed in a heartbeat."

The energy between them made her face heat up.

Vann reached for the phone without breaking eye contact. "Let's wrap this up so I can turn this thing off. So? Do you forgive Malcolm? Your call. No judgment either way from me."

Sophie pondered the question. "Tonight, I think I could forgive just about anything of just about anybody."

"Lucky Malcolm," he said. "So. I'm confirming the dinner reservation?"

"Yes."

Vann tapped the screen. Okay. Option B, duly confirmed, he typed. He thumbed the phone off, and placed it facedown on the table. "And now, I've got you all to myself until eight o'clock tomorrow evening. Malcolm can't bother us until then."

Sophie pushed her chair back, and rose to her feet, licking the cherry juice off her fingers, then slowly running her hand down the front of her dressing gown until the pressure loosened the knot of the silken tie. She spread it open, displaying herself to him.

"We should use the time well," she said. "So? Take advantage of the situation. Make me fall prey to your slick line. Lay it on me, you bad, seductive bastard."

"Oh, man," he said hoarsely, staring at her naked body. "You're so gorgeous. I still can't believe this is real."

She held out her arms. "Then get over here right now, and let me prove it to you."

* * * * *

Tall, Dark And Off Limits

Dear Reader,

I go for stories where the hero and heroine have been secretly crushing on each other for years. Add the lure of the forbidden (she's his best friend's little sister, and his boss's niece, ooh la la!), stir vigorously and voilà, you've got *Tall, Dark and Off Limits*, book three of the Men of Maddox Hill series.

To Zack, Ava is the golden girl of Maddox Hill, while Zack is a self-made man. He's worked his way up to be the chief security officer at a globe-spanning architecture firm, and he's proud of his achievements. But with Ava, he feels like a tongue-tied, overgrown soldier boy.

When Ava needs help with a security problem, Zack is as stiff and forbidding as he is gorgeous, but his protective instincts kick instantly into high gear. Is it an opportunity to break down the wall between them...or a powder keg destined to explode? Neither can resist finding out.

I hope you like the final installment of Men of Maddox Hill. Check out book one, Drew Maddox and Jenna Somerses' story, *His Perfect Fake Engagement*. Then give book two, *Corner Office Secrets*, Vann Acosta and Sophie Valente's story, a try! And I've got a delicious new series in the works, so sign up for my newsletter at shannonmckenna.com for updates!

Enjoy Zack and Ava's story, and let me know what you think! I love to hear from readers.

Much love,

Shannon McKenna

One

"How long has this been going on?"

The fury in Zack Austin's voice rocked Ava Maddox back in her chair.

Whoa. She'd come to his office for advice from him. Insights. Ideas. Professional experience. Maybe even a little comfort and reassurance.

She had *not* come here to be scolded like a bad little kid.

"A while now." She kept her voice cool. "I've been noticing the trolls for a year now. But it really escalated in the past few weeks. I started getting worried about it after I got back from my trip to Italy. Then the last couple of weeks, they started really swarming me. Then came the hack. So call it five weeks, give or take a couple of days."

"Five weeks." Zack's voice was savage. "Five goddamn weeks, Ava. That's how long it took you to say something to me about this."

"I'm saying something now." Ava's voice sharpened, despite her best efforts to stay calm. "It started small, you understand? In the comments section of my videos and posts. Cracks about my body, sexual stuff, 'shut up and make me a sandwich' comments. It's a shame, but professional women get used to it. I haven't been hiding anything from you. I'm just cultivating a thick skin and trying not to sweat it. As one does."

"And you let it get to this point before you said something? Seriously?"

Ava opened her mouth to let him have it, and then closed it. She inhaled. Let out a slow, relaxing breath, counting down. Five. Four. Three. Two. One. *Calm.*

Maybe coming to Zack hadn't been such a great idea after all. The chief security officer of her uncle's architecture firm, Maddox Hill, was totally beside himself. And Zack Austin was intimidating even in a good mood.

Why all this thundering intensity, for God's sake? She had not seen that coming. The general sense she got from Zack could best be described as chilly disapproval. And it had been even chillier ever since that fateful night at his apartment six years ago.

The one she could barely stand to think about without writhing in embarrassment.

Now look at him. Towering over her with those burning eyes and balled-up fists, a muscle twitching in his jaw. The exact opposite of chilly. It was almost scary.

"It started out about a year ago, on complaint sites," she told him, keeping her voice low and even. "Those are websites that let people anonymously harass anyone who pisses them off. I tried to get the posts taken down, but it's almost impossible without paying them off, and I will not give those leeches money. I've talked to the police at various times, but they made it clear that there's not much they can do, since I can't prove physical danger or monetary damages."

"They don't think this indicates physical danger?" Zack stabbed his finger at the photo, which she'd taken this morning with her cell phone.

Slut was spray-painted across her garage in big red letters.

Her haters knew exactly where she lived. And they wanted her to think about that fact. All the time.

"They'll investigate, of course," Ava said. "But up until now, it's just been toxic ugliness. No crimes."

"I'll set the cybersecurity team on it immediately," Zack said. "Sophie should be back from Italy soon. I want her to make this her first priority."

"I doubt she'll have much luck," Ava said. "Whoever these people are, they're very good. I've had my computer wizard friends look into it for me, and they told me that whoever's posting always masks their IP and scrubs their metadata."

"We'll see," Zack said darkly. "We'll just see about that."

"I was trying to look on the bright side until this morning," Ava admitted. "The posts were nasty, and they're engineered for good SEO, but I have a robust online presence and lots of preexisting content, so they never floated too high in the search engine results. Then yesterday I got hacked, and my social media feeds were flooded with this crap. And this morning was the vandalism. The detective I've been in touch with suggested a security camera. Which I already have, but it hasn't been working, and I've been too busy to get it fixed. I will, of course, take care of that as soon as possible."

"You don't have a working security camera?" Zack sounded personally offended. "Good God, Ava. I'll get someone over there first thing to get a system installed."

"Please, don't worry about it. I can take care of it myself."

"You haven't been taking care of anything, from what I can see. I should have known about this from the very first rude comment that showed up. And while your brother and your uncle are away, I'm responsible for—"

"Nothing." Her voice rang out, loud enough to be heard outside his closed office door. "You are responsible for nothing, Zack. I am a grown woman. I run my own company. I have spoken to the police. They don't think I'm in danger, but they suggest that I be cautious, and I intend to follow their advice.

Coming to you was just a courtesy. I wanted you in the loop. So would Drew and my uncle, I'm sure."

He flicked through the pictures and screenshots on her tablet again. "You've given all this to the police, I assume."

"Of course," she said. "I've been documenting it from the beginning."

"Jesus," he muttered. "LyingCheatingSluts. Scammerbot. NaughtyGirlsReports. It just pisses me off that these filthy scumbags can post absolutely anything they want, with no fact checking. No accountability."

"And no recourse," she said. "The sites won't respond to emails. It's a nightmare."

Zack paused over one post, one she recognized even from a distance and at an extreme angle, one of the ones posted on the She'sASkank site. A not-so-hot picture of her, in her black-rimmed nerd girl glasses, hair wildly mussed, mouth wide-open like she was yelling at someone, with a banner across her that read, *Impostor. Fraud. Skank.*

The caption on the bottom read, "This drug-addicted hooker and known sexual deviant is trying to go legit. She's passing herself off as a PR expert. Don't fall for it. She's nothing but trash. Remember…you were warned." The Gilchrist House address for Blazon PR & Branding Specialists, along with all their contact info, was included.

The whole thing was jacking up her anxiety to stratospheric heights. She would have called her brother, Drew, or her best friend, Jenna, for emotional support, but as it happened, they were off on their blissful honeymoon. She might even have confided in her moody and difficult uncle, Malcolm, but he was gone, too, off to Italy, to get to know his recently rediscovered biological daughter, Sophie Valente. Ava didn't want to upset the dynamics of that budding relationship. In fact, she'd gone to Italy herself at the beginning, just to check Sophie out for herself, and she'd concluded that Sophie was fabulous. Strong, kind, funny, smart. A cousin well worth having. So that was all good.

That said, being alone with this problem sucked. She was looking over her shoulder, and she felt nervous and vulnerable, even inside her own locked house.

So here she was with Zack, the security expert. But the look on his face made her doubt her judgment in having told him. She'd been afraid that he would think she was blowing things out of proportion. Trying to garner attention. Suddenly, out of nowhere, she was the one trying to calm him down.

"It makes me so angry, I want to kill someone," Zack said.

"Ah… I'm gratified at your concern," she said carefully. "But don't, okay? I have enough problems right now."

Zack made an irritated sound in the back of his throat and got up, turning his back to her to stare out the window at the downtown Seattle skyline, glittering in the darkness. Which gave her the always-welcome spectacle of the amazing way his white shirt fit over his big, broad, hard-muscled back. His long, strong legs. The way his dress pants hugged his taut, magnificent backside. *Wow.*

Noticing that made her pissed at herself. Because yes, in spite of his coldness, in spite of the hard, flinty look in his gray eyes, she still found the guy ridiculously hot.

He wore his hair buzzed to almost military shortness, a nod to his tours in Iraq with the marines. That was where he'd met her brother, Drew Maddox, the firm's CEO, and Vann Acosta, the CFO. A trio of overachievers, set to take over the world together—in a good way. Drew and Vann had let their hair grow back out to civilian lengths, but not Zack. He still had that tough, sexy-soldier-boy vibe going on, and it just got to her. Every time she saw the back of his muscular neck and his thick scrub brush of shiny brown hair fading to stubble on his nape and ears, she imagined how it would feel to touch it.

She'd bet it would feel both crisp and soft against her fingertips. Delicate friction.

But she'd never made any headway in charming the guy.

Maybe that was why she had such an outsize crush on him. How kinky and self-defeating was that.

And the insanity of that night six years ago didn't help. She still couldn't believe she'd gone to his apartment. He'd mixed up a pitcher of margaritas, and she had pounded those until she got up the nerve to throw herself at him. Tried to kiss him.

That was as far as she remembered. She'd woken up in his bed the next morning, fully clothed, a blanket laid over her. Head splitting. He'd brewed coffee, left a bottle of Advil on the counter next to it and gone to work. No word, no note, no call. No clue.

Zack had never said a word about it. And in six long years, she still hadn't worked up the nerve to ask him what the hell had happened that night. It was anybody's guess.

No wonder he was cold. Disapproving. God knew what he must think of her.

She had tried for years to convince herself that Zack just wasn't her type. Not mentally, not emotionally, even physically. He was too damn big, for one thing. Rough features, big head, broad face, square jaw. That deep, scratchy voice, usually barking orders to someone. Pale gray eyes, sharp and electric, and narrowed to suspicious slits, or at least they were whenever she was around. A grim, sealed mouth. She had seen him smile before. Just not at her. He had a gorgeous smile.

Even so, with his crooked, bumpy nose and the diagonal white slash through one of his thick eyebrows, he looked like he should be in full body armor with an M-4 carbine slung over his shoulder. He had that rough-and-ready warrior vibe, even in a bespoke suit.

He'd made it clear that he considered her public relations and social media management for Maddox Hill to be frivolous makework. Something to keep her busy. Her uncle was the firm's founder and her big brother was the CEO, so nepotism, right? Calling her to work as a PR consultant was just throwing the little rich girl a bone. Keeping her out of trouble.

She activated the inner mantra that she always used when dealing with Zack.

Repeat after me. You do not need to prove yourself to that man.

Yup, good thing she didn't need Zack Austin's approval to do her professional thing. And to crush it, too, for that matter.

"Which detective did you talk to at the police department?" he demanded.

"I spoke to Detective Leland MacKenzie. But there's no need for you to get involved. I can handle the police."

He turned back. "I'd rather be in the loop. If this escalates, I'll want to coordinate all possible resources to go after this filthy scum."

The violence in his voice startled her afresh. "Whoa," she said. "Don't overreact."

"That trash was right outside your house last night as you slept. With nothing but a lock between him and you. What kind of locks do you have on your door?"

"There's only one, and I can't tell you off the top of my head, but it looks big and substantial," she assured him. "I'll text you a picture of it when I get home."

"You aren't going home," he said. "Not alone, anyway. That's out of the question. You can't be anywhere alone until this bastard is pulped."

Ava held up her hands. "Zack, take a deep breath."

"Do not jerk me around. I know that's your specialty, but not today."

Ava shot to her feet, stung. "My specialty? Where the hell did that come from? When have I jerked you around?"

"I'm sorry. That came out wrong. But this is dead serious, and I can't let you—"

"I know! But I'm better off handling it on my own than watching you freak out about it! Excuse me, Zack. I'm out of here."

Zack stepped between her and the exit, blocking her. "Wait."

"No." She glared up at him. Damn, the man was tall. "Get the hell out of my way, and I'll get the hell out of yours. Now would be good. Scoot over, please."

"Ava." His voice was quieter now. "No."

The sound of her name, spoken by that deep, rough voice, made her shiver. And that pissed her off even more. "It's not up to you," she snapped. "Don't force me to make a scene. It would be embarrassing for us both." She fixed him with her best sudden-death glare. "I swear, I will screech like a banshee."

Zack didn't budge. "I shouldn't have said that. It was unfair."

She let out a sharp laugh. "Ya think?"

"I apologize," he said gruffly. "It just… This situation really got under my skin."

She swallowed. "Mine, too," she admitted.

"Please," he urged. "Sit down. Please, let's talk about this like normal people."

She realized, after her butt hit the chair, that the guy had herded her smoothly right back into her seat, using she knew not what tricks of mind magic and charisma.

She clutched the arms of the chair. "I should go now."

"Please understand, I can't just let this be," Zack told her. "I might not be responsible for your choices or your behavior, but as CSO of Maddox Hill, I am responsible for your safety, and I take that responsibility seriously."

He was casting a spell on her. Those intense eyes. This close, she could see his beard shadow. If she touched the stark angles of his jaw and ran her fingers against the grain, she'd feel that fine, sandpaper rasp. Supple and hot. She had to stop this. Right now.

"Zack," she said. "It's been a long day, so be clear. Are you apologizing to me or bullying me? Because you can't seem to make up your mind."

That actually got a smile out of him, because miracles did happen. It was brief and fleeting, but she saw it, and it involved amazing dimples. Long, deep-carved dimples that accented the gorgeous lines that bracketed his mouth.

"I'm apologizing," he said. "And I'm laying down the law. Respectfully."

She snorted. "I didn't know law could be laid down respectfully. I believe that's usually done by force. Which I'm not in the mood for, if you haven't noticed."

He studied her thoughtfully, like he was pondering how best to manage her.

Her heart thudded. Because he'd smiled. Because of all this intense interest he was displaying. She was reacting to him exactly like the kind of silly, attention-hungry bubblehead he already thought she was.

Pull yourself together, girl. Stay tough.

It took all her nerve, but she manufactured a cool, remote smile and twitched the tablet back. "I'll just take that, thanks." She closed the files, slipped the tablet into her briefcase and stood. "Lay down all the laws you want. I'll get on with my day. 'Bye."

He glanced at his watch. "It's eight forty p.m. You have more day to get through?"

She shrugged. "That's nobody's business but mine."

"At the risk of being rude, it's my business now. And your agenda for the evening just changed."

She blinked at him. "Did it? Good to know."

He ignored that. "Tonight, we're going through your life with a microscope and tweezers. I want to know everyone who could be angry at you. Disgruntled employees, professional rivals, ex-boyfriends, jealous girlfriends of ex-boyfriends, rejected would-be boyfriends—the sky's the limit. Anyone who might hold a grudge. Whatever you had planned for the evening, it's off. You're not leaving my sight until we fix this."

Ava was astonished. "I beg your pardon?"

"You heard me." His eyes were like points of bright, cold steel.

She tried to breathe, but the air wouldn't go in. She had not anticipated this intense, intractable, incredibly difficult version of Zack Austin.

"Let me get this straight," she said. "You want a comprehensive list of everyone who might disapprove of me before bedtime? That's not happening."

"You piss people off that much?"

"Yes, I do," she said. "Blazon does all kinds of different work, and some of my projects are controversial. I try to make them go viral, and often I succeed. Eliciting strong emotions is my stock-in-trade. It's an unfortunate law of nature that any time you try to change anything big, someone will get upset about it. Particularly if you're a woman."

Zack looked puzzled. "Change what? I thought your job was to boost Maddox Hill's search engine optimization and raise our profile on the social media platforms. What's controversial about that?"

Oh, God, where to even begin. "Maddox Hill is just a small slice out of the pie chart of my professional activity, Zack," she explained patiently. "I'm a consultant. Blazon has many different clients. Maddox Hill is only one of them."

"Ah," he said. "I did not know that."

"You learn something new every day," she said. "If you pay attention."

His eyes were locked with hers. The seconds ticked by. She held the connection.

"I'm paying attention now." He sat down at his desk and folded his arms, leaning toward her. "Tell me about the rest of the pie. Slice by slice. Go back as far as you can remember."

"We'd be here until tomorrow morning, and we'd have only just begun," Ava warned him. "I've got a lot of stuff happening. Blazon is a boutique branding and marketing company, so every project is different. We tell stories about products or services, in whatever manner or on whatever platform resonates with the target audience. We also design trade show exhibits.

An offshoot of a job I had a few years ago. I'm still partnered with the people who produce and deliver the physical booths. But my real love is making the videos. That's what I enjoy the most, and what I want to focus on."

"Like the videos you made for Jenna, for Arm's Reach?"

Ava was startled that he knew about those videos. She'd made them to help her best friend and now sister-in-law, Jenna, an engineer who designed cutting-edge prosthetic arms. "Exactly. They're becoming more like documentary films. I'm thinking of hiring more staff so that I can concentrate on that. When this troll problem is solved, of course."

"How many of these video projects have you done?"

She shrugged, trying to count. "I don't know," she said. "At least six or seven the past year or so. Maybe fifteen more in the three years before that."

He tapped his fingers against the desk, considering options. "We're going to need to get some dinner," he said. "Shall I order in, or do you want to go out?"

Ava realized something all at once. She'd had that sour, heavy feeling inside her for so long now. Whatever else she might be doing during the course of her day, she was also simultaneously worrying about her online haters and their toxic hostility. The anger, frustration, intimidation…it was like a cold rock inside her. Weighing her down.

But since she'd been in this room with Zack, she hadn't felt that cold weight inside. Not even a little bit. She'd had all the feels, for sure. But not that one.

And this dizzy, dangerous buzz was way more fun.

That did not, however, mean she had the nerve to hang out with Zack Austin in the Maddox Hill building all night, in his office, with darkness and silence all around.

"Let's go out," she said. "We can talk at the restaurant."

"Fine. Do you have any preferences? Italian, steakhouse, barbecue, sushi, fusion?"

"Anything is fine," she said. "Surprise me."

He hit his intercom. "Amelia? Are you still there?"

"Just heading out," his administrative assistant said through the speaker.

"Before you go, could you make a last-minute dinner reservation for two? Nearby. Something quiet, preferably with booths. We're ready to go now."

"I'll see what I can do," Amelia told him.

"Thanks." He put the phone down and met her gaze again. "So? Make the call."

"What call?" she asked.

His brows came together. "To cancel your evening plans."

She almost laughed. Her evening plans had involved going back to the Blazon office at Gilchrist House to take care of some final paperwork for the trade show and calling a car to take her home. Then maybe some yogurt and a piece of fruit, and she'd at least try to get some sleep. She probably wouldn't succeed, but hope sprang eternal.

And Zack thought she was going out clubbing in a sequined gown. Wild thing.

She'd almost prefer he keep thinking that, but she didn't have the energy to lie.

"No plans," she admitted.

His eyes narrowed for a moment before he spoke. "Good."

The rough satisfaction in that single word felt like a physical touch. It set off a million tiny fireworks inside her. Fizzy excitement, keeping bad feelings at bay.

Damn. It was just body chemistry. A cheap trick. Endorphins buzzing through her body. It was an absolutely terrible idea. She'd end up feeling worse before she was done.

But in Zack's current bulldog mood, she couldn't shake him off anyhow. So what the hell?

She might as well indulge.

Two

"No wine," Zack told the waiter brusquely, realizing too late how stuffy and uptight that sounded. "For me, of course," he said to Ava. "Feel free to have some. I never drink when I'm working."

"Good for you." She smiled up at the waiter, whose name was Martin, according to the tag on his shirt. "I'll have a glass of red wine, please."

"I have a beautiful 2016 Romanée-Conti that's open," Martin told her.

"Sounds lovely." She gave the waiter that trademarked blinding smile that brought men to their knees. Martin stumbled off, probably to walk into walls and tables.

And Zack just sat there, tongue-tied. When Ava Maddox was around, his foot always ended up stuck so far into his mouth, he needed surgical intervention to get it out. She was giving him that look. Big, sharp blue eyes that missed nothing. So on to him.

The restaurant had low light and a hushed ambience, and they were in the back, tucked in a wood-paneled corner booth.

Now the challenge was to kick-start his brain into operation, instead of just staring at how beautiful she was in the flickering candlelight.

She just waited, patiently. Like she was all too used to men losing their train of thought as soon as they made eye contact with her. Like she was accustomed to cutting the poor stammering chumps some slack while they pulled themselves together.

Her cell rang, and she gave him an apologetic glance when she saw the display. "Gotta take this. One sec." She tapped the screen and held it to her ear. "Ernest? Thanks for getting back to me. Are you still in the office?... Yeah? Could you get a cab to swing by the Mathesson Pub and Grill on your way home?... Yeah, I need my laptop, the pink one with the collage cover. I'm talking to the Maddox Hill CSO about the online harassment...yeah, I know, but still...uh-huh. Okay, thanks. You're my hero. Later, then."

She laid the phone down. "Ernest is my assistant. He'll bring my computer here so I can show you the master list of the last few of years' worth of Blazon's projects."

"I'm surprised you don't have your laptop with you at all times," he said.

"I usually do," she said. "But I had every intention of going back to Gilchrist House tonight. I have a crazy weekend coming up. Ernest and I are flying down to the Future Innovation trade show in Los Angeles tomorrow. It's a very big deal."

Zack couldn't hide his disapproval. "Traveling to Los Angeles? Going back to a deserted office late in the evening? Leaving by yourself, going home by yourself? With all this going on?"

Ava sighed. "Zack, Gilchrist House has a twenty-four-hour doorman. And I would call a car to take me from doorstep to doorstep. I'm not an idiot."

"I never suggested that you were."

"I'm not in physical danger," Ava assured him. "Really. This is just, you know, the new normal. The incivility of our modern electronic age. It's ugly and unsavory, but I've got to get used to it and learn to roll with it."

"The hell you do," he said. "New normal, my ass. I'll tell you what's normal. When I find that bottom-feeding son of a bitch and grind him into paste."

Ava gave him that narrow, nervous look, which by now he recognized. It was a signal that he wasn't behaving professionally. He was too intense. Making it personal.

In a word, scaring her.

"Ah, wow, Zack," she murmured. "I'm surprised at your reaction."

"Why? This situation is a disgrace. Why should you be surprised that I'm horrified?"

Her eyes slid away. "Well, I don't know. It's just that you've never taken me seriously before, so why would you suddenly take me seriously now?"

"I'm sorry I gave you that impression," he said stiffly. "It wasn't intentional."

"Oh, don't be that way." Her tone was light. "I'm used to it. I rub a lot of people the wrong way. I'm just too much for people sometimes. Drew's always on my case about it, telling me to tone it down. And I try, I really do. But it never works. Boom, out it comes. The real Ava, right in your face."

"He shouldn't do that," Zack said forcefully.

"Shouldn't what? Sorry, but I'm not following you."

"Drew. He shouldn't be on your case. He shouldn't tell you to tone it down."

Her eyes were big. "Ah… I didn't mean to get you all wound up."

"You're goddamn right, I'm wound up. I'm freaking furious, Ava. That sewer-rat troll who's bothering you? He doesn't have the right to even look at you. Let alone throw his filth at you. It pisses me off to see a lady treated that way. You don't deserve it."

She laughed under her breath. "Lady, hmm? That's sweet,

but I'm sure Uncle Malcolm would have something pointed to say about that characterization of me."

"Malcolm can say anything he wants," Zack retorted. "I mean it like my mom used to mean it. It has nothing to do with manners or clothes or social status or that crap. A lady is any woman who commands respect as her due. That means you. Absolutely."

Ava appeared, for once in her life, at a loss for words. She turned away, letting her hair swing forward. A silent moment passed, and it wasn't until she pulled a tissue out of her purse that he realized, to his horror, that she was crying.

"Oh, God," he said. "Was it something I said?"

"Yes, actually," she said, blowing her nose. "That was a really great thing to hear right now, Zack. After all that nasty filth that's been coming at me. So thank you for that."

"Ah, you're welcome," he said, helplessly bemused. "You sure you're okay?"

She tossed her hair back and gave him a reassuring smile. Her long black eyelashes were wet with tears all the way around those gorgeous, mascara-smudged eyes.

"I hadn't let myself feel how much the trolling bothered me," she said, wiping the smudges away. "Even though it's stupid and insignificant, it made me feel stained. Then you said just exactly the right thing. It made me feel better. Cleaner."

Huh. Talk about a lucky freak accident. Saying just exactly the right thing to make a hot, classy, fascinating woman feel better? That was something he'd never been accused of before. But whatever. He'd take it and run with it.

"I shouldn't let myself get upset," Ava went on. "It comes with the territory."

"What? Online harassment, you mean?"

"Making enemies, in general," she said. "If you try to make a difference, you're going to make a few. It's a mathematical certainty. And I like it when people like me. I really try to be everyone's friend. I try to be thick-skinned, but this time it got to me."

"So this has happened before?" He was freshly horrified.

She smiled at him, sniffling into her tissue. "On a much smaller scale," she said. "It's never been quite this bad. It started about four years ago, while I was working on the Colby Hoyt thing."

"Name sounds familiar," he said.

"It got a lot of press. He got pushed down the stairs and broke his back. He accused his girlfriend, Judy Whelan, of pushing him, and she ended up in prison for assault, but no one knew the truth, because she had brain damage that impaired her memory, inflicted by Colby himself. His lawyers flattened Judy's public defender, and it all went to hell. But one of Judy's girlfriends was a college roommate of mine, and came to me to help get the word out. We got it all over the internet. Public interest spiked, the case was reopened and, long story short, Judy's free and Colby's in for fifteen to twenty. And a bunch of angry trolls on anonymous message boards thought that Colby was really hard done by. They like to tell me how they feel. Often, and in very strong, descriptive terms."

"I remember Hoyt," Zack said. "Spooky guy. White eyebrows and lashes."

"Yeah, that was him. That was when the trolling began in my comments sections. Then, about a year ago, Colby was up for parole, and Judy's friends and protectors were having none of that. So we pushed the video again, and his parole was denied. That was when the posts on the complaint sites started to show up. I wonder if it's connected."

"I'll be sure to look into it," Zack said as the waiter reappeared.

The guy ogled Ava's chest as he presented several plates in front of them, directing his highest-wattage smile at Ava. "Here's a sampling of our appetizers for the day. Bacon-wrapped asparagus tips deep-fried in beer batter, portobello mushrooms with three-cheese stuffing and pan-fried sage and butternut squash dumplings."

Ava stared at the tempting array of finger food, startled. "Ah, wow," she said blankly. "Are these for someone else? I don't think we ordered—"

"On the house," Martin assured her. "Our treat."

"Why, thank you," Ava said graciously. "That's so lovely. They look delicious."

Zack followed Martin's retreat with unfriendly eyes. "Does that happen a lot?"

"You mean free food, raining down from the sky?" Ava shrugged airily and popped a squash dumpling into her mouth. "Sometimes. It happens. These are really good. Try one before I eat them all."

The disgruntled sound that came out of him made her hide a smile behind the napkin she was using to dab at her mouth. So he was entertaining her. Like a vaudeville act.

This was so tricky. He had been walking this tightrope for years. Ever since he met her, back when she was barely more than dewy-eyed jailbait. His best friend's little sister, always there at the parties and the holidays and the barbecues. The perfect little golden-haired princess, stealing the show.

She just seemed like a different type of creature to him. Born rich, and he hadn't been, but it was more than just that. It was like the fairies had flocked to her christening, like in that old Disney cartoon, and loaded her up with gifts. She was smart, classy, talented, well-spoken, funny. She had a gorgeous body. She sparkled; she shone. Waiters brought her unsolicited bacon-wrapped batter-fried asparagus tips, for God's sake.

And she was so damn beautiful, he had to struggle to keep his jaw off the floor. He'd found himself catching flies more than once. Gawking at her, like the overgrown West Virginia farm boy that he was inside, in spite of the fancy suit and the corporate title. So intensely aware of his big, crooked nose, broken in a bar fight. The knife scar through his eyebrow. Souvenirs of when he was a runt getting his ass kicked. To say nothing of the battle scars from Iraq. Not that she'd judge him for that, of course. Drew had scars, too. But it was just one more thing that set her apart from him. Worlds apart.

She always seemed defensive with him. Maybe it was that night six years ago, when she'd gotten drunk at his place and then cried herself to sleep in his arms.

He still thought of those hours he'd spent, just gazing at her sleeping face.

She was probably embarrassed. Angry at herself for the lapse in judgment.

And he needed to focus on something external, something that wasn't Ava herself. He pulled his notepad out of his bag. "Let's get started. I want you to list all the—"

"Ava! There you are, hiding in the back!" It was a young, skinny guy with white-blond hair and perfectly round glasses that gave him an owl-like, steampunk appearance. Had to be Ernest, the assistant.

Ernest placed a shiny pink laptop that was covered with a laminate mosaic of photos on the table and leaned over to sniff the appetizers. "Mmm, those look great."

"Go ahead and try one," Ava suggested. "They're delicious."

Ernest popped a fried asparagus tip into his mouth and sighed with delight as he chewed it. "Oh boy. I think I need a whole plate of these. It's a cholesterol bonanza."

"Do it, with my compliments. Put it on my card," Ava offered. "Least I can do."

"Ooh! Thanks! I will!" Ernest tried a dumpling. "Wow, yum. So, am I swinging by your place at six thirty?"

"For what? Going where?" Zack asked.

Ernest turned to him. "The airport," he said. "We're flying down to LA for the Future Innovation Trade Fair. The Bloom brothers have been nominated for the grand prize for their new soil inoculation antidesertification process. Half a million bucks. It would be a total kick in the butt if they won."

"Let's do seven a.m.," Ava said.

"No," Zack said. He turned to Ernest. "Never mind the

pickup. I'll bring her directly to the airport, and we'll meet you there."

Ava's face was bewildered. "Excuse me? You'll do *what*?"

"You're not staying in your house alone tonight," he informed her. "It's not safe."

"Oh, really? Where will you be?" Ernest's eyes lit up with speculative curiosity.

"We're still working that out," Zack said.

"*I'm* working it out, Zack," she said crisply. "Last I checked, I was still making all these decisions for myself."

"You tell him, Av! Rawr!" Ernest's eyes zipped back and forth between them.

Ava made a frustrated sound and flapped her hand at him. "Go order your food, Ernest. I'll call you in the morning and let you know what's going on."

"Will do."

But Ernest just stood there expectantly. The sparkle in his eye annoyed Zack. This was not a cage fight for this bozo's entertainment. "Good night," Zack said pointedly.

Ernest looked crestfallen. "See you in the morning!" He waggled his eyebrows at Ava. "Have fun!"

Ava put her fingers to her temples once he was gone. "Damn," she said sourly. "That I did not need, Zack."

"You still think it's okay to just run around like everything's normal?" Zack asked. "Working late, coming home late, sleeping alone, flying all over the country—"

"This is my work!" she shot back. "I will not let some mouth-breathing troll knock me off my stride! And with all due respect, I won't let you knock me off it, either!"

"So I'm in the same category as the mouth-breathing trolls?"

She rolled her eyes. "Stop it. You know perfectly well I didn't mean that. But I will continue to conduct my life exactly the way I want to. And I don't appreciate—" She cut herself off as the waiter approached.

"The rib eye for you, sir, and the pistachio-crusted salmon for you!" Martin placed the entrées in front of them with a flourish.

Zack waited until the waiter was gone before he went on. "You'll have a bodyguard 24-7 until I get to the bottom of this. But I can't pull that out of thin air at such short notice, so tonight and tomorrow, you're stuck with me. Give me the flight info so I can pass it on to Amelia. She needs to book me on your flight ASAP."

"Stuck with you? You want to fly down to LA with me? For real?"

"In normal times, the obvious solution would be for you to stay with your uncle out on Vashon Island," Zack said. "He's got good staff and a very good security system. But he's not here, and neither are Jenna or Drew. So I'm stepping up."

Zack suddenly realized that he had no clue if Ava might have a boyfriend who would not welcome his nighttime presence in her house. "Unless, ah…unless you have some other, uh, friend," he said stiffly. "That could come to stay with you. Overnight."

"No, I don't want to burden any of my friends with this," she said. "Other than you, of course. I was afraid of looking like a whiner and a wuss."

"You are neither," he told her. "On the contrary. So? Your place or mine?"

He instantly regretted the words. They sounded too suggestive. Fortunately, Ava didn't react. She was busy shaking her head back and forth like she couldn't stop herself.

"Zack, no. I'm going home. To my life. Besides, you're Maddox Hill's chief security officer. You're a busy guy with a complicated job, and you do not have time to do close protection work for me."

"I can make that call for myself," Zack said.

"I appreciate your zeal, I really do. We'll have a meeting after I get back from Los Angeles, and we'll get to work on my list then. Deal?"

"You are not staying alone tonight. End of story."

"You're not getting it." Ava shook her head, frustrated. "It's not up to you."

"I cover you until I have your security people in place, or I'll be forced to call Drew right now and tell him the situation," Zack told her. "He's in, let's see, is it Bali? I can't even remember. Then I'll call Malcolm in Italy and tell him, too. I don't know the time differences off the top of my head, and I really don't care. This is an emergency."

Ava's mouth dropped in outrage. "No way," she said. "You wouldn't."

"Oh, yeah." Zack brought out his phone and pulled Drew's number up onto the display. He let his finger hover over Call. "Your decision," he told her.

"But you can't! They'll freak out and come rushing home!"

"Rightly so," he said. "I would. If it was my sister, or my niece. In a heartbeat."

"But this is Drew's honeymoon!" she said. "And Malcolm's finally getting to know Sophie. It's important! I don't want to interrupt that!"

"Yeah, it would be a big shame," he agreed.

"You're jerking me around," she said.

"Maybe. But I'll let your family weigh in, if that's what it takes to keep you safe. We're all in this together."

Ava looked outraged, but that was just too bad. Her safety was more important than her approval.

The deathly silence stretched on and on. Ava grimly tucked away her salmon and salad, ignoring his existence. He kept himself busy with his steak.

That was only good for a few minutes, though. When the busboy whisked away their plates, there was nothing to focus on but the conversation she refused to have.

Martin reappeared, this time bearing a long, oblong platter with several bite-size portions of various desserts. "I thought you might like a sampling of our dessert menu," he told Ava. "Chocolate rum soufflé, apple tart with brandy sauce, key lime pie with shortbread crust, salted-caramel custard brownie cake and panna cotta with berries."

"Oh, boy," she murmured. "Martin, you are a very bad boy."

"I do try." Martin fluttered his lashes modestly. "Enjoy."

When Martin was gone, Ava took the dessert fork and delicately scooped up a bite of the salted-caramel custard brownie. She closed her eyes as she savored it.

His lower body tightened up in response. Her eyes fluttered open, and she smiled at him. Those bright, mysterious eyes, taunting him. Owning him.

"Well?" she said. "You're not leaving me alone with this temptation, are you?"

"Martin didn't bring those sweets out here for me," he said.

"We're in this together. Isn't that what you said?" She nudged the tray his way, then stabbed a square of caramel brownie cake and held it out. "It takes energy to shove people around. It's going to be a long night, buddy. Do some carb-loading."

He blew out a sigh of frustration. "Goddamn it, Ava."

Her lips curved in a smile that made his heart speed up. "Come on, tough guy," she murmured. "Better take your medicine. You're going to need it."

Three

Ava's hands shook as she shoved her things into her travel case.

Damn. What was wrong with this picture? So many things, she couldn't keep them all straight. She should not let Zack win so easily. His administrative assistant had already booked him a flight to LA tomorrow, with her and Ernest. He'd booked a room at the hotel where they were staying. There was no way to stop him from climbing all over her life.

And he had the advantage, holding the threat of calling Uncle Malcolm and her brother over her. While she was at a huge disadvantage, still not knowing what the hell had really happened on the night of the margaritas.

It made her feel so embarrassed. On top of being shaky and fluttery after that intense, sexually charged dinner date. To say nothing of weeks of worrying about vicious trolls trashing her professional reputation. She was a mess.

Zack's expression tended toward grim at the best of times, but his face had gone thunderous when she showed him the ugly graffiti spray-painted on the garage door.

Of course, a compulsory lecture followed about the complete

inadequacy of her door locks and her lack of an alarm system. No surprises there. He'd also called his security staff and set a team to come and remedy that the following day. He'd called another team to work on analyzing her online harassment problem, and still a third one to set up a team of close protection agents to follow her around everywhere she went. *Yikes.*

Zack took pictures of all of it with his phone, sent them to his teams and then insisted on taking her house keys from her hand to go into her house first. He insisted on preceding her into every room.

Now, as she packed her bags, Zack was waiting out there in her living room. Probably wandering around, cataloging all the other security breaches in her house. While she stood here with her hand in her lingerie drawer, pulling out sexy, silky nighties and little bits of things with spaghetti straps and lace.

Oh, hell no. Ava whipped her hand out of that drawer as if the garments had burned her and went rummaging into the bag she'd stuffed in the closet, the one she meant to take down to the charity clothing drive. In the bottom of that bag was a set of thick fleece pajamas in hideous red plaid. It was two sizes too big and had been a Secret Santa gag gift from one of her friends. She practically swam in the thing.

Those were the pajamas for Zack Austin's house. They projected a loud, blaring signal: *Don't even think about sex. Because I'm not thinking about it. Nope, not me.*

Somehow, she got her stuff for tonight into the travel bag, and the clothes she was wearing tomorrow to the airport. Thank God she'd already packed for the trip to Los Angeles, because she would have bungled that completely in her addled state.

She gathered up the last-minute electronic bits and pieces that had to go—phone, tablet, laptop, chargers. Toiletries for tonight, since a guy with a buzz cut wasn't likely to have hair-care stuff. She took some clips and pins and scrunchies, to cover any possible hair whims for tomorrow. Then she started out into the living room, and just stopped.

Trying to slow down the frantic gallop of her heart. Calm. Collected. Adult.

She walked in to find Zack standing at the fireplace, holding her mother's high school graduation portrait in his hands. He lifted the photo, turning to her. "Your mom?"

"Yes, that's her."

He set it down carefully. "You look exactly like her." He bent to peer more closely at Mom and Dad's wedding photo. "And Drew looks just like your dad."

"So they tell me," she said, rolling her travel bag and suitcase into the living room. "It's hard for me to see. Have you finished compiling the list of all my security fails?"

"Don't be so defensive, but yes, pretty much." He sounded faintly amused. "We'll leave a set of your keys at my house for pickup, and tomorrow a team will come in here to solve them all."

"I could handle this myself, you know," she told him.

Zack gave her a level look. "Ava, this is what I do. Just let me do it."

She shrugged. "Fine, I guess. I appreciate the thought. But you're overdoing it."

"Not at all." He looked up at her Chihuly glass vase, perched on a high shelf on her bookcase. "This place really looks like you."

"What does that means? Aside from the poor security, of course."

Zack looked trapped. "I don't really know what I meant, so I shouldn't have said it in the first place. I guess, colorful, eclectic, creative, chaotic?"

"Chaotic, huh? Cluttered, you mean. That's what Uncle Malcolm says."

Zack slanted her an ironic look. "I'm not criticizing you. Not in the least. I wish you wouldn't fight me about this."

"I'm in the habit, I suppose," she said. "I fight Uncle Malcolm and Drew all the time. I can't afford to back down for one second or those two would just roll over me like a tank. So I've got this knee-jerk defensive reaction going. I know it's a pain in the butt."

"You could try just trusting me," he suggested. "I promise. It's not a trap."

She thought about that night six years ago. That morning hangover in his downtown apartment when she woke and found him gone.

The confusion and shame. The agonized curiosity.

And yet, at the restaurant, he'd called her a lady. Deserving of respect. Huh.

"My house is more secure than yours," Zack said. "That's the only reason I wanted to drag you out there tonight. I would have stayed here, if you preferred to be in your own space, but I need to pack for the trip to LA, so there's that. Maybe I am overdoing it, and I'm sorry to inconvenience you. But I will not leave you unprotected. I just can't do it."

Ava was disarmed by the intensity in his voice. "It's okay," she said. "I'm packed up for tomorrow already. I guess your place makes more sense."

He gave a brief, fleeting smile and grabbed her bags to haul them out to his car.

She tried to analyze the conflicting emotions inside her, all fighting for airtime, as she followed him out. It was nice that he cared. Nice to feel safe. No doubt about it.

But giving him his way like this…it set a bad precedent. But a precedent for what?

Her mind was running down some very dangerous paths.

When Zack was a kid, his granddad had been a local expert at breaking horses to ride. Granddad was famous in the area for his technique, the main ingredient of which was patience. He'd taught Zack his secrets, which mostly consisted of being able to let go of his own agenda and adjust completely to the animal's wavelength. To be prepared for hours to pass just waiting. Force had no part in the process. Attunement was everything.

God knew, Ava Maddox was no horse. She was proud, touchy, high-strung. But if he tried to manipulate her with force, he was going to get hammered. Eventually she was going to get sick of him holding her brother's and uncle's interference over her. She'd tell him to piss off and do his worst. At which point he wouldn't be able to protect her at all.

Patience was the only way. But having patience presupposed confidence.

With Ava, he was anything but.

The drive to his house was very quiet, giving him plenty of time to second-guess himself and quietly freak out about things he couldn't control or change. Now that he'd seen her house, he could imagine what she'd think of his own. Her place was an explosion of color and images. Provocative works of art hung on the wall, and she probably had strong, smart, articulate opinions about every one of them. Corkboards with mosaics of photos, drawings, brochures, maps, Post-it notes, quotes. Wood carvings, wind chimes. Colorful rugs and jewel-toned accent walls. Her quirky chairs and couches were upholstered with antiqued colored velvet and strewn with big puffy pillows in contrasting prints. Her outsize creative personality blazed from her living space like heat from a bonfire.

Ava Maddox didn't need an interior designer to decorate her space. It came from directly inside her head. He could wander around for hours, staring at the all the bits of stuff that interested and intrigued her. Wondering what she saw in it, and why.

His own house, large and comfortable though it was, was going to look as bland and dull as an unadorned shoebox to someone like her. He didn't have a zillion little conversation-starting windows into his soul to show off when she walked into it.

Nor was it like him to give a damn what people thought of his home. It was comfortable; it suited him. If it was good enough for him, it was good enough for anyone.

But this was Ava. Nothing could be taken for granted where she was concerned.

The gate to his driveway ground open. He drove up and parked in front of his house. They sat there in acutely uncomfortable silence for a moment.

Zack was the first to move, but Ava was out of the car before he had the chance to open her door for her. He took her suitcase and garment bag from the trunk. "This way."

She smiled in silent amusement as he unlocked the three different locks on the door, pushed it open and punched a code to disarm the alarm. "Wow. Secure."

"It's who I am," he said, flipping the lights on.

Ava walked in and looked around. The foyer with the thirty-foot-high solarium window and the slanted skylights was surrounded by a huge open-plan space, kitchen and dining room on one side and the sunken living room and big fireplace on the other. Huge windows lined both rooms. The living room had French doors leading out to a big flagstone patio. There were high ceilings with dark-stained wooden beams, a beige Berber rug. Big, long, soft couches that could handle his size, upholstered in plain, dark colors that didn't show dirt. Simple, plain table lamps. The main decoration for his living space was the view and the greenery outside, but that didn't register at night. His walls were mostly blank. No paintings or sculptures other than his gallery of family photos.

That was Zack Austin. Plain and utilitarian. What you see is what you get.

"Wow," she said. "Big."

"Yeah, I like my space." Growing up in a single-wide trailer would do that to a guy, especially a freakishly tall one. His head was probably still dented from all the ceilings and door frames he'd bashed it on.

She went down the steps into his living room, and Zack followed her down.

"I'll light a fire," he said.

"Please don't go to any trouble," she told him.

"No trouble at all. I make sure that a fire is always ready to light when I want one."

He knelt down, struck a match and touched it to the crumpled newspaper and wood shavings that lay under the little cone of kindling wood. Another of Granddad's tricks.

"You're right," she said as it blazed to life, crackling. "That was quick."

She moved closer to the fire, holding out her hands.

"Give me your jacket," he said. "I'll put it in the closet."

Ava shrugged off her jacket, releasing a soft, warm whiff of her incredible perfume. When he returned from the closet, she had wrapped her bright, patterned scarf around herself like a shawl and was studying his photo gallery.

"Your family, I take it," she said.

"Yeah, these are my nieces and nephew," he said, pointing. "That's Bree—she's eight. And Brody, who's almost seven. And that's little Brett. She's three. That's my younger sister, Joanna, with her husband, Rick." He pointed at another photo. "That's my mom. And that's Granddad. He passed away when I was nineteen."

She smiled at the pictures. "Your nieces and nephew are gorgeous," she said. "Do they live nearby?"

"No. I wish. They're in West Virginia. Mom's not too far from my sister. She likes being close to her grandkids. I get back to see them as often as I can."

Ava studied the entire wall and looked back at him. "What about your dad?"

"He took off not long after Joanna was born," he said. "I was about three. I barely remember him."

She had a thoughtful line between her brows. "You never looked for him?"

Zack shook his head. "I figure if someone's going that far out of his way to avoid me, I should just let him. We wouldn't have much to say to each other. Are you thinking about Sophie and Malcolm, finding each other after all these years?"

"I guess I am."

"I thought about it, too. But that's different. Malcolm didn't know Sophie even existed. My dad knew all about me. He knew where we lived. He knew my mom needed money and help to raise us. He knew all that, and he didn't step up. So fuck him."

Ava nodded. "Fair enough."

He felt suddenly awkward. "Sorry. Didn't mean to get all heavy and negative."

"You weren't," she said. "Just honest. Which I like."

Those words made his body react, which was ridiculous. It was an innocent comment, and here he was, breaking out in a sweat. Imagining how it would feel to find out more things that she liked. Everything that she liked.

Every sweet, sexy, dirty detail.

He dragged his mind back on track by sheer force of will. "I was lucky. I had Granddad. My mom's father. He more than made up for the shortfall."

Ava was moving down the wall, peering closer at another photo of Granddad.

"I bet you took that photo yourself," she said.

Zack glanced at it. "Yeah, I did. That wasn't too long before he died. I was home from Iraq on leave. How did you know I took that shot?"

"The look on his face," she said softly. "The way he smiles at you. Like he's so proud. I remember that look on my parents' faces." Her voice caught.

Damn. Now his own eyes were getting all hot and prickly. No way. Not now. He was on shaky ground as it was. He groped for the first comment that came to mind. "How about Malcolm?" he asked. "Isn't he like a surrogate dad for you and Drew?"

She let out a stifled laugh. "I suppose he is. And I know

he cares about me, but I have certainly never gotten that look from him."

Yikes. That was a can of worms. Thank God for the fire. The perfect distraction. He turned away swiftly to poke at the flames and lay a couple chunks of wood onto it.

Ava spoke behind him, still looking at the photo gallery. "When I first walked in, my sense was that your decorating scheme was a little impersonal. But that's not true. Looking closer at these photos, I see that it couldn't possibly be any more personal."

Zack was careful not to look up into her eyes. "I'm not much for decorating," he said. "And to be honest, I don't really have much to say about most of the art I come across. After all these years at Maddox Hill, I can talk intelligently about architecture, but not art. But photos of my family? Those I know are beautiful. No one has to tell me."

"Yes," she said. "That's exactly what I meant."

He was getting self-conscious. "How about I show you to your room and get you some fresh bedding? Then after, you can come have a nightcap by the fire, if you want."

"Thanks, that sounds great."

He grabbed her bags and led her down the corridor to the bedrooms, choosing the one closest to his own. "You've got your own bathroom," he told her. "I'll bring you some towels."

"I'm sorry for all the trouble," she said.

"Hey, I insisted, right? I even threw my weight around. No pity for me."

"You know what? You're absolutely right. Be inconvenienced, Zack. The more trouble I am to you, the better. I need Egyptian cotton for the sheets and at least three nonallergenic pillows. Cool-toned solid colors for the bedding, please. No busy prints."

He laughed at her. "I'm going to regret saying that to you."

"Oh, I'll make sure of it," she purred.

Oh, whoa. The husky laughter in her voice made his body tighten and throb.

Four

Every damn thing that came out of her mouth felt flirtatious.
The subtext was always, *I want to ride you off into the sunset,
you big hot hunk of burning love.*

Maybe it was just sexual deprivation. She didn't even know
how long it had been since she had sex. At all, let alone good
sex. Her last boyfriend had gotten all huffy and offended when
she wouldn't stay the night, and when she finally did give it
a shot, he'd been freaked out by her constant nightmares. As
usual. Par for the course.

At a certain point, it just got too depressing to keep track of
data like that. Better to measure life by different metrics. Concentrate on other things.

She turned her attention to his guest bedroom, which was a
pretty, harmonious room. Simple, high ceilinged, with a big,
gorgeous window that showed a broad expanse of city lights
glowing in the distance. A queen-size wooden bed dominated
the room. There was a standing mirror, an old-fashioned antique
wardrobe, a matching dark wood dresser. There was even an

old washstand with a pitcher and a washbasin. She'd bet good money that Zack Austin had not chosen those items.

Zack came back moments later with a heap of bedding in his arms and laid it on the wing-back chair. "Solid-tone slate-blue Egyptian cotton," he told her. "No busy prints."

"Thanks," she said. "You are aware, of course, that I was joking."

He grinned. "I'm not taking any chances. The thread count is high, I promise."

She rolled her eyes. "Oh, shut up."

"Here are towels for you, and take this, too, just in case." He laid a charcoal-gray fleece bathrobe down on top of the pile. "It's mine, so it'll be huge on you, but if you get cold, you can wrap yourself in it. That big front room out there is slow to heat up."

"Thank you," she said. "Very thoughtful of you."

"Now let me get this bed made," he said.

"Oh, don't be silly. I can handle making my own bed."

"I can handle it better," he told her. "I was a marine. I can make a bed as tight as a drum in record time."

"Well, damn. Don't hurt yourself. You don't have to bounce a quarter off it."

It was a pleasing spectacle, watching a big, athletic man lean and bend and twist and stretch, getting all the bedding shipshape.

"Great bedroom set," she said. "Very pretty. Did you pick out the furniture?"

He shot her a grin as he plumped up the pillows and sent them soaring up to the head of the bed. "Hell, no, as I'm sure you guessed. I flew Joanna and my mom out here when I got the place and gave them my credit card. They went hog wild. They got me the couches and chairs in the living room, the dining set, the bedroom sets. There's a kids' room, for when my nieces and nephew come to visit. Bunk beds, dressers, lamps."

"They did a great job," she said. "They must be so proud of you."

"Yeah, well. We're all proud of each other. So, have I forgotten anything, as your gracious host? Anything else you need from me?"

Loaded question. Ava looked over the bed. It looked great, with the puffy duvet, the heaped pillows at the head. *All that's missing is you stretched out in it, stark naked.*

She coughed. "Looks great," she said. "Thanks so much. You've been lovely."

"Okay, then. Come on out for a drink whenever you're ready. Would you like a glass of wine, or would you rather have a cocktail? I can make you a screwdriver, a gin and tonic. Or a margarita."

Her face flushed hot. "Um, no. Some wine would be fine."

"Red or white?"

"Red, please."

"Then I'll get out of your way and let you settle in."

When she was alone in the room, Ava sank down onto the bed, heart pounding.

Yikes. If he'd mentioned margaritas, then he had to be thinking about that night, too. That crazy, embarrassing night that made her feel so compromised and vulnerable.

She craved some kind of armor. Fortunately, she'd brought some with her. Those hideous pajamas were just the thing. Sexless, shapeless comfort. She dug into her suitcase and put on the oversize plaid jammies. Over them she layered the big gray fleece bathrobe that Zack had left for her. Fuzzy yellow house socks with plastic antislip soles completed the carefully curated look, which could only be described as "walking fuzz ball."

She came padding silently out of the bedroom and found him crouched in front of the fire, in jeans and a waffle-weave thermal sweatshirt. Looking great in them.

He turned to look. The expression in his eyes, for just an instant, looked territorial.

It was just a flash, a gut feeling, and it could be her imagination, but she sensed that he liked having maneuvered her into this. He liked having her right here, in his space, in her nightclothes. Swathed in his very own bathrobe. Under his protection.

Whew. Scary thought. But even scarier was the corollary realization.

She liked it, too.

Oh, man. This was so bad. She had to walk this back.

"The robe looks good on you," he said. "Come sit over here, close to the fire."

Ava did so, curling her feet up and accepting the goblet of dark red wine that he offered her. He opened a chest behind the couch, shook out a fluffy blanket in deep shades of burgundy and blue, and laid it over her, tucking it in on either side. "I have three of these in the chest," he confessed. "This is the first time I've used one."

"Let me guess," she said, sipping her wine. "Your mom and Joanna got you those couch throws, right?"

"You found me out," he said.

"They're gorgeous," she said, stroking them. "So soft. Cashmere?"

"I expect so." He sat down on the couch, a careful distance away from her, and they stared into the now roaring fire for a while.

"I guess we should be discussing your troll problem," he said. "But it's been a long day. I've looped in the cybersecurity team. We'll pick it up when we get back from your trade fair, after they've done some research, and dig into it then."

"Yes, I'd rather not dwell on it right now," she said. "It's been an intense day, and this time of year sucks for me even without my trolls."

She regretted the words the instant they came out of her mouth when she saw curiosity sharpen in his eyes. "Oh, yeah? Why is that?"

Damn. Why had she blurted that out? She never talked about

it. She stalled, rolling the swallow of wine around in her mouth. "No particular reason," she mumbled.

"Don't shine me on," he said. "You have to tell me now. And you wouldn't have set me up to be curious like that if some part of you didn't want to."

Ava dug her hands into the cashmere fuzz, trying to warm them. "The fourth of this month is the anniversary of my parents' plane crash," she admitted reluctantly. "It hits me really hard, every year. Some years I handle it better than others. Sometimes I fool myself into thinking I'm cool. That I beat it this time. And then, whammo, it takes me down. I get so low, it scares me."

"I'm so sorry," he said. "How old were you when it happened?"

"Almost thirteen," she said.

He winced. "Oh, God, Ava. That's awful."

"Yeah. It left a mark."

The silence after felt more peaceful, oddly enough. She'd gotten it outside of herself. She listened to the flames crackle, feeling like more air was going into her lungs.

"I know how it feels, to have a big hole in that part of my life where a parent should be," Zack said. "But I had Granddad. He made all the difference in the world. He filled the spot where my dad should've been. When he died…" Zack shook his head. "It was like I couldn't breathe, for a month."

"Yeah," she whispered. "Yeah, I felt that way, too."

"You call someone to be with you when you feel like that, right?" he asked her. "You don't tough it out all by yourself? Tell me you don't."

"It doesn't occur to me to reach out," she said. "I'm not fit for company."

"Who cares if you're fit for company? It's not about that. You stay all alone?" Zack sounded scandalized. "That's terrible. You should ask for help. You don't have to be so damn macho about it. It's okay to reach out."

"Yeah?" she shot back. "You know what, Zack? You're macho, too. And I bet you absolutely suck at reaching out when you feel like crap. So don't preach to me."

Zack smiled. "You've got me there. Maybe reaching out isn't my most shining talent. But I have Drew and Vann, and having them makes me stronger. If I was messed up about anything, they'd help me out."

"Good," she said. "I'm glad for you. You're very fortunate."

He kept on frowning, like he wanted something more. "What about Drew?" he asked. "Can't you call on him when you're in that state?"

"Drew understands," she said. "But it's his grief and loss, too. He's sad himself on that day, on his own account, so I try to let him be."

"And Jenna?"

A rush of old memories made her smile. "Jenna, yes," she admitted. "That was how we bonded, freshman year in college. We didn't hit it off at all at first. I thought she was a stuck-up nerd with no sense of humor, and she thought I was a frivolous, spoiled diva. We were like cats and dogs. Then one day, she came back to the dorm room and found me crying in the dark. She wouldn't let up until I told her that it was the anniversary of their plane crash. Then she told me about her brother, Chris, dying, and we finally opened up to each other. Now she's my best friend in the world."

"Well, then," he said. "So you do have someone."

"Yeah. She just happens to be a half a world away, on a blissful honeymoon with my big brother. Which is great, but life's funny. It never works out like you'd expect."

He hesitated. "You could call me, too. I don't know how much help I'd be, but I'd sure as hell show up. And I wouldn't expect you to be good company."

Ava cupped the glass with both her hands, gazing into the red liquid, too shy to meet his eyes. "That's very sweet of you," she said, her voice small. "And funny you should say that. Because, actually, you already have done that for me."

Zack's eyes narrowed in puzzlement. "How so?"

"That night," she said. "Remember? Six years ago? The margaritas?"

He inhaled sharply, eyes widening. "Oh. Holy shit."

"Yeah. It was their death anniversary that night," she said. "I didn't want to feel those feelings, so I tried to hold them off with alcohol. And distract myself with, ah…"

"Me," he finished.

The silence stretched out. Just the sound of the fire.

"I wish I'd known," he said finally.

"I wanted to tell you for a long time. I didn't want you to think that I was a habitual drunk. Or…you know. A sex addict. I'm really not."

"I never thought that," he assured her. "Not for one second."

"Thanks for saying that. Even so, I've wanted to apologize to you ever since."

"What?" He sounded shocked. "What for?"

"You know, for putting you in a compromising position. My brother is your best friend since forever. Plus, he's your boss. It just wasn't right to do that to you."

"All the more reason I'm glad nothing happened," he said.

Ava could have sworn she didn't change the expression on her face, but Zack felt the truth in the air. He looked over at her sharply.

"Wait," he said. "Hold on. You didn't know that nothing happened? You actually thought that I would… God, Ava, what kind of scumbag do you think I am?"

"I didn't know," she protested. "How could I know? I blacked out. When I woke up, you were gone. I missed my chance to ask what happened. After that, I was too mortified to ask. And the more time went by, the more mortified I got."

He closed his eyes, shaking his head. "Damn. I can't believe this."

"So, um." She cleared her throat. "Since I don't remember, please tell me. What did happen? Exactly?"

"You kissed me," he said. "And then you started to cry."

Ava winced. "Oh, no."

"I carried you to the bed and held you while you cried it out. After a while, you stopped crying and started snoring. I covered you up and slept on the couch. End of story."

"You must have thought I was crazy," she whispered.

"No," he corrected. "I thought you were sad. And very, very drunk."

Ava drank the last swallow of her wine and put the empty glass on the coffee table. "I apologize for falling all over you," she said. "It must have been embarrassing."

"No," he said. "But it was a challenge when you kissed me. To do the right thing."

Ava's face must have been cherry red, but it was gratifying to hear that he was not completely immune to her charms. "Then why did you push me away?"

He gave her a narrow look. "Like hell. You were drunk. I knew exactly what Drew would think. Also how I would feel if it were Joanna in your situation. Alone with some guy who could take advantage if he felt like it. No way would I ever do that to someone."

"You're a good guy," she said. "But then, I knew that. Always have."

He shrugged. "Plus, it sucks to be somebody's moment of bad judgment."

"Whose bad judgment?" she asked. "What are you talking about?"

His eyes slid away from hers. "Never mind. Just stupid old stuff."

"Don't you even," she said. "You make me spit out the painful, embarrassing things." She poked at his thick-muscled shoulder with her fingertips. "It's your turn."

He shrugged. "I know how it feels to be someone's big mistake. A choice she's not proud of. Been there, done that. Never want to do it again."

She was mystified. "Who on earth would ever see you that way?"

Zack grabbed the wine, refilling their glasses and handing hers back. "It was back when I was still in the marines. I'd gone to check on a wounded friend in a military hospital in Germany. I had some leave, so I traveled. Met this girl in Berlin. Aimee. She was doing a semester abroad to study art and architecture. A debutante from Dallas. Her daddy had oil wells."

"All right," she said. "And?"

"I fell pretty hard," he said. "I wanted to make it work with her. One day she ghosted me and went off to Prague. Like an idiot, I followed her. I should have followed my own rule. If she was making such a big effort to avoid me, I should've let her do it."

"Did you find her?"

"Yes," he said. "She tried to be nice, but there's no way to sugarcoat some things. I had no money, no college degree, no connections. I was just a big, dumb, overgrown, backwoods jarhead to her. She didn't see a future in it."

She sucked in air, infuriated. "That snobbish bitch."

"She was just being honest," he pointed out. "I thought you liked honesty."

"That's not honesty. That's arrogance. Ignorance. She had no idea who she was dealing with. No freaking clue what you were capable of. She only saw herself."

Zack waved that away. "Doesn't matter. It was a long time ago. But it left a mark."

Ava studied his profile. The stunning, chiseled angles and lines and planes of his cheekbones and jaw. She wished she could lean over and touch them with her fingertips.

"If you ran into Aimee again, she'd see you very differently now," she said.

"Maybe so. But the changes are just cosmetic. The only difference is years of hard work. Bigger skill set, bigger bank account, better wardrobe. But I'm still that guy."

"The guy she couldn't see," Ava said. "But neither do you. I think there's quite a disconnect between the man everyone else sees and your own vision of yourself."

"Oh, yeah? How's that?"

"Your staff loves you and fears you," she said. "Drew and Vann just plain love you. The company founders respect you, both Uncle Malcolm and Hendrick Hill. And now that Drew and Vann are both taken, you are the last, desperate hope of the single ladies at Maddox Hill. Behold, the last of the Maddox Hill heartthrobs left standing."

He snorted under his breath. "Oh, get out of here."

"True thing. While Aimee the brain-dead debutante is probably married to some dull, self-important Dallas businessman who's bad in bed. Which is exactly what she deserves."

Zack laughed. "I never let my imagination go that far. To be honest, I can't quite remember what she looks like."

"Good," Ava said savagely.

"That said, I still don't ever want to be anybody's embarrassing mistake again," he said. "And you know what? I'm not the only one with a big disconnect."

She tensed, bracing herself for God knew what. "I don't know what you mean."

"You said today that you like it when people like you. Well, guess what? They do. You're everybody's friend. You have a million friends. The whole damn city loves you."

"Oh, don't exaggerate. What are you getting at?"

He pressed on. "But you won't call any of them to help you with grieving your anniversary date. Or even just to vent about your troll problem. You're everybody's friend, but you won't let anyone be yours."

"That's nonsense," she snapped. "I'm close to a lot of friends. And Jenna is—"

"Jenna is another matter, and she's also out of the country.

No, I'm talking about the rest of the teeming multitudes. You couldn't call on any of them. Could you?"

"Well, I called on you, didn't I?"

He studied her for a long moment. "Yes." His voice was soft. "You called on me."

The air somehow turned electric. A shimmer of awareness got sharper and sharper, until suddenly, it was unbearable. She leaned forward, placing the wineglass on the coffee table. It rattled and almost fell. She steadied it with shaking hands.

"So, ah…yeah," she mumbled. "It's been a really long day, and I should—"

"Ava," he broke in.

She swallowed nervously. "Yes?"

"Something you should know."

"Well, then," she said. "Go on. Let's hear it."

"If you should ever end up in my bed for real? You wouldn't spend years wondering whether it happened or not."

"Zack, I'm so sorry about that. Really, I blacked out. I didn't mean to imply—"

"You'd remember every last second of it." His voice was silky. "I guarantee it."

Ava threw off the cashmere blanket and got to her feet, almost tripping over the overlong bathrobe. "Um, yes," she forced out. "Understood. 'Night."

She hiked up the bathrobe and fled.

Five

At a quarter to 5:00 a.m., coffee was brewing and bacon sizzled in the pan when Zack sensed that he wasn't alone. He turned to see Ava in the entryway to the corridor, fully dressed in jeans and a red sweater, hair twisted up onto her head. Her jacket was on, her suitcase and garment bag piled behind her, and her smartphone was in her hand.

From the guilty look on her face, she'd been planning to slip away before he woke.

He'd spooked her last night, with the inappropriate comments. Jerk move.

"I'm going with you to LA," he told her. "I'm not leaving you alone until I have a team in place to cover you. Until then, I'm reporting for duty."

Ava let out a sharp sigh. "Zack, please. Be reasonable."

"Call Ernest," he said. "Tell him we'll meet him at the gate."

Ava's mouth was tight. Their fireside chat had made things worse between them, not better. Too damn much information, and she didn't know how to process it. Plus, she was embarrassed to show vulnerability. It made her defensive and cranky.

He needed to back off. Keep it classy and professional. This girl was Drew's little sister. Malcolm's niece. The Maddox family's golden princess. Even after a decade of friendship, trust and mutual esteem, he wasn't sure he wanted to know how Drew and Malcolm would feel about Zack raising his eyes to their precious Ava.

Not that his eyes had any choice. Or certain other body parts, for that matter.

"I'd rather do my thing today alone, no distractions," she told him. "We have a lot to accomplish."

Zack flicked a drop of water onto the buttered-up griddle to see if it danced. "Whatever you want," he said, pouring out the pancakes. "It's nine hours ahead in Positano, so Malcolm should pick up when I call. Don't know about Drew, but wherever he is in the world, he'll forgive me for waking him up when I tell him about your trolls."

"Bullying is not a winning strategy, Zack."

"If you really want to feel bullied, I can't stop you," he said. "It won't change my behavior. I am staying with you until another bodyguard I trust is covering you. So let me accompany you, or else discuss the issue directly with your uncle and brother."

"You know damn well they'll both overreact," she said.

"No," Zack replied. "They'll feel as I do, and I could use the moral support. This issue is spot-on when it comes to my mission. Which is to keep you all safe."

Ava's eyes slid away. "I appreciate your zeal, but this is over-the-top."

"I'd rather err on the side of caution. I'll stay out of your way. I won't mess with your process. Call Ernest and let him know. How many slices of bacon do you want?"

"Oh, give me three," she snapped. "Fighting gives me an appetite."

"I'm not fighting," he called after her as she left the kitchen. "Just stating facts."

"You hush up. Your carrot-and-stick routine is bugging me."

He heard Ava murmuring into her phone in the other room. A few moments later, she came back into the kitchen. "How is it you're awake at this ungodly hour, anyhow?"

"I grew up on my granddad's farm in West Virginia," he told her. "We got up early to take care of the livestock. Then I joined the military. It doesn't matter how late I get to bed. I can't sleep late. Usually I go running or else work out at this hour."

Ava gestured at the stove. "Smells good. What's cooking?"

"Pancakes. Gotta keep my strength up. The carrot-and-stick routine burns a lot of calories. Get yourself some coffee. Cream's on the table. Hope you like it strong."

A couple minutes later, Zack set two plates with stacks of buttermilk pancakes on the table.

Ava drizzled syrup on hers and took a bite. "Wow. So fluffy. These are fabulous."

"Mom's recipe," he said.

"You're a man of many talents," she said, forking up another bite. "I'm usually not hungry in the morning. I mean, not at all. But this...mmm. So good."

"I'm no gourmet chef, but Mom made sure I could handle the basics."

Ava tucked in her breakfast, eyeing him as she nibbled her bacon. "Won't they miss you at Maddox Hill today? Don't you have a job? A life?"

"Sure, but I'm always working, except when I fly home to see Mom and Joanna and the kids, so I almost never take vacation or personal leave days. Amelia knows what to do. If they have issues, they'll call me. The stuff I was going to do can be pushed off. So I'm clear. Both my calendar and my conscience."

"So you finally take up a hobby, and it involves helicoptering me," she said sourly. "I hope you're packed, because it's time to scram if we want to catch this flight."

"I'm all packed," he said.

Ava dabbed at her mouth with a napkin. "Thanks for breakfast. Can I help with the dishes?"

"Don't worry about it. The cleaning service is coming this morning, and they'll take care of it."

The drive to the airport was quiet. Ava shut down any attempt he made at polite conversation, and after a while he let the effort go. If she wanted to be pissed at him, that was her privilege. But as they approached the airport, the words just popped out.

"You don't have to be so defensive with me," he announced.

She looked over at him, startled. "Excuse me?"

"The stuff you said yesterday," he said. "Feeling sad about your parents. Getting trashed on margaritas. Being scared of the shitty trolls. It doesn't mean you're weak. It just means you're human, and it's okay to be human."

"Oh." She chewed on her lip. "Um… I'm not sure where that came from, but— Whoa, whoa, whoa, yikes! Zack, you just passed the exit for our terminal!"

Zack cursed under his breath as he glanced at the exit in the rearview mirror and resolved to shut his great big mouth before he hurt himself.

They left Zack's car in the parking garage and powered through the whole airport process in grim silence. Ernest was already at the gate, and the younger guy's cheerful, nonstop chatter effectively covered up the tense silence between them.

As soon as the plane was airborne, Ava and Ernest fired up their laptops, but after a while, Ernest leaned over and tapped Zack's sleeve.

"Have you seen Ava's videos?"

"Ernest, don't bug him," Ava said. "It's not his—"

"I've seen the one about Arm's Reach," Zack said. "It was excellent. There are more?"

"Oh, yeah. She's done loads of them, and they always go viral. She's, like, a wizard that way. We're in the middle of producing a big one about the Blooms and the Desert Bloom Farm. Ava always narrates, because she's awesome at it."

"Ernest!" Ava protested. "Don't put him on the spot! He may not be interested."

"I am interested, very. Show me, please," Zack said.

"Okay. Check this out," Ernest said, passing over his laptop. "This is the first section of the Desert Bloom bit, and it'll run on one of the interactive video screens in the booth at the trade show. Put in your earphones."

Zack calmly ignored Ava's efforts to excuse him from watching, hooked himself up and settled in to watch. A minimalist fingerpicking guitar piece accompanied drone footage, swooping over a huge swath of desert. It was dry and bare, just a few scrubby thorns clinging to life, as Ava's clear, golden voice narrated the story of two pioneers of modern botany and soil research, most appropriately named the Blooms. How, by pure chance, some years ago they inherited a tract of arid desert in Southern California and decided to turn it green using their skills as biologists. Replenishing the depleted soil bacteria and fungi, refilling the aquifers. Then, with startling abruptness, the drone footage showed the desert turning green. The land was suddenly thick with long grass, bushes and small trees. Then the drone swooped over orchards, gardens, greenhouses.

Damn, he could listen to her gorgeous voice for-freaking-ever. So sexy.

The drone flew lower, along a meandering stream, then over a pond, where a flock of birds took flight as she talked about soil biota. How its symbiotic relationship with plants facilitated uptake of soil minerals. How fungi stabilized the soil against erosion by forming water-stable aggregates. How the Blooms' process of soil inoculation worked.

He watched to the end of the clip, pulled out his earbuds and looked at Ava.

"Incredible project," he said. "They're up for a cash prize?"

"Yeah, half a million," she said. "It's a drop in the bucket, but every little bit counts. I've also been trying to get Drew to meet with them, to talk about Beyond Earth."

He was surprised by the mention of Maddox Hill's speculative futuristic project, his friend Drew's darling, geared toward possible future construction on Mars. "These guys want to go off world?"

She laughed. "Oh, they'll start with Earth. We have plenty of dry, dusty deserts here to work on. Winning the prize would be great, but the real prize is to rub elbows with investors who can take them to the next level. Please, God. I really need for this to work."

"Yeah? Have you sunk your own personal money into this project?"

"Some," she admitted. "They really need the investors, but they have to make a big splash to attract the right ones, so I'm covering the cost of the Future Innovation booth. The Blooms will pay me back when they can. They've also offered me a percentage. It's a gamble, but I think there's a big payoff in store down the line."

Zack was startled. "A booth at a trade show like that is one hell of an expense."

"Tell me about it," she said fervently. "I had to dig deep to cover it. I've been pulling down research grants for the Blooms since my college days, back when I interned at the Maddox Hill Foundation during the summers. I helped Bobby and Wilbur write their first grant application back then. If Drew hadn't been on his honeymoon right now, I would have dragged him down to meet them. The Blooms would be great partners for his carbon-sink architecture projects. Green walls, hanging gardens, green roofs to moderate temperature and make building complexes carbon negative. It'll spawn a whole new service industry. High-rise gardening."

"Yes," he said. "Drew would be excited by this project."

"And there's Beyond Earth," she went on. "Who better than the two crazy soil biologists who are turning Earth's deserts green to work on terraforming Mars?"

"You think big," Zack commented.

"I believe in the Blooms," Ava said. "Wilbur's incredible at making dirt come to life, and Bobby is a wizard with bacteria and arbuscular mycorrhizal fungi. I've been pushing this narrative for years now. Two dedicated, monk-like nerds, saving the planet one petri dish and hyphal network at a time. They have this way of coming at problems from every angle you could think of and then a hundred more that you wouldn't. The two of them are one big brain that needed more than one body to function. And anyone who partners with them will end up extremely rich, in the long run. Those guys are laser focused. Brains like a nuclear furnace."

"Like you," Zack said.

Ava seemed taken aback. "Me? Hardly!"

"Laser focused, brain like a nuclear furnace?" Zack said. "Sounds like you." He paused at the stunned look on her face. "What? Did I say something bad?"

"Ah, no," Ava said. "Just surprising. I was under the impression that you thought I was, ah…you know. Bimbo fluff."

Zack felt his face get hot. "I'm sorry if I ever gave you that impression," he said stiffly. "Social graces haven't ever been one of my strongest points."

"More my fault than yours, most likely," Ava assured him. "Considering that night with the margaritas and all. God knows, that would make anyone feel awkward."

The phone vibrated in Zack's pocket. He pulled it out. It was Vikram, who managed the close protection agents. Zack had left a long, detailed voice mail message for him last night about the security detail they needed to set up for Ava.

He hit Talk. "Hey, Vikram."

"Zack. Sorry it took a while to get back to you, but I wanted to get the team in place before we spoke. I've got four guys who can cover her 24-7 on a rotating basis, and I've messaged you their names. They're ready now, so where is she located? Is she at the Gilchrist building or still at home?"

"Actually, she's on a plane, on her way down to Southern California right now."

"Southern California?" Vikram sounded scandalized. "On a plane? No security?"

"I'm with her on the plane," he assured Vikram. "She's covered."

"You? Uh...why you? That doesn't seem like a good use of your—"

"I took a few vacation days. I needed a change of scenery. I'll just cover her until she gets back. She's got this work thing, a trade fair in LA. We'll come back Tuesday night. I'll be in touch. Have the team ready for Wednesday. Thanks for the names."

Vikram was speechless for a moment. "So, it's, uh...it's that kind of thing?"

"Not at all," he said hastily. "This just caught me by surprise. She had to catch an early flight, and I couldn't let her leave without having her covered, so...here I am."

"Yeah. There you are," Vikram said slowly. "You know, the guys on my roster practically clubbed each other unconscious to be first in line to guard that woman's body."

"Talk to you Wednesday, Vikram. Later." Zack ended the call before Vikram could piss him off.

Ava gave him a questioning look.

"It's Vikram, one of my guys," he explained. "He's putting together your team."

She rolled her eyes. "Oh, joy."

Once they thrashed their way through LAX, the limo took them to the new convention center and hotel in West Hollywood. Zack heard an excited yell as they walked into the huge hotel lobby. He stepped in front of Ava as two tall, gangling figures pelted toward them and then recognized the huge foreheads, thick glasses, bushy clouds of hair. Huge, crazy grins that showed off all their gums. The Blooms.

Ava stepped out from behind him to meet them. One of them grabbed her, swinging her around, which made Zack's hackles rise, but Ava was laughing and smiling. Then the other guy took his turn with the hugging and swinging. The two were a perfectly matched set. Twins maybe, or if they weren't, they might as well be.

"Zack, meet Bobby and Wilbur Bloom," Ava said. "Old friends of mine. Bobby and Wilbur, this is Zack Austin, the chief security officer at Maddox Hill. He's keeping me company while I work out my online troll problems."

"Yeah, we heard about that," Bobby said. "If we find those nasty bastards, we'll totally mulch them for you."

"Yeah," Wilbur added darkly. "We'll bury those scumbags in a crap ton of hot compost. Take 'em apart on a molecular level and repurpose freaking everything they've got. Who knows, maybe they'll eventually turn into something useful."

Ava gave them each a smacking kiss of appreciation on the cheek. "Thanks, boys. That's very gratifying. Have you gone over to the convention center to see the booth?"

"We just got here now," one of them said. "We were just about to take the van over with the plants."

"Wonderful," Ava said briskly. "Just let us check in to our rooms really quick, and we'll all head over there together."

The only holdup was a sharp disagreement with Ava about room disposition. He insisted on a room that connected with hers, which put the two of them on a different floor from the Blooms and Ernest. Zack stood his ground, despite Ava's very vocal frustration.

He was good at his job. Being accommodating or nice wasn't part of that job.

Once they got through that barrier, they headed over to the convention center and the expo floor. It looked like Times Square, with all the colorful, lit-up screens, logos and displays, and the bustle of preparation for tomorrow.

Desert Bloom's booth was in a prized central location, so Ava must be paying dearly for the space. The interactive screens in the booth were up and running, so while Ava and the Blooms set up finishing touches and installed live plant displays, Zack situated himself where he could see Ava, stuck in his earbuds and listened to the presentation on the screen. Ava's caressing voice described the Blooms' game-changing work with bacteria and fungi and explained how the Earth's deserts could be made fertile, replenishing aquifers, producing food, supporting ecosystems, protecting biodiversity. By the time she got to the part about sequestering carbon, he was half aroused.

Whoever would have thought that soil biology could be so damn stimulating?

Six

Stop it. Just stop it. Right now.

The silent lecture wasn't working as well as usual. Ava had way too much to accomplish today to indulge in this nonsense. From the moment they arrived to check in at the convention hotel, Zack had been bugging her. On her nerves. In her face.

First that stupid fight over the hotel rooms. Weeks ago, she'd asked for a room next to Bobby, Wilbur and Ernest. Today, Zack had insisted on a room that connected with hers internally. Which necessitated being on a different floor from her crew. Not ergonomic at all, but when she put up a fight, he trotted out his usual big bully stick. The awful, dreaded call to Uncle Malcolm and Drew. Oh, the terror. His ploy worked, though, because she did not want to deal with a scolding rant from her brother and uncle on top of her other stress. So Zack won that fight.

This trade show was incredibly important, for the Blooms and for her, and she did not have extra thought cycles to spare for a brooding hunk who followed her around watching everything she did, overhearing everything she said, examining everyone she talked to. It was unsettling. Embarrassing. People were starting to notice. And speculate.

She tried so hard to project confidence, to appear put-together, competent, at the top of her game. It functioned like a force field. Shields up, and off she went. It worked, for the most part. People paid attention and hopped to it. Stuff got done.

But when Zack Austin looked at her, her force field vanished, like it didn't exist and never had. It didn't matter what she was doing or wearing. Whether she was in hideous oversize pajamas and a cashmere couch throw, or a power suit, or jeans and a sweater and boots, like today, his gaze made her feel naked.

The sensation was disturbingly intimate. She'd never felt anything like it. Not even with past lovers. And the constant tingle of sexual awareness didn't help, either. He looked so damn good, standing around with his muscular arms crossed over his barrel chest, looking suspicious. Protective. And handsome.

Frantic activity dampened down the anxiety, which was one of the reasons she always worked so hard. It was a family trait, of course, one she shared with Drew and her uncle, but working hard kept the howling emptiness at bay while getting tons of stuff accomplished. She could look at that situation as a win-win, if she squinted a little bit.

When they arrived this afternoon, Henly and Frank, her trade show associates, had already set the booth up. She'd worked with them for years. She designed the trade show booth concepts, layout, sales literature and show apps, and Henly and Frank developed her ideas and brought them to life. They did all the construction, furniture, graphics, interactive screens, storage, transport, setup and teardown, and they did it well.

The brand-new booth looked great. All that was left were finishing touches, like Bobby and Wilbur's more delicate plant exhibits that had to be set up at the last minute, and the catering, of course. The goodies served tomorrow were sustainably sourced from Bobby and Wilbur's Desert Bloom Farm, all made from crops grown on land the brothers had reclaimed from the arid desert. There would be freshly baked artisanal crackers with assorted pâtés made from sun-dried tomatoes, artichokes and olives. There would be wines from Bobby and Wilbur's vineyards, mojitos made with lemons from their orchard, and mint from their herb garden.

They had to kick butt at this show, for Bobby and Wilbur's sake. And for hers, too. Aside from the rental of the space and the juice required to run it, she was personally on the hook for Carl and Henly's latest bill, and it was a biggie. The snack bar and drinks for three days of free goodies weren't cheap, either, but it was all part of her wicked plan—sink Desert Bloom name recognition deep into the viewing public's fickle brains by assaulting all five of their senses with pleasure and delight. And alcohol, of course.

She could stomach the risk, and she was confident that she'd make her money back, plus a huge profit in the long run. But she needed to keep the Blooms absolutely on track, which would be a challenge. It was up to her to keep all the plates spinning in the air, and for that she needed focus. No sexy, brooding, smoldering distractions allowed.

Ten o'clock had come and gone, and Bobby and Wilbur were still fussing over their pet plants, so she gave them the usual big-sisterly lecture about eating something and getting enough sleep and left them to it. Frank and Henly had already gone off to the hotel to crash, and Ernest had left earlier to have dinner with a friend.

But Zack was still there, patiently waiting. While working, she could stay busy and focused enough to ignore him, but now she'd suddenly gone all breathless and fluttery again. It made her so irritated at herself. Reacting like a hormonal adolescent.

Zack joined her as she left the booth, walking alongside her out of the big convention center.

"It's late," she told him. "You must be hungry. You could have just gone ahead and gotten yourself dinner hours ago, you know."

He grunted. "That would entirely defeat the purpose of being here."

"I was never alone," she told him. "And really, Zack. I'm not in physical danger."

"I hope you're correct, and I'll continue to hope that while I watch your back at all times. And Vikram will have a team ready when we get back to Seattle to keep that up."

She winced. "Oh, God. You mean day and night? For real?"

"Absolutely. Until we are all satisfied that you are no longer in danger."

She contemplated that grim and inconvenient prospect as they strolled through the balmy Los Angeles evening and into the adjacent luxury hotel that housed the convention center's participants. The hotel had two towers, with an open outdoor space with a large swimming pool between them. The restaurant's open-air seating was on a second-floor terrace that overlooked the pool. Their rooms were in the second tower. A couple of teenagers were horsing around in the pool as they walked past it down the breezeway.

"Are you hungry?" Zack asked her. "The restaurant should still be serving."

"I'm too buzzed to eat," Ava told him. "I get that way when I'm on the road. Maybe I'll order something later. Please, feel free to grab some dinner on your own. I don't want to stop you from eating."

He let out a noncommittal grunt. "I'll see you to your room."

They entered the lobby of the second hotel tower and headed toward the elevator banks, and Ava heard a voice behind her.

"Ava? Ava Maddox? Is that you?"

Ava turned to see a familiar face approaching, a big, toothy smile spread over it, arms wide for a hug. Craig Redding, a man she'd known from college. She'd been briefly involved with him years ago, but it hadn't taken even her young-and-dumb self very long to conclude that the relationship had no future. Craig was smart and good-looking, even if his eyes were pinched a little too close together, but on closer acquaintance, he'd proved to be arrogant and condescending. The Reddings were vastly rich and well-connected, and Craig had grown up convinced that he was God's gift. He had expected her to be grateful for his attentions. The memory made her neck hairs prickle up.

However, the Reddings had also commissioned Maddox Hill to design several large buildings for them, and when that much money was involved, Malcolm had made it clear that she was expected to smile and nod like a good little girl.

Up until now, she'd managed to do so from a safe distance.

Zack stepped in front of her, effectively blocking Craig's move to embrace her. "Who are you?" he demanded.

"It's fine, Zack." She came forward, but not close enough to get dragged into a hug. "I know him. We went to school together. Hey, Craig. What brings you here? I thought you worked at your dad's hedge fund in Portland."

"I have my own venture capital firm now," Craig told her. "I make the rounds of the tech trade fairs to keep my finger on the pulse of the future. What is it you do these days? Aren't you some kind of social media influencer? Like, what? Instagram videos? Makeup, fashion, that kind of thing? Cat memes and all that?"

She smiled, teeth clenched. "Hey, someone's got to do it."

"Branding communication specialist is the best description for what she does, I'd say," Zack said. "But she wears so many hats, I can't even keep track of them all."

Ava was taken aback at his contribution. The elevator dinged and opened.

Craig waved his key card. "I'm going up, too. Share a ride?"

Zack's face darkened, but there was no socially acceptable way of refusing him, so they all got in. The elevator door sighed closed.

"So who's your friend, Ava?" Craig's voice got that insinuating tone that had always annoyed her.

Zack's voice never had that tone when he spoke to her. He

was so straightforward. An odd reflection to find herself making, but whatever. "Craig Redding, meet Zack Austin," she said. "Zack is the chief security officer of Maddox Hill Architecture."

Craig's eyebrows shot up. "Really? I took him for a bodyguard. He has the look."

"I expect he does," Zack said coolly. "He's here to make sure that Ava's not bothered by anyone she doesn't feel like talking to."

"Aw. There, there. Ava and I are old friends." Craig's big white teeth were on full display. "You don't have to puff out your chest with me, buddy."

The elevator dinged and opened. Ava stepped out, followed by Zack, grateful that this wasn't Craig's floor. She didn't particularly want Craig to have her room number.

"'Night, Craig," she crisply. "See you around tomorrow at the trade show."

When the door closed, she blew out a breath of relief. "Sorry about that," she muttered. "Craig's kind of a jerk."

"I noticed," he said. "Cat memes? For real?"

"Yeah, Craig never took me seriously, but God knows I was used to that, after all those years with Uncle Malcolm." She stopped at her door. "Anyhow. Good night."

She swiped her card, but Zack made no move toward his own door. His eyes looked troubled. "Malcolm really does that to you? He puts you down, like that guy?"

"Uncle Malcolm doesn't get the point of what I do, so he dismisses it as frivolous," she said. "I gave up looking for validation from him a long time ago. He loves me, in his clumsy way, and he knows I work hard. He just would really, really rather that I was an architect. That, he could appreciate. It's the only thing that makes sense to him."

"I wish he could see what I saw today," Zack said. "How well you work. The videos, too. You're damned talented at what you do."

"Ah...wow. Thanks," she said, flustered. "Um. Good night."

Once inside the room, that connecting door loomed large in her mind. Zack had used dirty tricks to get her into this situation, but this was new, and the dirtiest trick of all. Saying sweet, approving things to her about her professional skills? That was diabolical. He'd get her eating right out of his hand in no time, the sneaky bastard.

It was a new, crafty element of his Ava management strategy. That old carrot-and-stick routine. If the threat to call Drew and Uncle Malcolm home early from their traveling was the stick, then admiring compliments about her skill and talent must be the carrot.

And she was so hungry for approval, she fell like an overripe pear, ker-plop.

Screw it. She flipped through the hotel info for the pool hours. She had to blow off some steam, and swimming worked best if she wanted a hope in hell of sleeping. Sleep was always elusive for her, even when she wasn't challenged by menacing cybertrolls and a smoldering Zack Austin. Exercise made the nightmares ease off, too. A little bit.

The pool was open until late, so she dug out her bathing suit and her flip-flops. She twisted her hair back into a braid and then sat on the bed and listened intently for Zack's movements in the connecting room. She stopped short of putting her ear to the door, because that would be creepy. It was weird enough already to be listening for him, like a teenaged girl making to sneak out for a night of misbehavior.

She already felt acutely vulnerable with Zack Austin, even when she was fully clothed, made up and coiffed. She couldn't imagine how it would feel to have him see her naked, wet, dripping and shivering. No way. She couldn't. She would implode.

She pulled the door open and gasped to find Ernest standing right there, his big eyes wide and startled behind his glasses. "Hi," he said.

"You could have knocked!" she whispered fiercely.

"I was going to, but you beat me to it," Ernest whispered back. "Why are we whispering?"

"Shh." She glanced toward Zack's door. "I was just popping down for a quick swim, and I wanted to do it in blessed privacy. What do you need, Ernest?"

"Your computer," he told her. "Remember that invoice we needed to correct, for that extra interactive panel? I was supposed to fix that and send the corrected invoice back to Carl yesterday, but I spaced out. Now I need to get it from your computer, fix it and send it to him pronto. He needs it tomorrow morning. Sorry to bug you."

"All right. Come on in." Ava stepped back to let him in and pulled her pink laptop out of the case, opening it up. "I just got here, so I haven't set up the Wi-Fi password yet."

"I'll do it." Ernest's voice remained a conspiratorial whisper as he eyed the connecting door. "I know your logins. Go on down, get your swim. I'll be quick."

"You sure you don't need me?"

"Not at all," he assured her. "Go on, go on. Close the door quietly."

She followed his suggestion and ran down the hall toward the elevator. This was childish, but a few dozen laps in that pool and she'd be able to make it through the night.

More or less. With a little luck, and fingers crossed. Even with Zack Austin fulminating silently on the other side of an unlocked door.

Zack jerked his tie loose as he ran his eyes over the room service menu. He wondered if he dared to knock on the door and suggest that they eat together. Ava was so mercurial. Sometimes blazing that warm, generous energy straight at him, dazzling him. Then, just as fast, bam, she barricaded herself, and it felt like a door slamming in his face.

He had just decided to act like a professional adult and leave her the hell alone when he heard the room door next to his, falling to with a heavy thud.

What the hell? She wasn't supposed to leave without him in attendance. He lunged for his own door and looked out in both directions. No one was in the corridor, so he went to the connecting door and rapped on it.

"Ava?" he called. "Hey! Ava, are you in there? Everything good in there?"

No response. He knocked again, louder.

Still nothing. He banged on it. "Damn it, Ava! Answer me!"

When she still didn't answer, he cursed under his breath and shoved the door open.

Ava wasn't in the room. It was Ernest at the desk, tapping at Ava's laptop. He had earbuds on and was beating time with his feet to a song only he could hear.

"Ernest? What are you doing here?"

Ernest made no sign of hearing him, so Zack strode over to the desk and slammed his hand down on the surface, making the laptop rattle and bounce.

Ernest jumped, letting out a startled squeak, and popped out his earbuds. "Oh my flipping God! You scared me practically to death!"

"Where is Ava? And why are you in her room?"

"I just needed to use her computer!" Ernest yelled. "Jeez! Calm down!"

"Where is she?" Zack demanded.

"She went down for a swim, that's all. She always does that when we go on the road. Otherwise she can't sleep. She has insomnia, and it gets really bad sometimes."

"A *swim*?" Zack's voice cracked in outrage.

He strode over to the window and yanked the curtain back, peering down into the central space at the huge pool ten floors below, surrounded by deserted deck chairs.

No one down there at all but a single slim figure, knifing swiftly through the water.

Goddamn. He clenched and flexed his hands, fighting the fury and frustration.

He looked over at Ernest, who seemed bewildered. "You should head on back to your room, Ernest. It's very late."

The younger man nodded. "Yeah. I'll just, ah, scram now. 'Night."

Zack strolled to the elevator, keeping his pace measured and his breathing even more so. He couldn't go on the offensive with her. Ava was proud and stubborn, and if he pushed her too hard, she'd tell him to piss off. Carrot and stick notwithstanding.

He didn't usually struggle to control his temper. Something about Ava crossed his wires. But the more conflict there was between them, the less safe Ava would be.

Her safety was more important than his ego.

Seven

Ava pulled herself up on the side of the pool and shoved wet hair out of her eyes. Something was in front of her, blocking the light. Her eyes came into focus on a pair of shoes. Then gray suit pants. Up, up, up…to Zack's face, looming over her. Glaring down with that patented, terrifying, lightning-and-brimstone look that only he could pull off.

"Oh," she said, dismayed. "It's you."

"That's right," he said.

Zack was standing directly in front of her, so Ava scooted over a bit before vaulting up and out of the pool. She squeezed water out of her hair as she steeled herself. She tried to project confidence and calm. A big ask while dripping and mostly naked.

"Zack," she said. "I sense that you have something to say. Let's hear it."

"You're not taking me seriously." Zack's voice vibrated with tension. "There's online info about your whereabouts this weekend. Anyone at all with an interest in you can find out where you are, and at what hotel. And you blow off your security and sneak down for a swim in a deserted pool at night? In what universe is that a sane thing to do?"

Ava sidestepped his question. "Hardly deserted," she murmured. "It was full of yelling teenagers until just a few minutes ago, and there's a stream of people up and down the breezeway. Plus the restaurant." She gestured at the terrace full of late-night diners.

Zack didn't even glance toward the restaurant or breezeway. "Why are you making this so goddamned hard?"

"I'm not," she retorted. "The hard part is all you, Zack."

As soon as the words left her mouth, she regretted them. They sounded dismissive, which he did not deserve. "Look, I'm sorry," she said. "I'll go back on up to the room. And I promise I'll be good." She turned away to get the terry-cloth robe on the deck chair.

Zack's hand shot out and clamped around her wrist.

She looked down at his big hand. Contact with his skin sent a hot thrill of pure awareness through her body. A rush of energy. Anger, and something else.

Something even bigger, wilder. More dangerous.

"You're being a bully," she said slowly. "Take your hand off me right now."

His fingers tightened around her wrist. "Stop acting like a child."

That arrogant bastard. On impulse, she twisted her hand around to grip his wrist and pitched herself backward toward the pool.

Dragging him in along with her.

There was a huge splash, a moment of disorientation…and then disbelief as she swam up to face what she'd just done.

Holy crap. She'd just pulled Zack Austin into a swimming pool, fully clothed. Like a bad little kid. And in front of an audience, no less. Some of whom were applauding from the restaurant terrace. They had now officially become the evening's live entertainment.

Zack's head and shoulders emerged from the water, his white dress shirt clinging to every detail of his thickly muscled body. He wiped his face, eyes blazing.

"Are you fucking kidding me?" he said savagely.

Stay tough. She held herself as tall as she could, trying to match his energy.

"Never lay a hand on me in a controlling way, ever again," she told him. "Or I will mess you up so bad. Do you get me?"

A muscle pulsed in Zack's jaw. "I get you," he said.

"Good," she replied.

They stood motionless in the water, eyes locked as the sounds of the world around them retreated, leaving the two of them in a bubble of breathless silence.

"How did we get here, Ava?" he asked finally. "What the hell just happened?"

"I don't know," she said. "I... I wasn't thinking."

"That much was clear," he growled.

Ava's chin went up. "I'm not apologizing."

"I didn't ask you to," he replied. "Just be straight with me. Do you really believe that protecting you is stupid and unnecessary?"

"No. I wouldn't have come to you in the first place if I believed that," she said.

"Then why sneak off without telling me? Where's the sense in that?"

"No sense," she admitted. "Just necessity, I guess. I reached a sort of breaking point. I had to get clear of everything for a little while."

"Clear of being protected? Secure?"

"No," she said, her voice strangled. "Clear of you."

Zack's eyes widened, and the water between them boiled as he surged back, putting more distance between them. "If I'm the problem, then this situation can't go forward," he said stiffly. "I'll call Vikram when we get upstairs. He'll send a team on the first available flight tomorrow. As soon as they're here, I'll get out of your hair."

"No! I don't want anyone but you," she blurted.

Zack looked blank. "But you just told me that I'm the problem."

"Don't call Vikram," she repeated.

Zack sank down into the water and floated there for a moment, studying her face with those intense eyes. Trying to read her. "I'm lost, Ava," he said. "Help me out here."

"I'm lost, too," she said, her voice small.

"It's because of that night of the margaritas, right?" he said. "That's what your problem is with me. You want everyone to think that you're strong, all the time. You just can't stand it if somebody sees beneath your mask."

That might be true, but she couldn't comment. Her throat quivered too hard.

Zack moved so gradually, he hardly seemed to move at all, but suddenly, he was just inches from her. The slightest movement and they would touch.

"I can't make a move," he said. "Not after that epic smackdown. I've just gotten scolded, threatened and dunked in a pool. So I'm just going to float here and wait for a signal from you. If there's something you want from me, Ava, just take it."

The tiles of the pool wall pressed against her shoulder blades. She fought for breath. "It's a terrible idea," she whispered. "Totally bonkers."

"Agreed," he said. "And yet, here we are."

"Something about you just drives me nuts," she admitted.

His mouth curved in a devastating smile. "Hmm. I can work with that."

She almost laughed, but she was too unstable emotionally to risk it. But suddenly, her shoulders were no longer pressed against the tile. She was drifting toward him.

"It's going to be hard to put this back in the box," he warned. "Just be aware."

Ava laid her hands on Zack's shoulders. Her fingers twisted into the wet, sodden cotton of his shirt, and the thick, hard muscles beneath. She let her legs float up to twine around his. "I don't want it in a box," she whispered as their lips touched.

It started small, just the lightest contact, but the magic took hold instantly. The kiss burst into full bloom. The stroke of his tongue against hers was so sweet. Electric. The tantalizing taste of him, the deep, rumbling vibration of his low moan. And then the nudge of his very thick, very substantial erection against her bare belly.

The teasing contact made her shiver and moan. Her legs tightened around his, hips pulsing for deeper contact. She twined her arms around his neck, and her hands slid into the silky short hair, as aroused as if he'd been teasing her for hours.

Because he had been. She'd been intensely sexually aware of him ever since that meeting in his office the evening before. This entire day had been one long seductive foreplay session, and it was finally time for the main event. She ached for him. All of him, all over her, deep inside her. Nothing held back.

His hand wound into her wet hair, and his lips moved softly against her mouth, exploring the shape of her mouth. "Damn," he said thickly. "Our audience."

She suddenly heard the hoots and whistles coming from the terrace of the restaurant. Some people were leaning over the railing, shouting off-color advice.

She was not an exhibitionist. It was startling to realize that she'd forgotten their existence. "Um. Wow." She hugged him closer, arms and legs. "That was intense."

"Still is," Zack said, gasping with pleasure as she squeezed her thighs around his. "Let's take this upstairs."

She slid down until her feet hit the bottom of the pool after a reluctant moment. It had taken years of waiting and a huge leap of faith, courage and madness to do this, and she didn't want to turn her back on it. It might vanish like smoke.

"I'm afraid the moment will slip away," she whispered.

"Not a problem," he said. "I've been hot for you since you were barely more than jailbait. If you want this, it's yours. Standing at attention and awaiting your pleasure, as much as you can handle, for as long as you want. Guaranteed. Nothing will slip away."

Her face heated, but his words were the encouragement she needed. She climbed up out of the pool. Zack waited in the water as she retrieved her robe from the deck chair.

"Aren't you getting out?" she asked as she wrapped herself in it.

"I'm trying to chill down this hard-on enough to make it through the hotel lobby," he confessed. "It's tricky when your clothes are sopping wet. They cling."

Zack climbed out of the pool and strolled along beside her with a supremely casual air. As if it were perfectly normal to leave a river of water on the carpet behind him. By the time they got to the elevator, she was laughing at him.

"What?" he demanded. "What's so funny?"

"You're squelching," she murmured. "Sorry. It's just a funny sound."

Zack snorted under his breath and stepped into the elevator. Another couple moved to follow them in, took one look at the Zack, drenched and with the puddle of chlorinated water spreading around his feet, and stopped short, doubtful.

"Are you guys coming up?" Ava asked.

"We'll get the next one," the guy said as the door closed.

They exploded with stifled laughter, and Zack seized her as the elevator shot up to their floor, kissing her breathless. Ten floors just wasn't long enough for that wild kiss. It continued, frantically, outside the elevator and at intervals all the way down the hall.

At her door, Zack paused, leaning back. His breath was uneven. "You've had a minute to think about it," he said. "So where are you with this? Still with me?"

"I'm with you," she said. "I just want to get the chlorine off. A quick shower."

"You got it." He grinned at her as she swiped her card.

Once inside her room, Ava leaned on the inside of the door, shaking. This was really happening. She couldn't believe it. But she had no time to waste on disbelief.

She peeled off the bathing suit and showered, shaving her legs, washing and conditioning her hair. She went at it with the blow-dryer and the round brush until she was satisfied with the way it looked and was almost tempted to put on some mascara, but no. It was a night to be au naturel. Some scented lotion and she was done with body prep.

She pulled on her sleep stuff, wishing she'd brought something sexier. The little gray stretch cotton cami and boy shorts were nowhere near as seductive as she'd like, but they were better than the horrendous flannel she'd used as a sex repellant at Zack's house.

Then she sat down on the bed, wondering nervously if the ball was in her court now. If she should signal him. A knock on the door resolved that dilemma, thank God.

"Come in," she called.

Zack walked in barefoot, in black athletic pants that hung low on his hips. His body was big and barrel-chested. Heavily muscled, but lean and cut. "Hey," he said.

He looked uncertain, lurking by the door, so she sat up straighter and smiled at him. "I haven't changed my mind, if that's what you're wondering," she told him.

He closed the door behind himself. "Thank God," he said.

They just stood there, gazing at each other. "It's been a really long time for me," Ava told him. "I don't know if I even remember the rules."

"Screw the rules. We'll make up fresh ones as we go."

She let her eyes roam over his gorgeous chest, his dazzling smile. "Sounds good."

"One big issue still has to be addressed," he said. "I need to throw on a shirt and go out and hunt down some condoms. I don't carry them on me."

"Oh. About that," she said. "I've had my bloodwork done. Several times since I was last involved with anyone. I have no diseases."

"Same," he said. "It's been a while for me, too. I'm in the clear."

"Great. In that case, you should also know that I've been on the pill for years. I take it to regulate my cycle. So on that account, we're covered. You don't need to go out looking for latex."

Zack looked startled. "For real? You'd just trust me like that?"

Ava thought about it for a moment. "Yes," she said with conviction. "Absolutely. You're a straight-up guy. Honest to a fault. Even if it costs you."

"You, too," he said. "You never take the easy way out. I've seen that when I see you go toe-to-toe with Drew or Malcolm. You never back down from a fight."

"Well, we're good, then," she said. "No more distractions or delays. You aren't going anywhere until I have my wicked way with you." She stood up and slowly paced over to where Zack stood. Taking her time, until she was inside the heat that emanated from him and could smell his soap, toothpaste, aftershave.

She leaned closer with a dreamy smile, hungrily inhaling his scent. "You shaved for me," she whispered. "I'm touched." She caressed the sharp points and planes of his square jaw. "Sandalwood and spices. Yum, nice. You are delicious, and I—"

Her words were lost against his fierce, ravenous kiss.

Zack took her at her word. He didn't really have a choice. This energy has been building up for so long. Ten long years. Ever since that fateful barbecue out at Vashon Island, right after he arrived in Seattle. That was the night Drew had introduced him to his stunning kid sister, who quickly became the star of all his erotic fantasies.

Finally, he was kissing her for real. Like he wanted to devour her. Like he was afraid she'd melt into smoke if he let go, turned his back.

He'd never allowed himself think beyond a hot fantasy in the privacy of his own mind. Not with this girl, not even back at the beginning. God knew, in those days he'd still been fresh off that bad scene with Aimee, in Berlin. He'd sworn off pretty, pampered princesses forever.

But Ava didn't belong in Aimee's category. Or any other category. She was unique, a force of nature. Strong and lithe and pliant in his arms, and her sweet, full lips tasted incredible. So soft. Her mouth was open to him, letting him inside, welcoming his tongue, his touch as he explored every lush detail. She wrapped her arms around his neck and dragged him closer.

He leaned back to take a look. Her gorgeous blue eyes were dilated, and her breasts were high and tilted, the tight little nipples poking through the soft, stretchy fabric of her camisole. Taut and stiff against his stroking hands. She shivered with arousal.

"Av," he whispered. "You're perfect."

"Hardly. That's sweet, but extravagant," she said. "Even so... thanks."

She was so wrong about that. She shone. Her skin was so hot and smooth. Flower-petal soft. That soft, thick hair, sliding through his fingers. Her hands gripped his shoulders, her sharp little nails digging into him as she kissed him back.

Bad kitty. No mercy. Not that he wanted any.

She leaned back for air. "I packed my sleepwear before I knew I was going to be seduced," she said breathlessly. "Or I would have brought some sexy negligée or other."

"Are you kidding me? That cute gray outfit makes me so hot, I can't breathe."

She laughed at him. "A stretch cami and boy shorts? Dude, you are easy to please."

Hell yeah, if it's you. He stopped himself from saying it out loud. Didn't want to be clingy or grabby. Too soon for big confessions. She didn't necessarily need to know that she was his benchmark for female hotness. It must have been that fateful night he'd spent lying next to her while she wept and then slept off the margaritas. That night had nailed it down for him. All those hours spent stroking her soft, silky hair, watching her sleep. Wondering about her dreams, her thoughts. What made her so damn sad. Wishing he could fix it for her.

That night had done something to him. He was imprinted. Couldn't shake it.

That had put a hell of a damper on his love life. No one ever measured up to his fantasies. Nor was it fair to expect anyone to do so. Ava was one of a kind.

Like everyone else, of course. But he was stuck on her. No one else would do. Such a chump. His tried-and-true pattern, to fixate on a woman he could not have.

And now, here she was. Filling his eyes, his arms, his senses.

"There's a bed, you know," Ava murmured. "If you get tired of holding me up."

No danger of that, but still, the bed sounded good. He carried her over to it and sat down with her body still wrapped around his. Ava shifted, wiggling around until she was straddling him, perched on his thighs and giving him that hot, hungry look from behind the wild mess of blond hair that shadowed her face.

He stroked his hands up her thighs, gripped her hips and pressed the aching bulge of his erection right up against the soft cotton that covered her mound in a slow, pulsing rhythm. Watching her eyes, synchronizing with her breath. Looking straight into her soul.

She cupped his face and kissed him as she moved against him.

Eventually, she moved faster, writhing eagerly, gasping for breath as she sought out the beckoning climax.

She flung her head back with a choked cry when it hit her.

He held on to her, feeling the pleasure wrack her body in long, rippling shudders of pure sensation.

Afterward, she collapsed over him and hid her face against his shoulder for a long time. Catching her breath. Her body still vibrated with a high-frequency tremor.

"You good?" he asked gently.

Ava let out a soft, whispery laugh but didn't lift her face. "Oh, God," she whispered. "Yes. No. I'm destroyed. And it was amazing."

He pondered that for a moment. "Wow. Confusing. Talk about mixed messages."

"It's just so different with you," she murmured.

"Different how? Different from what?"

Ava lifted her head. "You just get so close," she said. "I know that sounds strange, but I've never felt anyone this close to me. It's like you're inside my head, and it all feels so raw. Stripped live wires. Too much power. I'm afraid I'll get fried."

He went still. "Was it too much?"

She smiled down at him. Her eyes glittered with tears. "Of course, but it's worth it," she whispered. "I didn't know it could feel like that. Like a supernova."

"I see," he said. "Supernova. Yeah. I'd call that a step in the right direction."

Ava giggled silently. "You are a master of understatement."

He lifted her up, shifting her on his lap. "Let's go for another one," he said. "I like the supernova thing. But first…"

He tugged at the bottom of her shirt. Ava let out a soft laugh and peeled it up over her head, giving him a mind-altering view of her gorgeous torso, stretching, arching, stripping. Shaking out her tousled hair. Giving him that teasing, seductive smile.

Oh, man. So beautiful. Every last damn detail. It was just killing him. His breath was ragged, too, and he lifted her up, impressed his mouth to the perfect, soft curves of her breasts. Delicious, fragrant. Smooth skin, smelling like spring flowers, and the tight bud of her nipple against his lips, his tongue, the delicate tug of his teeth.

She shivered and moaned as he loved on her gorgeous breasts, as if he was drawing pleasure from them for both of them. Because he was. He teased her nipple with his tongue as he stroked those slick, tender, secret folds between her legs, slipping inside to pet and stroke. Deliciously wet and soft. She moved helplessly against his hand.

He was so turned on, he could hardly breathe, but he sensed that she was almost there. She moved against his hand, clenching, clutching his head to her chest, her breath ragged. Those gasping whimpers. He had to see this through for her.

He could keep that going all night. An unbroken string of orgasms. Oh, yeah. He was strung out on sexy supernovas already.

Her pleasure crested and broke. He rode it out with her as she came right around his hand, gasping with sobs of pleasure. Those clutching pulses, squeezing him.

By some miracle of self-control, he held back from coming himself.

He was saving that for later.

Eight

Ava could taste the salt sweat on his muscular shoulder. Hot, intoxicating. She could lick him all over.

Something about this man moved her. Shook her. There was an endlessness to it. A sense of mortal danger, as if she were looking over a cliff so high, she couldn't see the bottom of the chasm.

Zack looked wary. "Good?" he asked again.

She nodded, and Zack set her gently on her feet and jerked the bedcover down.

He tugged her boy shorts down over her legs and tossed them away, running his hands over her bare hips with a groan of appreciation. "I can't believe how gorgeous you are," he said. "It takes my breath away."

Damn. She had to get over this goofy girlish act and start making some moves of her own, like a participating adult, but she felt so bashful and vulnerable.

But it was definitely time for him to be naked, too. She slid his athletic pants down, but the elastic waistline got hung up on his magnificent erection, so Zack reached into his pants, shifting himself around. He let the pants fall.

Oh, yeah. His bare body was just what she'd expected after writhing all over him in the pool and all that eager, exploratory petting. But that was one thick, enthusiastic erection to play with. Good thing he was wickedly good at making her wet and desperate for him. As it was, the very sight of him made her thighs clench in breathless eagerness.

He gasped at her strong grip, her slow, twisting strokes on his stiff penis. He was stone-hard, but covered with luscious velvet. Suede-smooth. Incredibly hot. Pulsing.

"You're so beautiful," she whispered.

"Glad you like it." His voice was strangled. "Please, slow down. I'm so turned on. I'm on a hair trigger right now, and I want to save it for when I'm inside you."

She squeezed his thick, solid shaft, feeling his heart throb heavily against her palm.

"It's really hard to stop," she whispered. "I love touching you."

He kissed her again, and his sensual onslaught overwhelmed her senses with pleasure and arousal. He shifted on the bed and tumbled her down on top of him.

Ava straddled him, returning his kiss with wild abandon. Stroking her own intimate flesh slowly, teasingly over the long, heavy shaft that lay against his belly. She shook with excitement as he positioned her above him, up on her knees to give him the space he needed to grip himself and caress her with the tip of his blunt phallus.

Each slow, wet, teasing, swirling stroke a sweet lash of delight.

Finally, he nudged inside, and she sank down onto him with a gasp, filled up.

Wow. She could barely move for a moment, or breathe. The sensation was overwhelming. So was the look in his eyes.

Then he started to move. She started to rock on top of him,

and they found the sway, the dance. The heaving perfection of each slow, gliding thrust. Her breasts bounced, her hair dangling. She took all of him inside and loved every slick stroke.

Deeper…faster…harder, and already it was happening. The shivering tension was growing, charging. Transforming into something huge and terrifying and wonderful.

Zack stopped, holding her tightly as the climax rushed through her whole being.

Ava's eyes opened, and she reached out, stroking his cheek. Bracing herself against his big chest.

"You good?" he asked.

She smiled. "You keep asking."

"I keep wondering. I need to be sure. I need it to be excellent for you. Top-tier. Peak experience. Best ever. Nothing less will do for you."

She nodded, but she felt dismantled, disassembled. Inside out. Floating on a cloud.

"You look scared," he said. "Talk to me. Please."

Ava pressed trembling lips together. "I'm fine. It's just that I'm kind of a control freak, and this thing…well, this is the opposite of control. I just fall to pieces with you."

"But you like it? You want more?"

"Hell, yeah, I want more. I love it. Just one thing, though."

His eyes narrowed. "Yeah? Let's hear it."

"Come along with me this time," she urged. "Don't just be a spectator. I don't want to go supernova while you watch. I want you in it with me. All the way."

He looked troubled as he slowly stroked her leg from knee to hip.

"What?" she asked. "What's the worried look?"

"I'm a control freak, too," he admitted. "The stakes have never been this high for me. I've never been this turned on in my life. I'm afraid to just go for it, no holds barred."

"I can't wait to watch you," she said. "Mmm. So sexy."

"It's different for me," he said gruffly. "I'm bigger. I have to be more careful than you do. To make sure it's good for you."

"Oh, I see." She leaned over, pressing her breasts against his chest, and laid slow, hot, sensual kisses against his collarbone while squeezing him inside herself. "I'm not worried," she whispered. "I trust you. And I've got you. Let's go for it together. See what's on the other side."

Their hands clasped, then clutched in a tight, shaking grip as he surged up inside her, plunging deep. Unleashed.

So...good. Again. Again. Every heavy stroke made her wild for the next one. The bed shook. Their breathing was ragged. Gasps, moans, whimpers.

They both felt the power bearing down. It was like a storm rolling over them, huge and terrifying and inexorable.

They met it together, souls fused. Soaring.

At some point, Zack finally managed to roll onto his side. Ava cuddled up next to him, her hand on his heart. He buried his face in her hair and moved his hands slowly down the soft skin of her back, practically hypnotizing himself with the rhythmic caress. He ran his hand down her spine, explored her ribs, settled into the curve of her waist and the swell of her hip, and then slowly made his way back up. He wanted to commit every last detail of her to memory. Tender warmth, silken texture, sweet smell.

Then his stomach rumbled, reminding him of more mundane issues.

"Oh, hey," he said. "When I came over to knock on your door, I was going to suggest that we order dinner from room service. Are you hungry?"

"Mmm. I could probably eat something now. Do they still serve at this hour?"

"They have a reduced after-hours menu," he said. "I was checking it out before I went down to the pool."

Ava pulled loose of his embrace. "I'll go look." She laughed at the bereft expression on his face. "Come on. One of us had to get out of bed to make this happen."

"I wasn't ready," he complained. "It was way too abrupt. Traumatizing."

"Poor baby. I'll be right back." Ava went to the desk and sorted through the hotel brochures. She picked out a menu, tossing her hair back, her sexy silhouette backlit by the light filtering out of the open bathroom door.

"The after-hours menu is short, but there are possibilities," she said. "A charcuterie board for two, with smoked Parma ham, sausage, capocollo, assorted cheeses, three types of olives and fresh fruit, and hot, crusty artisan bread. There's also a savory pastry platter. Tarts made with ricotta and zucchini flower, wild mushroom and feta, fresh asparagus and caramelized onion, and sun-dried tomatoes and goat cheese. Anything appeal to you?"

"Both of them," he said. "With a bottle of good red."

He admired her back view as she called down for room service. After a few minutes of being tormented by the visual stimulation, he got up and went closer to her, burying his face in her hair and sliding his hands over her hips as she finished ordering.

"...yes, please," she said into the phone. "And a bottle of red wine. Something that pairs well with the cheese... Yes, that sounds lovely. The sooner it's here, the happier we'll be. Yes, absolutely. Have a nice evening."

Ava put down the phone and spun around, looping her arms around his waist, and gave him that brazen temptress look that made his whole body hum. Her tousled hair cast sexy, mysterious shadows over her face, but her eyes were smiling. "So I just ordered us a picnic at one in the morning. How depraved. Oh, no. Don't you give me that look, Zack."

"What look?" he asked innocently.

"The scorching, sex-all-the-time look. No way are we getting it on again when I've just ordered food to be brought up."

"It's a great way to distract us from our hunger while we wait," he pointed out.

"And it's a foregone conclusion that if we do get busy, they will knock on the door at the worst possible moment. I would hate that. So stop smoldering at me."

"Come on. If you're going to stand there naked, I'm going to stare at you with my jaw on the ground. You're the most beautiful woman I've ever seen. Deal with it."

"Wow," Ava murmured. "Bold words."

"True words," he said forcefully.

Her eyes dropped. "Well, then. I'll make it easier for you by jumping into the bathroom to wash up before we eat."

"Need help? I could be your bath attendant. I'll soap you up and then use the detachable showerhead to slowly, carefully rinse every single inch of you."

"Not a chance," she said, laughing. "You stay out here and be good. Listen for room service. I don't want to miss out on our dinner."

She disappeared into the bathroom, so Zack pulled on his sweatpants and went into the adjoining room to grab the terry-cloth robe. When he came back in, the hiss of water in the bathroom made sexy images form in his mind—Ava naked, hot water streaming over her perfect body. Beading on the tight tips of her breasts. Rushing over her gorgeous dips and curves to converge at the puffy little dark blond swirl of ringlets on her mound. That got him all worked up, just in time for the knock on the door. Their meal had arrived.

Zack opened the door and let the waiter push the rolling cart into the room. The guy left with a big smile on his face when Zack pushed the tip into his hand.

He tapped on the bathroom door. "Food's here," he called out.

"Be right out!" she called back.

Ava emerged from the bathroom, pulling the tie that had held up her hair up and letting it tumble luxuriously over her shoulders. He had the wine poured and the food laid out. She accepted the goblet from him and sipped it with a smile. "Oh, that's nice."

"It is," he agreed. "The food looks great. And the pastries are hot, so let's get to it."

The food was incredible. As if being with Ava had sharpened his senses. The bread was chewy and flavorful, and the tarts were delicious, the crusts flaky and buttery. Thin-sliced salt-cured ham was melt-in-your-mouth tender. The cheeses exploded with flavor. There were bowls of fat, shiny Greek and Italian olives, big aromatic green grapes, sliced black figs and fat golden pears to finish. Everything tasted freaking perfect.

They polished off all of it, leaving just crumbs, pits, grape stems and pear cores.

Ava looked oddly shy in the silence that followed. Her cheeks were very red.

"Damn," he said. "This hotel gets points for kick-ass midnight feast capability. Usually, it's a club sandwich if you're lucky and a frozen pizza if you're not. Only one thing missing. Dessert."

"I didn't even think of it," Ava said. "Shall we look at the menu again? We can see if they have anything that's—"

"I had a different treat in mind."

Her eyes widened as he stood up, circling the table in two strides, and knelt down in front of her, then gently tugged and spun her in the chair so that she sat facing him.

The movement made the terry-cloth robe fall wider open over her perfect thighs, and gave him a teasing glimpse of that shadowy perfection between them. He stroked his hands slowly over her warm skin, all the way up to her hips, feeling her shiver in response.

He bent down to kiss the soft skin over her knees. "I don't need the menu," he told her. "Everything I want is right here." He worked his way up her thigh with slow, languid, lazy kisses. No hurry. He'd get to the gates of paradise soon enough.

Ava covered her face, laughing under her breath. "I don't know what my problem is," she whispered. "It's ridiculous to be embarrassed after what we just did. You have such a strange effect on me, Zack. You make me all bashful and fluttery."

"I hope that's not a bad thing."

She dropped her hands, smiling at him. "Not bad," she assured him. "Just super-intense. Every sensation is amplified. The stakes feel so much higher."

Yeah, she had it exactly right. The stakes were higher. Infinitely high. But he didn't want to discuss that right now, not with his mouth watering for her intoxicating taste. So he just kissed his way slowly up her thighs, letting his hands slide into the velvety warmth of her secret places. Exploring the dips and swells and sensitive places. Caressing her tender folds. Hot, sweet, softer than a cloud. So perfect. Probing, petting. Coaxing.

Finally, he felt that ripple and sigh of total surrender go through her, and her legs relaxed. He gently pushed them open and tugged her forward to the edge of her chair, pressing his face to her belly. Her slender fingers held his head, stroking his short hair.

She let out a choked gasp as he put his mouth to her. "Oh, Zack."

So damn good. Her taste, her texture. It blasted off fireworks in his mind, his body. Even so, some part of him was hyper-aware of how fine a line he was walking right now. He hadn't understood the danger of the Ava paradox, not before being so deep inside her. Moving in her, melded with her, like he'd always fantasized about.

But getting what he wanted so badly had not satisfied him. This craving was insatiable.

When it came to Ava, the more he feasted, the hungrier he got.

Nine

Mom's eyes were full of fear as she clutched both Ava's hands and stared into her eyes. Her mouth moved and she was yelling something urgent, but there was too much noise to make out the words. Black smoke filled the plane cabin, sparks, flames. Things flew past them. All she heard was panicked screaming and the roar of wind in their ears as the plane was torn apart in the sky—

Her hands were ripped from Mom's and she was alone, spinning through empty space. The ground below rose to meet her, faster and faster—

Ava jolted awake with a gasp. Choking off the shriek of terror just in time.

Her heart was pounding. Her body shook violently. Zack stirred, and his arms tightened around her. "Av? You okay?" he murmured.

She twisted away and sat up, letting her hair fall forward to curtain her face. Gasping for breath, but trying to do it quietly. She didn't want him to see her face, even in the dim half-light from the bathroom. "Sure," she forced out, breathless. "Fine."

But he was on to her now. He lifted himself up onto his elbow, putting his hand on her back. "Are you?" he asked. "You don't seem fine. Bad dream?"

She jerked away from his touch, still shivering. "I'm fine," she repeated.

She slid off the bed and hurried to the bathroom, fighting tears and the cold, sucking emptiness behind them. It was pulling her down. Dragging her under.

Even now, even tonight, after the absolute best sex she'd ever had or even imagined having, with the man she'd always wanted. Even now, here she was again, in her usual dark pit. It had been childish and stupid to hope that just the magic of getting thoroughly and magnificently laid would suddenly fix all her problems for her.

That was too much to ask of a roll in the hay. Even a spectacular one.

She twisted up her hair, set the shower running and stepped inside. It was easier to cry if her face was already wet, and crying gave relief sometimes. She didn't know what to do with Zack. She couldn't manage him and her dark pit at the same time, with all his charisma and his potent emotional charge. He wanted so much from her.

She would disintegrate from the pressure.

She wasn't really surprised. She'd felt that desperate intensity the last time they made love, as the morning drew closer. As if they were trying to outrun something.

Yeah, right. That was because she was. But in the end, it always took her down.

A memory from her high school physics class flitted across her mind. Newton's third law of motion. *For every action there is an equal and opposite reaction.* One of the few physics facts that had stuck with her. But Newton's third law had lingered in her mind because it made emotional sense to her. It rang in her mind like a bell.

This fear, clawing inside her. This was the equal and opposite reaction. The price that had to be paid for anything that wonderful. Nothing came for free.

She took her time once she finished with her shower, styling her hair, putting moisturizer on her face. Hoping the feelings would subside if she focused completely on something else. Anything else. Sometimes it worked. For a while.

No such luck today, though. She dabbed a little concealer under her reddened eyes.

Her face was pale, but not her lips. They were hot red, and a little swollen, from hours of desperate, frantic kissing. Just thinking about it sent the sense memories pulsing through her body, making her thighs clench and her breath catch in her chest.

Stop stalling. Just do this. It has to be done.

She put in her gold and ruby earrings, pulled on the terry-cloth bathrobe and marched out into the room.

Zack was sitting up in bed, waiting for her. Her gaze locked with his for an unbearable instant and skittered away as if she'd touched a raw current of electricity. She got to work laying out clothes for the day. Underwear, stockings, skirt, blouse, coat, boots.

"Ava," he said. "Please. Just tell me. What's wrong? What did I do?"

"Nothing. Really, nothing," she said, because it was the simple truth. He was wonderful. That was what made this so awful. The unfairness of it. What a goddamn waste, that she couldn't let herself enjoy this as it should be enjoyed.

But she just couldn't. She was too raw. Too wrecked.

Zack studied her as she pulled her underwear on and hooked her bra, a frown of focused concentration in his eyes. "Bullshit," he said. "Tell me. Please."

She sat down on the other bed to pull her stockings on. "Really. It's nothing. Just this time of day. I'm at a really low ebb. Not a morning person. No fun to be with."

"Don't put your clothes on yet," he said. "It's early. I could make you forget what time of day it is if you gave me a chance. That's a challenge I'm willing to embrace."

She tugged her stockings up and slipped on her blouse. "No," she said tightly. "I, um…sorry, Zack, but I actually could use a little privacy right now."

Zack's face stiffened. He slid out of bed and picked up his sweatpants, pulling them on. "Okay. I get it."

"You—you don't. Really. It doesn't have anything to do with you," she told him swiftly. "It's just me. My own weird issues. Please don't take it personally."

He let out a bitter laugh. "Sorry, but that's not an option right now," he said. "This whole thing has gotten pretty damn personal for me. So don't even try."

"I didn't mean to—"

"I don't care what you meant or didn't mean. I'll get out of your way while you dress, but don't leave the room without me. I still want you covered at all times." He stopped by the door, careful not to meet her eyes. "It'll take me maybe ten minutes to grab a shower, get shaved and dressed. I'll be waiting for your knock."

"All right, but Zack, please don't get upset," she begged.

"How could I not? After what happened last night, the way you're acting sucks for me. You can't talk it away."

"I didn't mean to make you feel—"

"Too bad. It happened anyway. You think you're the only one with feelings? The rest of us should just suck it up? Play it cool so that you won't be inconvenienced?"

"No," she said miserably. "I don't think that at all."

Zack shook his head. "Get ready for your day, Ava." His voice was colorless. "Don't sweat it. I don't want to embarrass you or make things complicated. We're adults. It's fine. Take it easy."

The door closed. She fell forward onto the bed and buried her face in the pillow. It still smelled of him. Keeping her scream silent hurt. Like a screw turning in her throat.

She'd struck out in love before. Often. But it had been different the other times. Her past lovers had just backed away when things got difficult. Sometimes she'd even felt a sense of numb relief when they were gone. One less thing to stress about.

Not this time.

Zack scanned the stream of people cycling through the Blooms' trade show booth, which was packed and buzzing with activity. Apparently, Desert Bloom was the hottest prospect of Future Innovation. The food and drinks being served created a party atmosphere, with tray after tray of fresh-baked, artisanal crackers smeared with olive, artichoke or sun-dried tomato paste continually brought in by the catering crew, all treats prepared exclusively with Desert Bloom Farm products. Visitors devoured them as fast as they were delivered and kept Ernest busy pouring out Desert Bloom wines and mojitos.

Ava had not looked Zack's way once all morning and into the afternoon. Not that she'd had time. She was busy being whatever the situation required her to be, on the spot. Marketer, storyteller, branding specialist, crisis manager, cheerleader, shrink. She never strayed from the Blooms, who looked hunched and spiderlike in their black turtleneck sweaters and jeans, but they were relatively well-groomed today, having attempted to tame their bushy clouds of hair. They were wound up so tight, they tended to babble, so Ava was always at their elbows, nudging the conversation where it needed to go, but she did it so expertly, only someone watching as closely as he was would ever notice.

At least in this context, no one could call his intense, focused attention creepy. It was his goddamn job to hover over her, staring like a madman. Lucky for him.

He'd been such an idiot, getting his poor, tender feelings all hurt this morning. But the real idiocy was in giving in to temptation in the first place. What the hell did he expect from her? Birds and flowers and true love, after one night? It was just great sex. Any other guy with a brain would have been more than happy to settle for that, at face value.

But not him. Oh, no. He just had to make it as hard as possible for himself.

Wanting more. Wanting it all. Wanting it right freaking *now*.

On some level, he'd known he would crash and burn if he gave in to this urge. He'd known it for years, but a man could only hold out for so long. Ava Maddox, dripping wet, in a bikini, her gorgeous blue eyes hot with desire…how could he resist that?

He couldn't. And now he was paying for his lustful stupidity.

Craig Redding happened to be in the large group of men that were clustered around her, which did not thrill him. The guy was handsy as all hell. He kept touching Ava's shoulder, her arm, her back, her hair. Throwing a possessive arm over her shoulder. There he was, doing it again, even after she slipped his grip. At one point, he even pinched her cheek. Ava jerked away and wagged a warning finger at him, laughing. Too bad there was no pool here for her to dunk the presumptuous bonehead. Just as well, though, since Zack would be tempted to hold that entitled jerk's head underwater until he stopped flopping.

A raucous burst of laughter from the direction of the bar caught his attention.

It was Ernest, at the bar. He was giggling, his head together with another young guy. Tall, skinny, with straight black hair.

Ernest saw Zack look over and lifted the pitcher of mojito that he'd freshly replenished from the chilled urn behind him. "We're celebrating. You want some?"

"What's the occasion?" Zack asked.

Ernest beckoned him to come closer and leaned to whisper in his ear, his breath heavy with alcohol. "See that guy who's talking to Ava?" Ernest whispered. "Brown coat, balding, ears sticking out like jug handles? That's Trevor Wexford."

Ernest saw Zack's expression and nodded. "I see you've heard the name?"

"Big venture capitalist, right?" Zack said.

"Duh," Ernest said. "Like, huge. And that's his wife next to him, Callista. She's a real piece of work. The two of them have been here talking to Ava and the Blooms for over forty minutes. He's taken all their literature and given her his card. He's interested. Which is huge." Ernest dragged over the big pitcher and hoisted it up, slopping some of the liquid onto the bar. "Want a mojito? Sustainably farmed sugar and rum, lemons and fresh mint from the Desert Bloom farm. Or wine, from the organic Desert Bloom vineyard?"

The two young men dissolved into drunken giggles once again. Zack studied them for a moment. "Looks like the two of you have done some quality control already."

"Um, well." Ernest's new friend smirked. "Someone had to do it, right?"

"Who are you?" Zack asked.

"Oh, sorry," Ernest said. "I should have introduced you. This is Malik. He's Craig Redding's assistant."

"Ah. I see," Zack said.

"So can I pour you a drink?" Ernest asked. "Or some wine? The wine's good, too."

"I'm on the job," Zack told him.

Ernest tittered. "No problem. I've got you covered, along with all the other teetotalers." He pulled another big pitcher from the shelf behind him. "Here's your no-alcohol option, a virgin Desert Bloom. Basically, it's just a glass of really fabulous minty lemonade." Ernest poured out a cup and presented it to Zack. "The cups are sustainable, too. Made from leaves, each one stamped with a flower from the Desert Bloom garden. Same with the plates. Ava's branding idea."

Zack took the cup and admired the stamped dried flower that adorned the delicate veined surface of the leaf. "Nice design."

"Yeah, and one hundred percent compostable," Ernest told him. "And I'm the lucky guy who gets to load up the biodegradable garbage bags full of all the plates and cups and drag them out to the truck to haul back to the Desert Bloom compost center. Gotta be flex in this brave new world, right? I'm not just a marketer now. I'm also a janitor, garbage man, busboy, waiter and bartender! All the things! Wow, lucky me!"

Zack waited until Ernest and Malik got through their fresh snorting fit of laughter before he replied. "Your boss is over there working a whole lot more jobs than you are," he said. "I don't see her bitching and moaning about it. Or drinking, either."

Ernest and Malik abruptly swallowed their laughter, exchanging nervous glances.

Zack went on. "Seems to me that a big, important trade show where a lot is at stake for your employer isn't the best venue for you to get hammered with your buddy." He looked at Malik. "And I'm guessing that your boss would agree with me. Am I right?"

Malik's eyes slid away. "Uh…uh…dude," he muttered to Ernest. "I better go and, uh, check on some stuff. Catch up with you later."

Malik vanished, and Ernest just stood there for a moment, red-faced. "You don't have to get all moralistic about it, you know," he said. "It's not like I'm sloshed. Just a tiny buzz. I had barely a taste of the mojitos. I'm totally on top of my game."

"Good," Zack said. "Stay there. It's what she pays you for." He took a sip of his virgin Desert Bloom mojito. "Good stuff. Very minty. My compliments."

"I'm going to get another case of lemons," Ernest said, slinking away.

Zack drained his compostable cup of virgin mojito and tossed it into the receptacle provided, then shifted his position to get Ava back into his unbroken line of vision. She was still chatting with the guy Ernest had identified as Trevor Wexford. His wife and Ava were laughing at something he'd said.

"Hey, there, Zackie! Wasn't that your first name?"

Zack turned at the sound of that oily voice to see Craig Redding shoving a cracker smeared with artichoke paste into his mouth. The guy smiled at him as he chewed and washed it all down with a big gulp of mojito.

"The name is Zack," he said.

"Right," Craig said. "Chief security officer at Maddox Hill, eh? Quite a job. Huge company. Thousands of far-flung workers all over the globe. A crap ton of priceless intellectual property to protect. I'm surprised to see you straying so far from your flock."

"I've got an excellent team," Zack told him. "I have complete confidence in them to manage for a few days without me."

"That's nice to hear," Craig said. "A high-functioning workplace is a thing of beauty, right?"

"Absolutely," Zack said.

"I guess you'd know," Craig said. "You've been in the game at every level. From the very bottom on up. Right?"

Zack crossed his arms and studied the other man. "I suppose," he said. "Where exactly are you going with this?"

"Not anywhere in particular," Craig said, his voice elaborately casual. "I read a profile on you in the *C-Suite* magazine."

"Oh, yeah. They did one a couple years ago," Zack said.

"Yeah. I remember reading it a while back," Craig said. "Nice article. The writer must have had a crush on you. They just went on and on."

Huh. Craig had stalked him online, reading archived articles. That was weird.

"I'm gratified at your interest," he said guardedly. "I just don't get the point of it."

"I take an interest in the arcs of people's careers," Craig said. "You started out as a bodyguard back in the day, right? An army buddy of Drew Maddox, current CEO. The founder's nephew. He got you a job doing close protection for Hendrick Hill when he traveled to Africa after you got out of the army. Am I right?"

"Not exactly," Zack said. "It was the marines, not the army. And yes, Drew suggested that I apply for the job, but he didn't hand it to me. He wasn't even working at Maddox Hill back then. He was still in architecture school."

"Yeah, yeah, right. So it was all on your own merit, of course. Quite the success story. Real inspiring. Rags to riches, huh?"

Zack gazed at Redding, thinking about his single mom, a small-town social worker, and how she'd worked two jobs, scraping and scrambling to make sure he and Joanna had decent clothes.

"I wouldn't exactly say rags," he replied.

"You wouldn't? Huh. Guess everything's relative, right?" Craig's exposed teeth had a stringy wad of sustainably farmed Desert Bloom garden mint stuck between them.

"Guess so," Zack agreed.

"So this thing with Ava," Craig pressed on. "It's a career flashback? You're, what…devolving, professionally? Regressing? How should I call it?"

"Call it doing a favor for a friend," Zack said. "Then go about your business."

Craig's eyes narrowed. "That was rude and hostile. Fighting words, eh?"

"Not at all," Zack said. "I don't need to fight you. I'm just saving you time and energy. This conversation serves no purpose. Go talk to someone who cares."

Craig's nostrils flared, but he turned around and walked away, right back to Ava. He bent down and murmured in her ear. Probably something about Zack's fighting words. Running to tattle on him, like the whining, gutless twerp that he was.

Ava flashed Zack a startled look. *Ooh, busted.* He held his breath, wondering if she was going to come over and scold him for being such a bad, rude boy.

She turned away. Nope, no such luck. That brief, fleeting glance was all he got.

She was just so damn beautiful. Even if it hadn't literally been his job to keep his eyes glued to her, he wouldn't have been able to do anything else. And he wasn't the only one. Every man in her orbit rubbernecked. And he didn't blame them one goddamn bit.

However, if a rubbernecker happened to catch Zack's eye, he whipped his gaze away from Ava instantly and marched right onward without stopping to look at the Blooms' booth. That was Zack's small personal superpower. Silent intimidation.

Or so he had been told.

Using it like this displayed a distinct lack of professionalism on his part, but that was just too damn bad. God knew, the booth got plenty of cracker-chomping, mojito-guzzling traffic anyway.

He was doing them a favor by helping them sort out the wheat from the chaff.

The man just wiped her out. No matter where she went or whom she talked to, Zack was there, blasting out a frequency so intense, it exhausted her.

When she wrapped things up on the expo floor and said good night to the Blooms, she went to the bar to meet some old friends for a late drink. She'd known Marcus and Caleb Moss, the CTO and CEO of MossTech, for years. Caleb had been one of her first clients in the way back, when he'd opened a start-up tech business with a friend of his years ago. Sadly, the start-up had ended in catastrophe, through no fault of hers or Caleb's. But they had remained friends since then, and they'd made plans that morning to talk about the MossTech expo project, which was on the short list of candidates for the Future Innovation prize, along with the Blooms'.

Nothing would persuade Zack to leave her alone for a drink with her friends in the hotel bar. His only concession was to sit on the other side of the bar, with clear sight lines, and watch them all stonily from afar while nursing a club soda with lime.

Stoic, expressionless and unnerving as hell.

It didn't help that the Moss brothers were both extremely good-looking. No doubt that jacked up Zack's hellfire-and-brimstone stare an extra couple of notches in intensity.

Marcus and Caleb's conversation kept trailing off to nothing as they shot quick, unsettled glances in Zack's direction.

"Ava," Caleb said cautiously. "In the interests of personal safety, what's the deal with the guy fixated on you from across the bar? Is there something we should know?"

Ava rubbed her forehead with a sigh. "Some interpersonal conflict," she said, her voice weary. "Nothing to do with you. I imagine you heard about my problem with online trolls, right?"

"Yes," Marcus said. "Bottom-feeding scum. I hope you crush whoever it is."

"Yeah, thanks. Anyhow, it kind of blew up this week, so I went to Zack for advice. He's Maddox Hill's CSO, and he got all twisted up and upset about it. He insisted on coming down from Seattle to keep an eye on me down here, but somehow it's gotten really, ah...complicated."

"Yeah, no kidding," Caleb said.

"Do us a favor, babe," Marcus said. "Just make sure he knows that the two of us don't have designs on you, okay? Stunning though you are, you've never given either one of us a break, and at this point, I have no reason to think you ever will. And it's a sure thing we aren't going to try any funny stuff with that big, scary dude looming over you."

She swatted him on the shoulder. "Oh, shut up. I'm not involved with him."

Caleb and Marcus exchanged dubious glances. "I wouldn't want to be the one to tell him that," Caleb said.

Ava fought back a startling wave of tears, but she did not want to inflict that embarrassment on her friends. "There's attraction, yes," she admitted, her voice tight. "Big-time. But we just hit a wall, and it's better to stop now. Before we hurt ourselves."

Marcus studied her face. "I think that ship has sailed, Av. For him, anyway."

Her gaze dropped, and she bit her lip to keep it steady.

"Right," Marcus said. "Just as I thought. That ship already sailed for you, too."

"I'm sorry, Av," Caleb said awkwardly. "That sucks."

"Oh, stop it, guys," she snapped. "Enough already. I came here to talk about your plant DNA diagnostic techniques, not my love life. Moving on. You should consider having Moss-Tech partner with Bobby and Wilbur. Your research could really complement theirs. I want to set up a meeting sometime."

She turned the conversation to business, and the Mosses played along. They discussed DNA diagnostics at some length. Finally, she gave them both a peck on the cheek and promised to visit their booth the next day.

Zack materialized beside her as she walked to the elevator.

"Zack, for God's sake," she whispered. "Would you just stop?"

"Doing what? My job? No, I won't stop."

"That's not what I meant, and you know it. I'm referring to the glaring and the scolding and the general negativity. It's embarrassing. You got Ernest all upset—"

"He needed his ass kicked. He got sloppy today."

"Maybe so, but that's my problem, not yours. I'm the one who pays him. And that thing you said to Craig was just rude and ridiculous. I know he's annoying, but seriously?"

"I didn't like the way he was sliming you," Zack said. "He was bugging me."

She blew out a breath through her teeth. "You are making problems for me, Zack."

"Sorry. I should have gotten someone else to come down here to replace me, but this event wraps up soon. Once we're back in Seattle, Vikram's team will cover you and I'll monitor the situation from a distance. You'll never have to see my face again."

She stopped in front of her door. "Goddammit, Zack," she whispered. "This is just unbearable."

"It'll be over soon," he said. "Grit your teeth."

The stony quality in his voice made her as angry as she was miserable. "I never let people bug me," she said. "Living with Uncle Malcolm gave me a very thick skin, and I'm good at letting things roll off my back. But you just drive me totally nuts."

The look on his face was more like a brick wall than ever before. He wasn't going to risk letting her hurt him again. And she didn't blame him after the way she'd panicked this morning. Like she always did when the tide went out and left her sick and stranded.

No, this raw voltage was just too dangerous. They scared each other to death.

"If you need to swim tonight, let me know," he said.

"God, no," she said. "I'm exhausted."

"Then I'll let you rest. Good night." He stood there waiting until she swiped her key card and the light clicked green.

"Good night," she whispered.

Ava dropped her purse on the table and sank down onto the bed. Some part of her was always listening for sounds of Zack in the other room. She wondered if he would order dinner. Her eyes fell on the room service menu, the wine list. The memories of last night burned in her mind. The longing to reach out to him was physically painful.

But any attempt to make this better would definitely only make it worse.

Zack was not the kind of guy one could dally with and then send back to his room when she was done. If Zack did something at all, he did it all the way.

And all night long, with devastating, tireless energy and skill.

And when he was angry, oh God. The whole world felt it.

Ten

Twenty-five hours to go.

Zack ran that through his mind. He heard Ava's easy laughter while she chatted with the people outside the booth. She looked as stunning as ever in a tailored dark pantsuit and an ice-blue silk blouse.

Then a flash of coral pink caught his eye. He turned to see Callista Wexford enter the exhibition booth and approach Bobby and Wilbur, who were bent over a glass case full of flowering plants. Callista flashed them a brilliant smile and tossed her mane of glossy mahogany hair back. "Excuse me, gentlemen. I've noticed that fungi appear to be the mainstay of your seed conditioner potion. More so than the other microbes in your inoculation brew, which makes it different from some of the other projects of this kind that I've reviewed. Why this focus on the fungi?"

Callista waited expectantly, but her smile seemed to freeze in place as the Bloom brothers just stared back, eyes blank, mouths agape.

Damn. They were glitching. Their circuits were just not built to handle the massive charge of Callista's feminine splendor. She'd flash-fried them.

Zack racked his brains to remember everything he'd learned in the past day as he stepped forward. "I think the issue is to reduce the soil's exposure to erosive force," he offered. "The fungi stabilize the soil by making it into sticky lumps, which makes it more resistant to erosion. Did I get that more or less right, Wilbur?"

Wilbur blinked as his brain stuttered back online, his eyes darting between Zack and Callista. "Uh...uh...yes," he stammered. "It's, uh...glomalin. The soil particles form water-stable aggregates, and root entanglements, fungal hyphae and exudates pull it all together and help the soil hold water and resist erosion."

"But we haven't discounted rhizosphere bacteria," Bobby assured her. "Everything has its place in the process. But our focus here is to match the right fungi to the right plant to bring the soil to life as fast as possible. Which helps it hold the rain that falls on it."

And the Blooms were off and running, blasting out info about vegetation dynamics, soil stability and anionic-hydrophilic polymers. Not long after that, Callista extricated herself and joined Zack outside the booth.

"Wow," she murmured. "That was intense. Like turning on a fire hose."

"Yeah, the Blooms are really something," Zack agreed. "Great project, isn't it?"

"Oh, marvelous. So what's your role in all this?" Callista fluttered her eyelashes at him expertly. "Do you have a horse in this race?"

"Not yet, but it looks like a great investment," he said. "I just recently learned about it. I work at Maddox Hill myself. I'm just here because I accompanied Ava to the trade show."

"So you two are, ah...together?"

"I'm just here to provide security," Zack said, leaving it at that.

But Callista would not leave it where he put it. "I see. Is that why you never leave her side?"

His jaw clenched painfully. "Yes, I guess it would explain that."

Callista's smile widened. She eased closer to him. "So you're based in Seattle?"

She made a small, satisfied sound when he nodded. "Trevor and I have a place up there," she said. "We own a small island in Puget Sound, just a short boat trip from the city. Gorgeous place. Just water, birds and trees as far as the eyes can see. I spend a lot of time there. Sadly, Trevor's almost always working, so he practically never comes up with me." Callista placed her hand on his forearm. "I'm spending the next couple of weeks at the island, since I'm planning to attend the Maddox Hill Foundation gala." Her voice was throaty. "Come see me. I'll send a boat for you. Just tell me when."

Zack gazed down at the slender, perfectly manicured hand resting on his sleeve, adorned with costly rings and bracelets, and realized several surprising things all at once.

One, he wasn't into her. She was a stunner, sure. A man would have to be dead not to notice. But he was hooked on Ava's incandescent glow. Ava's beauty seemed deeper, more vivid. Other women looked flat to him by comparison.

He didn't know what to say to Callista. He wasn't talented at fabricating convincing social lies. He tended to default to the plain truth, but in this case, the truth sounded churlish and ugly. *You're married, and I don't want to go through that particular wood chipper. I'm not intrigued by neglected trophy wives on the prowl for fresh meat.*

Or worst of all, the most stark and naked truth of all. *Sorry, but I'm all hung up someone else.* God help him.

"Oh, hey, Callista." He turned when he heard Ava's voice. She was smiling when he turned to look, but with none of her usual warmth. "See something that you like?"

"Oh, yes," Callista purred. "Most definitely."

The women's brilliant smiles were like blades clashing. "Wilbur and Bobby were just telling Callista about soil stabilization via inoculation with AM fungi," Zack said, just to break the tension.

"Yes, they told me a lot of things, very quickly," Callista said, tittering. "But Zack's simple explanation about sticky dirt clumps really made it pop for me. Zack is an excellent brand ambassador. You should hire him to make the science digestible for us normal folk."

"He'd be far too expensive," Ava said crisply. "He's a busy man. A chief executive at Maddox Hill Architecture. No time for side hustles or science projects."

"No? Like, say, doing close protection work for you?" Callista blinked at her innocently.

"That's a special case," Zack said.

"I am sure that it is," Callista murmured. "Very special." She fished a card from her small purse and tucked it into his suit pocket. "If you feel like talking about that thing we discussed, or if you decide to carve out time for a side hustle, call me. Later, Ava. Be sure to tell Wilbur and Bobby that Trevor and I are rooting for them tonight."

"Certainly I will. Thanks," Ava said.

Her smile vanished as soon as Callista turned the corner. Ava turned toward Zack.

She finally broke the odd silence. "So what did you discuss with Callista?" Her voice was casual, but her eyes were anything but.

"Nothing in particular," Zack hedged. "She asked Bobby and Wilbur about arbuscular mycorrhizal fungi, and they both froze up. Either her cleavage or her perfume, or both. I primed the pump for them, got them talking, and after that, they were fine. And lucky for me, because I put out everything I had."

"Oh, I just bet you did," Ava said.

The hackles rose on Zack's neck. "Excuse me? What is that supposed to mean?"

"Oh, nothing," she said, her voice light. "I really appreciate you pulling Wilbur and Bobby back on track. I should have been covering them myself. They aren't equipped to function with a woman like Callista Wexford." She paused for a moment. "And I hope you'll forgive me for saying this, but I don't think you are, either."

Zack gaped at her. "Where the hell did that come from?"

"I know, I know," Ava said. "You're a free man. Do anything you want with that card in your pocket. But I've known Callista for years. She'll stomp right on your face to get what she wants. Keep that in mind before you wander into her sticky web."

"I have no intention of wandering into anybody's sticky web," he growled. "The warning isn't necessary. Or appropriate."

"So sorry. My bad," she murmured, looking unrepentant. "Oh, hey. Looks like they're calling me back out there. Excuse me." She slipped away.

He set off to follow her, keeping his eyes fixed on that honey-colored updo as it bobbed through the throng. She stopped at a group of Bobby and Wilbur's best prospects. Trevor Wexford and Craig Redding were in the group.

Zack forced his way closer, and Craig spotted him. Zack saw a contemptuous smile flit across his face, and before Zack could close the distance, Ava stumbled and fought for balance as Craig grabbed her arm and pulled her in the opposite direction. The *hell*?

Zack pushed through the crowd as fast as he could without knocking people over. He followed Craig and Ava into an adjoining room, filled with tables, not as crowded as the expo floor. Craig pulled her into a quieter corner and turned in mock surprise as Zack approached. "Well, if it isn't Zackie the guard dog, sniffing along behind."

"Let go of her," Zack said.

Ava turned her head with a gasp, her eyes wide. "Zack, please don't—"

"Don't overreact, pal." Craig raised both hands, smirking. "Keep it mellow."

"Step away from her, right now."

"Zack!" Ava's eyes were horrified. "Calm down! I've known Craig for ten years. We went to school together. He's not a danger to me. Relax!"

"Yeah, Zack," Craig taunted. "Relax. She's safe. We're just going to get lunch."

"She's not going anywhere without a bodyguard," Zack said.

"You've got to be kidding." Craig gave Ava a disbelieving glance, then looked back at Zack. "Rest easy, buddy. We're grabbing lunch to talk about old times and future opportunities. She'll be fine. What could possibly happen?"

"We'll never find out," Zack said. "I'm not leaving her, with you or anyone."

"And this stupid power struggle is beside the point!" Ava interjected. "I don't have time for lunch with you, Craig, as I already told you. The brothers need me as a go-between. I'm networking! And Zack, you are out of line."

"No, I am not," Zack replied, still staring at Craig. "By no means."

"What is it with this guy?" Craig asked. "Is he your guard dog or your boyfriend?"

Ava recoiled, her mouth tightening. "That was uncalled-for, Craig. Back off."

"I get it." Craig's voice had a tone of discovery. "This poor bozo doesn't know which one he is. Eenie, meenie, miney, mo, right? Guard dog or boyfriend? You've got his pointy little jarhead all confused."

"You're pissing me off, Craig," Ava told him. "Get lost."

"Dirty girl." Craig clucked his tongue. "You should know better, Ava. Things get messy real fast when you start screwing the help."

Zack had no memory of getting there, but he was suddenly nose to nose with Craig Redding, his hand twisted into the other man's shirt collar, pinning him against the wall. Craig's feet dangled over empty air, and his face was red. His eyes bulged.

"Apologize to her, you foulmouthed son of a bitch." Zack shook the guy to get him going, but Craig just gurgled and coughed, wiggling frantically. "Let's hear it. Speak up."

From far away, he heard Ava's frantic voice, far outside the roar in his own ears. Then he noticed her hands, smacking at his shoulders and his chest, then scrabbling with her nails at his fingers, still clenched around Craig's collar.

Ava was yelling in his face. "Let him go! Damn it, Zack!"

It went against every instinct to let that trash-talking punk stand on own his feet after what he'd said to Ava. Craig was in desperate need of a pounding.

Wrong place. Wrong time. He was doing himself no favors with this floor show.

Zack exhaled slowly and dropped Craig back on his feet. He stepped back.

Craig pitched forward, almost falling, and hunched there with his hands braced on his knees, coughing and sputtering.

Ava put her hand on his shoulder. "Craig, are you all—"

"Don't touch me!" Craig flinched away from her hand. His face was dark red with rage as he pointed at Zack. "You are a goddamn animal!"

"Better that than an asshole," Zack told him.

Craig sucked in a gasp of fresh outrage. "Leash your damned dog, Ava!"

"Just go, Craig," Ava said tightly. "Please. You've caused enough trouble."

Craig slouched out of the room, muttering.

Ava turned to him. "What in the hell was that? Never do that to me again!"

"I didn't do anything to you. I did it to him. For insulting you."

"I can fight my own battles!"

"Yeah? Then why did you come to me with your problem in the first place, if you're completely on top of it?"

"That is unfair," she said furiously. "My trolls are another issue. You are here to defend my physical safety, not my honor, and you're here at your own insistence, not mine. Craig is no threat to my physical safety! And I'm no fragile Victorian damsel with her smelling salts. I can defend my own goddamn honor!"

"He disrespected you," he said. "I can't allow that."

"It's not up to you!" Ava yelled. "I am not helpless! I can answer any disrespect that comes my way in person! I don't need a champion. Do you understand?"

Zack just gazed back at her and said nothing.

Ava's eyes widened. "Zack?" she prompted. "Hello? This is the part where you promise me that you won't do this to me again."

"I don't make promises unless I'm sure that I can keep them. If that sleazy punk insults you or gets up in my face again, I can't promise I won't break his jaw." He held up his hand as she opened her mouth. "Let me finish. He's a slimy little weasel, so I doubt it'll come to that. He doesn't have a death wish. It's a nonissue. He won't get near me."

Or you. The silent subtext.

Ava made an impatient sound. "I don't have time for your Neanderthal posturing right now. I'm going to get back to work. And you will not get in my way. Understood?"

"Absolutely," he said. "No one will get in your way. That's what I'm here for. To scare away the riffraff. That's my particular specialty."

She glared at him. "You just never stop, do you?"

"Never," he said.

Eleven

Ava didn't hear another word out of Zack for the rest of that frenetic afternoon, but she was intensely aware of his presence. He just stood there like a colossus, a few steps away from wherever she was, letting people sidle nervously around him.

His burning focus never relented, not even as she, Ernest and the Bloom brothers walked together to the elevator to prepare for the dinner and the awards ceremony. Zack paced along quietly beside them as she tried to calm down the Blooms, but three days of constant extroversion had taken its toll. Wilbur and Bobby were exhausted. Both of the brothers were pale and sweaty, with wild eyes and trembling hands.

"We'll come to your room in a half an hour," Ava reminded, patting Wilbur on the shoulder. "Take it easy. You guys will be great. I know it."

"But I can't knot a tie," Wilbur lamented. "And Bobby's even worse at it. Can I just wear a T-shirt under my suit coat? It's black, at least. I hate button-down shirts."

"Not tonight, Wilbur. Wear the shirt, please," Ava urged. "And relax. You guys just blew everybody's minds with your beautiful project. It will change the course of history. Remember, you're selling the one thing every person here or anywhere would pay any price for—hope for the future. A healthier, richer planet for our kids and grandkids. You two are the good guys, answering the call of duty to the whole world, so stand tall and own it. Chests out. Heads up. Be the guys who can make that dream a reality."

"Um…okay," Bobby said, wiping his broad, shiny forehead. "But…the ties?"

"Zack will help you knot the ties before we go down. Right, Zack?"

"Sure I will," Zack calmly assured them. "I've got your back. My granddad taught me to do it when I was ten. You guys will rock this. I'll bet you'll win that prize, too."

Ernest got off at the same floor as the Blooms and hustled them off the elevator.

"See you in a half hour," Ava called. "Wear the button-down shirt, Wilbur! And drink a glass of water, both of you!"

The elevator door closed, and she was alone with Zack Austin, which at this point made her just as jumpy and shaky as Bobby and Wilbur.

Zack gave her a thoughtful look. "You take this whole thing so personally."

"Of course I do," she replied. "How else could I take it? Those guys are my buddies. I've known them since freshman year in college. They're like my goofy little brothers. And they need my help like no client of mine has ever needed it before."

"Really? More than Jenna? You did incredible things for Arm's Reach when you started working for her foundation."

The door slid open on their floor, and Ava considered his question as they walked together. "Not the same," she said. "Jenna is a perfectly competent brand ambassador in her own right. She just needed me to pump energy into her project, mostly to free up more of her time for design work. Jenn can advocate for herself if she needs to. The Blooms are different.

They need someone to mediate with the world, or else they'll hurt themselves."

"So it's your job to carry them?"

"Somebody has to," she said. "The world needs their gifts. And I am not letting them blow this opportunity because of social awkwardness. Nor will I let anyone use them, or cheat them, or steal from them. I will flatten any son of a bitch who tries."

The smile that flashed over his face put her on the defensive. "What's so funny?"

He stopped by her door. "Nothing at all," he said. "I just hope the Blooms know how lucky they are to have you on their side."

Her face felt suddenly hot. "Okay. Well, thanks."

Her phone chirped in her bag, and she pulled it out and took a look at it, in case it was Ernest with a fresh crisis. It was a text from Drew.

Hey sis. Flying home day after tomorrow. Uncle Malcolm, Vann and Sophie coming home too. Bev wants us all back for the foundation gala. Jenna sends love. I'll call when we touch down. Be good. ttyl

She looked up at him. "Drew and Malcolm and the rest are coming home soon."

His face did not change expression. "Good. I'll be glad to have as many more people as possible circling the wagons around you until we solve this troll thing. Twenty minutes, okay? That gives us time to knot Bobby and Wilbur's ties and be downstairs on time. Knock on the inside door when you're ready."

"Sounds good," she said.

Once alone in her room, Ava wanted to have a mini meltdown, but she didn't have that luxury with mere minutes to put on her game face. The dress was an old favorite, midnight-blue silk with low-cut black velvet bodice. It fit looser than it should, since appetite-killing stress had been shrinking her lately. She twisted her hair up into a loose updo with dangling locks around her chin and put on some bolder makeup. Stepped into black heels, draped a blue silk and black velvet stole around her shoulders, and examined the results with a critical eye.

Whatever. The deep red of her lipstick made her skin ghostly pale, and her eyes looked worried and shadowy, but this was as good as it was going to get tonight.

She dropped her key card into her evening bag and rapped on the connecting door.

Zack opened it. He looked big and imposing and impossibly handsome in his slim-cut dark suit. He stared down at her, looking startled.

"What is it?" she demanded after an uncomfortably long pause. "Is something wrong? Is my makeup smeared? Have I a grown another head?"

"Nothing," he said gruffly. "Sorry. We better move if we want to get downstairs in time to help Bobby and Wilbur."

Ava squared her shoulders and ran her inner pep talk in her mind. She was woman to be reckoned with. The Bloom brothers' champion was on the rampage tonight.

Watch out, world.

It took longer than Zack anticipated to talk Bobby and Wilbur down off the ledge of their incipient panic attacks, but Ava pulled it off. Ernest had managed to smooth down the brothers' frizzy tufts into tidy ponytails, with the help of his own hair wax. The final emergency was Wilbur's nervous sweat attack, necessitating a last-minute fresh shirt.

Zack was fascinated with Ava's expert Bloom wrangling. She somehow managed to settle the nerves of the rattled brothers and bolster their confidence at the same time. Her nonstop patter as he knotted the Blooms' ties was both soothing and bracing.

The crowded ballroom downstairs was lit by an enormous art-piece chandelier with dangling prisms and lantern cutouts that spun, swirling slow, shifting patterns of gold-tinted light around the room like a lazy kaleidoscope. It was a perfect foil for Ava, who was already tinted gold. He did not understand how that dress stayed put on her stunning body. Women's mysteries. The big challenge was in not gawking like a meathead.

Dinner was pretty good, by mass banquet standards. Then the lights dimmed and it was time for the entertainment, a set from a hot new band, which consisted of a drummer, a guitarist and a waiflike young girl with blue hair in a baggy yellow athletic suit. She sang doleful but catchy ballads in a wispy little voice, about being lonesome, depressed, misunderstood, angry and ignored. Not exactly the message he wanted to dwell on right now, but it was something to stare at that wasn't Ava's décolletage.

Not that Ava would notice if he did gawk at her bosom. She was icily ignoring him. Embarrassed about their night together. Then, like a bad joke, the blue-haired girl belted out a song about her lover being embarrassed about having had sex with her. It was her big set closer. Sweet. His cup of awkward had officially overflowed.

The speechifying began, and all the big shots who had been involved with Future Innovation had to be heard from: a senator, a famous movie star, a university president, a handful of industry titans. They droned on and on.

Finally, the emcee announced the award and called up a famous biologist who had a highly popular science show on a big TV streaming platform to present it. Portia La Grasta walked up onto the stage in a sequined caftan, her long gray dreadlocks swaying, and proceeded to introduce the top six candidates. The audience watched a two-minute video presentation for each. It was all awesome stuff—a brilliant new solution for seawater desalination, a cutting-edge new plant micropropagation technique, a scalable hydrogen-powered vehicle, a hyperefficient desert solar farm. The Blooms were in good company.

Portia La Grasta finally brandished the oversize envelope. "And the Future Innovation prize for the most promising scientific innovation with the potential to transform our world goes to… Bobby and Wilbur Bloom, for the Desert Bloom project!"

Ava shot to her feet with a shriek of joy. The Bloom brothers jumped up, howling and capering and embracing each other. Pandemonium ensued. Wineglasses fell; wine was splashed. No one cared. A beaming Bobby and Wilbur made their way through the room and up onto the stage. Portia La Grasta and the emcee embraced them and handed Wilbur a plaque while Bobby stepped up to the mic, adjusting his glasses with shaking fingers.

"We, um, want to thank our lab techs, and the Maddox Hill Foundation for the research grants that made this work possible." Bobby's voice wobbled with emotion. "And a special thanks to our friend and publicist, Ava Maddox of Blazon PR and Branding, for telling our story and making everyone listen, and I mean from all the way back to the start of our research. None of this would have happened without her."

"She's brilliant," Wilbur interjected, leaning into the mic. "And fabulous." He pumped the plaque in the air. "This one's for you, Ava! Thanks! You rock!"

The crowd roared with appreciative laughter, and the spotlight swung around the room and lit upon their table, illuminating Ava in all her glory. She seemed right at home in that brilliant beam of light, smiling and clapping, her eyes wet. She gracefully blew the Bloom brothers a kiss, like a blessing from a benevolent deity. The crowd roared and applauded, eating it up.

Not surprisingly, everybody wanted a piece of her and the Blooms after that. It took forever to grind through that process. After the official proceedings concluded, Zack waited while Ava and the Blooms accepted congratulations and collected business cards and fawning compliments. Trevor Wexford was there, Callista on his arm. She was looking fine in a flesh-toned, sequined, mostly see-through sheath that was far more low-cut than Ava's. The end visual result was naked but sparkling. Not a bad look for her, but he couldn't drag his eyes away from Ava to appreciate it. Which Callista of course noticed.

At long last, he had the whole lot of them all herded into the elevator. The Blooms were still bubbling with euphoria, talking a mile a minute.

"All the big investors want us now," Wilbur exulted. "We have a meeting with Wexford next week! And four others!"

"Be careful with those guys," Ava reminded them. "They are predatory animals. They will chew you up and spit out your bones if you let them."

"But they won't, because thanks to you, we have great lawyers lined up to help us negotiate," Bobby assured her.

The elevator door opened, and Zack stuck his foot in the door to give them time for the last round of emotional hugs. Then the door shut behind Ernest and the Blooms, leaving Ava and Zack alone. The elevator ascended, in cut-it-with-a-knife silence.

He worked up the nerve to speak as they walked toward the rooms. "I'm glad the Blooms had the presence of mind to thank you properly. When Bobby took the mic, I was braced for anything. But he nailed it. Short, sweet and appropriate. You deserved it."

She shrugged. "Thanks, but I just polish the gems. I don't make them."

"You know damn well it's more than that. Particularly with the Blooms."

Ava swiped her key card, opened the door and beckoned him in. He willed his heart to stop racing as he followed her in. His heart ignored the directive.

Ava laid down her evening bag. "It's a rush to get a compliment from you, considering."

"Considering what?"

Her eyebrow tilted up. "Don't play dumb. You've been radiating Arctic disapproval at me for two days. It makes it hard to concentrate."

"I'm sorry you feel that way," he said stiffly. "I didn't mean to make you uncomfortable. And you're wrong. I don't disapprove of you. On the contrary."

"How can you say that after what happened with Craig? And two days of glaring and grunted monosyllables? Get real."

Zack's hands clenched as the energy built up. "Ava," he said tightly. "That's not fair. You ask too damn much. I've got to protect myself somehow."

She threw up her hands, baffled. "Protect yourself from what?"

"From you," he blurted out. "I've been trying for years. I should have kept trying, but no. I gave in. And sure enough, I regret how it played out."

Her stole dropped with a whispery thud around her feet.

"I should never have gone to bed with you," he said. "I know myself. I can't play it cool, pretend it's no big deal. I suck at that. I get that this was a one and done for you. But what a surprise, I'm not okay with it. I'm an all-or-nothing kind of guy."

"Am I really such a heartless femme fatale?" she asked.

"For me, you sure as hell are," he said. "I've had a massive crush on you ever since we first met. You must have noticed. It had to be impossible to miss."

"Um…actually," she faltered. "I, um, I didn't know that. In the least."

His voice was bitter. "Like always, I've got champagne tastes and a lemonade budget. I'm your brother's battle buddy from Iraq, and you're, like, Marie freaking Antoinette. It was stupid to lay myself wide-open, but I can't take it back. We're both embarrassed. But we'll live. After tomorrow, we'll avoid each other and move on."

"Zack…but I—"

"I didn't make mean to make this harder for you," he said. "I'll go now."

He turned toward the connecting door, but she lunged toward him, grabbing his wrist. "Wait," she said. "You've got it wrong. I don't want to move on."

His heart did that triple somersault again, then started off on a frantic gallop.

Her slender hand clamped around his wrist, although her fingers couldn't close around it. Her eyes were wet. *Oh, man.* He was out of his depth and sinking fast.

"Ava," he said. "Really. Don't sweat it. I won't give you a hard time. I get it."

"No. You don't get it, Zack. You don't get a goddamn thing."

"What, then? Help me out here. What is it I don't get?"

"How much I want this." Her voice quivered and broke. "But I just can't have it."

"Can't have what? Me?" He was utterly confused. "Why not? Here I am, on my knees. If you want me, what the hell is holding you back?"

She made a choked, desperate sound. "Me. It's just…me."

He was silent for a moment. "Please, don't give me the old it's-not-you-it's-me treatment," he said. "That never comforted anybody."

"I wasn't trying to comfort you. Far from it. Would you be quiet and let me explain?"

Zack made a lip-zipping gesture and gestured for her to go ahead.

Ava twisted her hands together until her fingers turned white. "That thing that happened the other morning," she said. "That's me every morning. I'm always like that."

"You mean…"

"Miserable. Nights and early mornings are just bad for me. I sink really low. But it has nothing to do with you. It's been years since I let anyone stay a whole night with me. I'm always in that dark place in the morning. If I sleep at all, I have screaming nightmares. Usually my parents' plane going down." She stopped to calm her shaking voice.

"Did you have that nightmare the other morning, when you woke up with me?"

"Yes," she said. "It was a bad one. Sometimes I can keep

myself from screaming, but I can't stop the tears. Either one is a huge buzzkill for anyone sharing my bed. And even if I skip the nightmare, I still have the feeling. It spills all over anyone who's with me. I just can't seem to hide it, or control it."

He waited for more. "Tell me about the feeling," he urged.

She hesitated. "It's like the tide going out," she said. "In a bad way. Something vital is draining away, no way to stop it, and I'm stranded on the rocks. I'm just not fit to be seen like that. And I don't want to burden anyone with it. Certainly not you."

"Oh, baby," he whispered.

"I'm not looking for pity," she said forcefully. "I'm very grateful for what life has given me. I'm healthy, privileged. Pampered, even. I have people who care about me, and I have work that I like, and I'm grateful for all that. No one has to tell me."

"I wasn't going to tell you that," he said. "Have you talked to anyone?"

"Yes. I've tried various things. Therapy, medications. So far, nothing works all that well. Exercise helps some. And being really busy. During the day, I can hold it off if I just keep moving. Sometimes it feels like my life is one long con job. Me, running around to show the world that I am just fine, thank you very much. Busy, busy. Sparkle, sparkle."

"That sounds exhausting," he said.

"Oh, it is," she said fervently. "But when I wake up in the night, I just can't fake it. Not even with you. I haven't had a boyfriend in years. I can only go so far with someone, and then it all just…falls apart on me."

"I'm so sorry," he said gently.

"But you want to know something funny? I've never wanted to try again as much as I want to try with you. But I can't run my con on you, Zack. Not at all. Not even during the daytime. It just doesn't work. I feel completely naked. I can't hide it from you."

"So don't," he said simply.

"Oh, stop," she muttered. "You don't know what you're asking."

"So teach me. I'm listening. My ears are wide-open."

"I told you," she said. "Believe me. It's not pretty."

"You're not pretty, Av, you're beautiful. Even when you're sad. Even when you're falling apart. You're amazing, and brave, and tough. You leave me speechless."

Ava shook with silent laughter. "I wouldn't call you speechless, Zack. You sound pretty damn eloquent to me."

Her hand was still clutching his arm. She seemed to have forgotten it was there. Zack rotated his arm, careful not to break her grip, and clasped her wrist gently with his fingers.

"You know what?" He bent down, pressing a kiss against the back of her hand. "If I had a pool behind me right now, I'd pull you into it and kiss you senseless."

Ava's mouth opened, forming words with no sound. Her eyes were wide, dilated.

"Well, actually," she whispered. "We don't need a pool for that."

Twelve

And in a heartbeat, they were at it. With all the thundering intensity of racehorses out of the gate.

Ava just wrapped her arms around his neck and hung on. She felt cherished by the way he cradled her head, made love to her mouth. She felt precious, adored, desired. His craving intensified her own. Reality could rip and tear under this kind of pressure.

But it didn't. It stayed intact. Nothing would fall to pieces with Zack around to hold it together. He had absolute command of himself.

His long, stiff erection burned through the fabric of her dress, and she burned to get closer to him. She wound one of her legs around him, and when that wasn't enough, she clutched his shoulders and hiked up the other one, too.

Zack let out a hoarse growl of approval and hoisted her up so that her legs were wrapped around his waist, not his thighs, and she was rubbing the stiff bulge of his erection right against the party spot. Straddling him, squeezing. He cupped her bottom and helped, grinding their bodies together. Driving her to distraction.

So good. She moved helplessly, driven by some primal imperative, one she couldn't control. She clutched him, panting as her climax build up, and up…and shattered, in a blaze of stars. Huge pleasure pulsed through her.

It washed the whole world clean.

After, her shaking legs were still twined around him, but she was limp and soft. Zack hoisted her up and carried her to the bed, laying her down with exquisite gentleness. He positioned himself above her, distributing his weight right where she needed to feel it, and moved, expertly, deepening the pressure. A slow, sensual pulse and grind, rocking and surging. Working her right back up to a screaming pitch of excitement.

Soon, she was clutching his shirt, nails digging in, scrabbling for the buttons. "Get this shirt off. I want to run my hands over your chest. I need to feel your skin."

"As my lady commands." He lifted himself up, flung off the suit jacket. Made short work of the buttons.

Ava took the opportunity to pry open the buckles of her ankle straps, staring at him as she tossed her shoes away. Zack wrenched his belt loose and sat down next to her. He slid his fingers into her hair with a groan, pulling the pins out and unwinding the locks, sliding them through his fingers. He slowly stroked her skin into shuddering bliss as he pushed the black velvet straps over her arms, tugging the bodice of her dress down until it cradled her bare breasts.

He pressed his face against her breasts with a groan, kissing her. Caressing her sensitive skin with his swirling, skillful tongue.

She clutched his shoulders. Her breath heaved in her chest at the incredible sensations. Light, heat, pleasure. The stiffened tips of her breasts seemed to glow with delight at his passionate appreciation. Then he slid his hand up the inside of her thigh, stroking her mound, then sliding under the elastic of the damp fabric. Tugging her panties off. Then opening her. Entering her with skillful fingers. Thrusting, caressing, finding the perfect spot. *Oh, please.* A shocked moan, a ripple of sweet surrender and her legs opened, lifting eagerly for more of the same. "Help me get this dress off," she said breathlessly.

"No," Zack said. "The dress totally does it for me. With your breasts bare like that, the skirt thrown up." He pushed her thighs open. "So perfect. Silky smooth." He thrust his finger inside her, tenderly, rhythmically, seeking out the sweet spots that made her shiver and squirm and gasp. "Hot and tight. You hug me. I'm about to come right now."

"Don't you dare waste it. Get your pants off and stop driving me crazy, you big tease. I want all that excellent bounty for me, me, me. At my service. You get me?"

"But I love driving you crazy. How about we go for at least one more of those supernova orgasms before we move on to the next part of the evening's entertainment?"

She reached up to cup his face. "I want to supernova with you," she told him. "We've got the rest of the night for the fun and games."

His eyes lit up. "Well, then. If you put it that way."

Zack slid off the bed, kicked off his shoes and swiftly shucked pants, socks and briefs, freeing that impressive erection. There was no doubt at all about his enthusiasm.

"Get over here, you," she said. "Give me what's mine."

He complied in an instant, bearing her over backward onto the bed.

"First, the mutual supernova," he murmured. "Then the fun and games."

He positioned himself on his knees between her legs, lifting her up so he could use the tip of his broad shaft to caress her secret inner flesh. Swirling, teasing, stroking. She lifted herself, silently straining for more as he nudged inside and pressed deeper.

They both cried out as he entered her, the pleasure was so

intense. Their hands clenched, shaking with emotion as they found the rhythm together. Deep…slick…heavy strokes. The only sounds the faint squeak of the bed and their panting breath. They were beyond words, merged, in the danger zone where she was stark naked, revealed to him. All her hopes and fears and pain, all her desires and fantasies, wide-open to him.

And safe, with him.

Every deep thrust of his big body brought the truth closer. Each tender, slick stroke of pure pleasure, as deep and intimate as a kiss. Revelation after sweet, passionate, tender revelation. Zack sensed the explosion building and let go of his own control, racing for the finish. Their beautiful supernova, getting closer.

Her shining light in the darkness.

Thirteen

Zack cradled Ava's soft, warm weight, staring at the ceiling in stunned disbelief.

It was real. It had actually happened. Over and over. Ava had drifted off after their last bout of luxurious lovemaking, her slender, silken limbs twined trustingly around his.

It was too good to be true. He was afraid to let himself believe it. He'd tried to be lighthearted and playful. Fun and games, that was the vibe he'd shot for, but he hadn't hit the mark. Not even close. Every time they came together, they were seized by that crazy, desperate, end-of-the-world intensity. Every time it got wilder, more abandoned.

There was no taking the edge off these feelings. No breaking this tension. No end to how deep he could go. It was bottomless. It left him in a state of terrified joy.

He needed to knock down walls inside his head make enough room for her there. He never wanted her to feel cramped. Ava was special. She had a destiny to fulfill, and he wanted her to reach it.

He wanted to see her shine like the goddamn star that she was.

He was too stirred up to even think of sleeping. The sky had started to lighten when he felt her stir in his arms and then stretch.

He felt the exact moment when she realized where she was, and he felt her stiffen.

This was the moment of truth. He steeled himself for freaking anything at all.

Ava pushed back from his tight embrace, propping herself up onto her elbow, and gave him a shy, tentative smile. "Hi," she said softly. "How long was I out?"

"Maybe three hours," he told her. "Maybe more. Sleep some more. It's still early."

Ava laughed. "You know, of course, that it's a miracle I slept that long at all," she told him. She sat up, swinging her legs around, her back to him, her long, honey-blond curls catching the light that still filtered out the bathroom door.

Zack waited for a moment before he worked up the nerve to break the silence. "So?" he asked her. "How do you feel right now? Did the tide go out?"

She looked back over her shoulder with wide, wondering eyes. "No," she said softly. "I feel…okay. Better than okay. I can hardly believe it. I actually feel pretty good."

"It wouldn't scare me, if you were struggling," he told her. "It's sure to show up again from time to time. Don't try to hide it from me. We'll cope with it together."

She gave him a smile so sweet, it made his heart squeeze and twist. "Thanks. I will. But I'm telling you the absolute truth, I swear. I feel good today. It's amazing."

He grinned, ridiculously happy. "Awesome."

"Yeah, fingers crossed. I don't know how long it'll last, or what it means, but I'll take it."

"I know exactly what it means," he told her.

Ava gave him a teasing smile, head tilted. "Oh, really, Zack? Enlighten me."

Now she was messing with him for making pronouncements,

but he was too euphoric to mind. "Three things," he said. "It means that it can get better. It doesn't define you. And it won't limit you. That's what it means. Good, hopeful, positive things."

Her smile widened into a grin, showing her gorgeous white teeth. "Why, you seductive bastard," she said. "Whispering your irresistible sweet nothings in my ear."

"What can I say," he murmured. "We all have our gifts."

"True thing." Ava pulled the cover down, baring his body, and swung her shapely thigh over his, straddling him. She leaned over him, stroking his chest. Reaching down to grasp his thick, pulsing shaft. Boldly stroking it. "So, ah...speaking of gifts..."

"Again?" he asked hopefully. "You're not tired?"

"Not yet." Her voice was husky and seductive. "I like feeling this way." She wiggled down his thighs, leaning over to let her satiny hair brush down his chest. "I have a few sweet nothings of my own for you, Zack."

Then she put her hot mouth to him, and all he could do was clutch the sheets, shudder and gasp.

Something felt strange when Ava opened her eyes. It took her a while to figure out what it was. It wasn't so much the marvelous novelty of being in the arms of a gorgeous man, though that itself was quite excellent.

It was the slice of light that slanted down from between the heavy blackout curtains. It was brilliantly bright. Not the usual faint, grayish glow of dawn.

She twisted around, squinting through her tousled mop of hair at the digital clock, and gasped. "Ten fifteen a.m.?" she squawked. "Oh my God! Holy...freaking...*crap*!"

Zack jumped as she leaped up. "What the hell? Are you okay? What's wrong?"

"I'm three hours late, that's what's wrong!"

"Oh. Okay." Zack rubbed his eyes and sat up. "You didn't set an alarm clock?"

"No! Why would I? I barely ever sleep! I've never needed an alarm in my whole life! I don't even know how the alarm clock function on my smartphone works!"

"Oh. So rolling around in bed all night with me makes you oversleep? Cool."

Ava grabbed a pillow and swung it at his head. "Don't you dare get smug about that."

"Don't worry," he urged. "The Blooms will survive for a few hours on their own. They're the darlings of Future Innovation. They're probably down there holding court with hungry venture capitalists right now."

"Uh-huh, right! With no contract lawyers present. That's exactly the problem."

"I see. Well, Ernest is with them, right? He'll run interference."

"Yeah, and he's probably wondering where the hell I am. Get dressed quick, you lazy, lounging naked man. As soon as I'm decent, I am out the door, with or without you."

"You're not going anywhere alone," he told her sternly.

She stopped at the bathroom door. "Actually, Zack. Drew and Uncle Malcolm will soon be getting on a plane headed back to the States, remember. And this new development will eliminate all your bully leverage."

"Oh, yeah? Meaning?"

She smiled. "Meaning, your carrot-and-stick routine will soon be officially obsolete, big guy," she informed him softly. "And I, for one, will not miss it."

"Ava," he said, in a warning tone. "Nothing has changed. You need to stay safe."

"I guess you'll just have to come up with a clever, creative new way to manage me after that," she said throatily. "With a new carrot, or, ah…a new stick." Her eyes dropped to his lap. "A nice, big, substantial one."

His erection tented the sheet up, and he sat up, all smoldering, sexy bedroom eyes.

"Let Ernest handle things down there," he said. "Get over here and let's see how this new leverage is going to work. We should start working out the kinks."

Ava backed away, laughing, her face already hot. "Kinks, ha! Put it on ice, you crazy sex demon. I have a counterproposal for you."

He gave her a lazy grin that made her heart throb heavily. "I'm listening."

"When we get back to Seattle, come to my house," she said. "We'll open a bottle of wine. Light some candles. Order some good takeout. Maybe run a bath. I have a big old claw-foot cast iron bathtub, big enough for two, if they're very friendly. And we can discuss our complicated new power arrangement for hours. Or even, um…days."

"What time is our plane?" he asked roughly. "I can't wait to get started."

When the bathroom door closed, she was giggling like a schoolgirl.

Fourteen

"So which of your hot evening dresses are you wearing to the foundation gala?"

Ava smiled across the restaurant table at Zack. "I'm still vacillating between the black beaded velvet or the crimson taffeta with the big full skirt."

"You look awesome in both," Zack said. "But the strapless red one just does something to me. I don't understand how those things stay up."

"Pro trick," Ava said. "Don't let your boyfriend touch you until you get home."

"Whoa," he said. "That'll be a challenge."

"You'll get your moment later, I promise. That deep crimson is my absolute favorite. It's my signature color."

Ava twined her fingers with Zack's and leaned toward him over the espresso cups and the plate of lemon profiterole they'd shared. It was the same restaurant he'd chosen for their first evening together, hardly more than a week ago. This place had become their go-to spot for workday lunches.

"I have to get back to work," Ava said regretfully. "I told

Ernest to check on Wilbur and Bobby, and sure enough, they have a wardrobe crisis. He's been sending me frantic texts about last-minute tuxedos for them. The rest of my afternoon will be spent on damage control. No rest for the wicked."

"Gregson will accompany you anytime you leave the Blazon office, right?"

Ava slid her foot out of her shoe and ran it up the side of his calf. "Of course," she said. "I know you want me to keep me safe, but I think my trolls are losing interest. There's been no new activity for the last few days. Maybe the worst is over."

He pulled her hand up and kissed it. "I still don't want you to risk it."

"I won't," she assured him. "I'll be careful, I promise."

"Meet you after work?" he offered. "Want to get dinner?"

"Or we could just meet at my place. I might not get back to Gilchrist House at all if I have to find tuxes for the Blooms. And I'll be famished for you."

Zack's smile widened. "Your place. Keep me posted on your timing. We'll figure out dinner later."

"Perfect." She beamed as she sipped her espresso.

Strange, to be so giddy and giggly after all her troubles, but she was having more fun than she'd ever had in her life. Apart from being a total god in bed, Zack was fun to be with. Smart, funny, thoughtful, opinionated. They had spirited disputes about movies, music, current events and everything else under the sun. She loved cooking with him, lolling in bed with him, sipping coffee. He saw who she really was, and he seemed to like it, just as she liked him. And between frequent erotic interludes, she slept like a rock and woke deliciously rested, smiling and ready for anything.

It felt incredible. She was flying high. Hoping desperately not to crash.

Vikram's crew of close protection agents covered her during Zack's work hours. At every other moment, Zack covered her himself. Quite literally, much of the time. To her knee-wobbling, thigh-clenching, toe-curling delight.

Her phone did its classic guitar riff ringtone in her purse, and she dug around for it.

"Dammit, Ernest, stop hounding me," she muttered. "I'll get there when I get there." She pulled out the phone and froze. "Not Ernest," she said blankly. "It's Drew."

In the startled silence that followed, the guitar riff played again. Again.

"You going to answer that?" Zack asked.

"Of course," Ava said.

It rang again. "Are you going to tell him about us?" Zack asked.

"When the time is right." Ava hit Talk. "Hey, big brother! I meant to call, but I thought you'd be conked out. Have you and Jenna emerged from the fog of jet lag?"

"Hell, no," Drew replied. "It feels like I'm walking on the moon. But I'm sharp enough to be pissed off at you."

Ava rolled her eyes and sighed silently. "So what else is new."

"How is it that I just learned about your trolls now?" Drew demanded. "Sophie told me this morning! The security team that Zack appointed for you filled her in. You should have told us!"

"I didn't want to wreck your honeymoon, Drew."

"That's my decision to make, and Jenna feels the same way. We can go play on a beach anytime, Av. Nothing is more important to us than you being safe. Nothing. Get it?"

Aww. It sucked to be yelled at, but she was used to it, and she was touched that Drew felt so passionately about keeping her safe. "I appreciate the sentiment," she told him. "And I'm glad you're back. I really missed you guys. But I'm fine. Zack had my back."

He grunted under his breath. "We'll discuss it with Uncle Malcolm tonight. Dinner at his house on the island. I'll pick

you up. Bring everything you'll need to dress for the gala tomorrow night. We'll all go together from Vashon."

"But, ah…actually, tonight I've got a thing that I need to…"

"Cancel it. Malcolm is on edge already. He wants to formally
welcome Sophie into the family tonight, and you have absolutely
got to be there. No choice."

Ava sighed. "Whatever. It'll be great to see you, even spit-
ting mad. Love you, bro."

She ended the call and dropped the phone into her purse.
"I'm so sorry," she said to Zack ruefully. "I'm in for it tonight.
Drew is taking me to Uncle Malcolm's house on Vashon for a
welcome-Sophie-to-the-family dinner. Or maybe it'll be more
like a rake-Ava-over-the-coals dinner."

"Are you ready to let them know that we're seeing each
other?"

Ava considered her words. This was his tender spot, the one
she had to tiptoe around. "Let's not steal Sophie and Vann's
thunder yet. They're just starting to plan their wedding."

"So you're still nervous."

"No," she retorted. "Not nervous, exactly. It's just that this
is private. It's fresh and new. It's also kind of miraculous, and
outside eyes wouldn't be able to see that."

"It might be fresh and new," Zack said. "But it's not delicate."

Ava squeezed his hand. "By no means," she said. "I just want
to leave it unmolested for a while longer before I expose it to
Uncle Malcolm's judgment."

"So you think he won't approve?" Zack said.

"Of me, no," she said ruefully. "Never. Just out of habit. It's
beyond him to approve of anything I decide to do. He's far more
likely to approve of you, Zack. He likes you. He thinks you're
rock solid. Otherwise you wouldn't be the company's CSO."

"Maybe I should come with you tonight," he said.

"Stay clear," Ava advised him. "It's going to be stressful.
He'll be horrified at my trolls, and he will almost certainly

blame me for it. You know, my unfortunate life choices that opened me up to that kind of abuse. So spare yourself."

"I should be standing with you for that," he said.

"And you will, tomorrow. At the gala, and going forward," she assured him.

They dealt with the bill and strolled back toward Gilchrist House holding hands. Gregson, her bodyguard for the day, waited for her at the front entrance as requested.

She smiled at him. "'Bye," she whispered. "Until tomorrow."

Zack pulled her close and gave her a fierce kiss that promised infinite sensual bliss. The man was voracious. He couldn't get enough, and neither could she. She stepped back gasping for breath.

Tomorrow couldn't come too soon.

Imagining that strapless crimson evening gown clinging to Ava's stunning body soon became impractical for a city street in broad daylight. He had to do deep breathing to chill himself down to normal dimensions. In the middle of that effort at self-mastery, his eyes fell on the display window of a high-end jewelry store.

He gazed thoughtfully at the gems in the window, thinking about Ava's red dress. *It's my signature color.* He went inside and approached the woman behind the counter.

"Show me your ruby rings," he said.

Some time later, he'd narrowed the choices down to a few front-runners. He had a clear favorite, by far the most expensive of the lot. But he made better money at this job then he'd ever dreamed of making, and he didn't have time to spend much of it. He could afford something worthy of her beauty. Better yet, something that would look good with that red dress, and with those gold and ruby drop earrings Ava often wore. She looked so good in those and absolutely nothing else. It was a great look for her.

A ruby ring would be a perfect addition to that winning ensemble.

The setting was modern, a twisted rope of differently colored golds, with a big ruby nested inside it. It was bold, eye-catching, unique, unusual. Risky. Like Ava.

If it was the wrong ring, he'd bring her back and let her pick out whatever she wanted. Probably he was pushing his luck. It might be too soon. But he knew where he wanted this to go. He'd always known, if he was honest with himself.

His phone buzzed, and he pulled it out, hoping for Ava. No such luck. Drew.

Zack hit Talk. "Hey, man," he said. "Welcome back."

"Where the hell have you been?" Drew sounded peeved. "I drag my tired, jet-lagged ass into the office today to talk to you and find that you've disappeared for a long lunch? Since when do you take long lunches?"

"I had some business to deal with," Zack said. "We didn't expect you guys back for another week or so. Did the honeymoon go well?"

"The honeymoon was awesome. We were summoned back by royal decree. Bev Hill insisted that Jenna and I be present for the foundation gala, and Ava's been telling me that I should talk to the Bloom brothers about Beyond Earth before they get too rich and famous to talk to me. From the looks of things, it might already be too late. In any case, we'll be there tomorrow night, jet lag and all."

"Great," Zack said. "Looking forward to seeing you."

"So tell me about this security issue that Ava has?" Drew's voice had an edge. "How the hell did you decide not to let Malcolm and me know about that situation?"

"Ava didn't want to disturb you guys. She was afraid you'd cut short your travels."

Drew let out a grunt of disapproval. "That decision was not Ava's to make. Going forward, when it come to my family's security, keep me in the loop. Always."

"Understood," Zack said.

"We'll discuss it tonight at Uncle Malcolm's," Drew said. "He told me to invite you. It'll be Jenna and me, Ava, Uncle Malcolm, Sophie, and Vann. Pack what you need for the gala, because it'll be too late after dinner to get the ferry to the mainland. There's room at Malcolm's house. We'll have the housekeeper make up a room."

"So Malcolm wants to scold me about Ava's problem?"

"I think his exact words were 'Tell Zack to get his secretive ass out to the island tonight, or we will have a problem.'"

"Ah," Zack said. "Great. Fun times ahead."

"Definitely, but the food will be good, and Malcolm shipped a bunch of cases of really good Italian wine back from Positano. Just get buzzed and tune him out. That's what Ava and I do." Drew paused. "Of course, that'll be after I pound you myself for not keeping me clued in. You can relax and get drunk when honor has been satisfied."

Zack was too busy secretly exulting at the idea of being in the same house with Ava tonight to be troubled by that prospect. "Do what you have to do. I'm there for it."

He slid his phone into his pocket and pulled out his wallet as he turned back to the woman behind the jewelry counter. He pointed at the most expensive ruby ring.

"I'll take that one," he said.

Fifteen

"I told you, Uncle," Ava repeated stubbornly. "As soon as I got nervous, I went to Zack and asked his advice. I was reluctant to interrupt your important trip for something unimportant. I was absolutely covered, so I just don't know what you're so upset about."

"I don't like being kept in the dark!" Uncle Malcolm sputtered. "I saw the disgusting things they posted. I want to hunt that filth down and crush them!"

Ava opened her mouth to snap back but stopped herself. After a week with Zack with her emotional defenses down, she saw her uncle's face differently. For the first time, she saw the fear behind his bluster.

"I'm fine," she said gently. "And I've been careful. Since I told Zack my problem, I have not been left alone without protection even once."

"I hate it. I hate that you were exposed to something so obscene!"

"I'm tough," she assured him. "I'm a Maddox, Uncle. Welsh warrior stock. Name-calling doesn't rattle me. You were the one who taught me not to back down from a bully."

"Well." Malcolm harrumphed. "This is quite different."

"As far as I'm concerned, you did the right things." Sophie's mild, soothing tone indicated that even after only a few weeks of acquaintance with her biological father, her cousin had already firmly grasped the basics of Malcolm management.

Probably better than Ava had over the course of a lifetime.

Not for the first time, it occurred to her that it was a good thing Sophie was such fun to be with in her own right, or Ava would've been hopelessly jealous. Her own relationship with her uncle had always been fraught with tension, but Sophie had swiftly forged a real friendship with her biological father. They enjoyed each other's company, and Malcolm did not harangue or criticize Sophie the way he did Ava and Drew.

Maybe because he hadn't seen her through her awkward teens. Sophie had already been a highly functioning adult when he met her. Like Athena, springing from the head of Zeus fully formed. Brilliant, funny, gorgeous. Vann Acosta, Maddox Hill's chief financial officer, had fallen for her like a ton of broken rock. Vann had always struck Ava as cool and distant, so it warmed her heart to watch him so devoted to her. Crazy in love.

Even now, Vann was stuck to Sophie like glue, arm wound through her arm, thigh pressed against hers, nuzzling her hair. Not that Ava could criticize. If she were alone with Zack right now, she would climb that guy like a tree.

"Nothing bad happened," Jenna pointed out to the room at large. "And nothing bad will happen now that her entire family is lurking around every corner. Malcolm, look at you. You got a tan in Positano. It looks good on you!"

"My dermatologist would disagree in the strongest of terms," Malcolm grumbled. "It was impossible to avoid. And believe me, I tried. The place is a damn oven."

They heard the front door open. Ava heard her brother talking. Then Drew walked in, followed by Zack. Seeing him unexpectedly made her heart bump hard in her chest.

"There you are!" Malcolm said. "Good! I have some things to say to you."

"You didn't say you were coming," Ava blurted. "You should have texted me."

An odd silence followed her words, but Malcolm quickly broke it. "So, Zack! What the hell do you have to say for yourself? Keeping secrets from us?"

Zack gazed calmly back at him. "I stand by all my choices."

"Really? You concluded that keeping us all in the dark about a security issue in our immediate family was a good choice? I should have you fired!"

Zack looked unrepentant. "That would be a shame. But do what you need to do."

Ava shot to her feet. "Like hell will you fire him! That would be stupid. He has been nothing but professional. He made me his first priority, the minute I told him about my problem, so back off!"

The antique mantel clock over the fireplace tick-ticked loudly after her words.

"Ava," Zack said. "You don't have to defend me. I'll be fine."

"I'm finished with this conversation," she announced. "Everyone just be polite and speak of other things, or Zack and I will catch the ferry back to the city right now."

"You will do no such thing," Malcolm snapped. "We are going to have dinner together tonight, like a civilized family. Jeffries?" he bawled out. "Where are you?"

The bald head of Malcolm's butler poked through the door. "Yes, Mr. Maddox?"

"Tell Mrs. Alvarez we're ready for dinner as soon as she can serve it."

"Yes, sir."

Dinner was surreal. Ava had the strangest sensation that she was floating over the table, watching all of them from a distance. Her uncle had a talented cook, and the wine was great, but she couldn't seem to get anything down.

The one bright spot was when Jenna stood up, holding Drew's hand, and announced that she was pregnant. She was going to be an aunt. Ava did all the requisite hugging and jumping and crying, but some part of her still watched it all from afar.

Jenna and Drew's announcement put Uncle Malcolm in a somewhat better humor, at least for him. Zack seemed perfectly at ease, talking shop with Sophie about cybersecurity, analyzing Ava's online harassment problem for them. Then he started telling funny stories about the Blooms' antics at the trade show. The tale of the Bloom brothers' fateful encounter with Callista Wexford made everyone laugh.

Everyone managed to relax at dinner except for her. Lucky them.

She still felt like she was braced for a blow, but she had no clue from what quarter.

Zack waited on the freshly made bed in the guest room, staring at the little velvet box in his hand.

Maybe he should wait to take this step. But he'd been waiting for a goddamn decade. Trying so hard not to feel it. And now that he finally had permission, all the feelings were rushing out at once, full force, like a flash flood.

He knew exactly what he wanted. He was dead sure that asking Ava to marry him was his only chance at happiness. Even so, asking the question was going to take all his balls and then some.

He unzipped the side pocket on his athletic pants and stowed the ring box there. It would be ready whenever he worked up the nerve.

He waited until the silence had fully settled in, then made his quiet way, barefoot, down to the end of the upstairs corridor. Ava's was the only bedroom that had a thin slice of light shining out of it. The other two couples were tucked behind closed doors, but Ava had left him a beacon.

He looked inside the narrow opening and pushed the door open.

She stood by the window, looking out at the trees below her window. She wore turquoise-blue silk pajamas. They struck him as incredibly sexy, but as Ava had pointed out, every damn thing she wore had that effect on him. Even her ripped-up jeans with the paint stains made him get hot. If Ava wore it, it was sexy.

The room was large and pretty, furnished with a big four-poster canopy bed with a heap of lace-trimmed pillows on it and an antique patchwork quilt. There was a marble-topped dresser drawer, and a vanity with a tall, narrow makeup mirror with those lights all the way around it, like the backstage dressing room of a theater. The vanity lights were the only lamp lit, and they gave the room a soft golden glow.

Or maybe that was Ava herself. "Hey," he said.

Ava turned and smiled. "What took you so long? Come in and shut the door."

He walked over to the window and slid his hand under the warm mass of her beautiful hair. She was vibrating with tension.

"You shouldn't let Malcolm upset you," he said. "He just had to unload."

Her shoulders twitched in an angry shrug. "It pissed me off that he attacked you. He's so childish, with his goddamn tantrums. Threatening to fire you, my ass."

"It's just what he does," Zack said. "He fired Drew after that thing with Harold and his showgirl, remember? And he fired Vann, too, after that business with Tim and the deep fakes. I'm just part of that exclusive club now. Yay, me."

She harrumphed. "I appreciate your positive attitude and capacity for forgiveness, but it still just bugs me. And I bug him. I always have, and now look at him. He finally gets the perfect daughter, dropped from the heavens into his lap, boom. Instead of a couple of screwups that he inherited from his brother, like me and Drew."

"Oh, come on. You're not screwups. You love Sophie."

"Sure. What's not to love? She's brilliant, awesome, talented, wonderful."

"Yeah, and so are you," Zack said. "You're incredible. You dazzle me."

She laughed under her breath. "Aw, thanks. So I'm a little jealous and territorial after all. I'm not proud of it, but it bugs me that he brings this shiny, perfect new daughter home and tears me to pieces in front of her. Like any of this crap is my fault."

"He's scared and angry, like I was," Zack said. "Let him have his freak-out. It'll pass. Sophie certainly isn't judging you. She's a security expert. She's on your side."

Ava paced up and down the room as he watched. She stopped in front of the vanity, staring into it with eyes that looked far-away and sad. Which was unacceptable.

Zack came up behind her, dropping a soft kiss against the back of her head.

"It's more than that, isn't it?" he asked.

"No. I mean, yes," she admitted. "This is where Drew and I came to live after my parents died. I spent some very bad nights in this room. My ghosts haunt me harder here."

Zack slid his arms around her waist and tugged her until she leaned against him and her head rested on his shoulder. "I remember the very first time I saw this house," he told her. "It also happened to be the first time I ever saw you."

She looked up. "Oh, yeah. I remember. It was summertime, right? And Drew brought you and Vann home for a barbecue. Wasn't that right after you'd been hired to be a bodyguard for Hendrick when he went to South Africa?"

"Yeah, exactly. Drew was still in architecture school. Vann and I stayed overnight. My mind was blown by this place. I mean, I knew Drew came from money, that his uncle was a big-shot architect. We'd talked about his family. But seeing this house, the grounds, the indoor pool, the staff… It was still a big shock to my system. Vann had been working in the accounting department at Maddox Hill for a year, so he was used to it. I tried to act like it was no big deal. Then someone dropped you off at the driveway. You saw us as you went to the house and changed course. Came sashaying toward us across the lawn."

"Oh." She grinned at him. "Wow. Did I sashay?"

"You totally did," he assured her. "A sexy, hip-swaying femme fatale sashay, in that tight little sundress. Remember it? Big red flowers on black. Short skirt. Your hair, swaying in the breeze. A golden goddess bestowing her grace upon us unworthy mortals."

Ava shook with silent laughter. "Don't overdo it."

"I swear to God," he said. "I practically fell to my knees then and there. Drew introduced you. He was classy about it, but stern. This was his little sister, big emphasis on the 'little.' Just turned eighteen. Just graduated from high school. On her way to university. The message was clear. Hands off, eyes down, and don't even think about it."

"He's always been overprotective, but he's got nothing on you," she teased.

"I think they put me in that same guest bedroom I have now," he said, his hands settling into the deep, sexy curve of her waist. "But I couldn't sleep. I tossed and turned. Dreaming of all the hot scenarios, if I were that kind of guy."

"Yeah?" Her eyes had that sultry glow that made him crazy. "What kind of hot scenarios? What kind of guy? Be specific."

"Oh, real classic stuff." He turned his head and found the warm, sweet skin of her throat with his lips. "I thought about tossing pebbles at your window, luring you outside. Maybe to that pool. Or else sneaking into your room." He unfastened the buttons of the silky pajama top and slid it off her smooth, warm shoulders, cupping her perfect breasts. "The idea was to worship your entire body with my mouth."

Ava swayed on her feet, her breath ragged. He clamped her

closer to the front of his body and slid his hand down into the loose waistband of her pajama pants, caressing her skin, the thin stretchy lace and, under that, the warm little swatch of springy ringlets decorating her sweet, secret folds.

He got his fingers under the lace and probed deeper, caressing her slick, tight-furled folds with his fingers until she trembled. Taking his time, teasing and demanding.

When the first orgasm broke over her, he caught her cry against his devouring kiss and thrust his finger deeper. That strong pulse of her pleasure clutching him, anointing his finger with that hot, sweet liquid balm. So damn good. Only one thing could be better, and he was working slowly, steadily toward it. Taking his time.

She stirred and looked up at him. "Wow," she whispered.

"Yeah," he muttered, his voice hoarse. His body shook with need. "In my fantasies, I made you come over and over. Multiple times, until you were so primed and ready, you were begging me to have my way with you."

She shook with silent giggles. "Begging? Really?"

"Oh, give me a break," he protested. "It was a horny badboy fantasy, okay?"

"I'm not complaining," she teased. "I'm so hot and bothered. Lay it on me. So what happened next in the fantasy? What did I beg you for? Be really, ah…specific."

Zack tagged the silky pajama bottoms off her hips, along with her panties. They pooled around her feet, and she kicked them away. Her eyes were dilated, locked with his in the illuminated mirror. Her lips were hot red, shadows painting her perfect naked body so sharp and bold. Every detail illuminated as he ran his hands over her sweet curves.

Zack seized her hips, tugging them back so she caught herself on the edge of the vanity for balance. He shoved down his own sweatpants, freeing his stiff, aching erection.

Ava licked her lips, making them gleam. That hot, luscious

pink that made his body clench and pulse with need. Her eyes, demanding everything he had to give her.

They were breathlessly silent. No need for words as he caressed the shadowy heat between her legs, opening her. Pressing himself inside, and then a slow, deep shove—

The vanity banged and rattled against the wall. A perfume bottle fell over with a tinkling clatter. They froze in dismay.

"Oh, crap," Ava whispered.

They held their breath in the silence, but no one called out.

"I think Drew and Jenna and Vann and Sophie are too busy in bed themselves to be bothered about us, thank God." Zack seized her hands and splayed them against the wall on either side of the narrow mirror. "I like the mirror," he said. "Looking at us makes me crazy. I can't give that up. Just don't touch the vanity. We won't make a sound."

Ava responded with a siren smile, arching her body sensually, hands braced against the wall, pushing back to take more of him. "Is this the part where I beg you?" she whispered. "Oh, please, Zack. Please. Do it. Give it all to me. I want it so bad."

Whoa. He almost lost it right then but hung on to his control.

He thrust inside her again, moving slowly and carefully until they found their rhythm. Once they did, it almost impossible to stay quiet. To not groan and bang and shout. Ava couldn't control the panting whimpers that jerked out of her at every slick, heavy stroke. He loved the jolt and sway of her perfect breasts, the way she caught her luscious lower lip between her teeth. It all drove him crazy. Spurred him onward.

At the end, he felt her orgasm crashing through her. The power seized him and he gave in to it, forgetting everything but their bodies, moving, melding. The wrenching throb of her pleasure drawing out his own until his climax exploded. Wiping him out.

He had no idea if he had made a racket. It was anyone's guess.

But amazingly, the house's silence held. He pulled Ava upright and held her against him. She trembled, damp with a sheen of sweat. "Are you cold?" he asked.

"Give me a sec." She pulled away and disappeared into a connecting bathroom.

Zack pulled his sweatpants back on and sat down on Ava's bed to wait. It seemed presumptuous to get into her bed, not knowing if she wanted him to sleep there with Drew next door and Malcolm right down the hall.

The bathroom door opened. Ava emerged, still gorgeously naked. She strolled over to the bed, stretching and tossing back her hair. Clearly enjoying his gaze on her.

"Should I go back to my room?" he said. "I don't want to risk causing any tension."

She considered that for a moment, and shook her head. "No. Stay. We're not doing anything wrong. And I want you. Right here."

He let out a slow, relieved breath. *Oh, thank God.*

"Well?" she said. "Pull down the covers, you horny, opportunistic bad boy, you. Let's get comfy."

He did as she asked and stretched out on her bed. Ava leaned over to him for a kiss, letting her hair brush the length of his torso like a long, delicately stimulating kiss.

"So, Zack," she said. "You know all those hot fantasies of yours?"

"What about them?" he asked warily.

"Well, you should know... I had my own corresponding fantasies. From the day of that barbecue and onward. I didn't sleep that night, either. I just lay there and I thought about you. I thought about you so hard. And I did things. You know. To myself."

"Oh my God," he whispered. "Tell me more. Or you could show me, too."

"Yeah? Would you like that?" She slid lower, trailing her fingers down the treasure trail of hair on his belly, toward his newly stiffened penis.

"Oh, yeah," he muttered.

"My fantasies were even naughtier than yours," she whispered. "Want to see?"

Zack shuddered with helpless excitement. "Yes, please," he said hoarsely.

Sixteen

Zack woke up with Ava wrapped in his arms, his legs tangled with hers. He lay there for a moment just enjoying the heat and the closeness. He watched her face as her eyes fluttered open, and she smiled at him, stretching luxuriously. A good sign.

"Hey there, you," he said. "How's the tide line today?"

She thought about it. "Pretty good." Her husky, sleep-roughened voice had a smile in it. "Which is a miracle when I wake up in this house."

He grinned at her. "Music to my ears."

"I'm grabbing a shower," she said. "So you'd better sneak on back to your room. I don't want to be stark naked when I have this conversation with Drew or my uncle."

"Fair enough," he said. "I think I might lurk in here awhile longer, though. I hear some activity out there. People stumbling out of their rooms, looking for coffee."

"When I'm out, I'll do recon," she said. "You can go back when the coast is clear."

"Or we could just stay in bed for a while longer," he suggested hopefully. "We could kill some time. Until they're all downstairs having brunch. Could be fun."

"Ha. Nice try, buddy. It was kinky enough last night when we hoped they were all asleep. You be good."

"Oh, always."

She was giggling as she got into the shower. A good omen. He grabbed his athletic pants from the floor, unzipped the pocket and pulled out the ring box.

Balls out. When she came out of the shower, he was laying it on the line.

He was about to toss the blanket off his naked self when the room door flew open and Jenna burst in, in her bathrobe, a towel wrapped around her head. "Av, would you lend me some... Oh, holy shit!" Jenna jerked backward in shock, mouth open.

"Morning, Jenna," he said evenly.

Ava emerged from bathroom wrapped in a towel, gasping when she saw her friend.

"Yikes," she squeaked. "And so it begins. Hey, Jenn. Did you sleep well?"

"Uh...sure. I... I guess." Jenna gaped at him, then at Ava. "Damn. I'm so sorry."

"Close the door, at least," Ava told her. "Since we're both naked."

"Oh, of course." Jenna did so, her gaze skittering away from Zack's bare torso.

Zack's fingers closed around the velvet ring box. He slid it back into the pocket of the pants, still under the cover of the duvet. So it was not ordained that this business be wrapped up before breakfast. The moment has been well and truly burned.

"I am so sorry," Jenna said. "I just never... I mean, I heard the shower running from the other side of the wall, so I knew you were up, so I thought I'd just pop in and knock on the bathroom door, you know, and ask if you had some old leggings I could borrow. Because all of a sudden, my jeans are too tight. From one day to the next."

"Sure thing." Ava pulled open a drawer of her bureau. "Color preference? Black, gray, dark blue, dark red?"

"Black is fine," Jenna said.

"There you go." Ava tossed them, and Jenna caught them one-handed.

"So, um...why did I not hear of this?" Jenna asked her. "Why the secrecy?"

"You've been out of the country for weeks, Jenn," Ava reminded her. "It's not secret. Just really new."

"I should've guessed after last night," Jenna said. "All those weird vibes pinging around the room. It gave me a weird, tingly feeling. And now I know why."

Ava smiled at her. "Good vibes, mostly. So? See you at breakfast?"

"Oh. Yeah. Of course. So sorry. Really. I'm out of here."

The door clicked shut after Jenna. Zack gave Ava a what-do-you-want-from-me shrug. "Cat's out of the bag."

"Don't you dare sound smug about it," Ava warned him. "You're not the one who'll have Uncle Malcolm breathing down your neck like a dragon."

"You don't think so? Let's go downstairs and find out."

"Sure," Ava said, pulling on her clothes. "I'll go down first. You get a shower and straggle in after a decent interval."

He did as Ava commanded and was the last person to join the brunch table.

Mrs. Alvarez had laid out a spectacular buffet, and he was grateful for it. A night like that generated a hell of an appetite. There was strong coffee, fresh-squeezed orange juice, a cheesy breakfast casserole, grilled bacon and sausages, smoked salmon and cream cheese with bagels, and freshly baked lemon scones, still steaming from the oven.

Conversation suddenly ceased when he walked in. Zack loaded up his plate and took the place next to Ava. What the hell. Might as well start as he meant to go on.

Drew and Jenna exchanged meaningful glances. Vann and

Drew did the same. Then Sophie and Vann. Sophie and Jenna stifled their giggles with coughing fits.

Then the silence was broken only by the clink of his coffee spoon.

Malcolm stared around at all of them, eyes slitted and suspicious. "What in the hell is going on here?" he demanded. "What are you kids all chortling about? Spit it out!"

No one said a word. Ava placed her cup down in the saucer with a rattle.

To hell with this. Zack put down his fork and placed his hand over Ava's on the table. He clasped her fingers, lifted her hand and pressed a slow kiss against her knuckles. A silent declaration of intent.

Ava gave him a startled look.

"Let's do this," he said to her. "I can't stand the suspense any longer."

"What the hell is this?" Malcolm barked. "What have you been doing behind my back?"

"It's not behind your back," Zack told him. "It's right front and center."

"Don't you give me any sass," Malcolm snarled. He turned his glower upon Ava. "Just what do you have to say for yourself, young lady?"

Ava sighed. "I'm not a young lady," she said. "I am an adult woman. Zack and I really connected down at the trade show in LA. We're really enjoying each other's company and seeing where it goes."

"And I assume that last night, it went straight into your childhood bedroom?"

"That is none of your business," Ava said coolly.

"The hell it's not!" Malcolm turned on Zack, his eyes popping. "You opportunistic bastard! I thought it was fishy, dropping everything to run down to LA with her. Not so altruistic after all, eh? Was that your plan all along? Get close to her and seduce her?"

"That's offensive and ridiculous," Ava snapped. "Control yourself, Uncle. You're being a bully."

"No, he's right," Zack said.

Ava froze and turned to stare at him. "What?"

"What exactly do you mean by that?" Drew's voice was suddenly hard.

"Malcolm's right," Zack told them. "It was a golden opportunity to do what I've wanted to do for years." His hand tightening around Ava's. "I've wanted you since the moment I laid eyes on you," he said to her. "Like I told you last night. I saw my chance to get close to you, and I took it. And I'll fight anyone or anything to stay close to you." He looked around the table. "For the rest of my life. So you all know where I stand."

"Zack!" Ava hissed. "For God's sake! Cool it!"

"I can't," he said. "I care too much."

The silence was broken by a sniffle across the table. "Aw," Jenna said, her eyes wet. "That's beautiful, Zack. God, I'm so emotional right now. Gets me in the feels."

"Absolutely. Me, too." Sophie dabbed at her eyes with her napkin and reached across Vann's plate to pat Zack's hand. "May true love prevail. Always."

"For God's sake, spare me." Uncle Malcolm shoved back from the table, hard enough to rattle the plates and jiggle the cups in their saucers. "Finding out that my houseguest debauched my niece under my own roof puts me off my breakfast. Be ready to catch the ferry this evening, all of you. No one bother me until then!"

He grabbed his cane and stomped out of the room, muttering darkly.

Ava covered her face with her hand. "Ouch," she whispered. "That went well."

"He's just wound up," Jenna soothed her. "Don't worry. He's still jet-lagged, and there's been so much stress and change the last few months. But he'll come around."

Drew grunted. "He's never handled stress or change well. Not even when he was younger. He's not likely to improve now."

Jenna frowned at him and gave Ava a hug from behind, kissing the top of her head. "Don't listen to him, babe," she said. "Come upstairs and let me show you the dresses I have to choose from for tonight. You, too, Sophie. And tell us everything."

Ava gave Zack a speaking glance as she rose from the chair and allowed herself to be pulled out of the room by her friend and her newfound cousin. The men listened to the sound of the women's voices retreating up the stairs.

Then Drew shoved his chair back, slouching in his chair, and looked Zack straight in the eye. "So let me get this straight," he said. "You've lusted after my little sister for the last ten years. Then you found out that she had a serious security issue. And while she was feeling attacked and vulnerable, while the rest of her family was out of the country, with no clue that all this was going on, you swept in on your white charger to be her sole rescuer. And took the opportunity to travel out of town with her. To hover over her 24-7. And finally, to seduce her. Wow, Zack. What a prince of a guy. I'm impressed."

"That's not exactly how I would describe what happened," Zack said.

"Yeah?" Drew crossed his arms over his chest, one of Malcolm's gestures. "Tell me how it really was, then. After all, we have all the time in the world. We have hours to discuss this situation. All day, in fact. Have at, buddy. I'm all ears."

Zack drained his coffee, steeling himself against his friend's cold anger.

No way out of this but through.

Seventeen

"Try not to worry about them, honey," Jenna urged her. "Wilbur and Bobby are not quite as helpless as they let you think they are. They like it when you do the heavy lifting, but they know it's not in their best interests to play dumb. They'll keep their act together."

"I suppose you're right," Ava replied, but she kept an anxious eye the Blooms, who were talking with her brother across the grand ballroom. The tuxedos she and Ernest had found fit pretty well, considering. It had been no easy feat to find them, as the Blooms were six foot three and skeletally thin. But they looked quite respectable and like they were enjoying themselves. So far, so good.

"I'm glad you went with the red dress," Sophie told her. "Zack couldn't take his eyes off you."

Ava smiled at her. "It fits the theme. Being the scarlet woman of the hour."

"Don't worry about that," Jenna urged. "Malcolm has already started to calm down. He just has to make room for the idea in his head. At his age, that takes time."

"Agreed," Sophie said. "He even laughed at Vann's jokes on the ferry."

"He may laugh and smile with you guys, but when it comes to Uncle Malcolm, I'm afraid my mileage may vary," Ava said ruefully.

Ava watched Jenna and Sophie exchange meaningful glances. She didn't wonder that Malcolm was glad to have the two of them around. His new niece-in-law and newfound daughter were wonderful additions to the family—bright, passionate and accomplished, and they both looked stunning tonight, Jenna in an empire waist gown beaded with silver and gold beads, and Sophie in a glittering, metallic bronze halter dress that clung lovingly to her lush, elegant body, leaving her tanned back completely bare.

Things were still tense for her and Zack, but Drew had calmed down. He and Zack had evidently thrashed it out after breakfast, although Zack was unwilling to tell her about that conversation. She got the sense of an uneasy truce. Weird, tense undercurrents.

Then she felt the hairs on the back of her neck prickle up. A low, excited ripple of conversation. Someone caught her eye and looked swiftly away. Then another. The hell?

Suddenly, people were quickly making way for Trevor Wexford, who was charging across the room toward her. And he looked pissed.

"What do those idiots think they're doing?" Trevor demanded. "That absentminded genius bullshit will only go so far. I don't buy it anymore."

"What on earth are you talking about?" Ava demanded, bewildered.

Trevor held up his phone. "This is from the Blooms' social media accounts!"

Ava focused on the screen and gasped. Trevor helpfully swiped up, making the images scroll. They were horribly familiar. Callista's head, clumsily photoshopped over naked bodies or dressed in dominatrix garb. Banner captions about frauds, sluts, skanks.

"It's not the Blooms," she said swiftly. "I swear it. They've been hacked."

"Then fix it! Make it stop! Or I will end them, and you! Do you understand me?"

"Certainly. Calm down, Trevor. I swear, this is not Bobby or Wilbur's—"

"Prove it!"

"I will. Just give me a little time." Ava glanced wildly around for backup.

Sophie was right behind her, already talking into her phone in a businesslike voice. "...to interrupt your Saturday evening, but this is life or death, Mindy. Get the whole team moving. We have to find out who hacked the Blooms right away. Get back to me the instant you have news. Thanks." She closed the call. "My cybersecurity team is on it, Mr. Wexford. They're the best in the business."

"They'd better be." He gave them a dark look and strode away.

Ava gave Sophie a grateful glance. "Thanks. I have to find Wilbur and Bobby, quick. They'd better find out about this from me."

Then she spotted them hurrying toward her. Too late. As she watched, Wilbur tripped over his feet, and Bobby knocked a glass of champagne from the hands of a portly matron, splashing it over her ample bosom. He compounded his gaffe by grabbing a napkin from a table and trying to sponge the lady's cleavage off himself.

Ava grabbed Bobby's arm and towed him away from the sputtering lady. "Sorry, Mrs. Winthrop!" she called out as she dragged the two out of the ballroom, into the stairwell and swiftly down a flight of stairs, out of harm's way. "What the hell, guys?"

"Someone's trying to ruin us!" Bobby moaned. "Ernest told

us about the hack! Someone is trolling Callista and making it look like it's us!"

Damn. She was going to kill that graceless clod Ernest for getting them agitated. "Calm down, Bobby," she soothed. "We'll fix this."

"But that smut is all over Callista Wexford's socials!" Wilbur gnawed his nails, blinking frantically. "We should never have come here! This kind of place just gives the haters a chance to mess with us."

"Wrong attitude, boys," Ava said bracingly. "We fight back. Sophie's team is working on it. They'll see that it's not you two. You two just lie low here for a few minutes while I run and find Zack. I want his take on this. Just chill."

She couldn't help thinking, as she ran back upstairs, how much had changed in the past week. Tough, independent Ava, running off to her new boyfriend for help, like a little kid with a skinned knee who wanted her owie fussed over.

But having a smart, fiercely competent, protective security expert for a boyfriend was a luxury. She was damn well going to take advantage of it.

She loved having Zack at her side when things got scary.

Eighteen

There they went again. Zack caught the eye of another guy in a group nearby, saw his gaze flick away and then heard a burst of smothered laughter. Not for the first time.

He forced himself to focus in on what Drew was saying about his conversation with the Bloom brothers. "...the Beyond Earth project," Drew was saying. "Ava's right. The work they're doing is the missing link that could make the program viable. I hope we can pin them down for talks now that they're the flavor of the month."

Again. Another nervous snort of laughter. "What's with those bozos?" he snarled.

"Who?" Drew looked back over his shoulder, but the clot of people had dispersed.

"Never mind. People giving me the side-eye. I started noticing it a few minutes ago."

Drew's eyebrows climbed. "Guilty conscience, after spending the night rolling around in my sister's bed?"

"No guilt," Zack said. "Not even a little."

"Come on, Drew," Vann said wearily. "I thought we put

this to bed. Let's not get wound up again out here in full public view."

"Better yet," Zack said. "I'll just go find my girlfriend, if you'll excuse me. I'm ready for some civil, reasonable conversation."

He strode away and was halfway across the crowded ballroom when it occurred to him that maybe Drew was right and he was hypersensitive. Who wouldn't be, after a long day of massive, relentless ball breaking from the overprotective, wiseass older brother? Damn.

"Zack! Thank God you're here!"

He spun around. It was Ernest, his white-blond hair sticking up like he'd been electrified. "What is it?" he demanded. "Is Ava okay?"

"She's fine, but we have a problem! I wanted to give you a heads-up, because—"

"Zack! Did you know?" A loud, penetrating female voice behind him.

He turned to see Callista Wexford striking a dramatic pose in the door to the room, clad in skintight black velvet. Lots of draped diamonds, bosom way out to there, but this was no time to contemplate the marvels of nature. She looked like she wanted to tear his head off. "Excuse me?" he asked. "Know what?"

"This!" she shrilled, holding up her phone.

Zack leaned forward, wincing at the ugly images. "Oh, no. Damn it."

"Can you believe this?" Callista's strident voice drew attention from all sides. "Trevor offered those two lunatics everything they could ever dream of, and this is the thanks they give us?"

"The Blooms are not responsible," he said.

"But it's coming from them! They're generating it all!"

"Bobby and Wilbur would never do this, even if they had the actual capability, which I doubt they do," Zack said. "I'd be surprised if those two even know how social media platforms work. Let's find out who runs their accounts first, and then we can start pointing fingers at—"

"Ava," Ernest said.

Zack turned to him, bewildered. "The hell?"

"Ava runs their social media accounts," Ernest clarified helpfully. "You're right about the Blooms. Those two don't have the first clue about any of it. Ava set all those accounts up for them years ago. She runs it all for them."

Callista's eyes widened. "Ah! I'm starting to get it. Ava got jealous down in LA, right? When I chatted you up at the trade show? She wants to show me who's boss. That conniving little slut really thinks she can survive a catfight with me?"

"No way," Zack said hastily. "Absolutely not. I'm sure she'd never—"

"Don't even try defending her," Callista hissed. "I hope you see what that woman is made of before you hurt yourself. Fair warning, Zack. I'm taking Ava Maddox down in a big, public way. So back away slowly if you don't want to crash with her."

Callista spun around and marched away, her heels clicking angrily.

Zack turned to Ernest. "I've got to find Ava, quickly."

"I think I saw her run upstairs," Ernest said. "Up toward the Blazon office."

"Thanks." Zack ignored the glances and murmuring as he wove through the throng. He raced up one flight of the big, spiraling Gilded Age staircase.

He stopped to look for her in the library, just in case, striding swiftly through a dark-paneled room lined with books, between leather sofas and reading tables. No Ava.

He made his way back toward the stairwell, but stopped when Vikram came through the doorway. His face was grim, and his dark eyes looked worried.

"Zack," he said. "I'm glad I caught you."

"Can't talk now, Vikram. I'm trying to find Ava. We have a serious problem."

"I know. That's what I need to discuss with you."

Something about Vikram's tone gave Zack a twinge of dread. "What is it?"

"Um...damn, Zack. I don't know how to say this. It's really embarrassing—"

"Just say it. Please."

Vikram's face tightened. "Okay, here goes." He pulled out his smartphone and tapped on it. "One of the guys on Ava's team of bodyguards found this online. It was posted a couple of hours ago." He set the video clip to play, and handed the phone to Zack.

Zack held the device gingerly, as if it might blow up in his hand. The link was titled The First Kiss... Part 1: Her Bad Boy Bodyguard!

It was Ava's hotel room in Los Angeles, and the camera was directed at the bed. Suddenly Zack appeared in the camera's field, carrying Ava, still in her gray cami and boy shorts. Her legs were wrapped around his waist. He sat down on the bed and dragged her closer, letting her hair tumble around his face as she straddled him, moving against his body, starting to kiss him.

The video cut off. A pop-up appeared on the menu.

You like? Lots more coming! Like and share! Part Two coming soon!

Vikram reached out, gently taking his phone back out of Zack's numb hand.

"I can see from your face that this is a surprise," he said.

"Yes," Zack forced out.

"Okay. I was afraid that... I mean, I didn't know if maybe the two of you had recorded that for fun, or—"

"Fun?" His voice was getting louder. "For *fun?*"

Vikram put both his hands up. "No judgment if you did, right? Lots of people use video for their—"

"I do not use video." He bit the words out one by one."

"Don't get pissed at me," Vikram said swiftly. "I'm just the messenger."

Zack shook his head. "I'm not. I'm just... I don't understand how this could have happened."

"Well, um. About that." Vikram gulped. "Given the situation that's come up with Callista Wexford, it really, you know, makes you wonder, right?"

"Wonder what?" Zack's voice got harder.

"Well, the video is already going viral. And just look how Ava Maddox and Blazon have been trending since it posted."

Zack shook his head. "No."

Vikram shrank from the rage in Zack's eyes. "Sorry. I just had to get it out there. It's what she does, Zack. Attention, buzz, likes, follows, eyeballs, that's her stock in trade. It's very telling that it appears right when the thing with Callista breaks."

"You're wrong," Zack said. "She would never hurt the Blooms. She loves those guys. Watch what you say, Vikram."

Vikram took a careful step back "I'm sorry," he said stiffly. "I shouldn't have said anything. I thought I was doing my job. Telling you what I saw, and what I really think. Even if it's hard to hear."

"I'm not mad at you," Zack said. "I appreciate the info, and your candor. But let's let this go for now. We'll talk more later."

Vikram backed away out the door, looking relieved.

Zack stood there, trying to square reality with the volcanic buildup of rage inside him. *Bad boy bodyguard?* He pulled out his phone, pulled up the platform Vikram had been using and entered the title into the search bar.

Sure enough. Three thousand and seventy views already. It was only a fragment of their encounter, twenty-five seconds of video, but there was no reason to think that hours more had not been recorded. Hours of wild sex, starring him and Ava, out there for the world to watch and know about. His friends, colleagues, bosses. His sister. His mother.

The door opened, and Ava burst through, talking on her phone. Her eyes lit up as she saw him, but she kept talking. "No, I can't yet. I just found him in the library, so don't worry about it... Just wait for me there, okay? I know it's an emergency. I'll be up there as soon as I can. I have to talk to Zack before I...yes. Fine. Later."

She ended the call and hurried toward him. "I'm so glad you're here!" Her voice was a breathless rush. "We have a problem. The Blooms just got hacked, like me."

"Did they?" he asked.

Her perfectly shaped brown eyebrows tilted up, puzzled at his tone. "Yes! And to my eye, it has the same style and vibe as whoever was trashing me."

"I see." His voice sounded dead to his own ears.

He had to sharpen up. Tease the facts from the fiction. Or rather, to tease facts out of his own romantic fantasies.

No matter what it cost him.

Something was very wrong.

Ava stopped short on her rush toward him. "Zack?" she asked. "Are you okay?"

"No," he said. "Not even close."

"Why are you looking at me like that?" she asked. "I was hoping you'd help me get ahead of this problem. Which you seem to already be aware of. Somehow."

"Ava," he said. "Just tell me what you know about this." Zack lifted his phone so she could see the screen.

The video was already playing. Ava stared at it in disbelief. Her phone slid out of her hand and thudded to the carpet at her feet.

The video clip stopped. The frozen still image was of her, cupping Zack's face as she came in for a kiss.

"That was filmed from your laptop in LA," he said. "The camera was on the desk."

She gazed at him, horrified. "You can't possibly think that I filmed that on purpose," she whispered. "Good God, Zack. Why would I?"

"I don't know. But no one knew that encounter was going to happen, Ava. God, not even me. How could someone else have possibly set us up?"

"You think that I'd make a...a sex tape?" Her voice cracked. "And post it online, for everyone to see? That's my worst nightmare! Why would I do that?"

"I don't know," Zack said. "I don't get it, either."

"I have never lied to you!" she said, her voice impassioned. "I've been more honest and real with you than I've ever been with anyone in my whole life!"

"Then explain this." He gestured with his phone. "What is this? Who could have done it, if not you?"

"I don't know," she said, her voice small. "I've got nothing."

But she could see that it was no use. He had that look on his face. A brick wall. Confusion, suspicion. And so much anger.

She backed away. "I think we're done here."

"I'll call a bodyguard to escort you home," Zack said.

"No, I think not. My security is my own concern from now on. Don't trouble yourself." She pulled her stole around herself, turned and ran.

People tried to talk to her as she stumbled down the stairway. She heard her name called. Saw Sophie, with a frown of concern in her eye. Drew's worried look across the ballroom. Thank God they were too far away to stop her as she hurried down the broad marble staircase toward the front door.

Seattle drizzle was soothing against her hot face and bare shoulders as she lurched down the street, hiking the skirt up into her hands.

She knew this sick falling feeling from her plane crash night-

mares. When the plane was already caught in the relentless grip
of gravity and was hurtling down, down, down.

Braced for impact.

Nineteen

Zack remembered this feeling from missions in the Anbar Province that had gone sideways. Bad intel, an unknown, unassessed threat flicking past the corner of his eye and mind. Unknown variables, nudging at his senses, but not nudging quite hard enough.

The hell? Someone had just planted a bomb right inside the most important part of his life. He'd already detonated it and *now* he was questioning the intel?

Of course he was questioning it. He was head over ass in love with that woman.

"...hear me, Zack? Hey! Earth to Zack!"

His gaze whipped around. Sophie was in the doorway, phone in hand.

"What?" he asked.

"We just saw Ava running off like her hair was on fire. What upset her?"

"Me," he admitted.

Sophie's mouth tightened. "Can you go after her and fix it?"

"I don't think it's fixable," he said.

"But she—" Sophie's phone rang again, and she picked it up. "Mindy? What have you got?" She listened for a moment. "Whoa. I'll go check it out right away. Call you right back." Sophie closed the call. "The latest attack against Callista Wexford originated from Blazon's IP address. Ava's own company, right here in the Gilchrist building. In real time. Whoever's doing it is there right now and isn't making the faintest attempt to mask it this time. Call Ava right now, and tell her to get back to the building. Let's all just go upstairs and see who it is."

If his guts could have dropped lower, they would have. "What do you mean, back in the building? Ava's right here."

"No, she is not. I saw her run out the door myself! Look out the window, and you'll still see her on the street. In that dress you could see her from space."

Zack leaned to look out the window. He caught sight of her instantly. The wind tunnel of tall buildings made her skirt billow out. Her updo had tumbled down, curls trailing over her bare back. Her stole fluttered behind her like a battle flag.

She wasn't involved in this. She wasn't upstairs, at Blazon. She wasn't even holding her phone.

The feeling that gripped him was a strange mix of horror, relief and guilt, but he had no time for feelings. Sophie joined him at the window and made a worried sound when she spotted Ava. She lifted her phone. "This has to be dealt with fast," she said, pulling up the number.

Ava's rock-and-roll ringtone started to play, right in the room. "Oh, no." Sophie bent to pick up Ava's phone and looked up at him. "I'm guessing that you might have jumped to some really dumb conclusions, Zack," she said.

"Scold me later." Zack was already in motion. "I'm going up to Blazon."

His feet flew up the stairs to the top floor. It was quiet and deserted up there. He sprinted down to the end of the hall, the last two doors, with the sign that read Blazon Public Relations

& Branding Specialists. The frenetic clack of a keyboard came from inside. Zack flung the door open.

Ernest was hunched over the keyboard. He jerked around with a startled squeak, eyes bugged, his mouth a big O. He spun around, hit a few keys and then sprinted hell for leather toward the emergency exit stairway.

Zack gave chase, catching him by the collar of his shirt just as he hit the panic bar of the door and reeling him back. "Hold it right there, Ernest."

"Let go of me! Let go! You're choking me!"

"Nope. I'm not letting go of you. What are you doing here?"

"Just some work I forgot about," Ernest said, his voice an aggrieved whine. "I just thought I'd pop up here and take care of it, and I'd be able to relax more tomorrow. You scared me to death."

Zack looked at the computer, which was now just a blank blue screen. "Trying to cover your tracks? Too late for that."

"Cover what?" Ernest wiggled in his grasp. "Dude, are you paranoid?"

"You were posting that garbage about Callista," Zack said. "No one else was up here. Ava's outside the building. Tell me what you've been up to. Or else."

Ernest licked his lips, blinking frantically. Zack just waited, letting the seconds tick by. Never easing the pressure on Ernest's shirt collar. Giving the younger man his best wrath-of-God stare.

It worked. Ernest went limp in his grasp, and his mouth started to shake. "Goddamn it," he said shakily. "You asshole. You ruined it. You ruined everything."

"Ruined what?" Zack demanded.

"Ava was supposed to come up here first, not you!"

Ernest started to sob. Zack had a disorienting moment of total, awful comprehension. Puzzle pieces clicked into place. He was a goddamn fool for not seeing it.

"Ava was on the phone with you when she came to the library to talk to me," he said slowly. "You were trying to lure her up so that I would find her here, after the team saw the posts about Callista coming straight from this IP address. You meant for me and Sophie's team to catch her red-handed. Or better yet, for Callista and Trevor to find her."

"You screwed it all up!" Ernest wailed.

"Guilty as charged." He pushed Ernest down onto the office chair and, with a shove, sent it rolling back to hit the wall. He advanced on Ernest. "Now tell me why."

"Let me go!" Ernest tried to stand up. Zack blocked him, and he dropped back into the chair, sniveling.

"No one's going to save you, Ernest," Zack said. "Talk fast."

"She deserved it!" Ernest burst out. "She got my brother thrown in prison! She got that lying, whining hag out of jail! None of that stuff she said about Colby is true! I know Colby didn't do that! I know Colby! He wouldn't do that!"

"Colby? Wait…are you talking about Colby Hoyt?" Zack asked. "You're Colby Hoyt's brother? But your last name isn't Hoyt."

"Different mom." Ernest sniffled loudly. "I'm eight years younger than him. Our dad never married my mom. His name wasn't on my documents. But Colby's still my brother. I can't just do nothing! He was up for parole a year ago, and she just pushed her goddamn lying bullshit video again and killed that, too! I had to do something for him!"

Zack thought back to the conversation he'd had with Ava that first night. He remembered seeing Colby Hoyt on the news. He'd had the same washed-out coloring as Ernest. The white-blond hair, the near-invisible brows and lashes, the oversize, droopy eyes. But Colby had seemed meaner and harder.

"You're getting back at Ava for helping Judy Whelan get out of jail and helping to convict your brother," Zack said, his voice stony. "So that's what this is about."

"She deserved it!" Ernest's voice was thick with trapped snot. "She just decides what the story is and makes one of her goddamn documentaries and it all looks so convincing. But it's a bunch of lies!"

He wanted to pound this little punk so badly, but he just breathed it out, slow and even. "So this is your punishment? Trashing her rep? Sex tapes? Hurting the Blooms?"

"It's just a game for her. But I can play that game, too. I used her own tricks against her. I want the world to know that she's a liar and a cheat. And a slut."

"She would have helped you," Zack said. "She believed in you. She would have helped you launch a brilliant career in marketing. But you flushed it all down the toilet for someone else's spite. Bad move, Ernest."

Ernest started to cry. "I had no choice!" he blubbered. "Colby's my brother. He asked me to—"

"Don't care," Zack said. "Not interested. Save it for your lawyer. Just one last thing before I call the cops. Did you post the rest of that video?"

"Only the teaser so far," Ernest admitted. "But I edited and uploaded the next installment. It's, like, two and a half hours of material, once you edit out the breaks and talking and naps. All I have to do is hit the go button." His eyes went crafty. "Maybe we can work out a deal? Say, I take that recording down, and you, like, um…let me go?"

"I'll tell you our deal," Zack said. "Take the recording down. Delete it while I watch. And maybe, just maybe, I won't break all your bones while we wait for the police. That's your prize. A functional skeleton. Do we understand each other?"

Ernest's face crumpled. "But I did it for Colby," he sobbed.

The police came, in due course. The hours ground by. All Zack wanted to do was to go after Ava, but instead, he was stuck there, following through on all the time-eating bureaucratic protocols that were put in motion when the police were summoned.

Then Ava's people piled on, demanding explanations. Sophie and Vann and Drew showed up, and then Malcolm stormed in with Bev and Hendrick, demanding to be debriefed.

The one bright spot was when Jenna called to confirm that Ava had gotten home safely. Ava was not, however, answering her phone, which Jenna had since returned to her. His calls went to voice mail. His texts were left unread. She was freezing him out.

He damn well deserved it. And it made him frantic.

She wouldn't answer Malcolm or Drew's calls, either, which prompted them to go check on her in person. Delaying still further the time he could go to her house himself.

Drew stopped halfway out the door and gazed back at Zack, his eyes troubled. "I gave you a really hard time today," he said. "But it's my job. You have a sister yourself, so I know you understand. Even so, thanks for watching her back. And for catching the troll. I just wanted to say good luck. With Ava, I mean."

Zack's jaw ached. "I'll need it," he said. "Ernest had me fooled for a few minutes, and Ava saw it. She feels betrayed. It's a bad scene."

"So fix it," Drew said forcefully. "Find a way. I haven't seen her as happy as she was today since before my parents' plane crash. I want her to have that. So make it work, bro. Figure it out."

Zack nodded. He didn't need to be told what was at stake.

Not to be outdone, Malcolm stepped forward and stared down at Zack from under his bushy white brows, his arms folded over his chest. He harrumphed. "You do know, of course, that if you hurt her, I'll rip your head off and use it for a bowling ball."

Zack suppressed the urge to laugh just in time. "I doubt it will come to that, sir."

When he was finally free to go, he drove straight to Ava's house and parked down the block, waiting until her family members came out and drove away.

When the cars had all gone, he walked up to her door, gazed up into the security camera he'd had installed and hit the buzzer.

Praying for mercy.

Twenty

Ava shivered as she stared at the security monitor on the wall by the door. This was all she needed, after all those hours on the phone trying to fix this godawful mess. The Blooms, the Wexfords, Uncle Malcolm, Drew, Sophie, the police. She was exhausted, but at this point, it seemed like everyone knew the score.

Everyone but her and Zack. That was still up in the air.

Zack gazed up into her eyes through the camera with that look he got when he was holding his heart wide-open. She wasn't pressing the intercom, so she didn't hear him, but saw his lips form the word. *Please.*

Damn the man. So the torture wasn't even over for the day. This was the final act.

She hit the intercom. "Zack, go home. I'm fine. Let's get some sleep."

"Please let me in," he said.

She'd given him keys, but he didn't use them. Because of course he wouldn't. He was an old-fashioned, righteous dude whose mama and granddad had brought him up right.

"My family just left," she said into the intercom. "They already wore me out."

"I know. I saw them go. I've been parked down the block, waiting."

"Oh. Well, I'm exhausted, and I've got nothing left for you. Besides, truthfully, Zack? There isn't anything left to say."

"There's everything to say," Zack said. "Please, open the door. I know I don't deserve it. But I'm ready to grovel."

That gave her pause. "Grovel? Really? Zack Austin, the great and powerful?"

"If groveling is what you need from me, I'll do it. Just let me in."

She hesitated, unwilling to unleash any fresh pain and turmoil. Besides, she hadn't taken off the makeup that had run under her eyes, or even bothered to comb her wind-snarled hair. She'd just pulled the tangled mess back into a scrunchie to deal with later.

She picked the simplest, lamest excuse. "I look like crap. We'll talk later, Zack."

"You know damn well I think you're the most beautiful woman I've ever seen. Just five minutes. Then I swear, I'll go."

She cursed under her breath, blew out a sharp breath and jerked the door open.

She stood there in her entry hall, swathed in her big, puffy, dark crimson fleece bathrobe. Bare feet sticking out, swollen and sore from the long, lonely walk in high heels before Jenna found her. Jenna had called a car, driven around in it until she spotted Ava, and given her a ride home. Saint Jenna.

Zack stepped inside and closed the door. He lifted up his open palm, which held the keys to the two new locks now on her door. The copies she'd given him when they got back from Los Angeles.

"These are yours," he said. "Having these keys means more to me than anything ever has before in my life." He laid them on the shelf by the door. "I hope you'll give them back to me."

Ava dragged her gaze away from the shiny, newly minted keys gleaming on the shelf. "Wow. You are the master of the symbolic gesture, Zack."

His eyes narrowed. "I'm not quite sure what that means tonight."

"Not much, I guess," she said. "I'm babbling. Long day. I need rest."

"With no one guarding you?"

Ava gave him an ironic look. "That's all over now. The threat has passed, and my life can return to normal. Whatever the hell that ever was."

"Ava—"

"It's really depressing and sad that it was Ernest all along, because I cared about that guy, and I tried to mentor him. I thought he was really bright and talented. And all along, he was just plotting to destroy me. Wow, there it is again. My incredibly poor judgment, on full display."

He waved that away. "I still want you covered," he said. "I can't turn it off just like that. I still want to protect you from anything that could possibly hurt you."

"Even you?" she asked.

He flinched. "Ava, please."

"Don't you 'Ava, please' me. You made your opinion of me clear. All that's left is for me to process the information, and I'd rather do that alone. Just go home."

Zack took a step forward, stopping short when she shrank back. "I got confused tonight, Av," he said. "Ernest really blew smoke in my eyes with that sex tape. And I just, ah…lost it."

She swallowed. "Yes. Ernest filmed us. I should have thought of that. But I trusted him. It just never occurred to me."

"Me either. If I'd been thinking straight, I would have remembered that Ernest was in your room that first night, before I went down to the pool to find you."

"But you weren't thinking straight," she said.

Zack shook his head. "No. I wasn't. Please, Ava. Forgive me."

She considered that for a moment. "Just like that?" she said.

"Take all the time you need," he said. "I'll wait. As long as it takes. Years, even."

He just stood there. It was impossible to meet his eyes. She was already on the edge, and if she looked at him, the tears would well up and she would be done for.

"I got bad intel," he said quietly. "It knocked me on my ass. Hit my weakest spot."

"Oh?" She crossed her arms over her chest, sniffing. "So what is your weakest spot, Zack? I should have that info, I guess. Considering what you're asking from me."

He stared at the floor as he considered the question. "My weakest spot," he repeated in a halting voice. "I guess my weakest spot is that I could never quite believe that getting with you was real in the first place. It seemed too good to be true. A woman like you, being into me. Wanting me. That's my weakest spot."

"Oh, Zack—"

"Some part of me was convinced that I didn't deserve it. I was always waiting for the other shoe to drop. So when Vikram showed me the video, suddenly I was there again. That big, dumb lug who got used and played by Aimee in Berlin. The meathead who'd been fooling himself all along. A million miles out of his league, and no freaking clue."

"I see." Her voice was small.

"I came to my senses fast," he went on. "About a minute after you left. Sophie told me about the activity at Blazon's IP address, and I realized what an idiot I was, but I couldn't chase you down. I had to clean up the mess first. With Ernest, and the cops."

Ava nodded, not trusting her voice.

"I never claimed to be perfect, Av." Zack's voice was stark. "I have my weak spots. My dark side. But I love you. I want to spend the rest of my life as close to you as I can get. You're everything to me." His voice broke. He looked down quickly.

It took a while to calm her shaky throat down enough to speak, but she was sure of what she wanted to say once she did. "Okay," she whispered.

Zack's head came up. His fierce gaze fastened onto her. "Okay...to what?"

She held her arms up, open to him. "To this," she said. "To us."

They stared at each other. The air between them charged.

"So you forgive me?" he asked slowly.

"I have my dark side, too. And my weak spots." Her voice was soft but steady and assured. "You made space for them."

The look on his face echoed the feeling in her own chest. Like light dawning.

"So...we're good?" he persisted. "Officially?"

She laughed at him, digging a pack of tissues out of her bathrobe pocket and taking a moment to dab at her nose. "Would you please stop it?" she complained. "You're acting like I've got a gun to your head, and it's weirding me out."

Zack took the shiny keys off the shelf. He took his keys out of his coat pocket and slowly reattached them to the ring as he moved closer to her.

She laughed at him. "There you go again with your symbolic gestures."

Zack put his hand into his pocket. "If you liked that symbolic gesture, get a load of this one." He sank to his knee, lifting a small black velvet box, flipping it open.

Ava gasped. "Oh my God. Zack."

It was the most stunning ring she'd ever seen. Sensuously coiled strands of multicolored gold, with a big, glowing ruby caught in the center. It was breathtaking.

"I wanted to give you this last night," Zack said. "We got distracted by our bad-boy fantasies. I tried again this morning, but Jenna walked in. I can't wait any longer to ask you for the honor of loving and cherishing and protecting you for the rest of my life."

She couldn't speak. Her eyes flooded. Her face shook, like a little earthquake.

"If the ring isn't right, we can change it," he told her. "If you'd prefer a diamond, maybe something more traditional. But I know you like red. I hoped you could wear it with that dress you wore tonight. But your bathrobe looks pretty damn good with it, too."

She shook with a shaky burst of laughter. "It does, actually."

"It was a risky choice," he said. "But that just kind of sum us up, you know? So what the hell. I risked it."

"It's perfect," she whispered, unsteadily. "It's gorgeous. I love it."

"So you'll wear it? You'll risk it?"

"Yes," she said. "Oh, God, yes. For you, I'd risk anything."

Zack slid the ruby ring onto her shaking finger. It fit perfectly. He kissed her cold hand, pressing it to his lips, to his cheek. His hand was shaking as much as hers. He rose to his feet, pulling her into his arms.

"We'll risk it together," he said as their lips met.

* * * * *

Keep reading for an excerpt of
The Troublemaker
by Maisey Yates.
Find it in
The Troublemaker anthology,
out now!

CHAPTER ONE

HE WAS THE very image of the Wild West, backlit by the setting sun, walking across the field that led directly to her house. He was wearing a black cowboy hat and a T-shirt that emphasized his broad shoulders; waist narrow and hips lean. His jaw square, his nose straight like a blade and his mouth set in a firm, uncompromising manner.

Lachlan McCloud was the epitome of a cowboy. She was proud to call him her best friend. He was loyal; he was—in spite of questionable behavior at times—an extremely good man, even if sometimes you had to look down deep to see it.

He was...

He was bleeding.

Charity sighed.

She had lost track of the amount of times that she had stitched Lachlan McCloud back together.

"I'll just get my kit, then," she muttered, digging around for it.

Not that there was any other reason Lachlan would be coming by unannounced. Usually now she went to his house for cards or for dinner; he didn't come here. Not since her dad had died.

She found her medical bag and opened up the front door, propping her hip against the door frame, holding the bag aloft.

He stopped. "How did you know?"

"I recognize your *I cut myself open and need to be sewn back together* walk."

"I have a...*need to be sewn back together* walk?"

"You do," she said, nodding.

"Thank you kindly."

She lived just on the other side of the property line from McCloud's Landing. One of the ranches that made up the vast spread that was Four Corners Ranch.

Thirty thousand acres, divided by four, amongst the original founding families.

Her father had been the large-animal vet in town and for the surrounding areas for years. With a mobile unit and all the supplies—granted, they were antiquated.

Charity had taken over a couple of years ago.

Her dad had always understood animals better than he did people. He'd told her people simply didn't speak his language, or he didn't speak theirs, but it didn't really matter which.

Charity had known how to speak her dad's language. He liked chamomile tea and *All Creatures Great and Small. Masterpiece Theatre* and movies made in the 1950s. Argyle socks—which she also loved—and cardigans. Again, something she loved, too.

He'd smoked a pipe and read from the paper every morning. He liked to do the crossword.

And just last month, he'd died. Without him the house seemed colder, emptier and just a whole lot less.

It was another reason she was thankful for Lachlan.

But then they'd both had a lot of changes recently. It wasn't just her. It wasn't just the loss of her father.

Lachlan was the last McCloud standing.

His brothers, resolute bachelors all—at least at one time—were now settled and having children. His brother Brody was an instant father, since he had just married Elizabeth, a single mother who had come to work at the equestrian center on McCloud's Landing a couple of months back.

But Lachlan was Lachlan. And if the changes had thrown him off, he certainly didn't show it.

He was still his hard-drinking, risk-taking, womanizing self.

But he'd always been that way. It was one reason she'd been so immediately drawn to him when they'd first met. He was nothing like her.

He was something so separate from her, something so different than she could ever be, that sometimes being friends with him was like being friends with someone from a totally different culture.

Sometimes she went with him and observed his native customs. She'd gone to Smokey's Tavern with the group of McClouds quite a few times, but she'd always found it noisy and the booze smelled bad. It gave her a headache.

And she didn't dance.

Lachlan had women fighting to dance with him, and she thought it was such a funny thing. Watching those women compete for his attention, for just a few moments of his time. They would probably never see him again.

She would see him again the next day and the day after that, and the day after that.

"What did you do?" she asked, looking at the nasty gash.

"I had a little run-in with some barbed wire."

He was at the door now, filling up the space. He did that. He wasn't the kind of person you could ignore. And given that she was the kind of person *all too* easy to ignore, she admired that about him.

"We've gotta stop meeting like this," he said, grinning.

She'd seen him turn that grin on women in the bar and they fell apart. She'd always been proud of herself for not behaving that way.

"I wish we could, Lachlan. But you insist on choosing violence."

"Every day."

"You could stop being in a fight with the world," she pointed out.

"I could. But you know the thing about that is it sounds boring."

"Well… A bored Lachlan McCloud is not anything I want to see." She jerked her head back toward the living room. "Come on in."

He did, and the air seemed to rush right out of her lungs as he entered the small, homey sitting room in her little house.

She still had everything of her father's sitting out, like he might come back any day.

His science-fiction novels and his medical journals. His field guides to different animals and the crocheted afghan that he had sat with, draped over his lap, in his burnt orange recliner, when at the end of his days he hadn't been able to do much.

She had been a very late-in-life surprise for her father.

She'd been born when he was in his fifties. And he had raised her alone, because that had been the agreement, so the story went. Amicable and easy. Which made sense. Because her father had been like that. Steady and calm. A nice man. Old-fashioned. But then… He had been in his eighties when he'd passed. He wasn't really old-fashioned so much as of his time.

He'd homeschooled her, brought her on all his veterinary calls. Her life had been simple. And it had been good.

She'd had her dad. And then… She'd had Lachlan.

And there was no reason at all that suddenly this room should feel tiny with Lachlan standing in it. Because he had been in here any number of times.

Especially in the end, visiting her dad and talking to him about baseball.

She sometimes thought her dad was the closest thing that Lachlan had to a father figure. His own dad had been a monster.

Of course, the unfairness of that was that Lachlan's dad was still alive out there somewhere. While her sweet dad was gone.

"It's quiet in here," Lachlan said, picking up on her train of thought.

"It would've been quiet in here if Dad was alive. Until you two started shouting about sports." She grinned just thinking about it. "You do know how to get him riled up." Then her smile fell slightly. "*Did.* You did know."

"I could still rile him up, I bet. But I don't know that we want séance levels of trouble."

She laughed, because she knew the joke came from a place of affection, and that was something she prized about her relationship with Lachlan. They just *knew* each other.

She hadn't really known anyone but adults before she'd met Lachlan. She'd known the people they'd done veterinary work for; she'd known the old men her dad had sat outside and smoked pipes with on summer evenings.

Lachlan had been her first friend.

He was her only friend. Still.

He'd taught her sarcasm. He'd introduced her to pop culture.

He'd once given her a sip of beer when she'd been eighteen.

He'd laughed at the face she'd made.

"I do not want that level of trouble. I also don't want *your* level of trouble," she said. "But here you are. Sit down and bite on something."

"I don't need to bite on anything to get a few stitches, Charity. Settle down. I know what I'm about."

"You can't flinch, Lachlan, and sometimes you're a bad patient. So brace yourself."

"You could numb me."

"I could," she said. "But I'm not just letting you use all my supplies. I'm stitching you for no cost."

"Considering you normally stitch up horses, you should pay me to let you do this."

"Please. Working on animals is more complicated than working on people. People all have the same set of organs right in the same places. Animals… It's all arranged differently. I have to know way more to take care of animals."

"Yes. I've heard the lecture before."

"But you've never taken it on board."

"All right," he said, resting his hand on the coffee table in front of her and revealing the big gash in his forearm.

She winced.

"Hardass doctor, wincing at this old thing," he said.

"It's different when it's on a person," she said.

Except it really was different when it was on him. Because he was hers.

He was special.

Seeing him injured in any capacity made her heart feel raw, even if she'd seen it a hundred times.

"All right, Doc."

"Okay," she said.

She took her curved needle out of her kit, along with the thread, and she poked it right through his skin.

He growled.

"I told you," she said.

She thought back to how they'd met. He'd been bruised and battered, and in bad need of medical attention.

His had been the first set of stitches she'd ever given.

She swallowed hard.

He winced and shifted when she pushed her needle through his skin again.

"I can't guarantee you that you're not going to have a scar," she said, her tone filled with warning.

"Just one to add to my collection of many."

"Yes. You're very tough."

"Oh, hell, sweetheart, I know that."

"Don't *sweetheart* me." He called every woman sweetheart. And she didn't like being lumped together with all that. She liked *their* things. Baseball and jokes about séances and *Doc*.

"How is everything going at the facility?"

She had a hands-on role in the veterinary care of the animals at the new therapy center on McCloud's Landing. But everything had taken a backseat when her dad had declined, then passed. She was working her way back up to it all, but it was slow.

"It's going well. Of course, I am tripping over all the happy couples. Tag and Nelly, Alaina and Gus, Hunter and Elsie, Brody and Elizabeth. It's ridiculous. It's like a Disney cartoon where it's spring and all the animals are hooking up and having babies."

"The domesticity must appall you," she said. But she wasn't even really joking.

She continued to work slowly on the stitches, taking her time and trying to get them small and straight to leave the least amount of damage, because whatever he said about scars, she was determined to stitch her friend back together as neatly as possible.

"I'm glad they're happy," she said.

"Yeah. Me, too. It's a good thing. It's a damn good thing."

But he sounded a bit gruff and a bit not like himself. She had to wonder if all the changes were getting to him. It was tough to tell with Lachlan, because his whole thing was to put on a brave face and pretend that things were all right.

He'd tried that when they'd first met.

She had been playing in the woods. By herself. She was always by herself. Even though she'd been fifteen, she'd been a young fifteen. She'd never really gotten to be around other children. So she was both vastly older and vastly younger in many different ways. She liked to wander the woods and imagine herself in a fairy tale. That she might encounter Prince Charming out there.

Then one day she'd been walking down a path, and there he'd been. Tall and rangy—even at sixteen—with messy brown hair and bright blue eyes.

But he'd been hurt.

Suddenly, he'd put his hand on his ribs and gone down onto his knees.

She could still remember the way she'd run over to him.

"ARE YOU ALL RIGHT?"

"Fine," he said, looking up at her, his lip split, a cut over his eye bleeding profusely.

"That's a lie," she said.

"Yeah." He wheezed out a cough. "No shit."

She'd never heard anyone say that word in real life before. Just overheard in movies and read in books.

Her father was against swearing. He thought that it was vulgar and common. He said that people ought to have more imagination than that.

"That is shocking language," she said.

"Shocking language… Okay. Look, you can just… Head on out. Don't worry about me. This is hardly the first time I've had my ribs broken."

He winced again.

"You need stitches," she said, looking at his forehead.

"I'm not going to be able to get them."

"Why not?"

"No insurance. Anyway, my dad's not gonna pay for me to go to the doctor."

"I… I can help," she said.

She could only hope that her dad was still at home.

He had a call to go out on later, but there was a chance he hadn't left yet.

"Can you stand up?"

"I can try."

She found herself taking hold of his hand, which was big and rough and masculine in comparison to hers.

Like he was a different thing altogether.

She'd seen the boys on the ranch from a distance before, but she'd never met one of them.

He might even be a *man*, he was so tall already.

He made her feel very small. Suddenly, her heart gave a great jump, like she'd been frightened. He made her feel like a rabbit, standing in front of a fox, and she couldn't say why.

But he wasn't a fox. And she wasn't a rabbit.

He was just a boy who needed help.

"Lean on me," she said.

He looked down at her. "I don't want to hurt you. You're a tiny little thing."

"I'm sturdy," she said. "Come on."

"All right."

He put his arm around her, and the two of them walked back to the house. Her father was gone. But his bag was still there.

"I've watched my dad do this a lot of times. I think I can do it."

"Your dad's a doctor?"

The best thing would be to lie. It was to make him feel better, not for nefarious reasons. It wasn't *really* a lie. But of course what this boy meant was a doctor for humans...and she was going to let him believe it.

"Yes. I've been on lots of calls with him. I can do this."

"Good."

She found a topical numbing cream in the bag and gingerly applied it around the wound on his forehead.

His breath hissed through his teeth.

She waited a few minutes before taking out a needle and thread. Beads of sweat formed on his forehead, his teeth gritted.

But when she finished, he looked up at her and smiled.

"Thanks, Doc."

SHE LOOKED DOWN at the stitches she was giving now.

"That ought to do it," she said.

"Thanks. Hey, Doc," he said and he lifted his head up so that they were practically sharing the same air.

His face was so close to hers; close enough she could see the bristles of his stubble, the blue of his eyes, that they were a darker ring of blue around the outside, and lighter toward the center.

What is happening?

Her throat felt scratchy, and her heart felt...sore.

"Yes?" It came out a near whisper.

"I need a favor."

"What?"

"I need you to reform me."

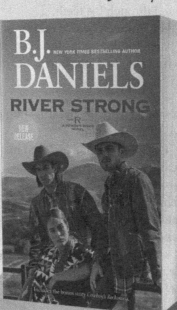